Read what people are already saying about

THE LONELY LIFE OF BIDDY WEIR

'If you're a bit of a weirdo, **you will love Biddy Weir**'
Ian Sansom, bestselling author of *The Norfolk Mystery*

'In Biddy Weir, Lesley Allen has created one of those characters that **gets under your skin and won't leave . . . A must-read** for anyone who has ever wondered about life and where we fit in'
Doreen Finn, author of *My Buried Life*

'**One of my favourite reads this year** . . . raw, real and authentic . . . You will be enthralled'
Bibliomaniac

'**Truly uplifting** . . . I cannot believe this is Lesley Allen's debut novel'
Steph and Chris's Book Review

'Never have I come across a book that I have felt **so compelled to share and talk about**'
Swirl and Thread

'I found it **authentic, compelling** and often uneasy reading'
Books and More Books

'This is **a touching story** of the effects of bullying and how it can change a person's view of themselves'
The Whispering of the Pages

Lesley Allen lives in Bangor, County Down, with her teenage daughter. She is a freelance copywriter and the press officer and assistant programme developer for Open House Festival. Lesley was named as one of the Arts Council of Northern Ireland's 2016 Artist Career Enhancement recipients for literature. She will be using the award to complete her second novel.

The Lonely Life of Biddy Weir

LESLEY ALLEN

twenty7

First published in Great Britain in 2016

This paperback edition published in 2016 by

Twenty7 Books
80–81 Wimpole St, London W1G 9RE
www.twenty7books.co.uk

A CIP catalogue record for this book is available from the British Library.

Paperback ISBN: 978-1-78577-038-8
Ebook ISBN: 978-1-78577-018-0

1 3 5 7 9 10 8 6 4 2

Printed and bound by Clays Ltd, St Ives Plc

Twenty7 Books is an imprint of Bonnier Zaffre,
a Bonnier Publishing company
www.bonnierzaffre.co.uk
www.bonnierpublishing.co.uk

For Aimee

'It's weird not to be weird'
John Lennon

Prologue

A phone call – Cove Cottage, Ballybrock, July 2000

It was the claws, digging at her chest, pulling her upwards, yanking at her pyjama top, that finally dragged Biddy from her sleep. That and the nokoise: the steady humming. She thought it was the falcons to begin with, come to rescue her again, lift her up and fly her to safety. But the sound confused her, displaced her. It wasn't their normal *keck*-ing call. She had never heard this sound from a bird before. And then suddenly she was aware of the weight. Something was pressing on her chest, pushing her down while the falcons tried to lift her up. Was it Alison? Was Alison trying to stop them? Would she never leave her alone?

'Go-way,' she mumbled, slightly panicked. 'Go-way. Leave-me-lone.'

The claws plucked again, this time piercing her skin, shocking her into consciousness.

'Bertie!' she squealed at the black, fluffy mass perched on her chest. The startled cat rolled onto the bed beside her as she sat up, rubbing at her eyes. The bedroom sparkled with warm speckled sunlight filtering in through the blue gingham curtains, bouncing off the gleaming white furniture. It was such a contrast from her bedroom at home, dull and heavy even on the brightest summer mornings.

The little blue clock on the bedside table said 10.35 a.m. 'No,' she gasped aloud. She never slept in, ever. Then again, it had

1

been almost 6 a.m., her normal rising time, before she'd finally climbed back under the duvet after the dream and gone back to sleep. She checked her watch, but yes, the clock was correct. Bertie meowed loudly, obviously irritated at having to wait so long for his breakfast. She wondered how late in the day she would have slept if he hadn't jumped on top of her, demanding to be fed.

As she began to prepare herself for the day ahead, Biddy's mood was buoyant and resolved, but tinged with nervous disquiet. She looked at herself in the bathroom mirror as she brushed her teeth. Although she was becoming more accustomed to her reflection, she still avoided close-up eye contact. But today she brought her face as far up to the mirror as her focus would allow. She noticed with surprise how green her eyes were. They looked exactly the same colour as the green-eyed double-breasted cormorant's. How come, in all her thirty years, she had never noticed that before?

She made herself a bacon and tomato sandwich: it was too late for porridge, but too early for lunch. Brunch, she thought, as she munched it on the patio, I'm having brunch. She thought about Penny Jordan and smiled a great big beaming smile at Bertie, who was sitting on the outdoor table staring at her, waiting patiently for some scraps of bacon.

It was another warm day and the light was perfect. But she wouldn't go down to the beach to paint today as she had previously planned. No, she mustn't tire herself out, or worse, lose track of time. She would still do Terri's painting, but it could wait until tomorrow. Today she had something else to do. Something much more important. So she stayed on the patio and sketched Bertie. He'd fallen asleep after feasting on her leftover bacon, and was now comfortably curled up on one of the patio chairs, drenched in a shaft of sunlight. There was something irresistible about his easy contentment and the soft curve of his body, and though she'd never drawn a cat before, never drawn any creature other than a bird, Biddy was pleased with the likeness. She'd give this to Terri too. She liked Bertie. He was good company, and he was too old and too fat to chase birds. She decided she wouldn't mind having a cat like him at home. Maybe Terri could help her find one.

Around 3 p.m., Biddy began to feel properly agitated. Butterflies as big as bats flapped ferociously in her stomach, thrashing against her ribcage, soaring into her chest. And a nagging doubt drummed in her head, spawning questions she didn't want to hear and was afraid to answer. What if it all goes wrong? What if they catch you out? What if you mess it up? What if you get into trouble? She tried to ignore the crescendo of *what ifs* and focus on the dream instead. She couldn't let herself give up now. She just couldn't. If she did, then she'd be exactly the same person she had been her whole life long: a worthless weirdo. Better to be a weirdo who had done something, who had stood up for herself at least once in her life, than a weak, pathetic, gutless one, who couldn't even be brave for just one single day.

She decided to write down the words she needed to say, like a script. That would help her to concentrate. When she was finished, she made herself a cup of tea and managed a bite from one of Terri's oatmeal biscuits.

Then she waited.

At ten minutes to five, Biddy went into the living room and sat down on the edge of the red velvet chair. She didn't want to slouch right back into it as she had yesterday afternoon, as she couldn't be too comfy. She had to stay focused and alert. Maybe the leather sofa would be better? But then she wouldn't see the screen quite as well, and she needed to. Even though she would have to turn the sound down, she absolutely must be able to see the screen. She settled on the chair, flicked onto the right channel and turned down the sound straightaway so that the last few minutes of the previous programme, a children's show, didn't distract her. The notebook she had used to write the script in sat on her lap and she held the telephone in her right hand. Perhaps she should have contacted Terri and asked her permission to use the phone? The call might be expensive. No, she dismissed the thought, Terri wouldn't mind. She was sure of it. Terri was going to be proud of her. And anyway, she'd pay her for the call.

Then another thought triggered a new panic. What if she didn't get through? What if she'd got herself all geared up for this, the bravest, most courageous, most outrageous thing she'd ever done in her whole life, and she didn't get through? She decided to dial the number there and then, before the show had even started. She knew it off by heart. Even though she'd never considered calling before, she'd heard that number repeated so many times that it was etched in her brain.

'Good afternoon and welcome to *Honey's Pot*. My name's Miranda. What can I do for you today?'

Biddy couldn't speak. The shock of actually getting through and hearing someone's voice, a real member of the *Honey's Pot* team who was right there in the studio, somewhere in the background, almost made her hang up.

'Hello? Hi? Hello? Anyone there?'

Biddy managed a noise. It wasn't decipherable, but it was enough to stop Miranda from hanging up.

'Are you calling about today's show?' Miranda asked softly. She sounded kind, thought Biddy. Sincere.

'Uh-huh.'

'Please don't be shy. I know it's a tricky subject today, one of the most difficult issues we've covered actually, but we all feel it's really important. Do you have personal experience?'

'Uh-huh.'

'Would you like to tell me about it?'

Biddy was sweating so much now that she was worried the phone might slip out of her hand. She didn't know what to do next. She hadn't rehearsed this bit in her script, hadn't really thought about this part of the procedure. She took a deep breath.

'Uh-huh.'

On the other end of the line, Miranda Moore waited patiently. She hoped to be in front of the camera herself someday and was using her researcher job to learn how to talk to people, how to coax them into telling her their problems and reveal their secrets, just like the show's famous host did. But unlike her boss, she definitely wasn't going to be a bitch to her team off camera.

'Listen, why don't I ask you a couple of questions,' she said gently, 'and if you feel like answering them, fine, and if you don't, fine. And we'll take it from there. Will that do?'

'Yes,' Biddy managed a whisper this time. 'Fine.'

'Good. Great. OK. Now then, first of all, can you tell me your name?'

Biddy panicked again. Her name! Of course they would want her name. Now what was she going to do?

'It doesn't have to be your real name,' Miranda had guessed her dilemma. She was used to it. 'You can use any name you like, really. It's your story, your experience we're interested in anyway, not your name.'

'Bridget,' Biddy said quickly, remembering the first day she had met Terri and she'd asked if that was her real name. 'Bridget . . .' she hesitated, what surname would she give? 'Just Bridget.'

'OK, Bridget. That's fine. Great. And where do you live? Again, you don't have to say the exact location, just the area, really, is all we need.'

'Erm, Northern Ireland.'

'Thought so,' Miranda sounded almost delighted. 'Love your accent. So, Bridget, were you bullied yourself?'

Biddy swallowed hard. What on earth was she doing? She hadn't thought this through at all. Who the hell did she think she was?

'Bridget?' Miranda's voice was low, concerned. 'Please don't be frightened. Maybe if you told your story it would help, you know. Kind of get rid of your demons, so to speak.'

Biddy let out a half gasp, half laugh. Get rid of your demons, this Miranda with the kind voice had just said. Face your demons, Terri had said. This was a sign. Surely, this was a sign that she was doing the right thing after all.

'Bridget, are you still there? Are you OK? Look, there's no pressure. You don't have to do this, rea—'

'No,' Biddy interrupted. 'No, I do. I do. I want to. I have to.'

'OK,' said Miranda, 'OK. Well, we'll take it slowly, and any time you want to stop, that's fine. So, Bridget from Northern Ireland, what happened to you, then? You were bullied, right?'

'Yes.'

'At school? Or work? Or somewhere else, perhaps?'

'School. At school.'

'And how long did it last, Bridget?'

'Seven years,' Biddy swallowed.

So did Miranda.

'Seven years! Right.' She hadn't expected that. She had assumed people were only bullied for a little while. A year or two at most. And then someone would stop it. She hadn't thought this through either. 'So, what did they do to you, Bridget, these bullies?'

'Things,' said Biddy tentatively, realising it would take all day to tell Miranda her full story. She saw from the TV screen that the programme had already started. She had to move quickly now, as other people would now be phoning in. 'Lots of things.'

'Was it physical, or psychological?' Miranda was aware that she needed to get a move on too. Between her and the other operators, Michael and Holly, they needed to select three callers and she had a hunch that Bridget would be a good one.

'Mostly psychological,' replied Biddy. 'But the main one, Al . . .' she hesitated, 'the main one, she shoved me a few times. And it was because of her I hurt myself.'

'You self-harmed?' Miranda was even more certain now that this caller would be excellent live, if she could just boost her confidence a little. She fitted the criteria exactly.

'Uh . . .' Biddy's voice trailed off. That wasn't exactly what she meant; she'd been referring to the fall on the mountain, but now she realised with a jolt that yes, the pins and the biting were indeed harmful and not the comfort mechanisms she'd believed them to be for years.

Miranda asked another couple of questions. Were the bullies ever reprimanded? Did she still see any of them? Did what happened still affect her? As Miranda talked, Biddy's breathing regulated and the thumping noise in her chest eased. She managed to give clear, if brief, replies to each query.

'OK, Bridget. I think you've been very brave calling us today, and I think we'll be asking you to speak live on the programme in a little while. Do you think you can do that?'

Biddy breathed in deeply.

'Yes,' she exhaled.

'Great. Fab. You'll be great. Now, just two more questions, Bridget, and then we'll get your number and phone you back in a minute or two. OK?'

'OK.'

'Great. I think you're very brave, Bridget, I really do, as I sense how difficult this is for you, and I'm so sorry to have to ask this, but can you tell me one really bad thing that this girl did to you? The main one you mentioned earlier. Or something really terrible that happened because of her?'

Biddy swallowed hard and ran her tongue over her dry lips.

'Well . . .' she paused and breathed in again. 'Well, I suppose I nearly died because of her.'

Part 1: the birth (and near death) of a weirdo
Ballybrock, November 1979

1.

Biddy Weir was two months shy of her tenth birthday when she discovered she was a bloody weirdo. The awful revelation was a shock, to her at any rate, and from that fateful day Biddy's life was defined not by her religion, the colour of her skin, or her sex; nor by what school she went to, her political persuasion or even which side of town she lived in: but by her oddness, by the undeniable, irrevocable fact that she was a weirdo, and a bloody one at that.

As far as Biddy knew, she was the only weirdo who lived in Ballybrock, a small quiet seaside town with church spires and hilly streets and seven fish and chip shops. And lots and lots of seagulls. There were others, of course, like the old lady with wispy pink hair and bright red lipstick who pushed her pet poodles around in a scruffy old Silver Cross pram. And the tall young man with the long wild beard who called himself The Poet. He walked up and down Ballybrock High Street fifty-one times each morning before going into Josie's corner shop to buy a quarter of midget gems and a packet of Rizlas. Josie always wondered where he bought his tobacco, but she never dared to ask. Then there were Billy and Ella, Ballybrock's resident drunks, who loved each other with a passion often openly displayed in public and lived for half of the year in the town's decaying bandstand. Nobody knew where they went for the other half.

But Biddy didn't *know* that these people were weirdos, for no one ever told her. They probably didn't even know themselves. For although the people of Ballybrock would snigger and whisper and look at each other knowingly when they passed them in the street, recoiling and pulling faces and talking about how 'bloody weird' they were, nobody actually called any one of them a bloody weirdo to their face. Not once.

But Biddy knew that she was one, for Biddy had been told.

Ballybrock was a nice enough kind of a place, not picture-postcard pretty, but generally pleasing. There was a rough pebble beach which ran the whole way along one end of the town and was shaded by a big stone wall. People would sit on the wall in summertime, eating their chips from crumpled old newspapers or licking their ice creams, shooing away the hordes of greedy gulls. Further along the promenade stood the bandstand where Billy and Ella lived, and a big old cannon sat proudly on the end of the pier. Right in the centre of Ballybrock was a small park with swings and a pond with a little island in the middle where peacocks and caged coloured birds lived.

There were never any bombs or shootings in Ballybrock, not like lots of other places in the Northern Ireland at that particular time. In Ballybrock 'The Troubles' rarely troubled anyone. The people were mostly friendly and, on the surface anyway, didn't seem to care if their neighbour was a Catholic or a Protestant. They looked out for one another and smiled and nodded as they passed each other on the street. And each year on the 12th July, regardless of what church they did or didn't go to, most of the residents of Ballybrock lined the High Street to watch the bands parade in all their finery.

Most folk who passed through Ballybrock concluded that it must be a pleasant place to live. And all things considered, it was. Just as long as you weren't a bloody weirdo like Biddy Weir.

Biddy had always known that she was different from the other girls at school. Her appearance, for a start, was a bit of a giveaway. Throughout her years at school, her uniform was either far too big or much too small. Regardless of her age, there never seemed to be a time when it was just the right fit. Her socks, which were supposed to be beige, were generally a strange colour of puce, and sometimes didn't even match. And her scruffy shoes were often laced with scraps of coloured wool from her grandmother's needlework box, which had sat on the sideboard since the old lady's death. But it was Biddy's hair that really made her look, shall we say, unusual. She was the only girl in her class who didn't have long glossy plaits or swishing pigtails tied at the top with shiny blue bows. Biddy's hair was copper and curly, neither long nor short, and it stuck out in every direction. But Biddy wasn't interested in pigtails or plaits. Looking pretty as a concept, or even an objective, never crossed her mind.

Biddy didn't have a proper school bag either, just an old string shopper with broken handles, which she tried to patch together with wool or thread, or even Sellotape.

And then there was her name. Her real name, that is, not the one she would become known by when she was almost ten years old. All of the other girls in her class had nice, sensible names like Julia or Jacqueline or Georgina. But Biddy's young mother, Gracie, who had not really been ready to have a child of her own when her daughter was born, named her after a cat who had adopted her family when Gracie was eight. There had been many Flynn family cats over the years, they came and went with regular ease. But Old Biddy was special. She stayed far longer than any of the other cats and had only died the week before Gracie went into labour.

'I'm not bloody well naming her after your mother,' Gracie had screamed hysterically at Biddy's father on his first visit to the hospital to meet his baby daughter, when he had tentatively suggested that Margaret might be a much more suitable name. 'And just be thankful it wasn't a boy.' He didn't dare ask what the boy's name might have been.

As it turned out, Gracie Weir had swiftly realised that she wasn't ready to be a mother and, in actual fact, had never really intended to become a wife. So, when Biddy was just six months old, Gracie ran away to join a travelling fair. The family never heard from her again.

So, that left Biddy, her middle-aged father and his elderly mother. Mrs Weir senior helped to rear the child as best she could while her darling son continued to work as a bookkeeper at Morrison's, the local hardware store. She cursed the day that Gracie, 'that little harlot', had come to work at the store. At fifty, her boy Howard was much too old to leave home, and Mrs Weir had assumed that she'd succeeded in her life's ambition – to keep him all to herself. The shame of the whole affair with Gracie and the child had nearly killed her.

'But you're more than twice her age,' old Mrs Weir had gasped when Howard sat her down in their dark parlour to break the news, thrusting a cup of sweet tea and two Marie biscuits into her hands. 'It's disgusting. Filthy. How could you let this happen, Howard? How could you do this to me?' It was even worse than when her late husband, Harold, had been hit by the train and killed.

Mrs Weir had consoled herself by believing that Gracie Flynn was nothing more than a shameless opportunist who had seduced her darling Howard for financial security and a roof over her head. None of this was Howard's doing, of course. Helen, the nice young secretary at Morrison's (not nice enough for her son, mind you), told her that Gracie had recently moved into one of those new council housing estates on the outskirts of town with her family – all ten of them. Nobody seemed to know where the Flynns had come from, but word was, they had a bit of a reputation for trouble. In Mrs Weir's mind, that explained everything. After all, Howard couldn't possibly have done the seducing himself as, quite frankly, he wouldn't have known where to start. She suspected that Gracie and her abundant family were really gypsies who'd been forced to live 'normal lives' by the powers that be. When she put her theory to Helen, it wasn't rebuffed.

'I knew it,' old Mrs Weir thought, pleased with herself, 'I just knew it.'

'Perhaps she got him drunk,' she whispered confidentially to Helen. 'Or perhaps she put one of her gypsy spells on him. He mustn't have realised what was happening.'

Helen, delighted with this exciting turn of events in her normally mundane existence at Morrison's, smiled and nodded. 'Perhaps,' she whispered back.

The truth of the matter was in fact pretty close to Mrs Weir's imagined version. Howard was as shocked as anyone when Gracie fell pregnant after their somewhat brief fumble in the sand dunes during the Morrison's annual Easter picnic. In almost fifty years, he'd never been drunk and he'd certainly never had sex and now here he was, getting pissed and making someone pregnant in the same afternoon.

As for Gracie, she didn't even fancy Howard. How could she? He was old and odd, and, with his thick brown spectacles, green cardigans and stinking breath, utterly unattractive. But, in her first week at the store, she'd boasted to Helen that she could bed any man she wanted.

'Not Howard, you can't,' laughed Helen, rolling her eyes. 'Not even you could do that.'

'Just you watch,' Gracie had smiled coyly, tossing her copper curls.

Once the damage had been done, so to speak, Howard had no option but to propose. A hasty, modest wedding at the town hall registry office ensued, with two staff drafted in as witnesses and Mrs Weir senior as the only guest. The reception was a cup of tea and a ham sandwich at the Peacock Café in the park. It wasn't quite what Gracie had imagined for her wedding day. But on the whole she was enjoying the drama of this new game, and decided to play along for a while, to see what happened. She could always leave, she reasoned to herself. If she'd learnt anything at all from her family's way of life it was that leaving was easy. And at least there was no need for any further awful sex with Howard. He showed no interest anyway, but even if he had, she wouldn't have hesitated to use the pregnancy as a get-out clause.

For a little while, Gracie almost enjoyed living in the dull but relatively comfortable environment of number 17, Stanley Street. It was quiet, such a change from what she was used to. Indeed, if it hadn't been for Howard's mother, she might have even found it a pleasurable experience. Until the child was born, that is.

Mrs Weir senior had glowed with relief when Gracie ran away, and was more than happy to resume the cosseting regime that had served her son so perfectly well before his ill-fated marriage. Her only regret was that her daughter-in-law hadn't taken the child with her. 'Perhaps that Flynn family will take her,' she quietly suggested to Helen on a rare trip into Morrison's with the pram. 'After all, there are more of them to help out. It's the least they could do.'

It soon became clear, however, that none of Gracie's relations were the least bit interested in the baby girl. When Gracie had married Howard Weir they may have been shocked by her choice of husband, and annoyed that there wasn't to be a boozy reception, but at least it meant they had one less mouth to feed. Gracie's hasty and mysterious departure was actually a relief to them, eliminating the concern that she would one day land back on their doorstep with the child in tow, as it was obvious the marriage wouldn't work. Marriages never did in the Flynn family. Ever. So, when a postcard from somewhere foreign arrived one day, informing them that Gracie was following her dream and would never return, they hastily made it known to Howard that they had neither the time, nor the inclination, to be involved in Biddy's life. For a short time, Mrs Weir hoped and prayed that the Flynns would come to their senses, change their minds and reclaim the child. Her prayers were shattered for good, however, when, a few months after Gracie had run away, the rest of her family upped sticks and moved yet again – this time, apparently, to Manchester, though no one really knew. And that was that.

So, Mrs Weir was stuck with Biddy. She didn't know quite what to do with a girl, as, apart from her own darling Howard, she had never really been one for children. Still, she made sure that Biddy was fed and clothed, and once or twice, when they had an unexpected visitor for one reason or another, she even bounced the child on her knee and patted her curls.

Mrs Weir's sudden demise from a massive, violent stroke coincided with the closure of Morrison's and Howard's premature entry to retirement. There really was very little hope of alternative employment for a fifty-three-year-old bookkeeper with a three-year-old daughter and no driving licence. But, as a man who was good with figures, he had made a number of small but canny investments in the past, particularly with the modest sum of money his father had left in trust when he died on Howard's tenth birthday.

Mrs Weir had always suspected that her husband, Harold, was a secret drinker and that his outings to the weekly evening mission meetings at the bandstand often included a trip to the local pub. It was the only time he would ever smell of peppermint – 'for my indigestion, dear,' – and Ralgex – 'my back is playing up today, and I didn't want to miss the meeting.' Her suspicions were confirmed when Harold's mangled body had been found on the railway line which ran directly behind the car park at Crawford's Inn. If Harold had come straight home from the meeting as they would do when they both went on Sundays, his journey would not have taken him anywhere near the Inn, or the railway. Mrs Weir never spoke of her suspicions, as her husband had been known as a good, God-fearing man, but she vowed that not a drop of alcohol would ever pass her son's lips.

And look what happened when it had.

Howard was a clever lad. He did well at school and could have gone to university, made something of his life. But his mother had other plans. Mrs Weir decided that her son should stay at home and get a decent, steady job with no real prospects. She also made sure he had few friends and limited interests, so that he could spend as much time with her as possible. She even stopped taking Howard to the Sunday mission meetings, deciding that, since He hadn't done a very good job with her husband, she couldn't trust God to keep an eye on her son. She'd just have to do it all herself.

When his mother died, Howard cashed in one of the saving policies he had set up with his father's inheritance fund and forgot about the rest. He put the money from the policy into a building society in the High Street. The interest from that, coupled with his meagre pension, would be quite enough for a man and a child with limited needs to live off for the foreseeable future. What point was there in having any more? He'd never been a spender, inheriting a tightness that had been in the Weir family for many generations. They were always keeping their money for a rainy day, but even when those rainy days arrived, they still went out with holes in their umbrellas. That was just the sort of them. And anyway, Ballybrock wasn't exactly the kind of place that required high living. It was more than a little bit backward in coming forward, and when Biddy was a baby, there had been no cinema, leisure complex, or big fancy shopping centre in the town. Even when those 'scourges of modern life', as Mr Weir called them, did start to arrive, he never went near them, so neither did Biddy.

All things considered, however, Mr Weir did the best he could with his daughter. He took her to the park, where they would feed stale bread to the ducks. They would walk along the shore and watch the noisy gulls dive for fish and swoop across their heads. He would sometimes read her stories and, for her fourth Christmas, he even withdrew enough money from the building society to buy a portable television so the two of them could sit together for *Watch with Mother*. Gradually, a bond of sorts began to grow between the quiet little girl and her almost silent father. Neither of them realised it was love at the time. But it was. It was just *their* love.

2.

As her school years passed, it gradually dawned on Biddy that she didn't quite fit in. She knew she wasn't pretty like the other girls at school, as during the ritual catchy-kissy sessions which had become customary in the playground, she was the only one in her class from whom the boys would run away, screaming.

'Ugh! She touched me, she touched me,' they would shout, cupping their hands over their mouths, pretending to vomit if one of them even brushed against her accidentally, or ran too close to her, as she wandered round the tarmac doing her daily count of bird poo patches. But Biddy didn't care. She never wanted to join in the game anyway. And she wasn't in the least bit jealous of the other girls, who all looked so similar that she sometimes had difficulty in telling them apart. Biddy wasn't worried about her wild frizzy hair or her badly fitting, grubby uniform. She was much more interested in bird poo.

Biddy had studied bird poo since she was little, after witnessing a seagull poo on another child's head, and over time she had become something of an expert. She knew, for example, that a large splatter of poo dotted with berries or seeds was probably deposited by a big black crow, or a magpie. A big white patch splashed with grey belonged to a seagull. That was the kind she liked best. A small whitish splodge, which could sometimes be mistaken for chewing gum, was the work of a tit or a sparrow. Biddy wasn't interested in dog's dirt or cat shit or rabbit droppings. Just bird poo. She was fascinated by the colours and textures, and loved the fact that birds could shit in mid-flight, hitting an unsuspecting human if they were lucky. She'd never been struck herself, but she'd seen it happen, often, and she couldn't understand why people always reacted with horror, screeching or wailing or swearing when they were hit. She'd often stand on the beach, perfectly still for minutes and minutes at a time, arms outstretched, staring up at the gulls, willing them to hit her. But the birds never did shit on Biddy.

So Biddy knew that she was different, and that was fine. But she didn't realise that she was actually a weirdo, never mind a bloody one – until, that is, Alison Flemming joined her class.

Alison Flemming was beautiful, smart, sporty and a talented pianist. With her honey-blonde hair, smooth skin, deep hazel eyes, and tantalising smile, she wooed people wherever she went. If Alison Flemming had lived in America, she would have been heading for the Prom Queen crown from the day she was born.

And Alison Flemming had another skill: even at the tender age of ten, she was a clever, accomplished and manipulative little bitch. It was a talent she would hone and develop over the years, becoming a master in the process. And like all good bitches, Alison liked to make sure she had a dependable team of devoted followers. Disciples, she liked to call them. It was only when she came to Ballybrock that she recognised her true potential, and fully comprehended the power she could have over others: both those who adored her, and those who did not. There were many hangers-on, but the true believers, the hardcore Alison Flemming fans, were Jackie McKelvey, Georgina Harte and Julia Gamble.

When Alison arrived at Prospect Park in November 1979 – the third month of Primary 6 – she was an instant hit with everyone in the class. Well, everyone except Biddy. At first there were fleeting feelings of jealousy from Jackie, Georgina and Julia, who until that day had generally been regarded as the collective leaders of the Primary 6 female pack. But the threesome quickly realised that Alison was something special and that, for the sake of their long-term prospects, they should become the new girl's closest allies. So, by the end of break time on Alison's first day, the three girls had cooed and clucked and flirted with sufficient eagerness to be awarded the honour of being regarded as the new girl's new best friends. And that was how it stayed, for years.

Alison knew that she would be adored, as that was all she had ever been used to. Well, apart from when the thing with Selina Burton had happened. But thankfully, that was all behind her now. The thought of moving to a new small town from the big city hadn't fazed Alison in the slightest, as she had had no real emotional attachment to any of her old friends, especially after the incident with Selina. She was looking forward to the challenge of making new people fall for her, and this time she was determined not to mess up. But even she didn't expect it to happen quite so quickly. The swiftness of her positioning as the most popular girl in the class was a pleasant surprise that inflated her already lofty ego to new heights, and gave her a formidable flush of bravado.

So when she noticed the odd-looking girl from her class with the horrible hair and the dirty, ill-fitting uniform, walking around the playground, head bent, hands clasped behind her back, stopping every so often to stare at – what? – her interest was instantly piqued.

The girl was the only female pupil who hadn't clamoured to talk to her, or flash her a toothy smile, or offer to show her where the cloakroom was, or the canteen, or the gymnasium. In fact, she hadn't even acknowledged her arrival in any way at all. How dare she?

Alison took a closer look. She really was quite repulsive. Her socks were a colour she couldn't put a name to. Her cardigan was missing several buttons. She was certain she smelled of something rotten. She kept glancing at her during the History lesson after break, and the Maths one before lunch, certain the girl would finally look her way, flash her a smile, try to befriend her – which, of course, she would not allow. But she didn't. It appeared that she, Alison Flemming, was entirely invisible to this, this 'thing'. Memories of Selina and the aftermath of the 'incident' flooded her, and she felt an irrational sense of rage. This hideous girl might not have noticed her yet. But she would. Oh, she would.

By the end of lunchtime, Biddy's fate was sealed.

'What's *her* name, then?' Alison asked her new admirers, glancing over at Biddy as they returned to the classroom.

'Oh, *her*,' sniggered Julia, 'that's just Biddy.'

'Biddy?' laughed Alison, almost choking. 'Biddy? What kind of a stupid name is that? Who on earth would call their child Biddy? Bet her parents are as odd as she is.'

'Yeah,' agreed Georgina with vigorous enthusiasm. 'Bet.'

'Actually, her dad's dead old,' said Jackie, keen to provide some juicy information for Alison. 'He looks like her grandpa. Don't think she has a mum.'

'No wonder she looks like that, then,' Alison sneered. 'What's her other name?'

'Weir,' said Georgina, Julia and Jackie in unison, 'Biddy Weir.'

'More like Biddy Weir*do*,' laughed Alison, flicking her long golden mane behind her, and her little group of admirers laughed with her.

'Biddy Weirdo,' screeched Georgina with glee, crossing her legs, as if she might wet herself. 'That's class.'

Alison was pleased with herself. She looked Biddy up and down with undisguised revulsion. '*Bloody* Weirdo, actually,' she ventured, and they all laughed even louder.

Until that point, Biddy had mostly been ignored by the girls in her class, and that was the way she liked it. Jackie, with her perfect snub nose, Georgina, with her brooding dark eyes and Julia, with her glossy blonde hair held back in a shiny Alice band, never included Biddy in the girly games or secret meetings they hosted in the school playground. Yet they didn't deliberately exclude her either. It was just one of those unspoken, taken-for-granted, shrug-your-shoulders kind of things. They didn't play with Biddy, and Biddy didn't play with them. They shared a silent, mutual understanding. Biddy got on with her thing and the other girls got on with theirs. That was just the way it was. But Alison quickly realised there were going to be advantages to having a weirdo like Biddy Weir in her class. Magnificent advantages. Ignoring Biddy, she decided, would not be an option, but neither, of course, was befriending her. She would have to find something else to do with her. As she made her way back to her desk after the lunch break she discreetly kicked a leg of Biddy's chair. Biddy glanced up from her reading book, a look of concerned confusion on her face.

'Bloody Weirdo,' hissed Alison, narrowing her eyes and holding Biddy's gaze for a second, finally making her notice her. Then she flicked her hair in that way of hers, and skipped across the room to take her seat.

Biddy wasn't prone to tears. Even as a baby, she had rarely cried and never had toddler sulks or terrible tantrums. And if she fell over and cut her knee or grazed her elbow, the sight of blood would intrigue her so much that it never occurred to her to cry or seek attention. It wasn't that she totally lacked emotion, for she knew what it was to be excited about birds and bird poo. It was just that because she had always been a bit of a loner, an outsider of sorts, she had developed her own private world, which no one had ever tried to penetrate. But on this day, for the first time ever, she experienced something very strange indeed. When the new blonde girl hissed at her and kicked her chair, she felt a jolt in her chest, like she had a big, sore lump in her throat, which she instinctively knew she had to get rid of. So she opened her mouth to let the lump out. It didn't come out of course – but a loud and rather unpleasant retching noise did.

'Bloody Weirdo,' muttered Alison Flemming again, loud enough for Biddy and some of the other P6 children to hear, but expertly pitched just outside the hearing range of Miss Justin.

A snigger quickly spread throughout the classroom, with some of the children almost peeing their pants at the thought of this great new girl, Alison, swearing and calling Biddy Weir a 'bloody weirdo'. They'd never seen or heard anything like it.

'Class! Class!' yelled Miss Justin. 'QUIET now or you'll all get extra homework!' Silence descended quickly upon the room, as the children looked at their teacher in nervous, wide-eyed apology.

'Now, who is going to tell me what is going on?'

Julia, obviously eager to impress her new best friend, smiled at Alison and raised her hand.

'Please, Miss Justin. It was Biddy, Miss Justin.' She paused, a flicker of panic creasing her face.

'Well, go on, Julia. What exactly did Biddy do to make you all so excitable?'

'Well, Miss, she erm, she burped and then she swore. She said b-b-bloody, Miss Justin.'

'Thank you, Julia. Please sit down now. Everyone, get out your reading books and turn to chapter four.'

Julia sat, smiling again at Alison who grinned back and nodded her obvious approval.

'Biddy, come to the front please,' said Miss Justin sharply. She reprimanded Biddy for being rude and disruptive, gave her lines, extra homework and made her sit at the front for the rest of the day. The girl repulsed her. She'd always wanted to punish her for something, and at last Julia Gamble had given her good reason.

Biddy said nothing, for she couldn't speak. The lump was still there, only now it was bigger. She thought it might burst out of her chest. Her tummy felt sick, her eyes felt hot and it felt like her body was shrinking. She didn't know what was happening, but she didn't like it at all and she wanted it to stop. It did stop eventually, but only for a while. Sadly for Biddy, that was just the start of it. That was the day that everything changed. The day that Biddy *Bloody* Weir*do* was born.

3.

The victimisation of Biddy was great sport for Alison and her cronies. Alison quickly realised that she could always get a laugh by throwing some new and clever insult at 'Bloody Weirdo', and as long as her bait was around, she would always have a captive audience. She could never have imagined that such a smelly, ugly, weird little girl would ever be useful to her in any way whatsoever. There had been a couple of unattractive oddities at her last school, but she had mostly just ignored them – unless of course, they ever got in her way. Her aggression towards Selina Burton had been based on the unfathomable comment from Selina that *she* was in fact the prettier of the two. Alison had been so shocked by this assumption, so completely shaken to the core by it, that for days she could barely eat or sleep. At school, she became obsessed by Selina's appearance. Her sea-blue eyes, fair skin and long, pale blonde hair began to really irk Alison. Particularly Selina's hair, which was at least four inches longer than her own. Selina could actually sit on hers. Alison realised that she had to do something about it all. So, she became Selina's best friend.

For a while, Selina and Alison did everything together. They linked arms in the playground, they went to each other's house for tea (which made Alison resent her new best friend even more, as she realised that Selina's parents were much wealthier than her own), and they even started riding lessons together. Then, one Saturday night, when Selina's parents were at a dinner dance in a big fancy hotel somewhere in the countryside, Selina was allowed to sleep over at Alison's house rather than stay at her grandparents as she usually did. They had so much fun. Alison's father brought in Hawaiian burgers from their local takeaway for dinner. They listened to music on Alison's portable record player, they ate sweets and popcorn in her bedroom, they dressed up in some of Alison's mother's clothes, and best of all, they played at makeovers. Selina made over Alison first, applying subtle make-up, and twisting her hair into a sophisticated chignon bun: she really was very good. You could see that she got her sense of style from her mother, who had once been a well-known model. Then it was Alison's turn. She did the make-up first, taking her time, telling Selina all the while how wonderful she looked. When she was done, she took a hairbrush and began to brush out Selina's long, glorious mane. Then she gathered it on top of her friend's head and tied a band around it. 'Ohh, I've had an idea. I know just the style for you, you'll love it,' Alison sang and clapped her hands with glee. 'But no peeking, not until it's done.' So Selina screwed her eyes tightly shut and didn't even think to peep, which was a shame, as then she might have seen Alison picking up her mother's kitchen scissors. Luckily for Alison, Selina's hair was very fine, enabling her to cut through the ponytail in almost one go. By the time Selina realised what was happening, it was too late. The damage was done. Alison had achieved her goal with spectacular success, as Selina's hair was well and truly ruined. Even the best, most expensive hairdresser in the city, to whom Selina's mother brought her at 9 a.m. the following Monday morning, couldn't do much to help. The damage was so catastrophic that even a 'Purdy' style was out of the question.

After that, Alison was, most definitely, the prettiest girl in the class. Or at least, the girl with the longest, most glossy hair. Soon she would even be able to sit on it. However, she hadn't thought through the repercussions. She hadn't considered that Selina, once she got over the shock, would actually benefit from having had all her hair cut off: she hadn't at all prepared herself for the reactions of the other girls in class, who now thought *she* was an utter cow and sided with Selina, oohing and aahing and petting over her when she returned to school. Alison was sure that they had only taken Selina's side because a few days after she lost most of her hair, her parents had bought her a pony to compensate for the 'accident'. That weekend Selina had invited over all the girls in the class to ride on Pippa, and then go to Pizza Pappa's for tea afterwards. All except Alison, that is.

So the level of popularity that Biddy Weir had inadvertently brought Alison at her new school was especially gratifying. She would lie in bed at night, scheming up new and brilliant ways of humiliating the Weirdo. But, having learnt from her past mistakes, Alison was clever enough not to actually perpetrate most of the misdemeanours herself. She recognised the value of delegation, and, as her gaggle of admirers were all so eager to please, it was never difficult to allocate Bloody Weirdo assignments. Tripping Biddy up in the playground, shoving her out of the line-up at assembly, hiding her clothes at P.E., cutting holes in her string schoolbag, sticking chewing gum onto the soles of her shoes, tearing her exercise books, spilling water over her finished artwork, planting 'stolen' apples or biscuits or packets of missing chalk in her desk. There were numerous little ways to keep the day-to-day harassment of Biddy Weir on a constant, steady roll.

Biddy quickly became accustomed to this relentless persecution. She hated it, of course, but after every episode, she carried on as though nothing had happened. When the teachers reprimanded her for being clumsy or forgetful or disruptive or punished her for whatever bad behaviour the others caused her to be accused of, she never protested her innocence. She instinctively knew that to do so would make it all so much worse, and so she just carried on whispering apologies for things that weren't her fault.

'Yes, Sir.' 'Sorry, Miss.' 'No, Sir.' 'I'll try, Miss.'

This was about the full extent of Biddy's interaction with the teachers at Prospect Park. It was evident the girl didn't have any friends, and now and then, one or two of them did get a vague notion that something wasn't right, but, as they didn't have any particular empathy with Biddy Weir, and as no complaint had ever been made by the girl or her father, they let it lie. Best not to get involved. God only knows what kind of a can of worms they might be in danger of opening. And none of them would ever have suspected that Alison Flemming, who had quickly established herself as a prize-winning pupil and a star of the school, was behind it all.

So, every day Biddy would go home with that big lump still in her throat and a knot of nausea in her stomach, and tell her father that yes, she had had a good day at school and no, nothing unusual had happened. Same old, same old. Then she would go to her bedroom and cry into her pillow and when the crying was done, she would sit on her chair by her dressing table and stare into the mirror. She grew to hate the person who glared back: the ugly, weak, pathetic, vile little girl. 'Bloody Weirdo,' she would hiss at her reflection, before going downstairs to do her homework. By the time she was eleven, Biddy was filled with as much self-loathing as Alison was with self-love.

4.

Now and then Alison came up with a really awesome idea, a cracking plan that would mortify Biddy even more than usual, and reaffirm her own popularity. And the older she got, the more inventive she became. Like the time she persuaded Georgina to accidentally spill a jug of cold custard over Biddy's hair in the canteen, and the day Jackie agreed to hide Biddy's vest and pants during an outing to the local swimming pool. Biddy, as usual, said nothing and put on her uniform, minus her underwear, while the others whispered and sniggered behind her back. And oh how they laughed later in the playground when, to chants of, 'Biddy's got no knickers on, Biddy's got no knickers on,' Jackie pulled up Biddy's skirt to reveal her pale, bare bottom.

But the best idea by far, the one that really worked a treat, and actually made Biddy cry, right there in the classroom in front of everyone and doddery old Mr Hendry into the bargain, was the one which became known as 'Red Paint Day'.

Alison matured quickly in every way – but particularly in the physical sense. In Primary 6 she was the first girl in the class to swap her plain white school vest for one of those pretty cropped bra tops with a hearts and flowers pattern and matching pants. The bra top wasn't strictly necessary to begin with, but Alison knew she had to make the first move towards grown-up underwear before anyone else from school pipped her to the post. That would have been humiliating. And anyway, by the time the autumn term of P7 arrived, the bra top most definitely was required. During that summer break, when Alison had turned eleven (she hated having her birthday during the school holidays, as she missed out on the fuss that would have been made of her at school, and there was always someone who couldn't come to her party because they were away on holiday somewhere or other, which meant fewer presents), she began to blossom from a girl to a young woman. Her pert little breasts started to push out the bra top, which was replaced by two tiny cotton triangles held together with pink satin straps. Her limbs appeared to lengthen overnight, she went up two shoe sizes, her long honey hair grew longer and glossier than ever before, and on their family holiday to France, her mother allowed her to wear blue eyeshadow for the very first time in public. Alison didn't miss for a second the admiring glances of the local boys in the village. She was in heaven. She took to wearing '4711' cologne. She also took her period.

When the new school term started, Alison wasted no time in telling the other P7 girls her wonderful news. She began with the disciples who, on her nod of approval, started to pass the word down the girls' line at assembly. From the top of the row, Alison watched with glowing pride as the news was greeted with gasps of awe and glances of respect. She was greatly relieved that this first and fundamental step to womanhood had not been experienced by anyone else that summer. Biddy, as always, stood at the back of the line, slightly apart from the rest of the class. No one had spoken to her, acknowledged her, or even noticed her. When Stephanie Hall, the last girl in the line before Biddy, turned to pass on Alison's news, she appeared to look straight through her and, apparently seeing no one, hastily turned back to discuss the exciting event with little Jill Cleaver. But Alison noticed Biddy, all alone, completely unaware of what the others were talking about, oblivious to their excitement. And it suddenly occurred to Alison that even if Biddy had been let in on the not-so-secret secret, she wouldn't have had the foggiest notion what they were talking about. Alison was as sure as she could be that Biddy Weir had never heard of 'periods', so there and then she dreamt up a plan to deliver the Weirdo's first ever sex education lesson.

Georgina, Jackie and Julia agreed that the plan was brilliant, Alison's best yet. The rest of the girls knew that something big was going to happen at Friday afternoon's Art class, but they weren't privy to the details. It was to be a surprise. Naturally, the boys were told nothing. There was no way that any of the girls were going to talk to them about periods and stuff, and anyway, keeping them in the dark would ensure maximum impact.

Biddy liked Friday afternoons. Art class was her favourite lesson, as she loved to draw, and because she was so good at it – by far the best in the class – no one ever made fun of her. They didn't praise her work or compliment her talent, and now and then a jar of water was 'accidentally' spilt over her compositions, but mostly they just ignored her. To Biddy, this was bliss.

But Alison was ragingly jealous of Biddy's artistic talent, as it was the only gift she apparently hadn't been blessed with herself. Since her arrival at the school, she had been waiting for an opportunity to humiliate Biddy during an Art lesson, and, at last, that day had come.

That first Friday afternoon of the Primary 7 term, the atmosphere in the Art lesson was charged with excitement. Even old

Mr Hendry, not noted for his powers of observation, sensed that something was up, but lazily put it down to the buzz of being in Primary 7, or the set task, which was to paint a scene from their summer holiday. And so, at the first opportunity, he went back to his copy of *Catch-22*, hidden inside the Headteacher's Prospectus for the new school year.

Alison gave Julia the nod. Julia put up her hand.

'Please, Mr Hendry,' said Julia sweetly, 'could you give me some help with my picture? I'm not sure how to paint the sand.'

Mr Hendry, irritated by the interruption to his reading, put down his cleverly disguised book and reluctantly began to show Julia how to mix yellow, brown and white, and speckle it on the page for the desired effect of sand. You'd never have known that he had once loved art himself. While he was otherwise occupied, Jackie, on Alison's next nod, walked to the back of the class, on the pretext of washing her paint brush, and carefully tipped a tiny jar of dark red paint onto the back of Biddy's chair. She glanced down briefly and watched the liquid run down the seat and soak into the desired area of Biddy's grubby school skirt before returning to her own chair, smiling sideways to Alison as she sat. As they had anticipated, Biddy was so immersed in her artwork that she neither noticed Jackie standing behind her nor felt the wetness of the paint on her bottom.

Next it was Georgina's turn to wash her paintbrush, but by this time Mr Hendry was seated and reading once again.

'Please, Mr Hendry, Sir, is it OK if I wash my paintbrush, please?'

'Yes, Georgina,' grunted Mr Hendry, without looking up. 'Quick as you can, then.'

Georgina moved slowly to the back of the class, glancing at Alison, holding her brush, thick with green paint, very deliberately out in front of her. She ran the brush under the tap for a few seconds too long for Alison's liking.

Come on, come on, just get on with it, Georgie, thought Alison, giving a little cough to remind Georgina she had a job to do.

Georgina obliged by tapping the paintbrush three times on the edge of the sink to get rid of the excess water, turning round to face the class, pausing for the tiniest second, then screaming at the top of her voice.

'Aaahhhhh! Aaahhhhh! Blood! Blood! Aaahhhhh! Biddy's covered in blood!'

Right on cue, Alison leapt up from her chair and rushed to console her frightened friend. Then, looking at Biddy with feigned horror and mock concern she shrieked, 'Oh, Mr Hendry, Mr Hendry, come quickly. Poor Biddy's got her period.'

The startled teacher, who was already halfway up the classroom to see what blooming fuss was disrupting his reading this time, stopped in his tracks. Sure enough, Biddy Weir's skirt and chair appeared to be covered in dark red blood, and the girl's face was as white as his chalk. She looked like she might be about to pass out. *Oh shit*, he thought. *What to do? What to do?* There was no way he was touching her or cleaning her up or even going any damn closer to her for that matter. Why in God's name did this bloody weird little girl have to go and take her bloody monthly thing in the middle of his class? This was a job for a woman.

'Julia!' he yelled.

'Yes, Mr Hendry?' said Julia, smirking over at Alison and Georgina.

'Go to the office. Get Mrs Martin. Tell her what has happened and say that we need some . . ' he paused, not quite sure what it was that they needed, 'things. And hurry, Julia, hurry.'

'Yes, Mr Hendry.'

Julia scuttled off to get the help that wasn't actually needed, wondering if they'd maybe gone a step too far this time: not out of any concern for Biddy, but fearing that they might get caught out. Still, Alison had promised them everything would work out fine. And Alison was never wrong.

Back in the classroom, mayhem had erupted. Georgina was still in full-blown melodramatic distress at the sight of the 'blood'. Alison was still feigning sympathy and concern for the girl everyone in the class, apart from Mr Hendry, knew she actually despised. Mr Hendry was still stuck to the spot, completely at a loss about how to handle the situation. The rest of the class started to join in the fun.

'Biddy's got her period. Biddy's got her period,' chanted some of the girls.

'Aw, gross! Disgusting! Yuck!' shouted the boys.

Most of them hadn't a clue what was going on, but it didn't matter. This was brilliant.

Biddy felt sick. She had no idea what was going on either. What on earth were Alison and Georgina shouting about? What had she done? What blood? What was her period? Why were they saying that?

WHAT IS A PERIOD?? she silently screamed.

Biddy looked round at her chair and saw the 'blood'. She put her hand down and felt the back of her skirt. She brought her fingers up to her face and examined the reddish liquid.

'Oh, double gross,' shouted Dennis Bailey, 'I'm going to puke!'

It's just paint, thought Biddy. *It's just red paint. Why do they think it's blood?*

But she couldn't say it out loud. The lump was there again, blocking her throat, stopping her words. She instinctively knew that this period business was something big, something important. Something not nice, but something significant. Something to do with being a girl. She looked around at the class. It seemed as though everyone was pointing at her and laughing at her and despising her even more than usual.

They all know, she thought. *They all know what it is, and they know that I don't.*

She ran her hand down her face, smearing it with dark red paint, which was soon dripping onto her shirt, helped on its way by warm, wet tears. And as the tears fell from Biddy's eyes as they never had before in public, she suddenly knew what she needed. The shock was overwhelming. 'I want my mummy,' she sobbed for the first time in her life. 'I want my mummy.'

Mrs Martin, the matronly school secretary, took Biddy to the office, where she cleaned her up as best she could and called her father. It took twenty-two minutes for him to walk to the school, as there was no one he could call on for a lift.

For twenty-two minutes, Mrs Martin battled with her conscience. Should she try to talk to the girl about what had happened: tell her that the incident had been an unfortunate misunderstanding? Explain why? Perhaps even run through the rudiments of puberty? After all, the poor wee mite had no mother of her own to do the job. But then again, maybe it wasn't her place to get involved. Surely there was an aunt or grandmother or some female member of the family who was a substitute mother figure? And anyway, Mrs Martin only had sons herself. Four of them. What did she know about sex education, as it was now called, for eleven-year-old girls? Besides, the child was obviously too distressed by the whole thing. Probably best not to get involved. She'd wait and see what the father had to say. And she'd say a prayer for the child tonight at bedtime. Bless her.

For twenty-two minutes, Biddy thought about her mother. She stood in the office with its salmon-pink walls and cream lace curtains and imagined that the plump, middle-aged woman with soft peachy skin and apricot lips, who was wiping down her skirt with a damp linen tea towel, was her mummy. She could smell her sweet scent and feel the warmth of her body as she busied around. Is this what her own mother looked like? Smelled like? Moved like? She'd never seen a photograph, never asked, never even really wondered. But now she did, and more than anything she wanted this lady to hold her, hug her, stroke her hair, kiss her forehead, tell her that everything would be OK, pretend to be her mummy for a minute.

'*Mummy, what's a period?*' she silently asked.

A knock at the door jolted Biddy, and for a split second she almost believed that her mother had come to save her.

'Oh, Mr Weir, she's fine. Come in, come in,' said Mrs Martin as she ushered Biddy's breathless, worried father into the room. 'It's all been a dreadful misunderstanding, Mr Weir. Somehow Biddy managed to spill some paint over her skirt, red paint, and some of the girls panicked. They thought she'd taken her, well, you know, her, ahem, monthly's, you see. Anyway, Biddy got a bit upset, and there were a few tears and . . . well, you're all right now, aren't you, Biddy?' she said, rather too loudly, rather too brightly.

Mr Weir nodded and looked at his daughter, standing by the window, a halo of sunlight highlighting her wild copper curls, her pasty cream skin sinking into the lace curtain behind, her pale green eyes glistening like slivers of broken glass. She looked like a miserable angel. She looked just like her mother.

'All right, lass, let's go home,' he said softly, reaching out for Biddy's hand. Biddy desperately wanted to be hugged. She couldn't remember having had a hug, from anyone, ever, not even her father, and it had never occurred to her to want one before. But suddenly she longed to escape to the shelter of someone else's arms, to feel protected from all her pain. But she took her father's hand, knowing it was the best that he could do.

'Mr Weir,' said Mrs Martin hesitantly, taking a book from the solitary thick shelf in her office that constituted the school's library. 'I hope you don't think it's out of place, coming from me, but perhaps you might find this useful,' she said, handing him a small hardback Ladybird book.

Mr Weir glanced at the cover. '*Your Body*,' he read and stared at the drawing of a human male skeleton alongside a sketch of a muscular man in a running pose. How could this help his little girl? 'Page forty-two,' whispered Mrs Martin, her smile oozing pity. 'All she needs to know.'

A flush rising in his cheeks, Mr Weir nodded and slipped the book into his inside coat pocket. He took Biddy home via the park, stopping at Mrs Henderson's corner shop to buy a packet of Kimberley biscuits and a sherbet dip. And when Mrs Thomas, their new neighbour at number 21, who was brushing down the path outside her house, asked if everything was OK – was Biddy ill, or had the whole school been sent home early and should she run now and get her boy Ian who'd be fretting if he was left standing at the gate? – he simply tipped his cap and ushered his daughter into their house without so much as a word.

The day after the 'incident', Mr Weir bought his daughter a packet of Dr. White's.

'You, ah, you can put this away for safe keeping,' he muttered, handing her a white plastic bag as she hung up her coat, shattered from enduring the relentless jibes and sniggers of her persecutors at school. It was the one and only time she had pleaded not to go, but her father had insisted.

She looked at him expectantly, waiting for an explanation as to the contents of the bag. Her father did not give gifts freely. It wasn't her birthday and Christmas was ages away. But he wouldn't meet her eyes and turned away, embarrassed and uncomfortable by this necessary gesture. 'I'll be in the shed if you need help with your homework. My tools need sorting.'

Biddy sat on the end of her creaking bed and removed the packet of sanitary towels from the bag, noticing they had been purchased in the big chemist store in town and not from their local pharmacist round the corner. It must have been the first time her father had broached its doors, and would probably be the last. She hugged the packet to her chest, wishing all at once to have a mother, to really have her period and to be normal like the other girls. Then she put the packet in her bottom drawer, tucked in beside the Ladybird book, where it would stay, untouched, for over four years, until her period finally came.

'Thank you, Papa,' Biddy said quietly to her father that evening at dinner. He nodded, knowing what she meant. 'Just let me know when you need some more, lass. I'll give you the money.'

And that was the last that was said about it. She often wondered if he wondered whether she had started. He sometimes thought that maybe she had, but was too shy to say. And as that first packet lasted for two whole periods, and Biddy started getting twenty pence a week of pocket money when she turned thirteen, she never did ask him for the money to buy some more.

5.

Biddy waded through the rest of her final year at primary school in a haze of despair. Her head bowed lower, and her body stooped over more than ever. From a distance she could have been mistaken for a shrunken old lady, and her classmates had great fun impersonating her strange and unconventional gait. But after Red Paint Day, nothing major happened for the rest of that year. It was generally agreed that nothing could top the success of that momentous day, and Alison knew when to back off. She couldn't risk being exposed as the master planner of Biddy's big humiliation and she suspected that some of her admirers had lost their enthusiasm for the game. Not that anyone actually befriended Biddy, or stopped referring to her as 'Bloody Weirdo', or stood up for her. Alison just had a feeling that she should let things settle. Besides, there was the 11-plus exam to concentrate on, and then the P7 cup – which, naturally, she expected to win.

The 11-plus was a breeze for Alison. There was never any doubt, from anyone, that she would do anything other than pass with flying colours, which she did. The wait for the results didn't cause Alison a second of concern, but, when the time came, the issue of which school she would go to most certainly did.

Since their move to Ballybrock, Alison had wholeheartedly believed that her father would pay for her to go to Belamore College, the prestigious private school further on down the coast. This was, after all, one of the main reasons that George and Felicity Flemming had decided to move from the city – or so they had told Alison, and everyone else in their extended social circle. Belamore was by far the best school in the whole

41

country. Sophia La Grue, the daughter of TV star, Lana La Grue, boarded at the Girls' College and her brother, Oliver, at the adjoining Boys' College. There were even rumours that a proper Lady someone or other was one of the pupils. Alison was almost beside herself with excitement.

'When I go to Belamore, I think I should board,' she told her parents on numerous occasions. The thought of midnight feasts and sliding down drainpipes for secret liaisons with some of the gorgeous floppy-haired boys from the Boy's College next door was beyond thrilling. 'Obviously, I'm only thinking about you, Mother,' she'd say. 'I mean, the long drive to and from the college each day would be far too much for you, wouldn't it, Daddy?'

And George Flemming would smile, and stroke his daughter's long golden hair and say, 'Let's just wait and see, honey.' Then he'd go into his study and remove the bottle of Black Bush from the cabinet, pour a large slug into a Waterford crystal tumbler, and knock it back in one. Then he'd pour another, and often, a third.

Alison knew he did this in the way that Alison knew everything: by snooping, by eavesdropping, by pretending to be asleep on car journeys and quietly lifting the telephone extension and holding glasses to walls and peeking through keyholes. She was as good at being a spy as she was at being a bitch, and she approached the activity in the same methodical and committed way that some of her fellow pupils might have applied themselves to, say, learning to play the cello, or becoming a county-level swimmer.

Thus Alison knew all along that the relocation to Ballybrock had actually nothing to do with her education at all. It turned out that her darling daddy had lost his very well-paid job as Company

Director due to a moment of madness involving the Chief Executive's wife. Well, six months of madness, actually. For some time prior to her mother's discovery of the affair with Muriel Clarke, Alison had taken to slipping out of her bedroom at nine o'clock each night and tiptoeing across the landing to the third step from the top of the stairs, from where she had a perfect view of the television through the glass panel at the top of the living-room door. Although the sound was often muffled, the pictures were good. So much more interesting than the boring children's programmes she was allowed to watch. *Blue Peter* didn't interest her in the slightest. At this particular time Alison's favourite programme was *Shoestring*, primarily because she found Trevor Eve, the actor who played the part of Eddie Shoestring, strangely alluring. Her parents' first major row about the affair happened to coincide with a *Shoestring* night, which distracted Alison's viewing and put her in a very bad mood. They, of course, were blissfully unaware that this interesting episode in their marriage was being witnessed by their ten-year-old daughter who, they assumed, was fast asleep in her pretty pink and white bedroom. That very afternoon, Felicity's dear friend, Diana James, had taken her to lunch and told her that she had virtually caught George and Muriel at it in the golf club locker room during the Night at the Races evening the previous Saturday. She'd wrestled with her conscious ever since, apparently, but felt Felicity deserved to know.

'And what was that toffee-nosed bitch doing in the locker room herself? Eh?' Alison heard her father sneer in response to the accusation, before denying it.

But Felicity knew the truth. And so, from her vantage point on the stairs, did Alison. She smelt the lie, like a trained dog sniffing out a truffle.

'I mean, Muriel Clarke,' her mother wailed. 'Muriel bloody Clarke. Why could you not have chosen someone less, well, less important?'

Alison had to cup her hands over her mouth to suppress the snigger bursting from her nose.

'Why your boss's wife, for heaven's sake? She's the Lady Captain of the Golf Club, George. She's President of the local Lady Taverners group. She even had a bloody rose named after her at the City's centenary flower show last year!'

Alison had to scuttle, mouse-like, back to her bedroom then, when her father hissed to her mother that she should calm down and shut the fuck up before she woke up their daughter, and that he'd better go and check on her, just in case. As he headed up the stairs she arranged her angelic face in a suitably sleep-like pose, her silky locks spread over the pillow like a plumage. But, to her annoyance, George didn't go directly into her room. Instead she heard the creak of his office door, the clink of a glass being removed from a cabinet, and the low groan of three soft 'fucks' in a row. When he finally came to check on her she smelt the whisky on his breath, and caught the edge of a sob in his throat as he tiptoed out of her room. Until that moment her father had been her hero, the man she knew no other would ever live up to. He was definitely handsome. Perhaps not quite as wealthy as she'd like him to be, but she knew from her snooping he had potential (there'd been recent talk of a promotion to Deputy Chief Executive, with a lucrative package). He was strong and capable and popular, especially with women, and charmingly flirtatious – which Alison found both thrilling and infuriating to watch. Of course he adored *her*: *she* was his number one, his hunny bunny, his princess. He was always buying her little presents, and pressing money into the palm of her hand, and stroking her hair, and telling her what a beauty she was. But that night, as well as the lie, as well as the whisky, Alison smelt something else from her father as he stood by the foot of her bed: weakness. And it turned her stomach.

The truth came out, of course, and, naturally, George lost his job. But the reason that Felicity gave for their move to Ballybrock, which, as everyone knew, was a small-time town in the back end of beyond, was Alison. Alison heard her: over the fence to neighbours, on the telephone to the ladies from the bridge group and the golf club, at the school gate, in the supermarket. They needed to be closer to Belamore College, she gushed to anyone who would listen, as it had always been their intention that Alison would go there. And she simply wouldn't agree to her boarding. Oh, no. She couldn't bear the idea of being parted from her darling daughter during the week. And, of course, the timing of George's wonderful new job was perfect. Yes, yes, he had indeed been looking for something in the area for quite some time. It might not be their ideal place to live, but their daughter came first. Alison was so talented, and so intelligent, that they owed it to her to give her the best education possible.

Alison sneered with contempt each time she heard her mother desperately relay her meticulously rehearsed story. She knew her mother didn't really care about her education. She probably did want Alison to go to Belamore – but only so that she could boast about it at her clubs, and committees and to anyone who would listen. When they moved to Ballybrock, she knew it would take her mother no time at all to join the golf club, the tennis club (even though she couldn't actually play), the bridge society, the Young Wives Club at the most socially attractive church, the PTA, the local Lady Taverners group (if Ballybrock was even big enough to have one, which Alison very much doubted) and any other group of influence she deemed to be worthy of her membership. And she would brag to every single new contact she made (to say 'friends' would be inaccurate, as Alison was well aware her mother didn't really invest in friendships as such) that her darling daughter would be attending Belamore. Alison despised her mother for the importance she put on social standing and the time she invested in securing it: yet she admired her for it too. And the older she became, the more Alison realised what an excellent role model her mother actually was. And, of course, she was secretly delighted about Belamore. The timing was perfect, as it coincided with the whole Selina Burton thing, and when she overheard her parents discuss the move, she was actually deeply relieved. Perhaps in this new place she really would be the richest and prettiest girl in the class. Perhaps *everyone* would adore her. Yes, she was sure that they would. She felt it in her blood. And if she encountered somebody who didn't, she would make damn sure she handled the situation much better than she had with Selina.

Naturally, George and Felicity Flemming had assumed the Selina Burton incident had all been a dreadful misunderstanding. A terrible accident. Child's play gone wrong. Alison heard them discuss it night after night from her secret spot on the stairs. It amused her that the notion of their darling daughter ever deliberately doing anything unsavoury to another child, never mind Selina Burton, her dearest best friend, the daughter of the Burtons, no less – eminent heart surgeon, Edward, and his wife Francesca who had once been a successful model – was, well, too preposterous for words. Alison was not a bad child, she heard them reiterate, time and time again. She was a sweetheart. An angel. A good, innocent girl. How could this have happened?

'I don't know which is worse,' she heard her mother sob one night, after an invitation to play bridge at Joyce Butler's house had inexplicitly been withdrawn, 'you being exposed as a philanderer, or the accusation that Alison is, of all things, a bully. A "malicious little bitch", I overheard Carol Mackey say in the playground the other day. This is your fault, George. Your fault. She must have known something was up. She must have been distracted. Not herself. Well, you owe it to both of us now to make sure she gets to that school. It's the bloody least you can do.'

For the first time in her life, Alison felt a swelling affinity with her mother, and realised that if she was really to get to Belamore, it was her mother she must focus on, and not her father.

The two Flemming females settled remarkably well into their new lives. Being big fish in a tiny pond suited each of them extremely well. Within their first year in Ballybrock, Felicity had become Chair of the school PTA, Secretary of their church Young Wives group and, as she told Alison and George on several occasions, was expecting an invitation to be Vice Lady Captain of the Golf Club at the next round of nominations. Apparently Charlotte Fox, the outgoing Lady Captain, had indicated so.

'According to Charlotte,' she heard her mother tell her father one evening when she was supposed to be doing her homework, 'no one has ever made it up the Ballybrock Golf Club ladder so quickly before.'

And, obviously, Alison's own star was shining brightly too. It was obvious for all to see. Her reception at Prospect Park had been astonishing: she was incredibly popular with the pupils and teachers alike, had made many new friends, and was, by all accounts, the brightest girl in the school. 'Oh, everyone loves Alison,' she heard her mother coo on the telephone to one of the few friends from the city she actually kept in touch with. 'She's even had her photograph in the *Ballybrock Chronicle* on five occasions' – a statistic which also delighted Alison.

'She's been amazing, George, hasn't she?' her mother would often cluck in the evenings, when she thought Alison was tucked up in bed. 'Such a credit to us. And she's never complained. Not once.'

In truth, the year since their move had been a doddle for Alison. Everyone at the new school did indeed love her, apart from Biddy Weir, of course, but Alison didn't really hold that against her, as creating the myth of Bloody Weirdo had merely added to her popularity. She did hate the girl, but not in the way she had hated Selina. Biddy disgusted her, repulsed her, but she was very, very useful.

So, everything was going swimmingly well for both Alison and Felicity. But as the day drew near when the anticipated acceptance letter from Belamore College would pop through the letterbox, it became clear that something was afoot. Alison began to notice that her father was spending more time than usual in his study, and, when the coast was clear and her mother wasn't around, she would kneel down on the bouncy hall carpet and peek through the keyhole. It wasn't quite as easy to spy on her parents in this house as it had been at their previous one, and now her father even had a lock on his study door. But Alison was terrifically light on her feet, and managed fairly well. She watched him sit behind his desk, either filling up his glass with whisky, or slumped across it, nursing his hands in his head.

She watched him pace the room, fingers held to his temples. She heard him snivel pathetic sentences such as, 'I'm so sorry, I'm so, so sorry,' and 'I don't deserve you, my sweetheart,' and 'you're such a good girl, such a good, good girl'. To begin with she thought he was referring to her mother, his conscience finally catching up with him, until the night she heard him cry into his whisky, 'How am I going to tell you, my hunny bunny? My hunny, hunny bunny.' Those words were like shattering glass to Alison. *She* was his hunny bunny, not her mother. And the only thing in the world he could be afraid of telling her, the *only* thing, was that she wasn't going to Belamore College. When her mother came home from yet another bridge game, she found Alison waiting for her in the kitchen, her eyes red from crying. Without even insisting that Alison go to her room, Felicity turned on her heels and marched to the study. Banging on the door, she screamed at George to let her in; tell her what the fuck was going on. It was the only time in her life that Alison heard her mother say fuck.

An almighty row ensued, and Alison, of course, heard every word. It transpired that her father's new sales job didn't even pay half of his previous salary, and that the hefty commissions he'd been banking on hadn't actually materialised.

'What about my bungalow, George?' her mother shrieked. 'You promised me a sea view and a bungalow within three years!'

'Screw your bungalow,' Alison whispered from the padded seat by the telephone table in the hall, having no need to spy from the stairs. 'What about Belamore?'

At that very same moment the penny dropped with Felicity and she screamed the same words. 'Belamore, George. Belamore. Don't you dare tell me . . .'

*

Alison's sense of shock when she discovered that she would not be going to Belamore College after all was overwhelming. She was truly devastated. She cried for hours and couldn't even go to school the following day because her eyes were much too swollen. Her mother cried too, and, for the first time in their lives, they sat on the edge of Alison's bed, arms around each other and wailed together in perfect harmony. It was a poignant, bonding experience, which may have even touched George if he had witnessed the moment. But he was still in his study, slumped over his desk, drunk as a skunk.

Alison could forgive her father his affair – indeed she almost admired him for it. She could forgive his secret drinking, and his long hours at the office, and the weekends spent locked inside his study. She could forgive him bringing them to this dump of a town. She could even forgive him not turning up at prize night when she was presented with the Prospect Park school cup, along with five other awards. But she would never, ever forgive him this.

It took until the end of the summer term for Alison to resign herself to the fact that she would be wearing the boring navy blue uniform of Ballybrock Grammar School and not the charming purple and yellow one she had set her heart on. One day, she resolved, as she tried her new uniform on, I will be rich enough myself to buy Belamore College if I want to.

But the biggest shock of all for Alison came on the very last day of school at Prospect Park. Miss Thornleigh, the headmistress, asked everyone who would be going to Ballybrock Grammar in September to stand at one side of the assembly hall, and all of those going to Mill Street Secondary School to stand on the other side, so that Mr Hendry and Mrs Thompson could talk to them separately about their new schools. Leanne Moore and Kenneth Smith were left standing in the middle, as they were moving to completely new towns to live. Kenneth's family were actually immigrating to New Zealand, which was a bit of a shame for Alison, as she quite fancied him.

Alison was glancing around the Ballybrock Grammar group. All the members of her 'gang' were there. Georgina, Jackie and Julia (who only got into the school as a paying pupil as she hadn't actually passed the 11-plus), along with other hangers-on like Jill Cleaver, Stephanie Hall, Beverley Brown and Sharon McKimm. Michael Williams, Bryan Murphy and Paul Blundell were there, which was fine as they all fancied her and were fanciable enough themselves, but greasy Johnny Sanders and speccy Richard Farrell she could do without. And there, hovering in the background, head bent, hands tightly clasped behind her back, was bloody Biddy Weir! Alison nearly choked. There must be some mistake: surely the Weirdo hadn't passed her 11-plus? Nobody had actually asked her, of course, when the results had come out three months before, but then there was no need. After all, she was a thicko, wasn't she?

Alison nudged Georgina. 'Look over there,' she nodded in the direction of where Biddy was standing. Georgina's eyes widened in amazement. 'No,' she whispered, 'she couldn't. She can't. Can she? Maybe her dad's paying for her, like Julia's.'

'Doubt it,' snarled Alison, nodding down towards Biddy's feet. Her big toe was sticking out of a hole in her sock. Her sandals looked a size too small. 'If he can't afford to buy her a pair of socks or sandals that actually fit, he'll hardly be able to pay for her education, will he?'

Alison sidled over to where Biddy was standing. 'I think you're in the wrong place,' she sniped. Biddy glanced up, saw Alison glaring at her, and quickly put her head down again. 'I said,' began Alison in a louder voice, 'I think . . .'

'Quiet, everyone, settle down,' shouted Miss Thornleigh, interrupting her. 'Those of you going to Mill Street Secondary, follow Mr Hendry to room 7. The Ballybrock Grammar group, please stay in the hall with Mrs Thompson. Leanne and Kenneth, you may wait in Mrs Martin's office until you are called back to class. Whichever school you are going to in September, I wish you all the very best for your future.' Coming from Miss Thornleigh, those were remarkably kind words, as she was not prone to sentiment of any description. She nodded at Mr Hendry and Mrs Thompson, and almost marched out of the hall, Leanne and Kenneth scurrying behind her.

Alison was still waiting for Biddy to realise she'd made a mistake, and go with the Mill Street thickos down to Hendry's room. But Biddy still stood rooted to the spot, head bloody bent as usual, toe poking out of her stinking socks. *God*, thought Alison, shaking her head in disbelief, *how the hell did this happen?*

Biddy was thinking exactly the same thing. She hadn't really paid that much attention to the 11-plus, and had ploughed through the test papers, sometimes getting an average mark, sometimes a poor one, but never a great one. She hovered around the borderline area, more below than above and had simply assumed that she would fail.

Biddy answered all but two questions in the first actual test. In the second, she completed the paper with two or three minutes to spare and spent the final seconds watching a seagull swoop up and down outside the window beside her desk. It landed on the sill and stared at her for a couple of seconds before flying off, just as the lady in charge of the exam said, 'Time's up, put your pencils down please.' When her father asked her after each test how it had gone, she replied: 'Fine, Papa,' and pointed to the plate laid out on the kitchen table. 'May I have a Kimberley biscuit, please?' That was the extent of their conversation about the 11-plus.

Mr Weir quietly hoped his daughter would pass and go to Ballybrock Grammar, as he himself had done. He also harboured a secret notion that one day she would go to university and live the life he had once hoped to have. But he knew that was just a dream, the only one he really had, and he didn't dare to share it with Biddy. What was the point? He settled himself with the more realistic expectation that she would be going to Mill Street Secondary, and that was fine.

Biddy's priority was to get away from Alison, and as she had overheard Alison boast on many occasions that she would be going to someplace called Belamore College, there was really nothing to worry about. And as no one had ever told her that she would pass, could pass, or might pass, she had simply assumed that she would be going to Mill Street Secondary – which was fine, really, since there was less of a chance that Georgina, Jackie and Julia would be going there.

When the letter had come and it had said 'PASS', Biddy assumed there had been a mistake. Her father had put on his coat and gone to the bakery to buy two apple turnovers to celebrate. Biddy waited and waited for another letter to tell her about the mistake, but none came. And now here she was, standing in the assembly hall on her last day at Prospect Park. The realisation that she really was going to Ballybrock Grammar finally hit her. And the fact that Alison Flemming was going there too was just too much to bear. This wasn't supposed to happen. Biddy's head began to spin, her throat felt as though it was closing over and sweat poured down her back. Mrs Thompson's voice sounded further and further away, and then the floor rose and smacked Biddy on the face. When she came round, Mrs Thompson was holding out a glass of water, Mrs Martin was dabbing her forehead with a damp cloth, and Alison Flemming was glaring at her with narrowed eyes, just the way an eagle might.

6.

With a brand new fan base at their big new school, Alison flourished and Jackie, Georgina and Julia continued to cherish their roles as her trusted servants. On her first day, Alison was relieved to discover that, despite the influx of new pupils from several different primary schools, she was still, by far, the fairest of them all; which was some consolation at least for not being able to go to Belamore College. And although there were one or two definite oddities amongst the fresh new first formers, none of them came close to the weirdness of Biddy Weir.

And of course, it wasn't long before news of the bloody weirdo in First Form spread throughout the school. As Alison's audience increased, her popularity soared and her ego expanded accordingly. Her perfect impersonation of Biddy's lonesome playground walks was replayed time and time again, to shrieks of delight from her old and new admirers. And her hilarious tales of Biddy's bare bottom and her first ever 'period' might as well have been printed in the school magazine, for almost every pupil in the junior school soon knew the stories. And even if they didn't find them funny, they laughed. Most of them knew it was better to laugh along than to be laughed at.

Biddy herself quickly realised that everyone at the new school knew about her weirdness. Everywhere she went she was shoved, tripped up or her path was blocked. She could hear the sneers, the sniggers and the murmurs. 'Whoa. Watch out. It's Bloody Weirdo.' 'Bloody Weirdo Alert. Bloody Weirdo Alert.' Sometimes she longed for the simplicity of her torment at Prospect Park. At least there she knew what to expect, most of the time, anyway, and she knew where she could hide. This place was just so vast, it terrified her. It was like being in a never-ending maze with no way out; a relentless nightmare she was doomed never to awaken from. There were so many more people here who knew who and what she was. Even the walls seemed to whisper, 'Bloody Weirdo, Bloody Weirdo, Bloody Weirdo' as she trudged along the school corridors, head down, shoulders hunched, willing herself to be invisible from the throngs of pupils, waiting for the next big humiliation.

Weeks, months, even, could pass by without any major incident, but they were always there, her tormentors, with their comments and sneers and expressions of utter disgust. And the threat of Alison delivering one of her trademark 'master plans' constantly clung to her, gripping her throat like a caught breath.

One sunny Thursday afternoon near the end of her second year at Ballybrock Grammar, Biddy was, as usual, hovering at the back of the bus queue after school. She always waited until the unruly mob started to push and shove their way onto the bus before joining the herd at the last minute, hoping that the driver would let her stand on the middle step. Sometimes, depending on who the driver was, she got her wish. Sometimes the door would swish shut, almost trapping her face as she tried to jump on, and she would have to wait for the next bus, or walk the thirty-minute journey home. She didn't mind the walk, but it was getting a lot more difficult now that her schoolbag was weighed down with more and more heavy textbooks. And on this particular day, it was much too hot to drag both herself and her bag up the steep Westhill Road.

'Hey, B.W.!' Biddy froze as Alison, Jackie, Georgina and Julia sauntered towards her, followed by two or three of the new Alison worshippers. 'I said, hey, B.W.! Didn't you hear me? Gone deaf or something, have you?' Alison spat. The others sniggered. B.W. was Alison's new abbreviated name for Biddy and they thought it was so cool.

'So, B.W. . . .' Alison continued, aware that some of the boys in the bus queue were looking over. Craig Black, the blond hunk from the fourth year whose attention she'd been trying to get for a week now, stood with his hands in his pockets, kicking some loose gravel onto the road. Their eyes met briefly and Alison slowly bit her bottom lip and ran her fingers through her hair before turning her attention back to Biddy. She knew that if she played this well she'd snare him. She might be just a second former, but she *was* almost fourteen – and knew she looked much older than her age. She also knew she'd go a hell of a lot further than most of the girls in his year would.

'So, B.W.,' she smiled, 'are you gonna enter the school talent competition?'

Biddy just stared at the ground, aware that her armpits were starting to drip with sweat.

'Eh, is that a "yes" or a "no", then?' Alison quipped, winking at the other girls and snatching a glance at Craig, who raised his eyebrows just enough to let her know he was watching. 'Well, probably best if you don't bother, B.W. After all, you wouldn't want to embarrass yourself any more than you usually do. Pity there isn't a category for bloody weirdos, though. You'd win that, for sure. Hands down. Just think, you could go through to represent the school at the national finals. And surely there isn't a bloody weirdo in the whole country who's weirder than you.'

Alison was on a roll now, and the sniggers from her expanding audience egged her on.

'Picture it: assembly, the day after the finals . . . Mr Duncan on the stage, all the teachers lined up behind him. "I'd like you all to put your hands together for our very own Biddy Weir, the best Bloody Weirdo in the country".'

A mock cheer went up from Alison's audience. Biddy's face burned as hot as the blazing sun. Her blouse was now soaked with sweat, her stomach churned with fear, and the lump in her throat was demanding release. *Please stop it, please stop it, please stop it*, she silently repeated, over and over.

But Alison was having fun.

'Anyway, B.W., don't be sad about not being able to enter the talent show. You'll be there in spirit, if not in body, because you, B.W., are the inspiration for our act. Isn't she, girls?'

'Sure is, Alison,' said Jackie.

'Abso-bloody-lutely,' laughed Georgina.

'Want to hear it, B.W.?' teased Alison, slyly. 'Want to hear *your* song?' Biddy swallowed hard. There was nowhere to run, and even if there were, she wouldn't have been able to move anyway.

'We do, we do,' chanted some of the onlookers, enjoying this unexpected afternoon entertainment more by the minute.

'OK, girls, ready?' Alison dropped her bag, loosened her already loose tie, undid the third button of her shirt to expose the teensiest bit of white lacy bra, and rolled up her sleeves. The others followed suit, only Julia not going the whole way with the buttons. They took their positions, bottoms stuck out, knees slightly bent, hands flicked out at the side of their hips, Alison standing slightly in front of the other three. The four of them had been practising their little routine in secret for two days and had perfected all the moves.

'After three,' said Alison, clearing her throat, adrenaline rushing through her veins. This was the best thing she'd come up with since Red Paint Day, and she could tell Craig was already impressed. Just wait until he heard the song!

'One. Two. Three . . .

Look out here she comes, stompin' down the street,
She's the bloodiest weirdo that you ever will meet.

Oh yes she's a weirdo
And she freaks us all out,
She's ugly and she's creepy,
There ain't no bloody doubt.

There she goes again talkin' to the birds
She's a definite nutter, she's a total nerd.

Oh yes she's a weirdo,
And she freaks us all out.
She's ugly and she's creepy,
There ain't no bloody doubt . . .'

A roar of appreciation went up from the crowd. Alison, Jackie, Georgina and Julia bowed and curtsied, loving the attention, delighted with their performance. Alison looked over at Craig, and tossed her hair. He rubbed his nose with the back of his hand, spat out his gum, and winked. Yes! She'd got him. She picked up her school bag, pushed her way past Jackie, Georgina and Julia and sashayed over to join Craig in the queue. The others, enjoying their fifteen seconds of fame, laughed and chatted with the crowd that had gathered around them.

Biddy stood alone, head bent, hot tears streaming down her face, snot dripping from her nose. The bus came. Everyone pushed on. Alison sat with Craig on the back seat. Jackie, Georgina and Julia were all given seats as reward for their fantastic performance. Everyone on board started singing the song as the bus pulled away from the stop, but no one noticed Biddy – still crying, still standing, head bent, at exactly the same spot. Another bus came and went. Then another, and another. But Biddy stayed where she was, rooted to the spot for over an hour, until the sun began to lose its heat and she finally found the strength to start the walk back to Stanley Street. She never took the school bus home again.

7.

The years dragged by. Biddy's life was heavy and weary, the persecution exhausting. On the worst days, the days when something big happened, 'episode days', as she came to call them, she wanted to curl up, go to sleep and never wake up. She lived for the good days, the days when Alison and the others completely ignored her. The best days of all were the ones when, for whatever reason, Alison wasn't at school – and, of course, weekends and holidays, when she could escape to the beach to draw.

Biddy's only true pleasure in life, the one thing that kept her going, was her drawing. She would often sit on the pebble beach, sketching the sea and the seagulls, oblivious to everything else around her. Now and again a shout of 'Hey, it's Bloody Weirdo,' or 'Talking to the birds again, B.W.?' came from the wall or the promenade. But no one ever came down to bother her on the beach. It was her sanctuary.

One cold Saturday afternoon in late January of Fourth Form, Biddy was sitting at her usual spot by the corner of some rocks, wrapped in the red and blue tartan shawl her father had given her for Christmas, along with a big artist's sketchpad and a new set of pencils. They were the best presents she had ever had from him.

'For your beach days,' he had said, smiling softly when Biddy gasped with delight.

They never discussed her art, but every now and then Mr Weir would go into her room when she was at school, and pull out the mound of sketches she kept stuffed under her bed. He could spend hours sitting on the end of her bed, staring at the pages, tracing his fingers over the dancing waves, caressing the wings of the seagulls. They looked so real, he almost expected them to leap off the page and fly away. Now and again he was moved to tears. But he never told Biddy he looked at her drawings, never told her how much he loved them, how very, very proud he was to have a daughter with such an outstanding talent. So she never knew.

The low winter sun cast a pale yellow glow across the sea. The light was beginning to fade as a shutter of blue-grey sky drew down towards the water. The seagulls swooped up and down, their shrieks calling the end of the day. Biddy looked up from her sketchpad, realising it was almost time to pack up, and noticed a young couple by the edge of the water wrapped up in colourful hats and scarves. They had their arms around each other. As they drew closer, she heard the girl laugh at something the boy had whispered in her ear, and her stomach sank. She would know that laugh anywhere.

It was Alison with an older boy she didn't recognise. He was tall and lean, with blond floppy hair and rosy cheeks, burning from the cold. His black and green stripy scarf told her he went to the private boys' school in Collingsford, the neighbouring town just a few miles away.

'Well, well, well, if it isn't B.W.,' Biddy heard Alison say to the boy as they drew nearer.

'Oh, I recognise her, I've seen her on the beach before,' he replied. 'She's always drawing. Do you know her?'

'Know her?!' laughed Alison as they drew level with Biddy, 'I made her what she is today, didn't I, B.W.?'

Biddy shivered and bit her lip. This was a Saturday. Episodes weren't supposed to happen on Saturdays. This had been a good day and now it was ruined. The lump started to rise in her throat.

'She's good,' said the boy, looking down at Biddy's drawing. His big brown eyes reminded her of chocolate buttons. 'Bloody good, in fact.'

Biddy's face reddened. She assumed he must be referring to her weirdness. She swallowed hard, pushing the lump down.

'Come on, Marcus,' said Alison huffily, realising that he was actually complimenting Biddy's obvious artistic talent. 'It's getting late. Mummy will be wondering where we've got to.'

Alison stomped off, turning back to pull Marcus's arm.

'Come *on*,' she screamed.

'All right, all right,' said the boy, obviously surprised at this sudden change in Alison's mood. 'I'm coming.'

He looked down again at Biddy's sketchpad and smiled.

'I mean it, that's great work. Keep it up,' he said softly, and smiled. He stood for a second, waiting for some kind of a response, but Biddy just stared back, unable to speak or move.

'Bye, then.' Marcus shrugged his shoulders and ran to catch up with Alison. Looking over his shoulder as he reached the wall, he saw that Biddy was still staring at him with unblinking eyes, her face expressionless.

'Hey Ali, who's the artist?' he asked, as he drew level with her. 'She's awfully shy.'

'I told you, B.W.,' she growled folding her arms, 'and she's not a bloody artist, OK?'

'Steady on, Ali,' said Marcus, shocked. 'I thought that sketch was pretty brilliant actually, and anyone who can draw like that is an artist, in my book.'

'Well, in my book she's just a bloody fucking weirdo, OK? B.W. – Bloody Weirdo. Get it?' she screamed in his face.

It was the first time that Alison had lost her composure in front of someone whom she only wanted to impress. She was normally such a proficient chameleon that she could charm anyone she chose to ensnare. And she desperately wanted to impress Marcus Baxter. Marcus had the most impressive credentials of any of her previous boyfriends and his prospects were nothing short of magnificent. Two years older than Alison, he was already a prefect and a House Captain at Collingsford School for Boys, and was tipped to be Head Boy next year. And although he hadn't told her so himself, she had heard, through a friend of her mother, that he was a cert for either Oxford or Cambridge. His only problem would be choosing which one to go to. As she was bound to be Head Girl herself when the time came, and as she'd always harboured Oxbridge aspirations, they made the perfect match. Marcus had such exquisite long-term potential that she was determined not to let the fact that he appeared to be a proper gentleman put her off. So far there had been no sign of anything more than a long, soft snog, which was nice enough: but she wanted more. But it was early days. She knew he fancied her rotten and it would only be a matter of time before he gave in – even to go to second base, though her ultimate goal was much farther than that. She just had to keep on doing what she was doing: woo him with her charm and beauty and multitude of talents.

But Alison screwed up that day on the beach. She let her mask slip and her unsavoury behaviour had a detrimental impact on Marcus. He dumped her the very next day. Alison wasn't used to rejection, and the shock of being dropped by a boy made her miss two days of school. She was utterly distraught, especially when her mother announced that Diana James had been on the phone that very afternoon and told her that Selina Burton was going out with Lana La Grue's son, Oliver.

'And I told her that you were dating Marcus Baxter,' gasped an equally distraught Felicity. 'Diana knows the Baxter family. The grandfather is something or other in the art world. Apparently they have an original Van Gogh. What am I going to say to her next time she phones?'

That was the last straw for Alison. The thought of Selina Burton going out with Oliver La Grue was like a knife twisting in her gut. All these years on and that snotty rich bitch was still getting one up on her. And now, because of that fucking stupid weirdo, she'd just lost the best catch she'd ever managed to snare. All the talents she possessed: her beauty, the multitude of cups and certificates she had been awarded at school, her recent Distinction at Grade 6 piano, her cert for the hockey captaincy next year – all of these things, yet Marcus had been more impressed by that weirdo's stupid scribbles. She collapsed on the sofa in a fit of violent, noisy, unattractive tears.

'George!' screamed her mother. 'Can't you do something?'

'Ahem, shall I . . . shall I get some tissues?' her father stammered, and shuffled from the room.

'You useless, spineless man,' Felicity yelled after him, starting to cry herself. 'This is all your fault.'

In that instant Alison realised just how much she had in common with her mother, although it galled her to admit it. She was right, it *was* all her father's fault. Alison had long since given up on her father's ability to provide an escape route from this small-town hellhole, so she'd started to look for other options.

Marcus may be a little intense at times, and somewhat dull at others, but his potential was enormous. And he drove his own car too, which was the icing on the cake: a brand new racing-green Mini with a cream roof, a present from his grandmother for passing his driving test. Alison saw Marcus as her ticket out of Ballybrock. And even if that ticket only took her as far as Collingsford, and on weekends, that would do for now.

But now her plan was in tatters. B.W. had as good as ripped that ticket up and flushed it down the toilet. Well, the weirdo would pay. This time it was personal. But she wouldn't rush into anything. She would bide her time, pick her moment and give the weirdo bitch the biggest kick in the stomach she'd ever had.

The day Alison returned to school following her 'illness' she followed Biddy into the toilets at lunchtime and grabbed her by the arm as she came out of the cubicle. 'You fucking weirdo bitch. Thanks to you my boyfriend is not my boyfriend anymore,' she hissed in Biddy's ear. 'But you'll pay for this. I promise. So you better watch your back, Bloody Weirdo, because you never know when I'm going to pounce.' Alison let go of Biddy's arm, grabbed her tie and leered in her face. 'Could be next week. Could be next month. Could be next year. Only I know when.'

She flicked Biddy's tie in her face then shoved her against the damp pink wall. 'Ugh,' she snarled in disgust, holding up her hands. She washed them using three squirts of soap, dried them with a paper towel, scrunched the towel into a ball and tossed it at Biddy before smoothing down her hair, checking herself in the mirror and swaying out of the toilets.

Biddy stood splayed against the wall, shaking. Alison's abuse wasn't normally physical. Biddy knew she didn't like to touch her, so why now? What had prompted this? And why would Alison's boyfriend stop being her boyfriend because of her? What had she done to make that happen?

Retching, she staggered into the closest cubicle, and when the bile had passed, she sat on the toilet, rocking back and forth, willing the pain in her stomach and chest to go away.

Bending over to rest her head on her knees, she noticed the large safety pin holding the strap of her schoolbag in place. She stared at it for a few seconds, focusing her attention on the curve of the pin head. There was something comforting about it, calming almost. The pain in her chest began to subside. She unfastened the pin and removed it from the strap, then slowly rolled up her sleeve and pierced the pin tip into her forearm, holding it firmly in place for a second or two. Then she did it again, and again, until the piercing became a frenzied attack that lasted for almost a minute. When she eventually stopped, she sat in a daze for several minutes, watching the tiny bubbles of blood burst and trickle down her arm like little red streams. The pattern they made was mesmerising, and for a few seconds, all thoughts of Alison vanished. The bell signalling the end of lunch break jolted Biddy back to reality. She tore off a few sheets of toilet roll and folded them into a neat square, spat on it and held it down hard on the prick marks until the bleeding stopped. Then, with another piece of toilet roll, she mopped up the blood, rolled down her sleeve, splashed her face in cold water, and went to class.

8.

Biddy still liked bird poo, but her interest in it began to wane when she discovered that sticking pins into her skin was a much more liberating pastime. The pain she felt in her arms from the sharp jab of the pins was a welcome relief from the constant, throbbing ache in her chest, her throat and her head. When her arms became numb to the pricking sensation, she moved down to her stomach, her thighs and the soles of her feet. She was careful not to mark herself on any part of her body that might be seen – not that she reckoned anyone would ever pay enough attention to her to notice. But just in case, she started wearing long-sleeved T-shirts and knee-length shorts at P.E., and she always got changed in a cubicle. It didn't matter if she looked ridiculous, as she always looked ridiculous: she might not be normal, she might be a weirdo, but at least she was aware of it. Besides, they'd ridicule her anyway, regardless of what she wore. Just so long as they didn't see her tiny scabs and scars, as that would make things so much worse. In a way she felt oddly protective about her scars. They were private, personal. Her little secret. She'd never had a secret before, and it felt good.

More and more often, Biddy made sure she got out of any games activity whenever she could, which wasn't difficult. She was pretty useless at ball games, and as no one wanted her on their team anyway, she was only selected if numbers were low as a last and extremely reluctant resort. And as track and field events were optional, she always opted out.

*

It was early May, in the last term of Fourth Form. Biddy had been sitting on the bench for the entire fifth period netball session, sketching birds in a notebook. Yet again there had been one girl too many for an equal team ratio, and yet again, Biddy had volunteered to sit on the side-lines and be the sub. She jumped when Miss Jordan, the new young P.E. teacher, sat down beside her. Teachers didn't normally get this close to Biddy and she instantly wondered what she'd done wrong. Was Miss Jordan going to insist that she had to participate more during P.E.?

But the teacher's tone caught Biddy unawares. 'Hello Biddy, pet, how are you?' she smiled. *Pet?* thought Biddy, looking around her to see who was watching, waiting for the whispers and sniggers. But the other girls were too busy with the goal-practice session after the game to notice. Biddy looked at Miss Jordan, her eyes wide and startled, not sure what to say.

'You don't like games, do you, Biddy?'

Biddy's heart sank. Just as she thought. Her evasion of P.E. was over. 'That's OK,' the teacher laughed lightly. 'P.E. isn't for everyone. Now, Art was never my thing, but I can see it most certainly is yours.' She nodded towards the open notebook in Biddy's lap, showing an exquisitely sketched seagull. 'That's quite exceptional, Biddy. You have a rare talent there. Mr Lynas must love you. I bet he doesn't often get an art genius in his class.' She smiled, and looked down at the sketch again.

Biddy's mind was racing. Nobody loved her, apart from her papa, of course. He had never actually said it, but she was certain he did. Mr Lynas, the Art teacher, certainly didn't love her. She doubted he even liked her. Nobody liked her, so why, just because she could draw, would he? He always gave her high marks, and occasionally he'd mutter a 'good, good' and nod in what Biddy assumed was an approving manner, but, as with most of the teachers, he didn't seem to pay much attention to her. But now here was this new teacher being nice to her. She had called her 'pet'; she had complimented her art. She looked up, again expecting to see a row of faces laughing down at her, but the others were still engrossed in their goal practice.

Miss Jordan stood up and blew her whistle. 'Right, girls, that's it for today. Julia and Jill, please collect all the bibs from your teams and return them to the store with the balls. Karen, you help too. The rest of you head on to the changing room.'

Biddy went to stand up, but the teacher sat down beside her again.

'Why don't you just stay here while the others get changed, Biddy?' she smiled again. 'I thought it might be nice to have a little chat.'

Biddy sat down again. A chat? People didn't chat to her. Not even her papa. Well, not really. Obviously they spoke to each other, but they didn't actually have conversations. Most of their life was spent in a comfortable silence, which they were both accustomed to.

'Look, Biddy, I really don't want to offend you or anything, and I'm not prying, but I just wanted to see if everything is OK with you.'

Biddy couldn't answer. She couldn't move. All she could do was blink. She was both confused and terrified in equal measure. What was going on?

'It's just, well, growing up can be so complicated at times, and I know that this can be a tricky age. I am aware that there's only you and your dad in the house, and I've been thinking that maybe sometimes some growing up, girlie type things might be a bit difficult for you.'

Biddy's stomach lurched and her head dropped. *She's going to tell me about periods,* she thought, mortified. *She knows what Alison and the others did in P7, and somehow she knows that I only started mine recently, and now she's going to humiliate me just like they did. They're all in it together. They must be watching or listening somewhere, having another laugh at me.* Her eyes stung and the lump started crawling up her throat.

But then the strangest thing happened. Miss Jordan took Biddy's hands in hers and then gently tilted up her chin. Biddy jumped with shock.

'Oh, Biddy, please don't be upset. It's probably none of my business, but I really do just want to help. And, well, you see it's not that long ago really that I was your age, so I do remember what it's like. Growing up, I mean. And I didn't have a mum either.' Biddy looked at the teacher, surprised. It had never occurred to her that other people didn't have mothers. Obviously she knew that grown-ups, like her father, would eventually lose their mothers, but she had always supposed that her own lack of a mother was unique. It was part of her oddness, part of what made her such a bloody weirdo. But here was this person, a teacher, a woman who was not much more than a girl herself, and she had grown up without a mother too. Her head felt fuzzy. She took in Miss Jordan's short dark hair, her tanned skin, bright blue eyes, and fit, slender figure. She couldn't be very many more years older than she was herself – she certainly wasn't old enough to be her mother. In fact, she thought, even though they didn't look remotely alike, she could almost be her big sister. Except, of course, that Biddy was a weirdo, and Miss Jordan clearly wasn't.

'It isn't easy, Biddy. I do know that.' Miss Jordan was talking again, and Biddy had to force herself back into a state of listening. 'I was lucky enough to have an auntie who sometimes lived with us. She had a job that took her away a lot, but when she came home, she'd always stay in our house. It was great, but it meant my little brother had to bunk in my room when she was around. And yuck, the smell!' she laughed, trying to put Biddy at ease.

It worked. Biddy laughed back, surprised at how light the sound of her own laughter made her feel. 'The best thing about Auntie Celia, apart from her colourful kaftans, was that she loved shopping, and with just my dad and that smelly little brother of mine in the house, I never got to shop for, you know, girlie things.' Biddy didn't know. Shopping? For girlie things? Did she mean Dr. White's? Was this going to be about periods after all?

9.

Penny Jordan could see that she wasn't making sense. All she wanted to do was reach out a helping hand to this sad, lonely girl, who, as far as she could see, had been ostracised by almost everyone in the school, pupils and teachers alike. But she felt she was making a mess of things. Since arriving at the school a couple of months back, there'd been something about Biddy that really bothered her. Not her strangeness – Penny believed that everyone was entitled to their own idiosyncrasies – but her desolation, her isolation, the heavy mist of persecution that clung to the girl. Penny knew all about persecution, and she sensed that Biddy was only going through the motions of life: alive, but not really living.

She knew, of course, that she'd need to tread carefully. Extremely carefully. She had turned this conversation over in her head time and time again, and her partner, Sam, had warned her against it. 'I know you feel sorry for the girl,' Sam had reasoned, 'but really, Pen, think of your position. You've only been there for the blink of a bloody eye; and you know you were lucky to get the flipping job in the first place.'

'Well thanks for the vote of confidence,' Penny had yelled.

'Oh, for God's sake, Penny, be reasonable: you know what I mean! Just think about it. If it comes out, and then you're seen to have a "special friendship" with this Biddy, well, you know as well as I do exactly what people will say.'

'Oh, don't be so bloody melodramatic, Samantha. Mr Duncan is the only person in the whole school who knows that I'm gay, and as I don't live, or socialise, in the town, how the hell is anyone going to find out? Biddy needs help. I just know it. And no one else appears to give a toss about her. As far as I can see, she has no friends and no home support, and, to make matters worse, I suspect she's being bullied.'

'Oh, Penny,' sighed Sam. 'Just promise me that you'll be careful?'

'Of course I will, Sam. I just really have to do this; you know?'

'I know,' said Sam, smiling. 'You know your trouble, don't you? You're just too nice for your own damn good.'

Sam's words echoed in Penny's ears as she sat on the gym bench now with Biddy, wondering how she could get to her point in the few minutes that were left before the bell. Biddy was staring at her expectantly, like a pathetic little puppy. It was obvious the girl didn't have a clue what she was talking about.

She drew in a deep breath.

'You know Biddy – clothes, make-up, underwear. That sort of thing,' she smiled, hoping that Biddy would respond with something. She hadn't spoken at all yet. But, no, she still didn't utter a word. She just shook her head slowly, still staring with that dazed expression, still so obviously bewildered.

'Don't you ever go out shopping, Biddy, for new clothes or shoes, or a nice handbag maybe? You know, something nice and smart for a special occasion?'

'No, Miss.' Biddy finally spoke, albeit in a virtual whisper. 'Not really. Sometimes when my shoes get too small, or I need a new school cardigan, or something like that, my dad takes me to the Chest, Heart and Stroke shop in the High Street. Or the Oxfam one. But we don't ever have any special occasions, so I really don't need anything smart.'

At last Penny saw a chink of light. 'Well, Biddy,' she smiled, 'there's the school disco coming up in a few weeks. That's a special occasion. Wouldn't it be nice to get something smart for it?'

'Oh no, Miss, I won't be going to the disco,' Biddy spluttered, almost choking.

'You won't be going?' said Penny. 'But I thought it was just about the highlight of the school year? Doesn't everyone go? I must say, I'm looking forward to it myself. And do you know, I think I might just splash out and get myself a nice new out-fit.' She rattled the words out, hardly stopping for breath, and beamed at Biddy when she finally finished speaking. To her dismay, there wasn't even the edge of a smile on Biddy's lips or a glint of excitement in her eyes. Instead, all Penny saw was fear.

'No, no, Miss Jordan. I d-don't go to the discos,' Biddy stammered.

'You don't go?' asked Penny, softly. 'Why ever not, Biddy? Sure they're great fun.'

'I don't like them,' said Biddy quickly, looking down at the floor, so Miss Jordan couldn't see the tears threatening.

'Have you ever been to a disco, Biddy?' asked Penny, trying very hard not to sound patronising. This could go either way and she had to keep Biddy on her side.

Biddy shook her head. Penny could see that she was forcing back tears.

'You know, Biddy, I've just had a fantastic idea. Since you've never been to the disco before, and since I've never been either, to the school one I mean, perhaps we could sort of go together? Well, not actually go together, as I have to be there early to help set up, but you know, look out for each other when it starts. I'll be a bit nervous myself, you see, as it's my first one at the school and I still don't know too many people. So it would be just great to have someone there for some moral support. Go on,' she nudged Biddy playfully, 'I bet you're a terrific dancer!'

Despite herself, Biddy started to smile. But almost as soon as the idea of going to the school disco formed the shadow of a possibility in her head, an image of Alison, Julia, Georgina and Jackie laughing and pointing at her shattered the illusion. She knew she couldn't go. Of course she couldn't go. How could a bloody weirdo like her go to a disco?

Penny saw Biddy's expression change from hope to despair in the blink of an eye. What was this poor child so frightened of? 'What is it, Biddy?' she asked softly. 'What's the matter? Please tell me. Perhaps I can help?'

'I can't go, I can't go. How can I go to a disco? I bet they don't let bloody weirdos into discos, do they?' Biddy almost shouted, finally bursting into tears. Why was Miss Jordan doing this to her: pretending she was normal when she wasn't? This was all just another big joke. She stood up and made to run for the door, but Miss Jordan blocked her way and held her shoulders.

'Biddy, Biddy, stop. Please calm down,' she soothed. 'What on earth is all this "weirdo" business? Has someone been saying this to you?' Penny gently guided Biddy back to the bench and pulled a tissue from her tracksuit pocket. 'Here, it may look a bit grubby, but I promise you, it hasn't been anywhere near my nose.' Biddy managed to smile a little through her sobs, and relaxed slightly. Maybe this wasn't a joke after all – maybe Miss Jordan didn't know she was a bloody weirdo. After all, she reasoned, she hadn't been at the school very long, so perhaps no one had told her yet.

'OK, Biddy, I want you to tell me what this is all about. Why would you think you are a weirdo?'

'Oh, but I'm not just a weirdo, Miss,' said Biddy. 'I'm a bloody weirdo. That's the weirdest kind of weirdo there is.'

'Someone has been telling you this?'

Biddy nodded. Penny took a deep breath. 'Biddy, has your father been saying this?'

'NO!' choked Biddy. 'Oh no, no, Miss Jordan. Not Papa. He doesn't know I'm one. Or if he does, he would never say. Really, it's not my papa.'

Penny felt a stab of relief; the girl's reaction was too instinctive to be a lie. 'I'm sorry, Biddy,' Penny said, taking her hand. 'Really, I'm sorry. Of course your father would never say anything like that to you. But someone has. Will you tell me who?'

'I can't,' said Biddy. 'I can't. If they found out, they'd . . .' Her voice trailed off.

'What would they do, Biddy?'

'I don't know. They'd think of something.'

'Biddy, look at me,' said Penny firmly, forcing Biddy to make eye contact. 'Now firstly, you are not a bloody weirdo, you are not a weirdo and you are not weird. Do you understand?'

Biddy shook her head. 'Yes, I am. They've always said that, so I must be.'

'Well, you are not. You may not be quite the same as them, but that is not a bad thing. Actually, that's a good thing, because, quite frankly, if that's the way they behave, would you want to be?' Biddy shook her head again.

'Good. Secondly, whoever *they* are, they need to be stopped because they're making you very unhappy. *They* are doing a bad thing. Do you understand, Biddy?'

This time Biddy nodded.

'Great. Good,' Penny nodded too. 'Now, I will completely understand if you don't want to tell me who these people are, but you need to tell someone. You absolutely must. Your father, perhaps?'

'No,' said Biddy quickly.

'All right. Well, what about someone else in your family? An aunt or a cousin or someone?'

'There is no one else. Just me and Papa.'

'Perhaps you could talk to Mr Duncan – he's a really nice man, you know.' Biddy shook her head. 'OK, well, what about a friend then, or a neighbour: someone you trust?'

Biddy bowed her head again: 'I don't have any friends, and the only neighbour I know is Mrs Thomas from number 21. She smiles sometimes, and she says hello to my papa, and once she gave us a lift when it was raining. But I don't actually know her.'

Penny felt her chest tighten. She wanted to hug Biddy close, she wanted to cry herself, but she knew she had to stay in control. 'Yes, Biddy, you do have a friend, you have me.'

Shocked, Biddy looked up at Miss Jordan's face. Her expression was serious, but there was an unmistakable kindness in her eyes. For the first time in her life, ever, someone had called her their friend. Miss Jordan may be a teacher, but she was a person too: a real person who didn't think she was a bloody weirdo. And she said she was her friend. It was almost too much for Biddy to comprehend and in a split second she made one of the most important decisions of her life.

'Promise you won't say anything?'

Miss Jordan nodded slowly. 'I promise, Biddy.'

'Alison Flemming and her gang,' she blurted quickly.

'You mean Jackie, Georgina and Julia?' asked Miss Jordan. Biddy nodded. She felt sick and lightheaded, but also strangely energised. 'And the other girls in your class?'

She swallowed and shook her head. 'Not so much. They just go along with it, but they aren't as bad. It's mainly Alison.'

'How long has this been going on, Biddy?'

'Since primary school,' sighed Biddy, the relief that she was finally telling someone almost overwhelming her. 'It started when I was nearly ten.'

Penny was trembling with an intense fury she had to fight very hard to contain. Her instincts had been right, and she understood something of Biddy's pain. She had been bullied herself at sixth-form college, when her sexuality was exposed by Joanna Dunne, a so-called friend in whom she'd mistakenly confided. But at least she'd had the confidence and maturity to stand up for herself, and she was able to lean on other friends outside of college for support. Biddy had been suffering this torture for almost half of her life with no support at all, and she was plainly deeply damaged as a result.

The bell shrilled, piercing Penny's thoughts and jolting Biddy back to the reality of her life.

'Oh, Miss,' she gasped, shaking. 'I'll be late for my next class.'

'It's all right, Biddy, don't worry. Who do you have next?' Penny asked calmly.

'Mr Matthews. History.'

'Well, I'll tell you what, you go and get changed and I'll write a note for Mr Matthews, explaining that I kept you behind to help me with something, and that if there's a problem, he can take it up with me later. OK?'

Biddy nodded and turned to go, suddenly aware of the sweat that was trickling down her armpits and an overwhelming need to go to the toilet. She couldn't make sense of what had just happened, and her body was reacting to it.

'Biddy,' Miss Jordan called after her. 'You did the right thing telling me. But this conversation isn't over. You do know that, don't you?'

Biddy stood with one hand on the gym door and looked down at the floor, unable to meet the teacher's gaze. The familiar feelings of shame and agitation rushed through her, churning her stomach, making her need to go to the toilet even more acute. But from somewhere, something else, a sensation totally unfamiliar and wholly unexpected, made her nod. 'Yes, Miss,' she croaked, not quite believing the words had come from her own mouth. And then she ran.

10.

'Hello, Biddy.'

Biddy looked up to find Miss Jordan beaming at her. 'Nearly bumped into each other there,' the teacher laughed. 'I can barely see over this lot,' she nodded at the pile of tennis rackets stacked in her arms.

Biddy stared at Miss Jordan. It had been three days since the incident in the gym, and she'd spent most of that time wondering if it had really happened. She mostly felt a sense of crushing mortification, horrified that she'd told a teacher about Alison, sick with fear about what the repercussions might be. She wished she'd kept her stupid mouth shut; or that Miss Jordan had never spoken to her in the first place. But then again, another part of her was glad it had happened. The kindness in the teacher's eyes, the softness of her smile and the gentle way in which she talked had been teasing her. And, the best thing of all was the fact that Miss Jordan had called her a 'friend'. She wanted more of it, that feeling – whatever it was.

'Have you lost something?' Miss Jordan asked.

Biddy shook her head. How could she tell the teacher that she'd just been staring at some bird poo to make her feel balanced after a particularly bad Alison day? Miss Jordan would realise what a weirdo she was after all.

'No-no, Miss,' she stammered.

'Stuart Smith!' Miss Jordan yelled as a boy ran past, bumping into her, almost knocking the rackets from her arms. 'Slow down! Honestly, the playground at home time is like a battlefield,' she grinned at Biddy and rolled her eyes.

Biddy just stared, not knowing what to say, or do, or what was coming next.

'Oh, are you rushing for a bus too? Am I holding you back?' Miss Jordan grimaced, trying to balance the rackets.

'N-no, Miss,' Biddy stammered again. 'I walk.'

'Oh, well, in that case, would you do me the biggest favour, Biddy, and help me take this lot back to the P.E. store? I think I underestimated their weight,' Miss Jordan laughed lightly.

Biddy continued to stare at the teacher, trying to process the request. A favour? She didn't think anyone had ever asked her for a favour. Not even her father. Obviously he asked her to do things: bring in the milk, take out the rubbish, get his pills from the chemist. But a favour? No. Never.

'Of course if you need to get off, don't worry about it. I'll manage.'

'No.' Biddy almost snapped. 'I mean yes. I mean no, I don't need to . . . erm . . . yes, I'll . . . here . . .' she slung the nylon shopper which was now serving as her schoolbag over her shoulder and snatched the top three tennis rackets from the pile in Miss Jordan's arms.

'Thank you, Biddy,' the teacher smiled. 'That's very kind of you. You're a star.'

As they walked across the playground towards the gym, Miss Jordan chatted away; but Biddy barely heard a word, as 'favour', 'star', and 'very kind' were ringing in her ears. No one had ever spoken to her in the way Miss Jordan did, and the effect was both surreal and intoxicating. It was almost as though she was having an out of body experience.

Neither did Biddy notice Georgina Harte pass them on her way to Mr Mackey's detention in Hut 4, for getting caught with cigarettes in her blazer on one of the Head of Year's random uniform inspections. The cigarettes, of course, were Alison's, but Georgina didn't mind taking the hit. Any opportunity to curry favour with Ali above Jackie and Julia was a welcome one. And any vague irritation she did feel about missing out on the bus ride home was instantly negated now she could report back her sighting of Bloody Weirdo sucking up to that new P.E. teacher Alison couldn't stand. What a stroke of luck.

Penny thought it was a stroke of luck bumping into Biddy too. She'd been thinking non-stop about the girl since their encounter in the gym hall, and had come up with several plans to help end her misery – then discounted them one by one. It wasn't as simple as just reporting Alison Flemming to Mr Duncan. She needed evidence, for a start, but stomping straight in and going for the little madam's jugular would actually be the worst way to tackle it for Biddy. There had been something about Alison that annoyed her from the very first time she encountered her. She couldn't quite put her finger on it, but something about the girl unnerved her. She was too sickly sweet. Too seemingly perfect. But everyone else seemed to be dying about her.

She also knew from her own experience that first and foremost what Biddy needed was a sense of self-worth, a feeling of empowerment; someone to show her that despite what she'd grown to believe, the whole world was not against her, and, most important of all, that she was not a flipping 'Bloody Weirdo'.

'Can you believe that?' she'd yelled at Sam that evening as they prepared dinner. 'Can you actually believe that the girl has been basically brainwashed into believing she is a bloody weirdo. Not just a weirdo, but a BLOODY weirdo? That's what she said. Her very words were, "*I'm not just a weirdo, I'm a bloody weirdo, and that's the worst kind of weirdo there is*". I mean it's sick, isn't it? It's fucking sick. She has done nothing to deserve this. Nothing. OK, she may be a bit "different", but that doesn't make her a weirdo. She's just a sad, lonely girl called Biddy.'

'Yes, Pen, it's sick,' agreed Sam, handing Penny a glass of wine. 'Now drink this, down in one if you have to, and calm down. And stop yelling please. It's not my fault.'

'Oh, Sam, I'm sorry,' she paused, almost downing the contents of the glass, 'but I've never been so angry in my life. Even when that bitch Joanna betrayed me all those years ago. So,' she held her glass out for a refill, 'what the hell am I going to do about it?'

'I don't know, Penny, really I don't. I'm rubbish at this kind of thing, you know that. But as I've said before, be careful. Please.'

'I will, Sam, I will.'

'Promise?'

'Promise,' Penny nodded, stroking Samantha's cheek.

She still hadn't made up her mind what to do when she, quite literally, stumbled upon Biddy in the playground. The girl seemed to be glued to the tarmac, staring at the ground in that trance-like way she'd witnessed several times before. Penny always wondered what on earth she was doing. As they walked together towards the gym hall she gabbled away ten to the dozen about none of the second years offering to help her with the rackets, and how she couldn't wait for the new tennis courts to be ready so they didn't have to use the back playground, and wasn't it just great to get some nice warm sunshine for a change, desperately trying to think of a way to turn this chance encounter to her benefit. But, just as before, Biddy said nothing. Not a word.

'Right then,' Penny said, locking the gym store door behind them, 'job done.' She beamed at Biddy. 'Thanks so much, Biddy, it's good to know that chivalry hasn't died out completely. Those second years could do with a lesson in manners from you,' she winked. Still nothing back.

'So, are you off home now?'

Biddy nodded.

'And you walk, you said?'

Biddy nodded again.

'Well, good for you. Walking's the best form of exercise. Never worry about playing netball, and tennis and rounders if you walk every day,' she beamed again, then looked around her conspiratorially and whispered, 'but never let on to Mrs Cunningham I said that. I'll get the sack.' She winked again, and this time Biddy smiled.

'So, any nice plans for the weekend?'

Biddy shook her head. She'd probably take her sketchpad to the beach, depending on homework and chores, but she suspected that wasn't what Miss Jordan meant.

'I'm going to do some baking myself. Start getting in some practice for the cake sale at the end of term. I haven't baked in years, and from what I hear there's quite a bit of competition amongst the staff,' she laughed. 'What about you? Will you be baking something?'

Biddy continued to stare, not knowing quite what to say. Wasn't it obvious? Of course she wouldn't be baking. She'd never baked at home, ever. She hadn't a clue how to do it, and Domestic Science hadn't helped her learn. Oh, she liked the idea of it, baking, cooking; but while Domestic Science lessons were a nightmare for her, they provided a dream opportunity for Alison and the others to ridicule yet another of her weird inadequacies. She often didn't have the correct ingredients for the practical lessons, and, naturally, never had a partner to borrow from either. Her current teacher, Miss McFettrick, generally just ignored her now, apparently not bothered whether she completed the tasks or not. It was as though she was completely invisible in her kitchen. But Biddy couldn't blame her, really. When she'd had to make a quiche lorraine for the Christmas exam last December, Miss McFettrick actually spat out the mouthful she was sampling, causing a roar of hilarity in the class.

'I didn't think it was possible for a female to make something quite so disgusting,' she had said, glaring at Biddy with undisguised disdain as she wiped her mouth with a tea towel. 'Your incompetence has reached a level I have never before experienced in all my years of teaching, and, I pray, I will never encounter again. How much salt did you put in here? A tablespoon? Do you not understand simple measurements, girl?'

The other girls broke into a round of applause, led, of course, by Alison. Needless to say, they devoured Miss McFettrick's words, quoting them to Biddy verbatim at every opportunity over the weeks that followed, and making sure that the entire school heard them too. Miss McFettrick hadn't tasted a thing that Biddy had attempted to make since. At least in the second and third year Mrs Hobart had been kinder, often using Biddy's work station to demonstrate the assignments and allowing her to take home the results. Although Biddy's father always cleaned his plate on these occasions, he never passed comment, and she often wondered if he believed she had actually made those things herself, or if he really knew the humiliating truth. Now she always tipped her woeful efforts in a bin on her way home from school, and as her papa never asked about her 'cooking classes', she never had to lie.

She felt a sudden wistful urge for her mother. Her mother would have been a wonderful baker; she just knew it. She would have taught Biddy in their kitchen, wearing matching pretty aprons with flowers on them. And together they would have baked delicious things for the school cake sale.

'Biddy?'

Biddy jolted and realised that Miss Jordan was actually expecting an answer, so she shook her head and simply said, 'No, Miss.'

'Just right,' the teacher smiled. 'Far better to go along and buy some delicious treats. Tell you what, I'll give you a heads-up on whatever my contribution ends up being, then you can buy it so I don't feel rubbish when it's the last cake standing.'

Miss Jordan laughed, so Biddy laughed her best forced laugh back and nodded. She was sure Miss Jordan's cake wouldn't be the last one left. She was sure it would be the most delicious cake in the whole of the sale, and that it would be the very first one to be bought, and that people would be clambering to buy it. But she wouldn't be one of them, because she wouldn't be there. They didn't do things like that, her father and her, and she'd never missed that they didn't. Until now.

'Well, I must be off.' They'd reached the school entrance and Miss Jordan looked at her watch. 'Need to go and get my stuff, then head home. I think it'll be takeaway in my house tonight. I was going to go shopping after work, but to be honest I can't be bothered.' She laughed again, and Biddy thought how she'd never heard someone laugh so much before in such a musical way. It was nice. It reminded her of a bird singing. She'd like to laugh like that herself, but of course she'd only sound ridiculous.

'There isn't a thing in my fridge,' Miss Jordan was saying now, 'save a big bar of Caramac. And I'm not going to get dinner out of that, never mind bake a cake. Have you been to that new supermarket yet?'

Biddy shook her head.

'Oh, it's great,' Miss Jordan clapped her hands together. 'Honestly, they have everything. And there's even a lovely coffee shop. I know I shouldn't admit this, being a P.E. teacher and all, but they do the most delicious donuts. Do you like donuts, Biddy?'

'I don't know, Miss,' Biddy answered honestly. To her knowledge she'd never eaten a donut before. Her father liked Kimberley biscuits, and that was that. But she suddenly had an overwhelming urge to eat one.

'Oh, well you must try one when you do go. That'll be my elevenses treat to myself tomorrow morning after I've finished the shopping. I might even buy an extra one; an emergency consolation just in case the baking turns out to be a disaster.' She beamed again, and giggled loudly. If Miss Jordan was a bird, thought Biddy, she'd be a Laughing Kookaburra.

'Well, cheerio, Biddy. Hope you have a lovely weekend. See you next week. And thanks again for your help.'

Biddy smiled weakly. She didn't want the conversation to be over, even though it wasn't really a proper conversation. She could stand here and listen to Miss Jordan talk for hours. No one had ever talked to her like this before, and the best thing of all was that Miss Jordan hadn't even mentioned Alison.

'You're welcome, Miss,' she managed to croak. And as she turned away and began the walk back to Stanley Street and her father, her weak, fake smile became a huge, helpless grin.

11.

Biddy left the house at a quarter past ten the following morning to walk to the supermarket. She told her father she was going to the beach early because she wanted to catch the mid-morning light, that he wasn't to worry as she'd very little homework to do, and that she'd pick up any odds and ends of shopping they needed on her way home. He presented her with a neatly written list, with the names of all the appropriate shops she was to purchase the item from beside each one: *6 pork sausages – McDaid's, 2lbs potatoes & 6 carrots – Gregg & Sons, 2 soda & 2 potato farls – Griddle, 1 tin Campbell's chicken soup (condensed), 1 packet of Bird's custard & packet of Kimberley biscuits – Mrs Henderson's.* He'd have had a fit if he'd known where she was really planning on doing the shopping. Even though the supermarket had been open for a couple of months now, her father still preferred to shop at McDaid's Butchers and Gregg & Sons greengrocers in town.

'What would I be wanting to go to that place for?' he had snarled when Biddy had tentatively suggested a trip shortly after it opened. 'Full of foreign things and people with high-falutin' ideas. I know what it's like to be put out of work because people are changing their ways, remember. Well, I won't be changing mine.'

If he was suspicious this morning, his voice did not reveal it, but on the way she almost turned back – several times. She felt sick, both with nerves and remorse. Biddy had never lied to her father before about what she was doing or where she was going, and now she felt as though she was doing something very wicked and deceitful. Waves of nauseating shame and embarrassment flushed through her, stopping her in her tracks every few minutes, but then the thought of Miss Jordan's smile and the sound of her voice kept her going.

The walk only took twenty minutes. There was a direct bus route from the main road just around the corner from their house, but even on a Saturday, Biddy couldn't bear the thought of it. Now she was finally here, the size of the supermarket unnerved her, and the range of products on the shelves was overwhelming. She watched as young mothers with children in trolleys, and middle-aged women, any one of whom could have been her own mother, glided around the aisles with ease and plucked things from the shelves with an air of efficient confidence. Her armpits began to sweat, the sick feeling churned in her stomach and panic started to rise in her throat. Her arms ached from the heavy basket, which was already weighed down with some of the items on her list: the tin of soup, the packet of custard, a packet of sausages and a bag of potatoes. She was finding it difficult to negotiate the unfamiliar aisles with the basket *and* the plastic bag containing her sketchpad and pencils. Finding herself in the household cleaning aisle, she stopped and put the basket on the ground, wiping her brow. What was she doing? She didn't belong here. And what was she actually going to do if she did bump into Miss Jordan? Go for elevenses with her? Stupid, stupid, stupid, bloody weirdo!

She was every bit as weird and as thick and as stupid as everyone said she was. Why hadn't she thought this through? Aside from not having a clue what she would say to the teacher if she did see her, she couldn't return home with the potatoes and the sausages anyway, as the supermarket wrapping meant it would be obvious to her father they hadn't come from McDaid's or Gregg & Sons. What was she going to do? Buy them, then dump them in a waste bin like she used to do with her Domestic Science efforts? She glanced at her watch: ten to eleven. Miss Jordan had said she took her elevenses in the café, after her shopping, so that would mean she was probably already here somewhere. Maybe she was in one of the long queues at the tills, or maybe she was already in the café. Biddy could feel the sweat running down between her breasts now too, saturating her vest. Her mouth felt dry and her head was dizzy. She thought she might be sick. She needed to get out of this place, now, before Miss Jordan saw her. She would just leave the basket here and run, and she'd never be so stupid again. Never.

'Hello, Biddy. What a lovely surprise. Doing some shopping?' Biddy looked up, startled to see Miss Jordan smiling at her. Even though just minutes before she'd been hoping to meet the teacher, she was instantly mortified: horribly conscious of her sweaty armpits and damp vest and the perspiration which must be evident on her forehead and upper lip. Her mouth opened, but no words came out.

'Oh my word, Biddy, are you all right? You look as though you're about to pass out.' Sensing Biddy's discomfort, Penny took control. 'It's really busy here today. I can't be doing with the crowds, to be honest. Look, do you fancy a quick cup of coffee? Come on, my treat. I was heading to the café anyway. You can bring your basket with you, then finish your shopping later.' She headed off in the direction of the café but Biddy stayed still, unable to move. Penny looked back at her and smiled encouragingly. 'Perhaps you'd rather have a Coke,' she called, 'or even a hot chocolate?'

Discovering her legs could actually move, Biddy followed Miss Jordan and joined her in the queue.

'What's it to be, then? Coffee? Tea? Coke?'

'Coke please, Miss Jordan,' said Biddy shyly. She'd never tasted Coca-Cola before, or Fanta, or even lemonade. Her father didn't allow fizzy drinks in the house, just cordial. Biddy used to watch from her bedroom window as the other children in her street queued up with their mothers at the Lemonade Man's van on a Friday afternoon, excitedly jumping up and down when it was their turn to get bottles of pink, orange, brown and green fizzy juice.

'What about a biscuit, or a donut, or some chocolate cake?' Biddy looked at the huge array of sweet things on offer and longed to try all of them. She really wanted to taste a donut, but she was too nervous to eat and she knew that any food just now would make her gag.

'No thank you, Miss Jordan, just a Coke, please,' she replied politely.

'Why don't you go and get us a seat,' said Penny, 'and I'll bring the drinks across.'

Biddy chose a table in the back corner of the café and tucked her basket under a chair, relieved to be rid of the weight of it. She watched Miss Jordan speak to the lady behind the till. The lady laughed at something Miss Jordan said and the yellow hair piled on top of her head like a lemon-top ice cream, wobbled like it might fall down. Were they laughing at her? Was Miss Jordan telling the lemon-top-haired lady that she was having to sit down for her coffee with some silly little schoolgirl? What was she doing here? Miss Jordan's back was now turned and it looked like she was placing bits and pieces on a tray. *If I leave now*, she thought, *I'll make it to the door before she turns around*. Biddy stood up, but she was too late, the teacher was already moving towards her, smiling.

'Here you are, Coke for you and a cappuccino for me. And I got you a donut just in case. Don't worry if you don't want it, I'll eat them both,' she winked.

Biddy took the drink without speaking and sucked the brown liquid through a red and white stripy straw. The fizz and flavour took her by surprise. She was shocked at how nice it was. It made her feel giddy and she smiled at Miss Jordan like an excited child.

'You know, Biddy, I'm really glad I bumped into you, as our chat the other day was cut short, and then yesterday, well, the playground really wasn't the place to resume it.' Miss Jordan took a bite from her donut and closed her eyes for a second. 'Mmmm . . . my guilty pleasure.' Biddy watched, mesmerised, as the teacher slowly chewed the bun and swallowed, then took a sip from her frothy drink. 'You've been on my mind a lot, Biddy, and, well, there's something else I really wanted to ask you.' Biddy nodded, still captivated by the taste of the Coke, which was bouncing around her mouth, and eyeing the donut sat on the plate in front of her. Could she be brave enough to take a bite? she wondered.

'This might sound entirely inappropriate, Biddy, but I promise you I'm just trying to help. The thing is, I've noticed that you look very uncomfortable during P.E. lessons; you know, when you are participating.'

I could maybe try a bite and see, thought Biddy, tentatively cutting the donut in half, then half again.

'I know you don't like P.E., and I was wondering if one of the reasons you'd rather not participate is because, well, because of your discomfort . . .'

Biddy put the quarter piece of donut into her mouth and let it sit on her tongue. It was like a cake version of a Kimberley: but the sugar was on top, and instead of a marshmallow filling there was the most delicious, bouncy bready stuff. She went straight in for a second piece.

'Biddy?'

Biddy looked at Miss Jordan, startled. Had she missed something? Had Miss Jordan asked her a question? *She must think me so rude*, she thought. *She's bought me a Coke and a donut and been kind to me for the third time, and I don't even know what she said to me.*

'Is that why you try to avoid games?'

'I don't like P.E.,' said Biddy, licking her fingers.

'Yes, I know, Biddy, and that's OK. You don't have to like it. But I'm afraid it is on the curriculum, so you really can't avoid it all the time. I know you walk a lot, which is great because exercise is really good for you, and very important.'

Biddy nodded and took another sip of her Coke. She wondered where Miss Jordan was going, but was finding it difficult to concentrate due to the explosion of new tastes and sensations in her mouth.

Penny cleared her throat ever so slightly. This was proving more difficult than she had anticipated, not that she'd actually rehearsed the conversation. And she certainly hadn't expected to be sitting with Biddy in the supermarket café when she left home this morning. Sam went to visit her elderly grandmother every Saturday morning, so Penny always did the shopping, and she quite enjoyed rambling around the aisles and the twenty minutes or so she spent in the café afterwards. It was the only 'me' time she really had to herself. She thought of Sam now, and, for the hundredth time considered that she really should heed her girlfriend's advice and mind her own business. It wasn't too late. She could leave it here, not say another word about it, change the direction of the conversation entirely. But her stubborn streak compelled her to carry on. She took a deep breath and went for it.

'The thing is, Biddy, I can't help thinking that perhaps if you wore a bra for P.E. lessons, it might make all the running around and so on a bit, well, easier for you. More comfortable. Then, maybe, you might enjoy P.E. a little bit more.'

There, she'd said it. This was what Penny had intended to talk to Biddy about from the beginning. A nagging doubt that Biddy didn't realise she needed a bra had disturbed her from the first time she had taken Biddy's class for P.E. But how in God's name were you supposed to bring up the subject of bras with a fifteen-year-old girl who was not just your pupil, but obviously had serious issues? Especially when you were gay? She'd asked a few of the teachers in the staff room about Biddy, but none of them seemed at all interested. 'Bit of an oddball, that one,' one had said. 'Hmm. Strange girl,' said another, raising his eyebrows. Most just shrugged their shoulders. She did manage to ascertain that Biddy lived alone with her father, who was also, by all accounts, a bit of a loner himself. 'An oddball,' was how one or two of her colleagues described him. She knew how difficult it was to grow up without a mother, especially through your teenage years. Auntie Celia had saved her, but it seemed that there was no one, no female at least, in Biddy's life to save her. So now, here she was, sitting in a supermarket café, trying to talk to the girl about bloody bras.

Biddy's hand stopped mid-way to her mouth, the last piece of the donut in it. She couldn't believe what Miss Jordan had just said. She'd learnt about bras from advertisements, and pictures she'd seen, and she'd thought many times that she probably should have one herself because of the way her breasts moved uncomfortably under her vest, but she hadn't realised it was obvious. Uncomfortable. That's exactly what Miss Jordan had said. She'd felt it earlier when the sweat was running down between her breasts, and wondered now if Miss Jordan could somehow see the dampness of her vest under her shirt. Glancing down, she was relieved to see no visible trace of sweat, but it did seem suddenly, glaringly obvious that she wasn't wearing a bra.

Biddy knew all the other girls in her year wore bras. Sometimes they were visible through their school shirts. Alison's always was. And though she always got changed in one of the three cubicles in the girls' changing room, she could see through the gap at the side of the curtains, and often caught glimpses of the others running around in their underwear, whooping and giggling. Alison's bra and pants always seemed to match. She always looked away quickly, not wanting to have seen, embarrassed by her faded knickers and saggy vest.

Biddy shook her head and put her hands up to her face, dropping the piece of donut on the table. If Miss Jordan knew she needed a bra, then so did everyone else. If Miss Jordan could see it, then so could they. And how they must laugh about it. More proof, if more was needed, of her weirdness.

The lump punched at the back of her throat. The donut and Coke, which a second ago had made her feel lighter and giddier than she'd ever felt before, now churned like lead in her stomach.

As the sickness stirred, the memory of the day not so long ago when she had finally plucked the courage from God knows where to go into Lorraine's Lingerie on the High Street, made her wince. It was going to be like that horror all over again. From the day it opened a year or so ago, Biddy knew the lingerie shop, which was next door to McDaid's Butchers, was a source of embarrassment to her father. Each time they passed it he spluttered a strange little cough, and visibly averted his eyes from the mannequins in the window adorned with bras and pants and short, frilly see-through night dresses. But she also knew he wouldn't stop going to McDaid's. Loyalty was important to her father. As far as she could remember they had never bought their meat from anywhere else, and it was unlikely that even a ladies' underwear shop would change that habit. Biddy felt embarrassed too, but mostly because she found herself wanting to have a closer look. She'd have liked to stop and stare at the mannequins, who all looked so pretty. Is this the type of stuff real grown-up women wear, she wondered? Did her mother have underwear like this, in soft creams and pale pinks, and deep reds trimmed with black? Did she wear turquoise blue frilly nighties, or pastel peach ones? Her own tatty flannel pyjamas and saggy, faded vests made her blush, as did her increasing suspicion that she needed to wear a bra herself. But she had no idea how she was supposed to get one. Was it just a case of going into this shop, picking a bra from a shelf or a rail, and then buying it? Or was there more to it than that? And how much did they cost? Should she bring all of the money in her piggy bank, and the coins stashed in a plastic bag under her bed with her? Would she even be allowed in a shop like that? Every time they passed Lorraine's, Biddy wished her mother was here to help. Her mother would know what to do; she'd show her what was what. She'd teach her about this part of growing up.

Eventually, when her vests began rubbing under her armpits, Biddy had tried the charity shops, but couldn't see any bras on display in any of them. And there was no way she was asking any of the assistants; not even the nice lady with the long grey hair in War on Want, the only one who ever smiled at her, and sometimes picked her out a cardigan, or a pair of trousers. So one Saturday, a couple of months back, when she was dispatched into town on her own to buy the groceries as her father had a heavy cold, she found herself pushing open the door of Lorraine's Lingerie and stepping inside. She wasn't sure what to expect, but what she saw made her gasp. Rows and rows of bras, some hanging on rails, some in boxes on slanted shelves. There were other rails displaying nighties like the ones in the window in a multitude of colours, most of them very short with matching pants. There were knickers, and stockings and slips and even swimsuits. Biddy had never seen anything like it. The clash of colours and patterns made her feel quite dizzy. She thought it must resemble a tropical aviary, but one where all of the poor birds were trapped in a small, tight space with no room to spread their wings, never mind fly. She could see the legs of the shop assistant – who, she wondered, was Lorraine? – on a set of stepladders in some kind of store room at the bottom of the shop. 'Won't be a minute,' a sing-song voice belonging to the legs shouted. 'Have a wee browse and I'll be down in a tick.' Biddy was relieved to have the shop to herself. It meant she could just grab the first bra she saw and take it to the till and have her money ready to pay for it when Lorraine, or whoever the legs belonged to, appeared. She went to the closest rail and lifted the first bra. It was white, which she thought was good, as her vests were all white – at least they used to be. But she hadn't expected it to be just as frilly, or quite so big. She picked up another one. It was cream, and not so frilly, but looked really big too. She was sure her breasts wouldn't fit into either of them. Maybe she wasn't ready for a bra after all. 'Nearly done,' the voice shouted. 'Just want to finish this stock take.' Biddy didn't know what the lady was talking about, but she began to worry that this wasn't going to be as straightforward as she'd hoped. Panic rose in her chest. Maybe one of the bras in a box would be better. She turned to the shelf behind her, knocking her elbow on the edge of it as she did. There were rows of boxes marked with numbers and letters. The pictures on the boxes looked less frilly, but the numbers and letters confused her. There were so many. What did they all mean? How was she supposed to know? And how much did bras cost anyway? She should never have come into the shop. Who did she think she was? How had she ever thought she'd be able to buy herself a bra, especially from here? Weirdos weren't meant to buy bras, or come into shops like this. She needed to leave now before the lady came down the ladders and screamed at her to get out.

She turned and ran, knocking over the rail of frilly bras as she did. She ran out of the shop, and down the High Street, and kept running until she got to the beach, where she threw herself on the farthest rock she could find, retching with shame and pain and exhaustion.

As they ate their sausages and champ that evening, Biddy wondered what her father would say if he knew the meat had come from Dempster's, the new butcher's on Market Lane, and not McDaid's, or what his reaction would be if she said to him, 'Papa, I think I might need a bra.'

Now sitting here opposite Miss Jordan, she felt as stupid and ashamed as she'd felt that day in Lorraine's. Why did she get herself into these situations? Would she never learn? Could she not just accept that as a weirdo she would never be able to do normal things, and leave it at that? She swallowed hard and pressed her palms hard into the sockets of her eyes, desperate to keep the vomit down and the tears at bay.

'Biddy?' said Penny softly. 'Biddy, are you OK? Biddy, what's wrong? Please look at me.'

She put her hands up to Biddy's and gently pulled them away from her face. Her eyes were screwed shut, but her lashes glistened with tears and her pale cheeks were almost translucent. Oh crap, she thought, what had she done?

'Biddy,' she said again, more forcefully this time.

Biddy jolted and opened her eyes, a huge tear pushing out of each one. Penny picked up one of the paper napkins on the table and dabbed the tears away. 'Oh, Biddy, I'm so sorry, pet,' she sighed. 'I really didn't mean to embarrass you. It's just, well, I remember what it's like. If I hadn't had my auntie to help me, I wouldn't have known about these things either,' she smiled gently, and handed Biddy a fresh napkin. 'Please, Biddy, you can trust me. I promise. I'm not trying to humiliate you, or interfere, or step on your father's toes. It's just that sometimes, as a girl, it's, well, it's good to have another girl on your side.' Biddy blew her nose and exhaled loudly. 'There now,' soothed Penny, 'big deep breath. That's my girl. No more tears, eh?'

She smiled at Biddy again and, miraculously, as Biddy settled, a half smile gradually formed on her lips. Penny's heart lurched. She took Biddy's hand and squeezed it, beaming back, and before she knew what she was doing, a thought danced through her head and out of her mouth.

'Listen, Biddy, are you busy next Saturday?'

Standing in the queue at the supermarket café, waiting to be served, a well-dressed woman in her early forties had been quietly observing the scene. She recognised Penny Jordan as the new P.E. teacher at her daughter's school and she was pretty sure the girl with her was that strange child in Alison's class – Biddy something or other. Just last week at the Young Wives meeting, Margaret Boal had told them she'd heard through someone at Ivan's office, who knew someone who used to work at the college in the city, that Miss Jordan was one of those lesbian types. She hadn't believed it, of course. It couldn't possibly be true. It was far too ridiculous for words. 'Oh really, Margaret,' she had laughed, 'do you honestly think someone like that would be employed at Ballybrock Grammar? Especially as a P.E. teacher? Don't be ridiculous, Mr Duncan would never allow it.' Felicity Flemming was in fact very put out that Margaret Boal had provided the group with such a juicy snippet of gossip, no matter how unlikely the truth was. Felicity prided herself on being the number one bearer of news, and didn't take kindly to anyone else stealing the limelight. Now, as she placed an almond square on her plate, her eyes widened in disbelief. Whatever the teacher and the girl were talking about looked very intense indeed. The girl put her hands up to her face and the teacher took them down again. Then the teacher wiped the girl's face with a napkin. And then, *then,* the teacher took the girl's hand in her own. *Well, I never,* she thought, as she moved up the queue. She was still certain the rumours were preposterous, as, quite frankly, she was inclined to believe that lesbianism was nothing more than a myth. But even so, the fact that a teacher and a pupil were fraternising together in public outside of school was simply staggering. It was unprofessional. Unacceptable. Unbelievable. Except, of course, she had witnessed it with her very own eyes. As she reached the till, her heart fluttered in anticipation of this week's Young Wives meeting.

12.

Biddy stood on the edge of the bath and peered into the big oval mirror that hung above the sink, arms outstretched to help her balance. There were no full-length mirrors in the house, and the one on her bedroom dressing table was too small to give a decent view. Not that she'd ever needed one before. Even in the changing room earlier today she hadn't wanted to look in the mirror. But now she did. Now it was time to see her body.

She didn't know what to make of the sight that greeted her. The pitiful spectacle started at her knees, which stuck out like two roughly peeled potatoes. The pasty skin that covered her spindly thighs was decorated with tiny pink scars forming an uneven pattern broken only by the odd yellow scab. Her pointy pelvic bones and concave belly were covered by a pair of saggy blue-grey pants she'd had since she was eleven. Every bone on her protruding rib cage was visible, like a female body builder or a Biafran baby. But then, there it was; gleaming white cotton with a tiny trim of shiny lace and fine elastic straps. Her bra. Her very own bra. Proof that no matter what the rest of her body looked like, she was definitely going to be a woman. She might still be a bloody weirdo, but at least she had breasts that needed a bra, just like Alison and the others. And just like them she now wore a bra too. She could almost be normal.

Penny Jordan had taken Biddy to Rankin and McMordie, the big department store in the city. The smaller one in Collingsford would have been more convenient, but Penny felt there was less chance of being spotted in the city. Despite being certain she was doing a good deed, she still had an uneasy feeling. Developing relationships with pupils outside of school was definitely frowned upon.

She'd arranged to meet Biddy outside the store at 11 a.m. It was exactly a week after their chance encounter in the café. That meeting had given her the opportunity to organise this one. Naturally she hadn't told Sam where she was going, as she knew she would only try to dissuade her. And in truth, she might just have just succeeded.

This is sheer bloody madness, Penny thought to herself, as she waited for Biddy to arrive. But she couldn't back out now. She'd managed to secure Biddy's confidence and to let her down at this stage would be devastating for the girl. Besides, it was only a bra, for God's sake, not kinky underwear! And the girl really needed a bra. And she really wanted to help. And it wasn't as though she was paying; Biddy was buying it herself. She said she had money: savings in her piggy bank.

So why was she feeling so goddamned uncomfortable about the whole thing? She spotted Biddy's wild copper hair bobbing its way through the crowded street before her anxious face came into view. Her pale complexion was almost grey with fear. She looked terrified; like she might turn and run away at any moment. Penny watched as Biddy's eyes darted down to the pavement after accidentally catching someone's gaze, and her stomach wrenched as Biddy almost walked into a lamppost.

'Biddy,' she shouted, 'over here.'

Biddy looked up to see Miss Jordan waving at her from the doorway of the store. She looked so pretty in her dark denim jeans and matching jacket. She even had a matching denim bag slung across her shoulder. And her turquoise T-shirt made her eyes sparkle like two sapphire gems. Instantly unnerved, Biddy stopped abruptly, suddenly unable to move. People tutted as they bumped into her, but she didn't notice. She was thinking about her own clothes. Pale blue elasticised cotton trousers which were too big around the waist and sat above her ankles. A cream nylon shirt with a round collar. A baggy, navy blue cardigan with two missing buttons. And to top it off, her white school P.E. plimsolls. She had no handbag, just a plastic bag full of change which was heavily weighing her down, making her walk with a slightly lopsided limp. Biddy had never considered her appearance before, but as she looked at Miss Jordan standing waving at her in her nice smart outfit, she knew with absolute certainty that she looked ridiculous. It was like a punch in the stomach. She wanted to turn and run, but suddenly Miss Jordan was standing in front of her, saying something she couldn't hear because of the rushing noise in her ears; and before she knew it they were in the store going up a moving staircase.

Biddy had never been on an escalator before and it took her by surprise. She felt the panic rise in her throat and the sickness churn in her tummy as she looked back at the people below moving further away from her. She closed her eyes and wished she was a bird who could fly away. She didn't like this place. She didn't like the city, or the department store or this moving staircase. There were too many people. There was too much noise. She wanted to go home. She'd lied to her father for the second Saturday in a row, and she felt wicked and ashamed. She had to get out of here: now.

'Are you OK, Biddy?' Penny's concerned voice jolted her back to reality. Biddy realised that she couldn't go home. Not now. Not when Miss Jordan had gone to so much trouble to organise this. How could she let Miss Jordan down? She was the only person apart from her father who had ever shown an interest in her. So she swallowed hard, nodded her head and smiled weakly.

'I thought you were going to fall on me there. Are you sure you're all right?'

'Yes. Fine, thank you,' she said politely. 'Just felt a bit dizzy.'

'Did you have any breakfast, Biddy?'

'A bit,' nodded Biddy.

'Well, I'll tell you what, when we're done here I'll take you to a little place I love that serves a fab brunch. Deal?' Biddy nodded and forced her mouth into a smile. She had no idea what a brunch was, or what it tasted like, but if Miss Jordan got her one, she would do her best to eat it. Maybe by then she wouldn't feel sick.

'There's the underwear department over there.'

Biddy gulped as Miss Jordan steered her in the direction of rows of bras and pants in white and black and pink and red and baby blue, the memory of Lorraine's Lingerie giving her palpitations. But the section was so vast it made Lorraine's Lingerie shop look like a market stall. Everything looked so pretty, so delicate and much less flamboyant than in Lorraine's. She had been so scared that she would feel overwhelmed again, terrified she would throw up in front of Miss Jordan, but rather than feeling sick, having her teacher with her was easing her anxiety. This time she wanted to touch the lacy cups and stroke the silk of the knickers. They were all so very beautiful, not as garish and terrifying as the ones in Lorraine's. She wanted to hold the fabrics up to her skin and breathe them in. But just as she was about to pick up a soft blue bra she froze. A tall slender shop assistant, with hair like Marilyn Monroe and glossy red lips suddenly bounced in front of them.

107

'Good morning, madam,' the assistant said to Miss Jordan in a voice pitched so high that she was almost singing. 'And what can we do for you and your, ah,' she hesitated, 'your little sister today?' She clasped her hands beneath her chin and fixed the full intensity of her gaze on Biddy.

Biddy jumped back, startled, and looked at Miss Jordan, who, registering the panic in her eyes quickly replied: 'Erm, it's OK, thank you. We're just browsing at the minute.'

'Not a problem,' sang the bra lady. 'I'll be right here if you need me for anything, and remember: it's better to measure, and do try before you buy. Our changing rooms are just behind you; three items at a time.' Her red lips pouted slightly, as she took in Biddy's appearance before turning her attention to a glamorous woman behind them.

'Right then, "little sister",' Miss Jordan winked. Biddy grinned, thinking how truly wonderful it would be to really have Miss Jordan as her big sister. 'This is the starter section, and I think you're probably about a 28A. Or maybe a 30A. Tell you what, why don't you pick one or two bras you like in both sizes and then you can go and try them on. I'll help you pick out a couple, and then I'll head over there to the gift section while you're in the changing room. I need to get a present for someone and I thought I might get a nice photo-frame or something here. I don't really think we need bother Miss Red Lips, do you?'

Biddy smiled and nodded, relieved that Miss Jordan didn't expect to join her in the trying on process. And if the red-lipped bra lady had insisted on measuring her, unlikely as it was, she knew she would have run down the moving stairs and right out of the door. No one, absolutely no one, must see her scars.

Penny felt a little more relaxed by now. Hopefully this wouldn't take too long. They could go for a bite to eat, she'd deliver Biddy back to the station, and then she could do a bit of shopping herself. She fancied a new jacket and could do with some nice Nike trainers for work. 'Now then,' she smiled at Biddy, 'how much money do you have, so we know what our budget is?'

Biddy handed her the plastic bag, relieved to be rid of the uncomfortable weight. It contained over two years of pocket money saved for nothing in particular. The only things she spent her money on were sketchpads and pencils when she needed them, and, since her period started, a few packets of Dr. Whites.

'Gosh, Biddy,' laughed Penny, 'did you raid your money box?'

'Yes,' came the deadpan reply.

Penny opened the bag and looked inside. It was filled with ten-pence pieces. 'Bloody hell,' she thought, working very hard to suppress a giggle, 'there must be nearly twenty quid here. Let's hope the assistant at the till is in a good mood.' She looked up at Biddy, who was staring at her expectantly, waiting to be told what to do next. The naked innocence on her face twisted Penny's heart.

'Well, Biddy,' she smiled, with all the positivity and encouragement she could muster, 'this is great. Fantastic. You could even buy two bras. Or maybe you'd like a new T-shirt or something nice for the disco. Now that would be a good idea, wouldn't it?'

Biddy continued to nod at the appropriate moments, still not trusting herself to speak, in case the wrong words came out. She wasn't going to the disco, but she didn't need to remind Miss Jordan of that now. So she pointed at two bras she thought were pretty and before she knew it she was in the changing room with both of them, plus another picked by Miss Jordan herself. That was the one she bought. Not because Miss Jordan had chosen it, but because it was by far the most comfortable of the three.

Biddy arrived home that afternoon with her new bra, a pair of denim jeans, the first she'd ever owned, and a long-sleeved blue and white stripy top with a slash neck. 'Now you're all set for the disco,' Miss Jordan had said as she left her at the station. 'A wee touch of blusher to highlight those cheekbones and you'll be the belle of the ball.'

Blusher, cheekbones, 'belle of the ball', bra, jeans, brunch. Biddy's head was spinning with new words and new experiences. She had bought her very own bra and her first pair of real jeans with her very own money. She had eaten a brunch of bacon and scrambled eggs and a funny kind of bread with a funny name and had a frothy coffee and she hadn't even felt sick once. And someone had thought that Miss Jordan was her big sister. *And*, best of all, she'd been invited to Miss Jordan's house for a baking lesson in a couple of weeks' time. Her actual own house, to do some proper actual baking. The teacher hadn't laughed when Biddy admitted that she didn't know how to bake, as the subject of the cake sale had been brought up again over their 'brunch'. 'Well, we'll have to sort that then, won't we?' she'd said, pulling out her diary. 'How about you come to mine and help me with my fairy cakes? With your artistic flair, I bet you'll be an ace cake decorator. I can't do next weekend, and the Saturday after that I'm on the clearing-up rota after the disco. So how about the following one? Saturday 8th June? Would that suit? It's the week before the sale.' Biddy didn't know if she was more astonished by the invitation, or by Miss Jordan's reference to her drawing, the second time she'd complimented her on it, but she did know that this was by far the best day she had ever had. And she didn't want it to end. So when she got off the bus at Ballybrock station, she headed straight for the big chemist shop before going home. Maybe she would go to the disco after all, and if she did, she ought to buy some blusher.

Penny was relieved when she waved Biddy off at the station. It had gone well, much better than she'd expected it to, but she felt exhausted. She'd managed to persuade the girl to buy some new clothes as well as the bra, and she'd watched her eat a decent lunch too. Not that she thought Biddy was starving herself, or that Mr Weir was deliberately neglecting the nutritional needs of his teenage daughter. She just had a suspicion that, more often than not, Biddy either forgot to eat or couldn't be bothered, and that her father simply didn't notice. Anyway, at least she would look semi-decent at the disco in her new clothes. Even though they weren't high fashion, they weren't from a charity shop either, so there was less of a chance that Alison and her gang would take the piss out of her. Thankfully she hadn't bumped into any-one she knew, or, more importantly, anyone from school. OK, perhaps inviting Biddy to her house to help her bake had been a bit of a step too far; but then again, what harm could it do. She felt she had made a genuine connection with Biddy, and knew the girl responded well to her. It was even more obvious now that she needed some form of female influence in her life. She'd chosen the 8th as Sam would be at her parents' that weekend for their wedding anniversary party, so there'd be no need to tell her. It would be a good distraction for her.

Penny felt so pleased with herself that she headed straight back to the store to buy a pair of black lacy pants she'd spotted earlier. 'Yup,' she thought, holding them up against her, 'Sam is really going to like these.'

Unbeknown to Penny, a couple of hours earlier, Susan Patterson had been holding up the very same pair for her husband, Clive, to inspect. 'What about these ones, honey?' she said, 'and look, there's a gorgeous bra to match.' When she got no response, she turned to see her husband standing with his back to her. 'Clive,' she hissed, 'you're supposed to be helping me choose. Don't be a shit. You promised.'

This was Susan's payback day for her husband's third night out with 'the boys' in less than two weeks. A new outfit with shoes, a bag and underwear to match. And she intended to squeeze in some jewellery and perfume as well. She suspected Clive was having another fling with someone at school. And he suspected that she suspected. So he suggested one of their shopping trips, which suited Susan just fine. She didn't really care about his little infidelities, as she had her own secret liaisons with the junior doctors at the hospital where she worked. But when Clive flexed his credit card at her, he always seemed so much more attractive.

'Clive!' she said again between gritted teeth, pulling at his elbow. But Clive wasn't listening. Clive was watching Penny Jordan, the new P.E. teacher at school, standing at the till buying a bra for that weird girl in Alison's class. At least that's what it looked like. She was counting out ten-pence pieces on the counter, and the girl was standing beside her holding a bra. Just last night, Alison had told him the rumour about Penny being a 'lesbo'. And here she was, right in front of his eyes, buying a fucking bra for a fourth year, fucked-up weirdo. Bloody hell! It made what he was up to seem like nothing at all.

'Clive!' Susan almost shouted this time.

'Jesus fucking Christ,' he said, scratching his head as he turned to face the black skimpy panties she was holding up for his inspection.

'Does that mean you like them, or you don't?'

13.

When her balance became unsteady, Biddy jumped down onto the bumpy bathroom lino and pulled on her dressing gown. She took a small paper bag from her pocket and tipped the contents onto the old rickety table beside the sink. A pale pink Miners lipstick, rose-coloured blusher, blue-black mascara and bright blue eye-shadow. The girl in the chemist shop said Miners was the best for teenagers, and that these colours were all the rage. Biddy hadn't asked for help, but the girl, Debbie, as her name badge said, decided she needed it.

Biddy didn't know where to start. Perhaps she should have let Debbie do a demonstration after all, as she'd wanted to do, then at least she'd know what to do with the stuff. She knew all the other girls at the disco would look perfect. She opened the jar of eye-shadow, rubbed her forefinger into the blue powder and smeared it once across both eyelids. Next was the lipstick. The shiny pink stick looked good enough to eat. She ran the tip of it over her lips in a circular motion as though she was colouring in, half expecting it to taste like a sweet: a bonbon, or a strawberry sherbet. She used her forefinger again to apply the cream blusher, smearing a rosy stripe, tinted blue from the remnants of the eye-shadow, below her cheekbones. Then she rubbed each cheek roughly in a circular motion, spreading the now purplish colour across most of her face. Finally she twisted out the long mascara brush, closed her eyes and rubbed it left to right across both sets of lashes. She had difficulty opening her eyes as her lashes instantly clogged together with lumps of the black liquid. She blinked furiously, her eyes stinging from bits of mascara that had escaped from her lashes. Now it was time to look in the mirror.

If Gracie Weir had not run away, she would, no doubt, have witnessed the scene that her daughter was now surveying at some stage of Biddy's younger life, just as most mothers who have little girls and bulging make-up bags inevitably do. But Biddy was fifteen, not five, and this make-up was hers, not her mother's. Yet the effect was virtually the same. And Biddy knew it. Her tears pulled streaks of black mascara with them as they ran down her cheeks, dripped off her chin and splashed onto her chest, staining her new crisp white bra. She rubbed furiously at her face, the blue and pink and purple colours blending with wet black tears like a toddler's first painting. 'Bloody Weirdo', she sobbed, rubbing at her face with the backs of her hands before collapsing on the bathroom floor. 'Bloody, bloody, fucking, Bloody Weirdo.'

14.

Biddy was shaking as she put her fifty-pence piece down on the table. 'Hand!' said a boy wearing a large white T-shirt with 'FRANKIE SAYS RELAX' slashed across it in bold black letters. His hair was stiffly swept back from his forehead and Biddy was sure he was wearing make-up, which confused her. She recognised him as a boy in her year, but didn't know his name. She was sure he didn't wear make-up at school, though. Did that make him a bit weird like her, she wondered? Or was it a normal thing that boys did? One of the many normal things that she just didn't know about? Then a similar-looking boy, who wore a similar T-shirt, except his said 'CHOOSE LIFE', appeared at the door of the staff cloakroom. Biddy's heart thumped. He was wearing make-up too, but just around his eyes. 'Coat,' he said, thrusting his arm out towards her.

Biddy winced and leant backwards.

'Are you going to give me your coat, or what?' snarled the boy.

Biddy thrust her navy blue Pac A Mac at him, then immediately regretted it. She should just leave now. This was a mistake. She shouldn't be here. She coughed, trying to push the acidy feeling away.

'Here,' the boy grunted, giving her a green ticket with the number 97 on it. 'So you get the right coat back. Not that anyone's likely to take this home by mistake.' He shared a snigger with RELAX, mouthing 'Bloody Weirdo' behind Biddy's back before turning back into the staff cloakroom. The RELAX boy glared at Biddy, who was staring at the blue bird stamped on her hand. It wasn't a very good image, she thought. There was no way of telling what kind of bird it was supposed to be. 'Are you going in, or what?' he said, obviously irritated. ''Cos it's too late to get your money back now.'

Biddy nodded, but she still didn't move. She couldn't. She could hear the beat of loud music coming from the assembly hall and feel the vibration beneath her feet. It suddenly dawned on her that everyone would be dancing, and she'd never danced in her life. Did her mother like to dance, she wondered? Had she ever danced with her father? She couldn't imagine her father dancing.

'Duh?' said RELAX, pointing to the doors with obvious irritation.

'Home,' whispered Biddy.

'What?'

'Ho—'

'Biddy! You made it. Wow, don't you look great.' Penny Jordan swung through the assembly hall doors, letting a snatch of Duran Duran's *The Reflex* out with her.

Biddy certainly looked more grown up than usual. The jeans and stripy T-shirt suited her, but they weren't exactly a fashion statement, and Penny feared she would feel out of place when she went into the hall. And her make-up was all wrong. Penny wanted to build up her confidence, but she knew, after seeing how all of the other teenagers were dressed, that if Biddy went inside looking like this, she would be as good as handing Alison the ammunition for an attack on a plate. Perhaps her insistence that Biddy come to the disco had been misjudged after all. Perhaps she had been wrong to interfere. She breathed in deeply, a smile still etched on her face. Well, whether she'd been right, or wrong, Biddy was here, and she had to do something to steer off a shipwreck.

'Phew, it's hot in there,' she said, fanning her face with her hand. 'I'm just nipping to the loo. How about you, Biddy? Do you need to go?'

'Erm, yes,' said Biddy quietly.

'Come on, then, nip in here with me and then you won't have to queue in the girls' loos.' Penny nodded towards the staff toilets. 'I'm sure Bryan and Tim won't let on, will you, boys?' She grinned and winked at them. 'Like the T-shirts, guys.'

Not knowing quite what to make of the situation, the boys shook their heads and when Miss Jordan and Biddy went into the toilet, they stared at each other in wide-eyed, open-mouthed amazement.

'What are you two gormless dickheads gawping at?!' Standing in front of them, chewing gum and tossing her shaggy permed, honey-coloured hair, was Alison Flemming, resplendent in full Bananarama regalia. Her white three-quarter length trousers were held up with black braces which sat over a tight white cropped boob tube. A long white unbuttoned shirt-coat was purposely falling down over her right honey-toned shoulder. Her black Doc Marten semi-laced up boots matched her heavily kohled eyes. To complete the effect she knew she was having on the boys, she slowly licked her bright red lips.

'Erm, nothing,' managed CHOOSE LIFE Tim.

'Yeah, nothing,' repeated RELAX Bryan, letting out an un-attractive snort, as he gazed at Alison's breasts.

'What's the matter, Piggy Boy, never seen a pair of tits before?' taunted Alison, pulling her baggy shirt further down over her shoulder and letting her fingers slide over her boob tube.

Bryan gulped and Tim covered the erection, which was glaringly obvious under his tight black jeans, with his hands.

'Be nice, boys, and let me go in there for a wee,' Alison pouted coyly, indicating the staff toilets. 'The queue in our loo is too long and I'm so close to peeing my pants.' Bryan looked at Tim and then looked at the toilet door.

'Can't.' He shook his head furiously and glared at the speechless Tim for backup. Tim just shook his head too.

'What do you mean, "can't"?' mimicked Alison. 'Afraid you'll get told off by old Morgan, or maybe even get detention?' she mocked. 'Wise up, and just let me in, for fuck's sake.'

She went to push past them, but Bryan blocked her way. If Miss Jordan hadn't been in there with Bloody Weirdo, he would have let Alison in, no problem. And strictly speaking, if Bloody Weirdo was having a pee in the female staff loo, then there was no reason why Alison shouldn't be allowed one too. But he didn't want to take the risk. Deep down, he was a good boy. Besides, he liked Miss Jordan and he didn't want to get in her bad books, especially as P.E. was his favourite subject.

'Look Alison, I just can't let you, OK.'

'Course you can, Bryan. If you really wanted to, that is. Maybe you just need a little incentive.' Alison put her finger on her chin and closed her eyes, pretending to think.

'I know, boys,' she smiled, and stuck out her chest. 'You can have a little peek. Would that help?'

Bryan gulped and his cheeks reddened. Tim's eyes got wider and his penis stiffer. He wanted to say, 'You're on. Deal. Yes, bloody please,' but he didn't trust himself to speak. *Go on, go on,* he willed Bryan. *Say yes, say yes.*

Bryan cleared his throat.

'Thing is, Alison, there's, ah, well there's already someone in there. A teacher. So you see you can't. Sorry and all. And thanks for the offer. But you can't go in.' Bryan could almost hear Tim's silent scream and it echoed the one inside his own head: *Fuck. Fuck, fuck, fuck, fuck, fuck.*

'Who is it?' Alison wasn't giving up. There were only a few teachers in the school she definitely wouldn't risk annoying. Most she could deal with. If it was Franklin, Scully, Pemrose or fat McFettrick, she'd give up. Anyone else and she'd try her luck. She could always cry and plead an emergency. She'd think of something. She always did.

'Miss Jordan.'

'Biddy Weir.'

Bryan and Tim spoke simultaneously.

'Well?' demanded Alison. 'Which one is it? Miss Jordan or Bloody Weirdo? It's not both of them, is it? Together? In the staff loo?' Her heart was beating furiously, as she looked from Bryan to Tim, from Tim to Bryan. *Bloody hell*, she thought. *Mum and Clive were right. There is something going on. Fantastic. Fannybloodytastic.*

'Sorry, lads, but I'm going in there. This I have to see.'

As Bryan lifted his hand in protest, Alison played her ace card: 'Oh, for fuck's sake here, have a look, and then piss off.' She slipped her hands under each strap of her braces and pulled down her boob tube allowing her more than ample teenage breasts to bounce out at Bryan and Tim. 'Now, move,' she hissed, pulling her top back in place. There was no resistance this time from Bryan, who was just as speechless as Tim.

Biddy was washing her hands at the sink when Penny came out of her cubicle. The staff toilets weren't all that much better than the pupils' ones, but they had a bigger mirror and proper towels and nice pink, rose-scented soap. Not that awful yellow sticky goo that smelt of cold porridge and glue. Miss Forester, the deputy headmistress and by far the oldest teacher in the school, took it upon herself to keep the Staff Ladies in nice condition. She supplied and laundered the towels herself and she bought the soap and room spray out of her own pocket. Sometimes she left in a tube of hand cream, and on special occasions, like tonight, she even set out a little vase of roses, cut from her own garden, regardless of whether she would be there or not.

'Looks like Miss Forester's been at her work again,' smiled Penny, squirting a blob of hand cream onto her left hand before offering some to Biddy. 'It's OK,' she whispered. 'She isn't here. And anyway, I'm sure she wouldn't mind. But I won't tell, if you won't,' she winked, rubbing the cream into her hands.

Biddy cautiously followed suit and copied Miss Jordan's actions. She'd never used proper hand cream before. Sometimes when her hands became rough and chapped from sketching out-side in the wintertime, she would rub in some Vaseline before going to bed. She supposed she'd have used her mother's hand cream, if her mother were here.

'Mmmm,' said Miss Jordan smelling her palms. 'Roses. I think Miss Forester likes roses, don't you?' Biddy nodded. *Would my mother have liked roses*, she wondered, *like Papa does. Or violets? Perhaps she would have preferred violets.*

'So, Biddy. Are you ready to rock?'

Biddy smiled nervously. Miss Jordan looked so pretty. She was wearing the same dark jeans she'd worn on Saturday, this time with a bright pink short-sleeved V-neck jumper with a big deep waistband that flattered her tiny waist. And she was wearing make-up, but it looked lovely on her. She obviously knew how to do it properly. Biddy wished she looked like Miss Jordan. She sighed and shuffled uncomfortably in her school plimsolls.

'You know what, Biddy, I think you might be a bit more comfortable if you took your socks off. Your feet might get a bit hot in there.'

'Oh. OK.' Biddy smiled nervously at Miss Jordan and slipped off her plimsolls. Then she pulled off her grey school socks and put her shoes back on again.

'Erm – what will I do with these?' Biddy held up her socks.

'Roll them up and give them to me. I'll put them in my bag in the staff room and you can get them back before you go. Now, let's have a look at you. How about if I turn your jeans up slightly at the bottom. Good, that looks better, doesn't it?'

Biddy nodded, taking Miss Jordan's word for it.

'And you see, if you pull your T-shirt slightly over your shoulders, like this . . .' Penny adjusted the slash neck top slightly to make it sit the way it should. 'Excellent,' she beamed. Biddy beamed back. She loved Miss Jordan helping her like this. Miss Jordan made her feel special, and she'd never felt special before.

'Biddy, I see you've bought yourself some nice new make-up,' said Miss Jordan, brightly. 'It's great fun buying make-up, isn't it?' Biddy nodded.

'It's a bit tricky, putting it on sometimes though, don't you think?'

Biddy nodded again, her smile fading. *She thinks I look stupid*, she thought.

'You know, I'm useless at putting on eye-shadow. I had to get my friend Sam to help me tonight. Do you think she's done a good job?' Penny closed her eyes for Biddy to examine.

'Yes, Miss. Your eyes look lovely,' she replied, shyly.

'Sam gave me a couple of tips. Shall I try them on you?'

'Erm, OK, Miss.' Biddy closed her eyes tight and tilted back her chin.

'Not so tight, Biddy. Just relax your eyes a little. That's it. Good.' Penny gently rubbed Biddy's eyelids with a tissue, removing some of the excess blue powder and blended in the remaining colour with her little finger. Then she took another tissue, ran it briefly under the tap and softly rubbed at Biddy's cheeks until she looked more like a flushed teenager and less like a painted doll. Next she removed most of Biddy's lipstick, took a tiny tin of Vaseline from her pocket, and smeared a little bit over her lips.

'Now, rub your lips together like this. Doesn't that feel nice? That's *my* secret make-up tip,' she smiled. 'Vaseline. I never go anywhere without it. Right, just let me fix this gorgeous hair of yours.'

Penny put her hands under the tap and then ran them through Biddy's frizzy mop, the moisture separating some of her curls. She pushed it back off her forehead and ran her fingers through the ends until she created something that at least resembled a style.

'You really do have fabulous hair, Biddy, you know. Many people would pay a fortune to have curls like yours, and I'm one of them.'

Biddy smiled nervously. She was sure Miss Jordan was just being nice. Why on earth would anyone want to look like any part of her? Especially someone as pretty as Miss Jordan? And as for her hair, she'd never seen anyone else with hair remotely like hers, and she knew it was part of what made her a weirdo. She knew that Miss Jordan was actually telling a lie, even though it was a kind lie.

'You know, I have a gorgeous hair clip I don't use anymore as my hair isn't long enough. It would look amazing in your hair,' said Miss Jordan as she continued to prise out Biddy's curls. 'To tell you the truth, it never looked good on me. It was made for your colouring. My dark, flat locks did nothing for it. I'd like you to have it, Biddy. I'll give it to you when you come round for our baking party.'

'Oh, n-no, Miss. I couldn't . . .'

'Nonsense. Of course you can. It's a present. Now, you're ready. Take a look.'

Miss Jordan swung Biddy round to the mirror. She barely recognised herself. Her eyes looked bright and sparkling, her lips looked plumper and her cheeks had a soft flush of colour. And her hair sat back off her face instead of falling all over it. Her heart was thumping. Miss Jordan hadn't forgotten about the invitation; she really was going to teach her how to bake, *and* she was going to give her a present. No one, apart from her father, had given her a present before. And Miss Jordan had made her look like this: almost normal.

'Oh,' she said quietly. 'I look different.'

'You look fabulous, Biddy,' smiled Penny. 'There's just one finishing touch we need now.'

Biddy looked at her expectantly.

'A smile, Biddy, a great, big, beaming smile.'

Biddy's face glowed and her smile broke into a laugh.

'There,' said Penny proudly, 'beautiful.' She gave Biddy a big hug. 'Now, I'm going to dart into the staffroom to put these socks away, then let's go and have some fun.'

15.

Alison turned sharply and darted out of the toilet before Miss Jordan or B.W. saw her.

'You assholes let them know I was here and you'll live to regret it. Got it?'

She glared at Bryan and Tim, who were still reeling from the sight of some real live breasts. They nodded obediently. There was no chance they'd tell anyway. If Jordan and Bloody Weirdo hadn't seen Alison, then they were off the hook. Come to think of it, though, they had been in there for quite a long time.

'Ah, is everything OK in there?' Bryan nodded to the toilet door.

'Oh yes,' smiled Alison slowly. 'I would say everything was perfect. Gotta go boys. And remember what I said.'

And off she ran to seek out Julia, Jackie and Georgie. She couldn't wait to tell them what she'd just witnessed. There was absolutely definitely something funny going on between Miss Jordan and Bloody Weirdo, and now she'd seen it with her very own eyes. The lezzie and the nutcase. What a scoop.

Alison hadn't witnessed the whole scene, of course. She'd come in just at the point when Penny was touching up Biddy's lips. But from her vantage point just inside the entrance, set back behind the cubicles, she saw the rest of the episode through the toilet mirror. And that was enough for her to conclude that the lesbian teacher was indeed having a fling with the fourth-year freak. She couldn't believe her luck. When her mother had told her the rumours about Jordan being gay a couple of weeks before, she was repulsed. She didn't really believe it, of course, not properly, but she had delighted in telling the others the next day in school.

'I always knew there was something funny about her,' she had said, screwing her face up in disgust.

'Yeah,' Georgina agreed. 'I mean, the way she looks at you in the changing room. Yeuck,' she shivered.

Julia and Jackie hadn't noticed anything, but not to be left out they nodded in agreement.

'Freaky,' said Julia.

'Bet Duncan doesn't know,' added Jackie. 'She shouldn't be allowed to get away with it.'

'Oh, she won't,' Alison had sneered. 'If it's true, of course.'

Then just the other night, Clive had relayed the story of his sighting in the underwear department at Rankin and McMordie in the city. Alison had been furious. She'd been stewing for days, red with rage that Clive had taken his wife shopping to Rankin and McMordie – and for underwear at that. And he hadn't even bought her a present. Even the thought of the disco hadn't lifted her mood. They may have only been 'seeing' each other for a few weeks, but Clive had assured Alison that his marriage was stale, that his wife was a frigid bitch who didn't understand him, that she turned a blind eye to his 'extra-curricular' activities. That had pissed her off too. It was well known amongst the pupils, and staff, at Ballybrock Grammar that Clive Patterson was a flirt, and as far back as the second year Alison had been aware of the rumours. Even then she'd been intrigued. Would a teacher really have a fling with a pupil? She'd felt a rush of admiration the first time one of the rumours was whispered to her harem in the playground one lunchtime by Georgie's older sister, Victoria. The other girls had all been horrified, but Alison was more than a little bit in awe. Mr Patterson and Amanda Loughrin. Mr Patterson and Sonia O'Hara. Mr Patterson and Miss Courtney, the young French teacher they'd had in the third year. Amanda and Sonia had been sixth-form pupils, and whilst Clive had told Alison to mind her own business when she'd quizzed him about them, he had admitted that he'd never dated anyone as young or as gorgeous as her. Dated. Young. Gorgeous. Those three words were enough to keep her sweet. But his blatant reference to his lothario reputation had enraged her. And now this. Well, there would be no more 'extra-curricular activities', and no more shopping trips to the city with his bloody wife, especially to buy underwear. Now that she was Clive's girlfriend, any little presents he'd be buying would be for her, and only her. She would make sure of that. OK, their 'dates' hadn't actually progressed beyond drives to secluded spots in the hills in Clive's new metallic blue 2.8 Ford Capri, but they would. Clive said so. He might be bringing her to the cinema in a couple of weeks to see *Witness*, that new film everyone was talking about, starring Harrison Ford. And maybe out for dinner too. They'd have to be careful, of course. They'd probably have to go to the city. But that was fine with her. All part of the fun; part of the thrill. And she had no trouble lying to her parents about her whereabouts: she was a professional in that department.

Although they hadn't actually had full-blown sex yet, they'd done plenty of other things. She'd certainly gone further with Clive than she had with any of her other boyfriends. They might have talked the talk, but none of them walked the walk. Not even Craig Black, though she'd let Georgie, Jackie and Julia think otherwise. (Well, they'd guessed 'it' had happened, and whilst she didn't confirm their assumption, she didn't deny it either.)

With Clive though, it was only a matter of time. And Alison was ready. So ready. She sometimes thought she'd been ready since the very first time she'd clapped eyes on Trevor Eve from her secret viewpoint at the top of the stairs in their house in the city. She was almost embarrassed that all these years later, at almost sixteen, she still hadn't gone the whole way, despite the fact that none of the other girls in her year had either. But she must be the first. She absolutely must.

For a time, Alison thought Marcus would be the one to take her virginity, but B.W. had ruined that possibility for her. Bitch. She'd never forgive her of course, but maybe she'd inadvertently done her a favour, as losing it to Clive would be better. Way better. He was so much more attractive for a start. In fact, he had a look of Trevor Eve about him. And, obviously, he was experienced: a man of the world. He'd be an amazing lover. Far better to lose it to a man, a proper man, than a boy. She couldn't be bothered with boys anymore. When she thought about it, she never really had. Older men had always been her thing. They were just so much more . . . interesting. Marcus had been dull; hadn't she even said that at the time? And though she wasn't in any way deluded into thinking that Clive would be a long-term catch, he was a hell of a short-term one. He had said he loved her, moaned it really, just the other night, as the car windows steamed up and Marvin Gaye crooned '*Let's get it on*' through the stereo system, and she'd muttered it back. Maybe she did, maybe she didn't; maybe he did, maybe he didn't. But she doubted it. She didn't really get love as a concept, and she suspected Clive felt the same, but ever since she'd caught him giving her 'that glance' as he'd asked her to deliver a letter to Mr Duncan during a Geography lesson back in March, the game had been on. She knew that day he wanted her, and she decided right there and then that she wanted him back.

Maybe tonight would be the night, she'd thought that afternoon, as she chose her outfit for the disco: her new white Bananarama-style dungarees, or her black Madonna 'Holiday' ensemble? She knew she looked sexier in the dungarees, and besides, there'd be loads of Madonna copycats there; rubbish ones, granted, but all the same, if ever there was a night she needed to make an impression, it was tonight. This afternoon in his store room, Clive had told Alison to meet him there at 9.15 p.m. 'I'll be waiting,' he'd said, stroking her cheek, 'and if you're a good girl, I might just have a surprise for you.' She was suddenly looking forward to the disco after all.

As she carefully and skilfully applied her make-up, Alison decided to forgive Clive for the shopping trip, which gave her the headspace to think about his other revelation: B.W. and Miss Jordan, shopping together for bras. She had been so consumed by rage and jealousy towards Clive's pathetic wife, that she really hadn't given this incredibly juicy piece of gossip any proper consideration. Part of her did think that Clive had somehow been mistaken, in the same way she thought her mother was mistaken too. The notion was frankly too absurd.

Well, now she knew for sure that it was true, absurd or not, she'd absolutely have to do something about it. And though she would never, ever admit it, a tiny part of her was jealous. Not because she fancied Miss Jordan, or had a thing about girls. Not in the slightest. But she couldn't stomach the glaringly obvious fact that Miss Jordan and Biddy Weirdo had some form of – oh, she didn't know quite what – connection? They *did* things together. They'd been spotted by her own mother in a café. They'd been caught buying underwear together by her boyfriend. She'd seen Miss Jordan touching B.W. in a sort of comfortable, intimate way with her very own eyes; the kind of comfortable intimate way in which she longed to be touched herself by Clive, or her mother, or father, or, well, anyone really. Not that she'd ever admit it. And she'd heard Miss Jordan, with her very own ears, tell Biddy that she had a present for her, a hairclip, and that she'd give it to her next time she was in her house, to bake. Miss Jordan had the fucking weirdo in her own home, and baked with her, and gave her presents. Clive wouldn't even be seen in public with Alison, never mind invite her to his house. And, so far, he hadn't bought her so much as a can of Coke. She knew he was embarrassed by their relationship, ashamed of it even. She knew he was. Not that she'd ever admit it.

As she made her way through the throng in the assembly hall, looking for the girls, she spotted Miss Jordan and B.W. on the dance floor. They were dancing. Together. Rage swept through her like a tornado. Bloody fucking Weirdo and Miss pretendy-goody-two-shoes-sweet-and-not-so-fucking-innocent Jordan were dancing, together, at the school fucking disco. Until that second she had been directing some of her anger at Clive. But now she realised it wasn't his fault at all. Not even remotely. He was as much a victim of their illicit love as she was. He was married, even though he didn't want to be. He was a teacher. He held a position of responsibility, for God's sake. He *had* to be careful. He *had* to be secretive. Of course he had to. He had no choice. But here were B.W. and Penny Jordan flaunting themselves in front of her fucking face. Well, she'd be fucked if a dyke teacher and the bane of her life school weirdo were going to have something she couldn't.

By the time she'd rounded up her gang from around the dance floor, Alison's plan was fully formed. It was a brilliant plan. Her best yet. Tonight was going to be even better than she'd hoped. Tonight she was finally going to get her own back on that bitch for screwing up her chance with Marcus Baxter, and for daring to be so blatantly close to a teacher, and for, well, for simply existing. She caught Clive looking at her as she strode along the back of the assembly hall, and held his gaze for a few seconds, slowly moving her tongue over her lips, both of them locked in a sheath of light from the disco. He looked gorgeous tonight. Even more like Trevor Eve than usual. Yes, she thought, tonight will be a brilliant night. My night.

She glanced at her watch but it was too dark in the hall to see the time properly. She looked up at the clock, illuminated by the disco lights. Ten to nine. Their rendezvous was at a quarter past nine. She'd have to work fast.

16.

As Biddy and Penny entered the disco, Steve Bailey, a former pupil who was trying to make it as a DJ, was crooning into his mike in a mid-Atlantic accent.

'OK, groovy guys and gorgeous girls, this is for all you beautiful wallflowers out there. It was a big hit a couple of years back for Kajagoogoo. They sure aren't the same now without the wonderful Limahl at the helm, but I hope you won't be "too shy-ai" tonight to get up on the dance floor.'

Biddy didn't have a clue what he was talking about. She'd never heard of Kajawhatever, and she'd no idea who or what Limahl was. But as she listened to them sing about a girl who was tongue-tied and short of breath and very, very shy, she thought the DJ was playing this song just for her.

Biddy looked at Miss Jordan and smiled, shyly. The music made her want to move, but she didn't know what to do.

'Oh, I love this one, don't you?' the teacher shouted in Biddy's ear. 'Come on, let's dance.'

And before Biddy knew what was happening, Miss Jordan had dragged her into the middle of the floor and was making all kinds of odd moves. As Biddy looked nervously around, she realised that everyone else was dancing the same way. For a second she panicked, her terror that she wouldn't be able to dance like all the normal people in the assembly hall quickly replaced by a gut-wrenching worry that she might get into trouble for trying to do it beside a teacher. Or worse, that Miss Jordan might get in trouble for trying to help her. She glanced anxiously around again, biting into her lip, and spotted Mrs Hobart dancing with the head girl and boy. And there was Mr Boyd dancing with a group of girls she recognised from her year. OK, she thought, her breathing easing, we won't get in trouble. Miss Jordan was still doing her funny dance, so Biddy tried her best to copy her, knowing how stupid she must look.

In actual fact, she didn't look any more ridiculous than anyone else, and as she danced, the music began to seep into her bones. She closed her eyes and felt like she was flying.

Biddy had never heard music like this before. They didn't have a record player in the house and her father only ever listened to Radio Four, so the only kind of music Biddy was familiar with was classical or Big Band Swing. She liked it well enough, but it didn't make her feel like this.

As Kajagoogoo faded out, Wham!'s 'Wake me up Before You Go-Go' blasted in, and the dance floor was suddenly packed. Biddy felt herself being pushed further into the middle of the throng, but a momentary flash of panic turned to relief when she realised that Miss Jordan, who was also being shoved, seemed oblivious to the crowd and continued dancing. Biddy threw her head back and lost herself in the music. Next came Madonna's 'Material Girl'. Miss Jordan cupped her hands and shouted in Biddy's ear, 'I love Madonna, don't you?'

'Yes,' Biddy shouted back, nodding furiously, 'I love her too.'

She'd heard of Madonna. She knew what she looked like and she knew she was a singer. And she'd heard of Wham! too. She'd caught snippets of arguments between girls in the classroom, or the canteen, or the library, debating which one was cuter: George, or Andrew. But she'd never actually heard any of their songs. And now she had, she loved them all. She loved

Kaja-whatever, and she loved Wham!, and she definitely loved Madonna. She grinned at Miss Jordan, and actually laughed out loud. I *can* be normal, she thought, as she moved her body to the music with increasing ease. I can. I can do normal things like drink Coke, and buy jeans, and wear a bra and dance. I can have fun. This is fun, and I like it. Maybe I'm not a complete weirdo after all.

Penny Jordan laughed too. She was thrilled to see Biddy relaxed and enjoying herself, and she wasn't a bad wee mover too. The girl actually had some natural rhythm; who'd have thought it? Now all she needed were some friends. That would be her next mission. Perhaps she'd invite someone else along to the baking session in a couple of weeks. Maybe Karen Robinson? She seemed like a nice girl, and didn't appear to be part of Alison's entourage. She'd witnessed her helping Biddy up from the floor last week after Alison had 'accidentally' bumped into her whilst going for a goal shoot. But maybe she was moving too quickly?

Penny was lost in her happy thoughts, and Biddy was lost in the music. Neither of them noticed that Julia and Jackie were suddenly dancing beside them. And they didn't see Alison join them a few moments later. And they were totally unaware of all the winking and thumbs-up signs and nudging that was going on between the girls.

'That Madonna sure is one hot chick,' crooned Steve as 'Material Girl' faded out. 'Talkin' about hot things, let's turn the temperature up a little bit with some lurve tunes for all you cool young couples out there to smooch to.'

At the back of the room, some of the teachers shuffled uncomfortably as the DJ spouted on in his cringing pseudo-American accent. This was a school disco – not an 18–30's Club Med outing. Penny, realising that she really shouldn't be on the dance floor when the slow songs came on, tried to signal to Biddy that she was going to sit down, but Biddy couldn't make her out. Penny took her elbow, drawing her closer.

'I'm whacked,' she said into her ear. 'I need a rest. And I'd better go and chat to some of the other teachers. Why don't you go and get yourself a Coke and a packet of crisps or something at the tuck shop? I'll see you later, OK?' She grinned at Biddy, giving her the thumbs-up sign.

Biddy nodded and dropped her head, reality crashing in. She completely understood that Miss Jordan couldn't spend the whole evening with her, but for the last ten minutes or so she'd been in a place that felt like heaven, and she didn't want to leave. What was she supposed to do now? There wasn't anyone else here she could talk to. Maybe she should just go home. As Miss Jordan turned to go, Biddy saw that someone was blocking her way. It was Jackie McKelvey. Instinctively Biddy turned around and saw Alison standing behind her. Even in the semi-darkness she could make out the twisted smile on her face. Biddy recognised that smile, that look, and she knew that something bad was coming.

'And to start off the sloooww session, it's Mister Peabo Bryson and Ms Roberta Flack with their big hit from back in 1982. And we have a very special request for two groovy young sweethearts out there in the crowd: Penny Jordan and B.W. who are joining with Peabo and Roberta in celebratin' their luurve tonight. Well, P.J. and B.W., get smoochin' and have a luurvelee night.'

Penny froze. 'Shit!' she whispered.

Biddy's head began to spin and the sickness started to stir. She must have misheard the DJ. She thought he'd said something about her and Miss Jordan. But he couldn't have. Could he?

Over by the door, Georgina took her cue and switched on all the lights. Biddy looked around, panic rising in her chest. The music was still playing, but everyone was pointing and whispering and sniggering in her direction. What was happening? What had Alison done? She looked at Miss Jordan, tears welling up in her eyes, unable to read the expression on the teacher's face.

Peabo and Roberta sang on. But nobody was dancing. Everybody, every single person in the room, was looking at Miss Jordan and Biddy Weir standing facing each other in the middle of the hall. Alison smiled at Georgina as she joined her, Julia and Jackie on the edge of the circle that had somehow formed around the teacher and the pupil.

'Knew she was a lezzie, but didn't realise she was into little girls,' Alison whispered to Jane Stewart, a sixth-form prefect who was standing, shocked, beside her. Jane gasped, her hand shooting up to her mouth, and stared at Alison in horror. Then she turned and relayed the astonishing truth to her own group of friends. Georgina, Julia and Jackie all whispered the same juicy snippet of gossip to someone standing beside or behind them, and within seconds the whole hall was gasping and murmuring.

'Give her a kiss then, Miss,' a boy bellowed from the crowd.

'Hey, Miss, do you fancy me too?' screeched a girl, to wails of laughter from her friends.

'Well, well, well. Turns out our resident weirdo is also a raving dyke,' laughed Alison.

Penny closed her eyes and lowered her head. She wanted to move, to get both herself and Biddy out of the hall, but for some reason she felt glued to the spot. Sam's words of warning rang in her ears.

Biddy started to shake. She had no idea what was going on, no idea what Alison was talking about, but she knew it wasn't good. In fact, it was definitely worse than not good. And this time it wasn't just aimed at her, but also at Miss Jordan. Lovely, kind, thoughtful Miss Jordan. And it was all *her* fault. She wanted to lie down on the floor and curl up in a ball with her hands over her head. She wanted to die.

'Did you two have a nice time together in the staff loo earlier?' Alison shouted, just as Mr Duncan arrived to see what all the fuss was about. 'Oh, and is anyone else invited to the baking party in your house, Miss Jordan? Or is it private – just for Biddy?'

More gasps ricocheted around the room. Penny looked at Mr Duncan and shook her head. Biddy crossed her arms over the top of her head and started to moan a low, deep groan.

Alison glanced at the clock. Ten past nine. She saw Clive hover by the door and held his gaze, tossing her head slightly. He smiled at her and pushed through the double doors. She knew her work here was over. The damage was done. Whatever happened next was out of her hands, but she'd a feeling it would be good. Well, good for her, anyway.

'I'm going outside for some air,' she whispered to Georgina. Georgina winked at her friend. She was the only person who knew about Alison and Mr Patterson and Alison knew she wouldn't jeopardise the privileged position she was in by blabbing about it to anyone else.

'Make up something if you need to,' Alison whispered. 'I'll be back before ten.'

And off she went through one set of doors to Clive Patterson's store room in classroom 10, while Mr Duncan ushered a shaking Biddy Weir and an ashen-faced Penny Jordan through the other.

17.

14 June 1985

Dearest Biddy,

I really don't know how to begin to say sorry to you for everything that has happened. Firstly, you must know that it was never my intention to cause you any kind of harm or pain or distress. The fact that you have suffered such hurt and humiliation because of my actions breaks my heart. I only ever wanted to help you. I truly wanted to be your friend. You must believe that, not just for my sake, but for your own. I like you for who you are, Biddy. And if I like you, if I wanted to be your friend, others will too.

Secondly, as I have told you before, you are absolutely not a weirdo. You are unique and special. You are a talented artist, and a caring person. The people who taunt and bully you are weak and shallow and cruel. For some reason they feel threatened by you, or are jealous of you. They see you as an easy target because you do not fit their profile of 'normality', and also because you have absolutely no desire to be one of them. But you are worth a hundred of them, Biddy – a thousand even.

And so what if you are different to them? Being different is not a bad thing. I am different, too, Biddy. I am gay. I share my life with another woman, a woman called Samantha, who I love very much indeed. She is wise and strong and funny and kind – and she is very feisty too! Being with her gives me the courage to be who I really am. You would like her, Biddy, and I can tell you, she would make mincemeat of Ms Flemming and her cronies!

Contrary to what a lot of people still think in this day and age, being gay does not make me a bad person. I am not evil, I am not immoral, and I am certainly not a weirdo either.

Samantha knows all about you, Biddy. She was very worried when we became friends, because she thought there was a chance that one or other of us might get hurt. But then she realised how important our friendship was to me, and every day when I got home from work she would ask me how you were. I am telling you all of this because I want you to understand why I was drawn to you. It was absolutely not in any way because I had malicious intent, or liked you in a way that I shouldn't have, despite what many people are saying. It was partly because I saw in you a sadness that disturbed me, and when I discovered the extent to which being bullied has affected your life, I really wanted to try and help you. I also felt a connection with you, Biddy, because we both grew up without our mothers, and as I have already told you, I know how difficult that is. Perhaps it was wrong, naive and unprofessional of me, but you know what – I liked your company, Biddy Weir. You are a girl of few words, yet I know there is a whole lot more to you than even you can see. I also know there will be a path that will lead you to a happy life, I'm just sorry that I can't be around anymore to help you find it. But another friend will come along, Biddy, I promise, and when they do, please don't be afraid to let them in.

Biddy, I should tell you that Sam and I are going on a very long trip. We've always talked about travelling and when I decided to leave the school (which was the best thing to do for all concerned) we realised this was the perfect time to go. Our plan is to work our way across Australia and then maybe go to New Zealand and the Far East. Who knows where we'll go, and what we'll do, but we're very excited. It will be a grand adventure.

But I won't forget you, Biddy, and I look forward to the day when we can meet up again. Perhaps you will be a famous artist by then. You certainly have the talent and there is no reason why you will not succeed if you decide that you want to. Always keep that in your heart.

Well, Biddy, it's time for me to go and do some more packing. I'm sorry again for what has happened, but I don't regret our friendship, and I hope you don't either. I know things are horrible for you at the moment, but time will pass and I know you will get through it. And please, Biddy, if things do become too difficult, and Alison and her gang decide to pull another of their vile stunts – you must go to Mr Duncan and tell him what has happened. He will listen, I promise, and he will help. He is a good man and a fair man – but he cannot help if he doesn't know what is going on. My hope is that those girls will now back off – but if they don't, you MUST tell Mr Duncan, or another teacher, or your father.

Take care of yourself, Biddy, and be strong. As Christopher Robin said to Winnie the Pooh, 'Promise me you'll always remember: you're braver than you believe, and stronger than you seem, and smarter than you think.' My Auntie Celia used to recite that to me. It brought me enormous comfort and for a while it became my mantra. I hope it helps you too!

With much affection, your friend,
Penny.

18.

Biddy folded the letter and slid it back under the neat pile of grey school knickers in the top drawer of her dresser. There was no chance of her father finding it there, as he would never venture into her underwear drawer. As far as she knew, he never actually came into her room at all, but just in case, she'd needed a good hiding place. She kept her little round box of pins and needles inside a pair of old socks at the back of the drawer, and he'd never found that, so she reckoned her underwear drawer was a safe haven for secrets, even when she wasn't there.

Biddy had read Miss Jordan's letter every single day for the past three months. Apart from her drawing, it was the one shred of solace she had had since the nightmare of the disco. The summer was normally her favourite time of the year: long days and clear bright nights to spend on the beach drawing. But the memory of what had happened darkened everything around her, and the thought of the impending school trip made her ill with fear. She ate even less than normal, she barely slept, and on the days when she did have the energy to go to the beach, she often found herself fantasising about walking into the sea and not stopping.

But then she would think of Miss Jordan, and all the things she had said in her letter, and she'd think about her papa and her heart would lurch. She knew she would never leave him.

The letter arrived one Saturday morning a couple of weeks after the disco. Biddy just happened to be in the hall doing her weekend hoovering when it fell through the letterbox, along with the electricity bill and an official looking letter for her father. The pale blue square envelope with the neat handwriting on the front had her name on it. Biddy shook as she picked it up. She'd never had a letter before. She'd never had anything addressed purely to her in her life. Was this a joke? she thought. A trick? What was Alison up to now? It had to be her – no one else would send her a letter. Well, she wouldn't read it. She wouldn't give Alison the pleasure of hurting her again: not this time anyway. She'd put it straight into the bin and never think of it again. But then her papa had shouted from the kitchen, 'Was that the post, lass?' and as she heard him make his way towards the hall, she quickly shoved the letter down the back of her trousers.

As soon as she could, she hid it under her pillow, still determined not to read it, but not quite sure why she had chosen not to put it in the bin. Every so often throughout the day she went into her room, slipped it out from under her pillow and turned it over in her shaking hands. It wasn't until her clock read 3.10 a.m. that she finally, carefully, tore back the seal and slowly pulled the matching blue paper from the envelope.

Since that day, the letter had become her most treasured possession, and whilst she didn't know how she would manage the next few days without it, she also knew, with absolute certainty, that she couldn't bring it with her. The prospect of Alison Flemming getting her hands on it was just not worth the risk.

She had woken up that morning feeling sick and exhausted. Her dreams, when she had managed to sleep, were haunted by Alison and the others, her hours of wakeful tossing and turning dominated by thoughts of escape. But she knew there wasn't one.

She lifted the socks containing the tin of pins and sat down on the edge of the bed, staring at the battered old brown suitcase which was lying open on the floor, awaiting the last couple of items she needed to pack for the trip.

'It was my grandfather's,' her father had said when he handed it to her a few days earlier. 'Glad it's getting an airing again. Don't think it's been used since before you were born. Long before,' he nodded to himself. Biddy caught a brief glimpse of something in his eyes. Sadness? Regret? A wistful memory? She wasn't sure, but she knew she couldn't object. 'Anyways, no point forking out for something new when we've a family heirloom that'll do the job rightly, eh, lass?'

Biddy nodded. 'Thank you, Papa. I'll just go and pack now.'

Her father had nodded and left the room, quietly closing the door behind him. Biddy knew that he was standing still outside her door as the wonky landing floorboard hadn't creaked. She waited, hoping that he would come back into her room, willing him to open the door, wanting him to tell her she didn't have to go. But then she heard the creak, and the slow, uneven sound of her father going down the stairs.

Her father had never talked to her about what had happened with Miss Jordan. But he must be curious. Surely he wanted to hear her side of the story? And she had wanted to talk to him about it. She still did. She wanted to tell him all about Miss Jordan and how kind she was and how much she missed having a friend, and how unhappy she was, and how Alison and the others made her want to be dead sometimes. But for some reason, neither of them said a word about it to each other. Three months had passed since the disco and Miss Jordan's departure. The summer had come and gone, and Biddy still wondered what Mr Duncan had said to her father that awful Monday morning in June.

She had sat outside the headmaster's office while her father and Mr Duncan spoke for a few minutes, terrified that something else really bad was about to happen, convinced that, after years of ignoring her, Mr Duncan was finally going to punish her for being a bloody weirdo. He had spoken to her kindly before her father arrived, told her that if she was having problems at school, she could talk to him. She would have liked to have said something about how nice Miss Jordan was to her, how kind she was and how she had helped her with clothes and things. She would have liked to have told him about Alison and Georgina and Julia and Jackie, and how much they frightened her and made her feel sick every single day. She had wanted to say that she didn't fully understand what had happened on Friday night at the disco and to ask him if she could see Miss Jordan. Please. And she had wanted to say she was sorry that she was a bloody weirdo and she really didn't mean to be one and she didn't like being one, and she would really like to stop sticking pins into herself, but she didn't know how. She would have liked to have said all these things, but the lump was there, of course, and it was really, really big that day. So she had said nothing. Nothing at all.

Biddy didn't know what had happened inside that office, what was said, but when the two men emerged, her father's pale face was unusually flushed, his expression strained. A flash of the memory of her father coming into Mrs Martin's room at Prospect Park made her shudder. Here they were again. Nothing had changed. All these long, agonising years later, Alison was still controlling her life.

'All right, Biddy,' Mr Duncan had smiled, 'your father and I have had a chat and we feel it's best if you take the rest of the day off. I know the misunderstanding at the disco was a bit stressful for you, and you do look a little bit tired, so I think perhaps a day of rest would be a good idea. And we'll see you back tomorrow morning, fresh as a daisy. OK?'

Biddy had nodded, wishing she could leave school forever and never come back.

'Let's go, lass,' her father had croaked, nodding at Mr Duncan before donning his cap and lifting Biddy's string bag from the floor. They had walked to the bus stop in silence. They rode the six-stop journey home in silence. They walked from the stop to their house in silence. The only time her father had spoken on the twenty-minute journey home was to ask Mrs Henderson at the corner shop for a packet of Kimberley biscuits and a sherbet dip.

Biddy placed an art pad, a couple of pencils and a battered packet of broken charcoal sticks on top of the small pile of neatly folded items she had packed for the field trip, then tucked the socks into the bottom corner of the case. At least she could smuggle a needle into a toilet cubicle without anyone seeing. All that was left to pack now was the blue nylon dressing gown she was wearing, and her toothbrush.

'Biddy!' her father called from the bottom of the stairs. 'Porridge is on the table.'

Biddy smoothed out the blankets on her bed and went downstairs to sit staring at the porridge she knew she couldn't eat.

19.

The letter had said they had to be at the school by 8.30 a.m. The bus was leaving at 8.45 sharp. Anyone who wasn't there would be left behind. Biddy wanted to be left behind. She had spent the summer in a haze of distress because of the disco, and a fog of dread at the prospect of September, the fifth year and the field trip. Normally it took place in the Spring term of the fourth year, but a week before they were due to go last April, a big strike which involved some of the teachers at the school meant the trip had to be cancelled at the last minute. Biddy had never been more relieved about anything in her life. It was the first time ever that one of her deepest, most important wishes had come true. But her relief and happiness were short-lived. Two days later, they were told that the trip had been rescheduled and would take place in the third week of September, well before revision for their Mock O Levels would start. It was like someone had given her the best present ever and then taken it away. And that was then, before the whole disco thing; before Miss Jordan left. It would be even worse now. So much worse. She just knew it. Just before she left the house, Biddy went to the toilet and threw up the little bit of porridge she had managed to eat at breakfast.

When she arrived at school in the taxi her father had booked the night before, Biddy was the only pupil without a parent to see her off. Her father had offered to come with her, to help carry her case. But she'd said it was OK. He didn't need to. Really, she reassured him, she'd manage. Besides, it wasn't at all heavy, as she didn't have a lot to pack. They were only going for three nights and she reckoned one change of clothes, her pyjamas, fresh underwear for each day and her Pac A Mac were all she needed, as well as a bar of soap, her toothbrush and toothpaste, a towel and a flannel. And of course, her sketchbook, pencils and her tin of needles. She thought that would be enough. Essentials, the letter had said, were T-shirts, trousers, a sweatshirt, a waterproof coat, trainers, thick socks and a strong pair of walking shoes. No skirts or high heels for the girls and no button-down shirts for the boys. Biddy didn't know what a strong pair of walking shoes really meant, so she wore her Wellington boots and packed her P.E. plimsolls in the case. She also wore the jeans and stripy top she'd bought the day she went shopping with Miss Jordan, and tied her baggy navy blue cardigan, which now had three missing buttons, around her waist.

Before she got into the taxi, Biddy's father hugged her. It was an awkward hug, not quite drawing her properly into him, almost not even touching her. But it was definitely a hug. She lifted her right arm behind his back and lightly touched his brown cardigan. He smelt of coal tar soap and fusty mothballs. She would have liked to have had a tighter hug, and to hug him tighter. She would have liked him to wish her luck or tell her to take care. But the half-hug was so much better than no hug at all and, in a way, said more than a few words ever could.

But Biddy had absolutely no idea just how worried her father was about her, and how much he really did not want her to go on this field trip either. If she'd given him any indication that she didn't want to go herself, he might have let her stay. But she hadn't. And he hadn't known how to ask. And anyway, she had to go. Rules were rules. And that was that. But as Mr Weir watched the taxi – a brown Cortina, which had clearly seen better days – turn right at the bottom of their road, he felt unsteady. He went back into the house, straight up the stairs into her room and pulled the sketches out from under her bed. By the time he came back down to put the kettle on, nearly two hours had passed.

'Going on a school trip then, love?' the taxi driver asked. 'Where are you off to then, somewhere nice?' he tried again, having had no response to his first question. This time, she nodded. But she still didn't answer. 'I know, bet it's that place up by Innis-brook Forest. I hear it's great. Supposed to be haunted though, mind you.'

Biddy swallowed hard and stared straight ahead. *Shut up, shut up, shut up*, she screamed inside her head. But the taxi driver kept on talking. 'My grandson goes to your school. Frank Simpson. Second year.' Biddy still said nothing. She knew she was being rude. People didn't often engage with her in such a friendly way, and she should have responded to his kindness. But she couldn't. Not today.

'Well, I suppose you wouldn't know him. You being a big girl, and all.' He shrugged and, to Biddy's relief, switched the radio on, drumming his fingers on the steering wheel in time to the music.

Biddy wasn't used to cars, and whilst she didn't want to reach their destination, the journey was adding to her anxiety and she willed it to be over. She'd only been in two cars before: another taxi several years ago when she'd been sent home from school with a vomiting bug, and the time Mrs Thomas had stopped halfway up Westhill Road to offer her father and her a lift. They'd been shopping in town and had missed the 4.15 p.m. bus. As it was Saturday, there wasn't another one for an hour, and so her father decided they should walk, but ten minutes later they got caught in an almighty downpour.

'No point in turning back now, lass,' her father had said, pulling up the collar of his old tweed jacket. 'Best just keep your head down and plough on. We'll be home soon enough.'

Biddy had no collar on her yellow cardigan, but she put her head down and carried on, a plastic carrier bag in each hand, one filled with bread from The Griddle, the other holding a packet of porridge oats and two packets of Kimberley biscuits. Her father carried the heavier stuff: the milk and the meat from McDaid's. As the rain ran down the back of her neck, soaking her cardigan and the blue nylon blouse below it, and her feet squelched around inside the Moses sandals she'd got from the Oxfam shop the previous Saturday, Biddy wondered what it would be like to be someone like Alison or Georgina or Jackie or Julia. To have a father who had a job he went to every morning where he earned enough money to buy a car. To have a mother to go shopping with. To not have to carry home bags of meat from the butcher's in town. To have had a party for your thirteenth birthday. To not be a bloody weirdo. These thoughts were all jumping around inside her head, when Mrs Thomas had pulled up beside them in her car, wound down the window and asked if they wanted a lift. Mrs Thomas often offered them lifts, but her father always politely declined. She was so sure her father would say no that she kept on walking. But then he was calling her back, and getting her into the back seat of the car and getting himself in the front seat and heaving in all the sodden bags of shopping. She was so shocked that he'd said yes that it took her a few minutes to settle. She was sure from the look on Mrs Thomas's face that she was equally surprised. Biddy wondered if the only reason she actually offered her father lifts in the first place was because she knew he'd say no. As they drove through the rain she pressed her face against the steamed-up window, and began to fantasise that Mrs Thomas was her mother, that this was their family car, and they were all going on a family trip to the city, or the swimming pool, or to visit people they knew. Then suddenly Mrs Thomas stopped outside their house and the most wonderful of daydreams was over.

As they headed towards the town centre, Biddy began another fantasy: she would ask the taxi driver to let her out at the station. Then she would get a bus to somewhere. Anywhere. Wherever the £10 she had in her purse would take her.

'*Please, Mister, could you stop at the station? Could you stop at the station please, Mister? I'd like to get out at the station. Just leave me at the station, please.*' She practised the possibilities inside her head, then she opened her mouth to see if anything would come out. But nothing would. And then it was too late. They had passed the station and were heading up the hill, past the town hall, towards the school.

'This do here, love?' The taxi driver pulled up outside the school gates. 'Your dad has paid me, so we're all sorted.'

Biddy nodded but she didn't move. She didn't want to be in the taxi for a moment longer, but she didn't want to get out either. But there was no escape now.

'Umm,' she cleared her throat nervously, 'OK. Thank you,' she said to the back seat as she pulled her case out of the taxi and closed the door.

Biddy stood apart from the others, glancing at the groups of chattering teenagers gathered around the Ulsterbus coach, sickness rising in her throat. It was already going wrong and she instantly felt humiliated. She was the only pupil there without a parent to kiss and hug and fuss over her. And worse, she was the only one with a stupid, battered, old brown suitcase. Everyone else had smart bright rucksacks. Everyone else was wearing trainers and sweatshirts and baseball caps and looked as if they were going on a school field trip. She looked like one of the war refugee exhibits from the Heritage Museum. Everyone else was excited. She was terrified.

Brook House, the residential centre at Innisbrook Forest, was a rambling old building smothered in ivy with lots of different shaped windows, most of which were covered in bird poo. Depending on your point of view, the old house was either horribly spoilt or brilliantly improved by a huge white-washed flat-roofed extension, which the local education authority had stuck on the side of it. Biddy didn't notice the extension: she didn't even take in the old house. All she saw, as the school bus crunched down the gravel drive, were the windows splattered with bird poo, and she felt a huge surge of relief.

The two-hour journey had been hell. She'd had to listen to the others singing stupid songs about meatballs and quartermaster's stores or something like that, and bantering with Mr Patterson, Mr Boyd and Mrs Abbott, calling them 'Clive' and 'Roy' and 'Ruth'. Their shrieks of laughter clattered like thunder inside Biddy's head. At least no one had had to sit beside her. And no one had spoken to her either, apart from Mrs Abbott when she was passing round some sweets.

'Lemon sherbet, Biddy?' the teacher had asked, holding out a white paper bag. Biddy shook her head and looked down, noticing Mrs Abbott's jeans as she did so. Miss Jordan was the only other female teacher she'd seen wearing jeans. The memory of the teacher shook through her, shoving the lump out of her stomach and up to her throat. Maybe if she hadn't caused Miss Jordan's dismissal, she'd be on this horrible trip instead of Mrs Abbott. After all, Mrs Abbott wasn't a Geography teacher like Mr Patterson and Mr Boyd. She taught Domestic Science. And if Miss Jordan was still a teacher, and she had been chosen to go instead of Mrs Abbott, then the trip wouldn't have been horrible after all. As Biddy was so busy with all these thoughts, she hadn't even heard Mrs Abbott offer her some rhubarb rock instead of the lemon sherbet, or seen her roll her eyes in exasperation when Biddy didn't respond. Not that she'd have taken one anyway. She was so nervous she couldn't risk gagging on it.

But when Biddy saw the poo-covered windows, her heart had skipped a beat. Birds, she thought, there are birds here. I will be OK. And as she watched a gang of big black crows to-ing and fro-ing from tall chimney to tall chimney, her eyes brightened and her mouth flicked up slightly at the edges.

20.

Biddy had never been to the mountains before, and the green stillness captivated her. It wasn't quite the same as being at the beach, and there weren't any seagulls, but there were other birds, bigger and darker than she'd seen before, circling high in the sky, calling to her with rough, deep squawks. The smells were different too. The breeze carried scents of turf and wild herbs that made her feel dizzy, and she had to concentrate really hard to focus her attention on the first assignment. She wished that she could just sit down on a mound of rough grass and draw, but Rory McBride, her unwilling partner, was grumpily striding several feet in front of her, telling her to 'get a fucking move on' every five minutes.

'At least she knows most of the fucking answers,' she heard him mutter as she completed question seven on the sheet. 'That'll get me off the hook with Patterson, the bastard.'

Rory McBride hadn't been one bit happy when Mr Patterson had partnered him with Biddy Weir before they set off on their afternoon hike up the mountain.

'Aw, come on, Sir,' he had pleaded, 'you can't be serious. I mean, look at her. She's wearing wellies, for fuck's sake.'

'Shut your face, McBride. You'll do what *I* decide,' snarled Clive Patterson in Rory's face. 'And you'd better get all the questions right, or you'll spend the evening in the classroom writing an essay on rock formation in the mountain. And if you swear at me again, you'll spend the whole bloody trip with her. Got it?'

Rory nodded, tossed his head in an 'I-don't-give-a-shit' kind of way, and sauntered over to the other, sniggering boys.

'What have you done to annoy Patterson, then?' laughed Paul Clarke.

'Fuck knows,' replied Rory, shrugging his shoulders and kicking at the gravel, glancing over at big-nose Patrick Burns who'd been picked to partner Alison Flemming. 'Bastard,' he muttered.

But Clive had seen the way Rory McBride was flirting with Alison on the bus down to Innisbrook Forest and he wasn't happy. Rory was tall and lean with dark, wavy hair and fancied himself as a bit of a stud. Clive had to admit he was a good-looking lad, and cocky with it in an irritatingly charming way. He was pretty sure Alison didn't fancy him, but decided it was best to keep them apart, just in case.

Biddy had had no idea what to expect on the field trip, and when she realised she'd have to share a bedroom with fourteen other girls, including Alison, she had to work harder than ever to keep the lump down in her throat. For a moment, she thought she might actually vomit or even soil her pants right there in front of all the others and Mrs Abbott, who was showing the girls to their dorm. At least she got a whole bunk bed to herself as, obviously, none of the girls wanted to share one with her. As soon as she could, she escaped to the toilet where she gagged and retched until the lump subsided. Then she sat on the toilet seat, took the tin of pins out of her pocket, and fiercely stabbed the tops of her legs until her racing heart settled. But her respite was short-lived. Before they set off on their afternoon hike, Mr Patterson started pairing them off and the fear that she'd have to partner Alison or one of the other girls almost overwhelmed her. She had to focus on the bird shit patterns on the windows to stop herself from passing out. When Mr Patterson partnered Rory McBride with her, she knew he was horrified. He looked revolted. He looked as if he might be sick himself. But Biddy was relieved. At least Rory McBride would leave her alone. The boys usually did, unless they were with Alison, of course.

Biddy and Rory managed to answer all the questions on the worksheet correctly, much to Rory's relief and Clive Patterson's annoyance. Now he'd have to watch McBride sniffing around Alison all evening. Still, he'd found a room at the top of the old house which would be perfect for a little midnight liaison. He watched Alison stride into the dining room, tossing her long honey mane, her tight jeans and low-cut top accentuating her delicious figure. She was one of the best fucks he'd ever had. He'd held off going the whole hog until she was sixteen, though he knew she'd have let him before then. She'd basically begged him the night of the disco, but the tease of keeping her waiting was part of the game. And he was good at the game. So good. He'd been looking forward to this trip for weeks, mostly because the risk of getting caught out added to the thrill. Not that he wanted to get caught, of course. He knew exactly what the ramifications would be, especially after the whole Penny Jordan debacle, for which he never felt an ounce of guilt. But the possibility, the danger, made the whole thing even sexier.

By the time the evening meal was served, Biddy was exhausted. They'd spent the afternoon walking up Innis Mountain behind the big house, studying maps and wild mountain flora, looking at stones and filling in activity sheets. She'd enjoyed being out on the mountain, the fresh air had taken her mind off the worry of bedtime, but her feet felt sore and swollen after three hot hours in tight Wellington boots, and her head was pounding. She had been right about Rory. He didn't even make eye contact with her and he kept as much physical distance from her as was humanly possible. Biddy was happy enough to complete all the questions on the sheet herself, as they were reasonably straight-forward and Geography was one subject she managed with relative ease. Especially if it was anything to do with nature. Throughout the three-hour hike, the pair didn't exchange one single word, apart from Rory's grumbles at Biddy to hurry up and a couple of incoherent grunts.

As the group headed back to the house, chatting and whoop-ing and laughing with each other, Biddy walked several feet behind the others. Despite her exhaustion and her sore feet, she had a sudden overwhelming desire to stay on the mountain. She'd love to sleep in the open air, under one of the huge fir trees. She wouldn't be scared, and she knew she'd be safe: the birds would look after her. The thought of sleeping in the same room as Alison and the others terrified her. But before that there was teatime to deal with.

By the time they got back to the house, Biddy was unusu-ally hungry. It must have been all the walking and the fresh air. She was used to the sea air, but the mountain air must be different. Maybe all the new smells and sounds had affected her appetite. Her tummy rumbled loudly. Lunch had been a picnic on the lawn outside the big house with cheese rolls, bruised apples and Penguin biscuits, washed down with car-tons of Kia-Ora orange juice. She had sat well away from everyone else, so she'd managed a few mouthfuls, despite her nerves, and she liked the Penguin biscuit – it had been a nice change from Kimberleys.

Despite her hunger now, however, the thought of dinner terrified her. They would all have to eat together in the dining room at big rectangular tables. During the hike, Biddy had managed to forget about the dining room dilemma, but now, as her tummy rumbled, her hunger turned to fear. She hadn't eaten in the school canteen since the day in the second year when Alison had spilled her tapioca pudding all over her and told everyone that she had made herself sick. She felt sick now. This would be so much worse than the canteen. When they were shown around the house after they'd arrived that morning, Biddy had counted five big tables in the dining room, four for the pupils and one for the teachers and the resident instructors. There were thirty pupils altogether: fifteen girls and fifteen boys. With a lurch in her stomach, she realised that she would have to share a table with at least six others. Her head began to spin and she leant against the slender trunk of a tall birch tree at the top of the driveway to steady herself. What if she was made to sit at Alison's table? Alison would be furious. She'd do something horrible. She knew that no one would want her at their table, but at least if she wasn't at Alison's, it might not be quite so bad. Maybe then she would be able to eat something.

She was wondering whether she should go into the dining room before all the others, or wait until everyone else had gone in and then take the last remaining seat, when Mr Boyd yelled 'grub's up,' from the top step of the entrance porch, his hands cupped around his mouth. 'And remember to wash your hands in the downstairs cloakrooms.'

Biddy watched from behind her tree as people streamed into the big house from every direction. Most of the boys had been playing football; some of the girls were gossiping and giggling together on the lawn; Paul Ballentine had been pushing Nicola Smart on the tyre swing under a huge oak tree at the side of the house. There was no sign of Alison Flemming.

'If anyone else is outside, you'd better get in here right now. Or else.' It was Mr Boyd, calling from the top step again. He didn't say what the 'or else' would be. As Biddy slid out from behind the birch, Mr Boyd spotted her.

'Come on, Biddy. Get a move on,' he yelled. She slowly made her way down the path, her heart hammering inside her chest.

Biddy was the last one into the dining room. There were three empty seats, one at a table with seven of the boys and two at a table with six boys. Rory and Paul were sitting with Alison, Georgina, Jackie, Julia, Nicola and Jill. All of the other girls were at the fourth table. Biddy hesitated then moved towards the table with two free seats and pulled out the chair at the far end. At least there would be nobody sitting on her left. At least there would only be six annoyed boys, and not six or seven very angry girls. At least she was nowhere near Alison.

'McBride. Ballentine.' Everyone looked up at Mr Patterson, who was standing shouting over at the mixed table. 'Shift. Go on, move. Get over there,' he nodded towards Biddy's chosen table. 'Biddy, go sit with the girls.'

'Bastard,' whispered Rory under his breath, noisily moving out of his chair and stomping over to the other table. Paul rolled his eyes, then winked at Nicola, who gave a disappointed smile in return. The six boys who had just had a lucky escape grinned at each other. Alison shared a confused look with Georgina.

'Are you moving, or what?' sniped Rory to Biddy, who was still sitting, afraid to move, in case her legs wouldn't work because they were shaking so badly. She stood up slowly and, trembling, made her way across the room to her new table, aware that Alison was glaring at her. Now there would be no chance of her eating anything at all.

Mrs Abbott stood up. 'OK, OK. Settle down everyone. Before we eat I have a couple of announcements. After dinner you all have an hour or so to relax.' A cheer went up from around the room. 'You can watch TV in the common room, play pool or table tennis in the games room, or just hang out in your dorms. At 7.30 p.m. sharp, everyone must meet in the seminar room where Mr Boyd and Mr Patterson will go through the results of today's study paper and talk us through the agenda for tomorrow.' The cheers turned to groans. 'All right, all right. That's what we're here for,' Mrs Abbott continued. 'Supper will be served in the common room at 8.30 p.m. Everyone must be in their dorm by 9.30 p.m. then it's lights out at 10 p.m., sharp. Now, tea tonight is vegetable broth followed by sausages, peas and mash. Then apple tart and custard for pudding. Eat up, everyone, you'll need your strength for tomorrow's five-hour hike.' More groans followed as Mrs Abbott winked and took her seat again.

Alison's blood was boiling. She glared at Biddy with contempt. She knew that Rory fancied her and while she wasn't about to get off with him, she did relish the attention. He wasn't bad looking, he was a good laugh and flirting with him kept Clive on his toes. Perhaps that was it, she thought. Perhaps Clive was jealous. The thought made her tingle. Well, fair enough, but why did he have to go and put that smelly oddball at *her* table. How in God's name was she going to eat her dinner now?

'I think I've just lost my appetite,' she whispered to Georgina as her soup was set down in front of her. 'How about we get rid of the bloody cow?'

Georgina raised her eyebrows.

'Yeah, but how are we gonna manage it, with that lot watching over us?' she whispered back, nodding towards the teachers.

Alison bit her lip, furiously trying to come up with something.

'Alison,' Georgina whispered, tentatively, 'I'm not sure this is the place to . . .'

'Shh, will you,' Alison interrupted, 'I'm thinking.'

Suddenly Mrs Abbott was on her feet again. 'Sorry, guys. I forgot to ask if one person from each table would go to the kitchen and collect a jug of water.'

Alison smiled. Here was her opportunity.

'I'll go,' chirped Julia, moving to stand up. But Alison signalled for her to sit.

'Why don't you go, Biddy,' she said slowly, smiling sweetly at Biddy. 'You're closest to the kitchen.'

All the girls at the table looked at each other, wondering what Alison was up to. Biddy gulped. She had just about managed to walk across the room and sit down without her legs caving in. Now Alison was telling her to go to the kitchen and bring back a jug of water. Why? Was Alison hoping that she would spill it all over the place or trip? What was it? She was obviously planning something.

'Get a move on, will you,' demanded Alison. 'I'm thirsty.'

Realising she had no option, Biddy stood and carefully made her way across the room, through the door and into the kitchen, concentrating on every step.

'Pass me the pepper, Jackie,' asked Alison, once Biddy was out of sight.

'Salt too?' asked Jackie.

'No thanks, Jack,' smiled Alison. 'The pepper will do just fine.' She screwed the lid off the little glass pepper mill, leant across the table and tipped most of the fine, pale brown powder into Biddy's soup. Then she stirred it around with her own spoon, replaced the lid, wiped her spoon with her napkin and took a spoonful of her own soup, just as Biddy came back into the room carrying the water jug with both hands.

'Mmm. Delicious soup,' Alison flashed her smile around the table at the other girls, some of whom were sniggering into their napkins, some sitting open-mouthed. Georgina, Julia and Jackie dutifully smiled back.

Biddy managed to carry the water jug over to the table without spilling any.

'Just set it down in the middle,' said Alison, still smiling. 'We'll serve ourselves, won't we, girls? Now, tuck into your soup, Biddy, before it gets cold. It's yum. Isn't it, girls?'

A rumble of agreement echoed around the table.

Biddy sat down and stared at her soup. Alison had called her Biddy. Twice. What was going on? What was she up to? She never called her Biddy unless a teacher was around, and right now they were all out of earshot. Biddy looked up. Alison smiled directly at her and carried on eating her soup. It looked like a normal smile. There was certainly no trace of malevolence, no hint of danger in it. Come to think of it, nothing bad had happened since the disco. For the first three weeks of term, Alison had left her alone. Maybe she'd, what – had enough? Maybe she felt nothing could ever top what she'd achieved at the disco, so she'd decided to stop? Biddy stared down at the soup bowl again. The soup looked nice. It was homemade, a bit like her father's. Not that gloopy stuff from a tin. Maybe she could try to eat some. After all, she wouldn't have to chew it. She could just swallow. That would be easier. Besides, she'd probably get into trouble if she didn't eat anything.

'Salt or pepper, Biddy?' Alison asked, smiling again. Biddy shook her head. She'd said it again, her real name, not her other name. Maybe this trip wasn't going to be so awful after all. 'No thank you very much,' she managed to squeak. She stirred her spoon around her dish a few times, then finally brought it up to her mouth and slurped.

'Oh my God, what the hell are you doing?' Alison screamed, as Biddy spat the soup out of her mouth, spraying it across the table. Biddy started to choke, gag and sneeze at the same time. She reached out for the water jug, but no one poured her a glass. Panicked, she jumped up, knocking the table heavily with her knees which caused her own bowl and three others to spill their contents over the red and white checked plastic tablecloth. Soup ran everywhere, dripping onto chairs and splashing the floor. Julia, Nicola and Jill stood on their chairs, for fear of getting covered. Jackie and Georgina stood back from the table. As the soup was not running in her direction, Alison sat where she was, calmly surveying the scene of glorious chaos.

'What on earth is going on?' shouted Mrs Abbott, as she ran across the room to see what had caused the commotion. Biddy stood slightly hunched, her hands covering her mouth. Little bits of carrot, leek and barley clung to her stripy T-shirt. Drips of soup trickled down her chin. She was wailing, gasping, sneezing and shaking.

'Biddy, calm down. Calm down, Biddy. Please calm down.' Mrs Abbott took Biddy by the shoulders and shook her gently.

But Biddy continued to gulp, the most extraordinary noise coming from her throat.

'She sounds like a donkey with constipation,' Alison murmured to Georgina and Jackie who started to snigger. Mrs Abbott flashed them a look.

'For heaven's sake, would someone pour her a glass of water? Can't you see she's choking?'

Julia went for the water jug but Alison snatched it from her, poured a glass and handed it to Mrs Abbott.

'Here you are, Mrs Abbott. Is she all right?' she asked with mock concern.

Biddy gulped down the glass of water and started to cry, big, heavy, throaty sobs.

'What on earth happened?' asked Mrs Abbott, giving Biddy a handful of paper napkins. No one spoke. Biddy blew her nose loudly in between the sobs and snorts. Most of the girls were feeling uncomfortable by now. How could a bit of white pepper have caused that reaction? Should they tell or not? One or two exchanged worried glances, wondering what to do. But Alison was loving it.

'Alison?' asked Mrs Abbott, hoping for a reasonable explanation.

'Don't know, Mrs Abbott,' Alison held out her hands, shook her head and shrugged her shoulders. 'One second, she was slurping her soup, the next she was spitting and screaming. Perhaps she doesn't like it. I thought it was quite nice.'

Georgina had to suppress more giggles. She sat down at a seat which had become vacant at the table behind theirs and crossed her legs in a double twist, worried that she might wet herself. By this stage Mr Boyd and Mr Patterson had joined Mrs Abbott and many of the other pupils had gathered around the table for a closer look.

'Is that vomit?' asked Laurence Moore.

'The soup's not that bloody bad,' muttered someone else.

'All right, all right, settle everyone,' shouted Mr Patterson over the din. 'Ruth, get her out of here before she hyperventilates. Roy, you'd better tell them in the kitchen that we need this mess cleared up. You lot, sit down.'

Mrs Abbott ushered Biddy, who was still sobbing and shaking, out of the room and into the ladies' toilet on the ground floor.

Alison smiled at Georgina. 'Told you I'd get rid of her,' she whispered.

'I can tell you this, I'm not friggin' being her partner tomorrow,' mumbled Rory, as he went back to his seat. 'Weirdo.'

21.

Biddy was initially relieved when Mrs Abbott came into the dorm to say it was lights-out time. She had been lying in her bunk, submerged under the quilt, since seven o'clock. Mrs Abbott had been nice enough as she'd helped to clean her up immediately after the soup incident. At least she had actually touched her, which didn't happen very often, and she genuinely seemed concerned.

'What happened, Biddy?' she asked, as she guided Biddy to the sink. Biddy shook her head. She was still gasping and shaking.

'Biddy, I really need to know what happened.'

'Hot,' was all that Biddy could manage.

'Hot?' the teacher asked, confused.

'Uh-huh,' Biddy nodded.

'But Biddy, the soup wasn't hot, it really wasn't. If anything, I thought it was too cold. Here,' she ran a hand towel under the taps, 'take this, and splash your face with water.'

The water eased the burning sensation in her eyes and up her nostrils, and her breathing began to settle.

'Maybe you put too much pepper in it?' asked Mrs Abbott, taking the towel back and rubbing Biddy's top with it.

'No,' Biddy shook her head. 'I don't like pepper. I don't use it.'

'Well, maybe you added pepper instead of salt? By mistake?'

Biddy shook her head. 'I didn't add anything.'

Mrs Abbott sighed and shrugged her shoulders.

'Well, look, whatever it was, you're OK now, right?'

Biddy nodded, but she didn't feel OK at all. She felt sick. Her head hurt and her mouth was sore and she wanted to go home. But she nodded anyway.

'Look, why don't you go upstairs and clean up properly. Take this with you,' Mrs Abbott handed her the towel. 'Change your top and rinse this one through in the bathroom sink. It will dry overnight on the radiator in your dorm. When you're done, you can come back into the dining room and finish your dinner. I'll get the girls in the kitchen to keep it in the oven.'

'No thank you, Miss,' Biddy managed. 'I'm really not hungry now. If it's all right with you I'd like to lie down?'

'Well, OK then,' Mrs Abbott sighed, 'I'll come and see you in a while, and if you want I'll get you some toast or something later. All right?'

Biddy nodded and managed a half smile. 'Thank you, Mrs Abbott. And I'm very sorry.'

'Nothing to be sorry for, Biddy,' the teacher smiled back. 'Just so long as you're OK. Now, I'm away back in to get my own dinner.'

When Mrs Abbott had gone, Biddy went upstairs to the girls' shower room where she sat in a toilet cubicle sticking pins into her thighs and the soles of her feet until she felt calm again. She rinsed out the T-shirt as instructed by Mrs Abbott and placed it over one of the long, low radiators in the dorm. Then she pulled on her spare off-white Aertex top and sat on the edge of her bed, hands folded in her lap, her body juddering every now and then.

'EEEHAWWWW. EEEHAWWW. Snort. Snort. EEEHAWWW.' Some of the girls burst into the dormitory, laughing hysterically at Alison's donkey impersonations.

'Alison, you're so naughty,' laughed Julia.

'How do you always get away with it, Alison?' asked Karen Robinson, who was sometimes irritated by Alison's attitude, and annoyed with the attention she attracted, but never did anything about it. When she'd heard that Alison was responsible for Biddy's outburst at dinner, she didn't find it quite as amusing as the others. She felt a shiver of pity for Biddy, just as she had after the disco, and thought that Alison was cutting too close to the bone.

'Don't you worry that someday you'll go too far and really damage her, or even that you'll get caught out?' she asked.

Alison wasn't used to being challenged. 'Don't know what you're talking about, Karen,' she snapped and glared at her for a few seconds, then looked over with disdain at Biddy, who was still sitting on the edge of her bed, head bent, hands folded on her lap. She sniffed a laugh, went over to her own bunk, rustled in her rucksack and took out a black portable tape recorder and a cassette of A-Ha's new album, *Hunting High and Low*. 'Come on, girls, let's bring this outside. If we go behind the greenhouse we might even be able to sneak a fag. Have you got the packet, Georgie?'

Georgina nodded. She skipped over to her own rucksack and removed a packet of Silk Cut, which was wrapped up in a face cloth inside her toilet bag, and slipped it inside the pocket of her Levi sweatshirt.

Alison headed towards the door. 'Coming, Karen?' She waved the tape in the air. 'Or are you going to stay here and keep the Weirdo company?'

Karen hesitated. Alison did piss her off, but there was no way she was staying on her own here with Biddy. Yes, she felt a bit sorry for her, but not that much. Besides, she loved that album, and also, the chance of a sneaky smoke was too good to miss. Everyone followed Alison out of the room, Georgina letting the door slam behind her. Seconds later, Biddy heard it creak open again. It was Alison.

'If you even *think* about telling Abbott that we've gone for a smoke, it'll be more than soup you'll be spitting out next time. Got it?' Biddy quivered, but made no response to Alison's threat. 'I said, got it?'

This time Biddy nodded, keeping her head bent so far that her chin rested on her bony chest. As the door slammed again, the tears began to run down her face and drip from her nose onto her T-shirt. She knew that Alison had been responsible for whatever had happened in the dining room. Her stomach turned and churned and the thought of the next two days living here in this house made her shake with fear. What would Alison do next? How would she manage to get through tonight, never mind the rest of the trip? Would Mrs Abbott send her home if she asked? But how would she get home? Her father couldn't come to collect her, as he didn't drive. And there was no one else. No one. Maybe if Miss Jordan wasn't away travelling the world, she could have come to get her. Or maybe if she'd had a mother, *she* would be able to drive, and she would have come for her. She might have allowed her not to go in the first place. She might have hugged her close and stroked her hair and said, 'There, there. Of course you don't have to go, of course you can stay with me.' But she didn't have a mother, did she? And she hadn't even had the guts to ask her father if she could stay at home anyway. It wasn't his fault. It was her fault: her own stupid fault.

The thought of her father caused a rapid, throbbing stab of homesickness. She wanted to be near him and smell his musty, coal-tar scent. She wanted his dry, wrinkly hands to give her a handkerchief to wipe away her tears. She wanted her own old creaky bed with its stripy cotton sheets and layers of thin, bally blankets and piles and piles of sketches stuffed underneath it. The dormitory door opened again making Biddy jump, and squeeze her eyes shut.

'How are you feeling now, Biddy?'

She sighed with relief. It was Mrs Abbott's voice, not Alison's.

'Biddy?' Biddy looked up, her face expressionless.

God, she looks a right sight, thought Ruth Abbott. It was obvious that she'd been crying: her face was pale with big red blotches, her eyes pink and puffy. She wanted to get back to the lounge for a bit of crack with Clive and Roy. They were going to have a game of poker and she was pretty sure she could beat them. But she also knew that it was her responsibility to make sure Biddy was all right. After that dreadful business with Penny Jordan last term, Mr Duncan had asked her to keep an eye on her. 'She may be a bit vulnerable,' he had said. *Aren't they bloody all at that age*, she had thought. Ruth had never actually taught Biddy Weir, but she knew the girl was a bit, well, odd. Still, she hadn't expected her to be quite so feeble, or so desperately introverted. Frankly, she'd been disgusted by that whole episode at the disco. She hadn't been there herself, but naturally she'd heard all about it from several of the teachers who were. But she hadn't bought it. She'd had some dealings with Penny, and she liked her. So what if she was gay? Her own cousin was gay, and that didn't make him a pervert. From her contact with Penny, she was certain it was all a ridiculous misunderstanding. And anyway, didn't Penny have a partner? She had been tempted to speak up, defend the young teacher, but as she was hoping for a promotion to Deputy Head of Department when Margot Russell left next term, she didn't want to do anything to get on the wrong side of Mr Duncan. So she kept her mouth shut. But seeing Biddy now she wondered if she should have spoken up. The concept of something untoward going on between them was even more ridiculous to her now she had actually had direct contact with the girl. Biddy was so innocent, so childlike. Look at her, she thought: she's like a little lost waif. She could be from the '50s; she certainly wasn't a child of the '80s. And she didn't appear to have any friends at all. Maybe she should ask one of the other girls to take her under her wing, just for the next two days. Alison Flemming, perhaps. Alison always seemed eager to please.

'Are you feeling a bit better?' she asked, softly.

Biddy nodded. Ruth knew this was a lie, but at least the girl was settled, and right now she was happy to settle for the fib.

'Good. Now, are you hungry yet? Shall I get you a snack?'

Biddy shook her head.

'You sure? How about some tea and toast?'

'No, thank you very much, Miss,' Biddy almost whispered. 'I'm just tired and my tummy's a bit sore.'

'Well, we've all had a busy day. Perhaps you've just overdone it a bit. Why don't you just get your jammies on and get into bed now?'

Biddy nodded.

'You could read a book or a magazine or something.'

Biddy nodded again.

'Have you got something with you to read?'

Biddy nodded again, even though she hadn't.

'All right then, Biddy. Just you stay here and relax. I'm sure you'll be feeling better in the morning after a good sleep. I'll be round again before lights out.'

Biddy nodded again.

'Bye, then.'

'Bye,' whispered Biddy, so softly that Ruth Abbott didn't even hear.

Biddy lay in bed with the duvet pulled up to her chin and watched silently as the other girls ran around the room, hitting each other with pillows and playing with each other's hair. Their behaviour fascinated her. It was all so foreign, so surreal: a bit like watching an episode of *The Living Planet*, only instead of jungles, or deserts, or mountains, or birds, David Attenborough's subjects were real-life teenage girls. This was very different to the way they behaved at school, thought Biddy. Well, maybe it wasn't; maybe she just spent so much time at school trying to avoid them, trying not to get in their way or make eye contact, or interact with them on any level, that she simply hadn't noticed. Now she couldn't tear her eyes away.

Some of them flicked through magazines, oohing and aahing at the pictures. 'Simon's my favourite,' said Jill. 'Look, isn't he gorgeous?'

'Ugh, no way!' Nicola was apparently horrified. 'Nick is definitely the cutest. Look at those eyes.' Biddy wondered who they were talking about: some pop group, obviously. She imagined herself sitting on the bed beside them, looking at the pictures too. Which one would she prefer? Simon, or Nick? If Nick had nice eyes, it would probably be him. Some of the girls sang songs she didn't recognise into their hairbrushes, and danced the kind of dances they'd all been doing at the disco; apart from Vanessa Park who was pirouetting around the room like a ballerina. Julia seemed to be poking at Jackie's eyebrows with a pair of tweezers. There was so much chatter, so much laughter; but for once it wasn't intimidating or menacing. Despite what had happened earlier, the high-pitched, musical hum around the room was sort of mesmerising. Something about the tone reminded Biddy of the aviary at the Botanical Gardens in the city.

She was equally fascinated by the bedtime outfits on display. Some of the girls wore big baggy T-shirts with pictures of Minnie Mouse or the Tweetie Pie bird on them, or big printed slogans like the ones Bryan and Tim had on at the disco. Some wore oversized shirts which looked like they belonged to their fathers, with the collars and cuffs cut off. One or two were dancing in their underwear. Georgina was admiring Alison's pink pants and matching vest top.

Biddy tugged at her own tartan flannelette pyjamas which were buttoned the whole way up to her neck and felt mortified. She'd worn the same type of pyjamas for as long as she could remember, and always loved the comfort of them – until now. The room was warm and she felt sticky and uncomfortable underneath the unfamiliar duvet. But she knew she daren't move, because then the spell would be broken, and another shameful secret would be revealed.

During her brief but brilliant friendship with Miss Jordan, Biddy had felt the unfamiliar rumblings of a yearning to be normal. It took her by surprise, as she'd never given much thought to being normal before; in truth her focus had always been on managing her weirdness, not letting it bother other people – and, of course, as much as possible, on staying out of Alison's way. There was never any energy left for thoughts of a normal life. But Miss Jordan had opened her eyes to that possibility, just a little bit. She knew she couldn't be properly normal, not ever, her weirdness was obviously too inherent for that – but she had started to think that she could maybe, perhaps, do some of the normal things that other girls her age could do: like wear clothes that didn't come from charity shops, and buy make-up, and dance to pop music, and bake cakes. And she was just beginning to do some of them, she was, when, well, when look what happened. *That'll teach you*, she'd told herself over and over, *you stupid, bloody weirdo*. Tonight, in this huge room in this strange old house, miles and miles away from the safety of Stanley Street, as she pretended to be invisible and silently, secretly watched the maze of little dramas all around her, she felt that rumble once again. *I wish*, she thought. *I wish, I wish, I wish . . .*

'Right, girls. Settle down.' The spell was broken. The girls started to leap into their bunks as Mrs Abbott strode into the room. 'It's lights-out time.'

There were groans of 'Aww, Miss,' from around the room. 'Just a wee while longer?' pleaded Julia.

'Go on, Miss, ten minutes?' ventured Jill. 'Five?'

'Please, Miss,' tried Karen.

Still peeping out from the top of her duvet, Biddy noticed Alison dabbing something from a tiny bottle behind her ears, and on her wrists and down the middle of her breasts. The other girls were still trying to persuade Mrs Abbott to delay lights out, but Alison just slipped into the bottom bed of the bunk she was sharing with Georgina and didn't say a word.

'No, seriously girls, that's it. You've got a long day ahead tomorrow and you all need a good night's sleep. You can chat for five minutes, but that's all. Anyone heard talking after that will be punished. And don't think I won't be listening. You never know when I'll be prowling outside your door. Night, girls.'

'Night, Miss,' some of the girls reluctantly groaned.

Biddy pulled the duvet over the top of her head, turned on her side and drew her knees up to her chest, hugging them. In the dense, black darkness she could almost pretend she was back in her own bed, except for the strange light spongy quilt and the breathing and whispers of the other girls. She'd been OK there for a while, lost in the curiousness of what she had been watching, but now she felt a surge of longing for her own heavy blankets, for the sound of her father snoring. She didn't want to hear these sounds. She unclasped her hands from around her knees and stuck her fingers in her ears. Now all she could hear was her own heavy breathing and the rush of blood inside her head. It sounded a bit like the waterfall they had come across on the mountain earlier that day.

Eventually she had to pull down the duvet to get some air. The girls continued to chatter and giggle. Mrs Abbott banged on the door twice and told them to settle down, which they did for a moment, before erupting into giggles again. But Biddy was aware that Alison's voice wasn't one of them, which was strange, and instantly unsettling. Mrs Abbott banged the door again, but still the giggles persisted.

'For God's sake, would you all shut up!' yelled Alison. 'I want to go to sleep.'

'Eeeeeuuuwww. What's up with *you*?' someone retorted.

'Nothing's *up* with me. I just want to get some sleep. Now, shut the fuck up.'

Alison obviously had more influence on the others than Mrs Abbott. Once or twice someone sniggered or cleared their throat, or whispered something to their bunk mate, but gradually the room fell silent.

Biddy had never shared a bedroom with another person before. In almost sixteen years, she had never slept anywhere but her own bed in her own bedroom with the same wallpaper on the wall and the same blankets and the same creaking floorboards. She lay still in the darkness, eyes wide open, arms now stiffly by her sides, and listened to the unfamiliar sound of other people sleeping. Deep, heavy breathing reverberated throughout the room. Someone started to snore, but it was light and high-pitched, unlike her father's deep wheezy rattle. Beds creaked, duvets rustled, someone near her sounded like they were grinding their teeth. Biddy was tired. She wanted to sleep, she knew she needed to sleep, but her eyes wouldn't let her. Every time she closed them, someone moved or coughed, and they sprang back open again. Gradually, she felt herself get heavy and her eyes began to droop. But then a noise from the other side of the room jolted her awake. Someone was getting out of bed. She could just make out their outline in the gloom, pulling on a dressing gown. They moved towards her bed. Biddy swallowed and screwed her eyes shut tight, waiting for whatever was coming. Were they going to put a pillow over her face? Or pour something over her? What? What were they going to do? But then she heard the door slowly creak and opened her eyes. Whoever it was, she was going out of the room. Biddy had a clear view from her bed, and as the door opened, the dim light which had been left on in the corridor highlighted Alison Flemming's long golden hair, like a halo.

Biddy breathed a sigh of relief, which was instantly drowned by a huge gulp of panic. What was Alison doing? Where had she gone? Was this all part of a plan? Was everyone else just pretending to be asleep, waiting for Alison to prepare her next trick? *Breathe*, she told herself, *breathe. Listen to the other breathing.* The snores. They were real. They were.

Maybe Alison had simply gone to the toilet.

As that thought hit her, that sensible, rational thought, Biddy realised she actually really needed to go to the toilet herself. She hadn't gone before lights out, as she hadn't wanted the others to see her pyjamas. And now she was worried if getting out of bed was against the rules, even to go to the toilet. What if Mrs Abbott was doing her prowling and caught her? But Alison had left the room, so she mustn't be worried about getting caught. But then again, Alison was never caught. The more she thought about it, the more Biddy's bladder seemed to cramp. She couldn't go now, obviously. Not while Alison was there. She'd just have to wait until she returned. Then wait some more until Alison fell asleep. And then she would go. Her bladder was getting heavier and more painful by the second. Alison was taking an awfully long time. Maybe she'd got locked in the bathroom? Maybe she'd lost her way back to the room? Biddy crossed her legs and sucked in her tummy. Maybe she should just risk it and go. No. She couldn't. Of course she couldn't. Her bladder was close to bursting now, and her kidneys began to ache. '*Please hurry up, please hurry up, please hurry up,*' she whispered, over and over again.

Eventually, a long time later, the door creaked slowly open and in came Alison. She closed it gently behind her, then tiptoed over to her bed. Biddy held her breath and waited for something to happen. Nothing did. The room stayed silent. Nobody stirred. Alison didn't speak to anyone. But it was too late anyway. Biddy pulled the duvet over her head, stuffed the corner of her pillow into her mouth and cried silently as the warm urine seeped through her pyjama bottoms, saturated her sheets and oozed into the mattress.

22.

The next day, their mountain hike soon eased Biddy's anxiety, the fresh, fragrant breeze blowing off the fog of a sleepless night. As they climbed higher and higher up the winding stony path, the smells and colours and sounds of the mountain increasingly enthralled her. She often dawdled behind to examine a wild flower or inhale the sharp scent of a mountain herb, and was frequently yelled at by their group leaders Mrs Abbott and Mr Price, one of the resident instructors at Brook House, to get a move on – despite the fact that she never once complained about the trek, unlike most of the others, who moaned and groaned throughout the day.

'How much further, Miss?'

'Can we sit down for a minute?'

'I'm knackered, Sir.'

Whenever Mr Price pointed out a rook or a fox's lair or a rare wild flower, the majority of pupils would roll their eyes at each other, or mutter 'big deal' under their breath. But Biddy quietly hung on his every word. The maze of stone walls zig-zagging across the landscape particularly fascinated her, and she wished she was brave enough to ask Mr Price about them. But Mr Price must have read her thoughts.

'You'll have noticed all the stone walls on the mountain,' he said, when they stopped beside one for a snack and water break. 'There are hundreds of them. Literally. In fact, Innis boasts some of the finest examples of dry stone walling in the world.'

Mr Price encouraged the pupils to examine the structure of the walls, which some approached with more enthusiasm than others. 'People used to come from all over the world to see these walls,' he continued, 'and sometimes to help to build them. From geologists to poets and students to walking groups. They don't come as often now, not since the Troubles started, even though you don't get any trouble on a mountain; not of that kind, anyway. But they'll come again one day, when it all settles.'

Biddy was intrigued by the notion of people from foreign countries visiting this mountain just to see a wall. When she looked more closely, however, she understood why. The silver-grey stones were piled together in seemingly random yet precisely positioned rows, with no cement to bind them together.

'This particular one is known as "Paddy's Wall",' Mr Price said, patting the wall. 'It starts on the far side of the stream down below, and runs for about half a mile up towards the heart of the mountain until just over there.' He nodded towards a mound of unused stones a few feet away from where they stood, where the wall came to an abrupt end.

'What's that, Sir?' Ben Creegan asked, pointing to a small wooden cross which was lodged into the earth, just beside the pile of stones.

'Well, Ben, why don't you go and take a look. Tell us what it says,' Mr Price smiled.

Ben wandered over and knelt down beside the cross. '*Paddy Joyce 1886–1951: a man of the mountains, a mountain of a man. RIP*,' he called back to the group.

'Paddy Joyce was a well-known local waller who spent his entire life on the mountain,' Mr Price explained, as the rest of the group gathered around the stone mound. 'He lived in a little stone cottage at the foot of Innis. It's still there, but it's basically a ruin now. You'll have passed it on your way through the village.

Anyway, it's said that Paddy's mother brought him to the mountain the very day he was born in a sling across her chest, and that he came back here every single day of his life for the next sixty-five years. In fact,' Mr Price paused and looked around the mountain, 'he single-handedly built many of the walls dotted across Innis. He died right here, on this spot, in April 1951 while building this wall. The locals didn't want Paddy to miss his daily fix of the mountain while waiting for a funeral to be arranged, so they carried him down, sorted him out a coffin, and between them managed to carry it back to this spot, where they buried him the very next day.'

'What, here, Sir?' Rory interrupted. 'Right here?'

'Yes, Rory, right here. Right underneath these very stones.'

Most of the group were horrified.

'Aw, no way, Sir,' said Paul.

'You mean, there's a dead body under there?' gasped Nicola.

'I feel all shivery,' shivered Clare.

Ben Creegan actually said, 'Shit.'

'Ben,' warned Mrs Abbott.

'Is that not, like, illegal, Sir?' asked Rory. 'I mean, do you not have to be buried in a proper graveyard? Or else get cremated like my grandma was?'

'Well, Rory, the mountain has its own laws,' smiled Mr Price. 'And I guess it was happy enough to keep the body of Patrick Joyce. After all, he truly was a man of the mountain. He knew it like the back of his hand. If a lone climber lost his way or got into a spot of bother, it was always Paddy who got him – or her – down. He could sniff out trouble on the mountain like the scent of burning turf floating on the breeze, and in his time he saved more lives than the mountain rescue service ever did.'

He paused, and raised his eyebrows. 'Some people claim they still see Paddy wandering the hills at twilight, especially around Clundaff Point. Which, as it happens, is where we'll be stopping for lunch.'

'Aw, no way, Sir. I'm not going anywhere haunted,' gasped Rory.

'Don't worry, guys, he doesn't appear until twilight,' Mr Price winked. 'We'll be long gone by then. Now, I guess we'd better get a move on, as my tummy is already rumbling.'

Biddy was immediately fascinated by Paddy Joyce and his wall. She lingered for a moment, looking at the cross. Imagine living your whole life on a mountain and never having to go anywhere else, she thought. Or on a beach. *I could do that.*

'Come on you lot. Move it!' Mrs Abbott called from further on up the hill, and Biddy reluctantly left the stone, following slightly behind Rory, Paul and Ben.

'Are you saying you believe in ghosts?' she heard Paul laugh as he nudged Ben.

'Yeah, ya big sissy,' teased Ben.

''Course not,' scoffed Rory. 'Don't be soft.'

'Whooooo! Whooaaa!!' Paul made mock ghostly movements with his arms in front of Rory's face. 'Rory's scared of the ghost of Paddy Joyce.'

Rory pushed him off: 'Piss off. Why the fuck would I be scared of a bloody weirdo like that?'

Biddy stopped in her tracks. Another one, she thought, and smiled. She liked Paddy Joyce even more now.

By the time they reached the heather-covered plateau dotted with huge grey boulders where they stopped for lunch, Biddy was already in love with the mountain, but the appearance of two peregrine falcons swooping and sweeping over a turret high above them triggered a sense of elation she had never experienced before.

She knew they were falcons immediately, recognising them from her big encyclopaedia of birds, and Mr Price confirmed it. 'They're common to Innis,' he said. She hadn't known that. The boys, excited at the sight of real live birds of prey, were hoping to see a kill. Maybe the birds would swoop down and grab a fox or a rabbit or a mountain hare. They quickly lost interest, however, when Mr Price told them that peregrines mostly only ate other birds, and that as there were no other birds around, a gory display was unlikely. But Biddy was entranced by the falcons' grace and beauty and their silent, elegant dance of flight. She wished she had her sketchbook with her. She wished she could fly like they could. To her, the mountain was like a magical paradise, a haven, a whole new world, where anything was possible. And when the time came to head back to the house, she didn't want to leave. She wanted to stay there forever, on her own, with the butterflies and the swooping falcons.

23.

'All right everyone, settle down,' Mr Patterson bellowed from the top step of the big porch. 'You've got one hour to chill out before tea, which, by the way, is stew tonight.'

'Aww no, Sir,' groaned Stewart Stevenson, 'I hate stew.'

'Shut it, Stevenson. You'll eat what you're damn well given. Now, bugger off the lot of you, and be back here at 5.30 p.m. sharp.'

Someone produced a football from somewhere and the boys began kicking it around on the grass at the side of the house. Most of the girls went up to the dorm, giggling and whispering, eager to exchange gossip about who was trying to get off with whom. The teachers went into the lounge to have a smoke and sort through the pile of worksheets. Biddy stood alone outside the big house while the others dispersed. Not knowing what to do or where to go, she walked back up the path to the big birch tree and sat on the grass with her back resting on its trunk. She picked at shoots of grass and thought about the stew. She liked stew. Food didn't generally excite her, but stew was one of her favourite meals. Her father made a big pot every other Monday, and it lasted two or three nights. It was his mother's recipe, he'd told her, and her mother's before that. He didn't know how far it went back – generations, probably. Anyway, he'd have to teach her someday. He said that every time he dolloped the first steaming spoonful of the fortnightly pot onto her plate, and every single time she inhaled the sweet, warm smell of meat, carrots, onions and something she didn't know the name of, she wondered when that 'someday' would be.

Her tummy gurgled, either with nerves or with hunger. It didn't matter which, as after last night she knew she wouldn't be able to eat anything anyway, no matter how good the stew looked. She'd eaten nothing at breakfast, even though she wasn't sitting at Alison's table, but she did wrap a piece of dry toast in a napkin which she slipped under her cardigan and ate in the toilet before they went off on the hike. Lunch was a picnic on up the mountain, the same as yesterday, only with a ham sandwich this time. She'd managed most of it as she sat alone on a moss-covered rock surrounded by clumps of wild purple heather, mesmerised by the peregrine falcons.

The sound of low voices coming from somewhere behind made her look up, just in time to see Alison and Georgina dart around the back of the big old greenhouse. They were probably going to smoke a cigarette, just like they had last night. They hadn't seen her, but just the sight of Alison unnerved Biddy. She had managed to avoid her for most of the day as they'd been put in different groups. Everyone in her group ignored her completely, but nobody did anything bad. Biddy could cope with people not talking to her. She was used to that. She liked it that way. But at teatime, she would be back in the same room as Alison, and then it would be bedtime, and somewhere along the course of the evening Alison was bound to have something or other planned for her. The lump started to move up her gullet into the back of her throat and she swallowed repeatedly to keep it from pushing into her mouth. She thought about her father and his stew and the half-hug they'd had yesterday morning before she left, and she really, really wanted to go home.

Alison and Georgina reappeared, arms linked, giggling together. Alison threw her head back, tossing her long golden hair, which glistened in the warm September sunshine. Biddy held her breath, willing them not to see her. But they were too busy gossiping about something or other more important than Biddy to notice her, and disappeared around the back of the house. She exhaled, sighing with relief. A crow squawked loudly above her head. Biddy looked up to see three of the large black birds high above her, swooping from the tallest chimney on the roof of the big house down to the glass roof of the greenhouse and back again, dipping closer to her with every dive, crying out as they passed. She was sure they were calling to her. Her father and his stew and that evening's dinner and Alison and Georgina were forgotten, as an urge to draw the crows consumed her. But her sketchbook was in her case, and that would mean going into the dormitory where some of the other girls were sure to be. Maybe they would just ignore her. Maybe they wouldn't even notice her. She decided to risk it. She'd get in and out as quickly as possible.

As Biddy pushed open the dormitory door, she briefly scanned the room. The scene was pretty similar to the one last night, only this time it didn't hold the same fascination. Georgina, Jackie and Julia were lying on Julia's bunk, flicking through a magazine. They were making the same familiar oohing and aahing noises that Jill and Nicola had been making last night. Vanessa Park was putting blue eye-shadow on Jane Gilbert's eyelids. Pamela Brown was brushing Karen Robinson's long black hair. Jill Cleaver was rifling through her rucksack looking for something. Clare Watson was showing Angela Duggan and Kathy Young her newly pierced ears which she thought might have gone septic. And Nicola appeared to be writing in her diary. There was no sign of Alison. Biddy scuttled over to her bunk, head down, teeth tightly clenched and pulled her case out from under her bunk. She hoped no one would notice her.

'Oh my God,' exclaimed Georgina loudly, 'what *is* that smell. Did somebody drop one? Oh. It's only B.W. God, has anyone got any perfume?' Some of the girls sniggered. Most just carried on doing what they were doing. Georgina tried again.

'Seriously, has anyone noticed the stink coming from B.W.'s bed? Like cat's wee? Maybe she wet herself.'

Julia and Jackie giggled.

'Hey, B.W. Did you wet the bed last night?'

Biddy's back was turned away from Julia's bunk. She started to shake and felt her cheeks flush with hot embarrassment. *How did they know*? she thought. She had stayed in bed that morning, with the quilt pulled over her head, waiting until all the other girls went into the bathroom together to use the toilet, have a wash and clean their teeth. She knew there was no one in the room to see her pull on her clean pants and trousers or stuff her damp pyjama bottoms under her pillow. Was there a smell? She couldn't tell. Had they looked under her pillow? She swallowed hard several times.

'Give over, Georgina, would you?' said Karen.

Biddy was surprised. No one ever spoke back to Alison or Georgina, but since they'd been here, Karen Robinson had done it to both of them.

Georgina herself was furious. She could never muster up the same enthusiasm from the others for goading Biddy as Alison could, a fact which always irked her. She glared at Biddy hoping to evoke a reaction at least from her, a sign that she was scared. But Biddy always looked scared, so Georgina didn't know if she was getting to her or not. She shrugged her shoulders in a 'see-if-I-care' kind of way, and returned her attention to the pictures of Duran Duran in Julia's *Jackie* magazine.

Biddy snatched her sketchbook and pencils from the case, shoved it back under the bunk, and slunk out of the room, keeping her head bent low, not wanting to risk eye contact with anyone. She was so relieved that Alison hadn't been there. Alison would probably somehow have discovered that Biddy really had wet herself. In her hurry to get away from the dorm and back to the birds, she lost her bearings. Turning left at the end of the corridor instead of right, she ended up on an unfamiliar large square landing. There were corridors running off in three directions, a staircase leading up to the next floor and two more flights of stairs at both sides of the landing going down. Disorientated, Biddy circled the landing before deciding to take the narrower of the two downstairs staircases, reckoning that there was less of a chance she would bump into anyone on that one. Just as she reached the turn halfway down, she heard the sound of laughter coming from above. It was a girl's laughter, light and high. Then someone's voice – a man's, low and deep.

Biddy stopped and backed up against the banister, afraid of getting caught somewhere she shouldn't be. The laughter came again. Instinctively she looked up, and there standing against the banister right above her head was Mr Patterson. And he was holding onto Alison. Then Alison reached up and ran her fingers through Mr Patterson's hair. Alison giggled and Mr Patterson made a sort of groaning noise. 'Christ, you're gorgeous,' he said in a low, croaky voice. 'You're so fucking hot.'

Biddy swallowed hard. She didn't want to see this. She didn't want to hear this. She didn't want to know this. She wanted to un-see and un-hear and un-know, and never think of it again. Terrified to move in case they heard her, she held her breath and closed her eyes tight, willing them to disappear. But when she opened her eyes again, she couldn't help but look up, and saw Mr Patterson kissing Alison on the mouth. And Alison was kissing him back. Biddy had never seen people kissing like this before, not in real life anyway, and whilst the idea of kissing did intrigue her, she wished she wasn't witnessing these two people doing it. Not them, not here, not now. Why did she look? Why? She closed her eyes again and squeezed them tight, still afraid to move. This was wrong. This was all so wrong. Alison and Mr Patterson were responsible for what happened to Miss Jordan. He was the one who had told Mr Duncan about the day in Rankin and McMordie. Alison was the one who told the Principal that Miss Jordan had been helping her in the toilets. How could they do that? How could they make something that was so nice and so good and so completely innocent look so ugly and bad and wrong – when they were doing *this*? When they'd probably been doing *this* all along? In those few seconds, Biddy Weir wasn't scared of Alison Flemming; she hated her. She hated her and she wanted her to pay for what she did. An unfamiliar rage pumped through her veins with such ferocity she felt that she might burst. But then she made a fatal error: she looked up again. The kissing had stopped, and Alison's head was resting on Mr Patterson's shoulder, her fingers still trailing through his hair. But she was staring down at Biddy, her hazel eyes brimming with venom. 'Weirdo,' she mouthed, slowly, deliberately. Then she closed her lips and ran her index finger along them in a menacing 'zip it' motion. And just like that, the unfamiliar sense of bravado Biddy had felt a few seconds earlier vanished, and the fear was back.

Biddy turned and ran down the rest of the stairs two at a time. At the bottom, she raced along a narrow corridor, past a scullery and some store rooms, until she eventually came to a fire door at the bottom which led her outside. She kept on running up the driveway and past the greenhouse, and past the birch tree, until, breathless and shaking, she came across a huge oak tree, and collapsed behind it, vomiting up the pitiful amount of food in her stomach.

24.

'Biddddeee! Biddddeee! Biddddeee Weir!'

Biddy was still crouched behind the tree, hugging her knees, trying to make sense of what she'd seen, of what she now knew was going on between Alison and Mr Patterson, when she heard Mrs Abbott calling her name. Startled, she glanced at her watch. It was twenty to six. She was late for dinner, but there was no way she was going down to the house. Not now. She felt confused, and disorientated. She knew what she wasn't going to do, but had no idea what she was going to do. Above her, a crow squawked twice. Biddy looked up at it and instinctively relaxed, albeit ever so slightly.

'Biddddeee! Where are you?! For goodness' sake, you're missing dinner. Biddddeee!'

Biddy was surprised that anyone had actually noticed she wasn't there. She felt a wave of nausea again. Alison would definitely be planning something now. She'd be busy working out how to make sure that Biddy kept quiet about seeing her and Mr Patterson kissing. Not that she would tell anyone. What would she say, and who would she say it to? And who would believe her anyway? No one would ever take her word over Alison's. Ever. But she knew that Alison wouldn't take her silence for granted, and that whatever plan she came up with, it would most likely be worse than anything she'd done before.

Biddy stood up and peered round the side of the tree. She could see Mrs Abbott walking back towards the front door of the house, shaking her head and raising her hands up to her shoulders in a shrug directed at Mr Boyd, who was now standing at the top of the steps. Mrs Abbott went into the house and Mr Boyd stood looking around for a second or two and then followed her. She didn't know what to do next. There was no trace of hunger in her stomach now at all, just waves of nervous cramps. Her heart was thudding, her head spinning, her hands shaking. If she did go back to the house now and ventured into the dining room, she'd be told off for being late, and she couldn't face seeing everyone staring and sniggering at her. She wouldn't be able to eat. And she really, really couldn't bear the thought of Alison's menacing stares. She couldn't go inside, she knew that for sure. But what else should she do? She sat down on the grass, then immediately stood up again, her back pressed against the tree, biting her lips and clenching her fists. Her pad and pencils lay, unused, at her feet. Her breathing accelerated and the sound of her banging heart grew louder. She felt herself becoming dizzy. She reached into the front pocket of her jeans, drew out the small silver tin, opened it, took out the longest needle and stabbed it through the denim into her thigh – two, three, four times. The thick fabric slowed down the force of the jab, but the effect was still enough to bring an immediate flood of relief. Biddy's heartbeat slowed down, the rushing noise in her ears faded and the dizzy feeling seeped away.

Exhausted, Biddy slid down the fat tree trunk and slumped back onto the ground. There had been a heavy shower earlier that afternoon and the clumpy grass around the rim of the trunk was still damp from the dripping leaves. Her bottom was getting wet from the repeated bouts of sitting down, but this time she didn't quite have the energy to stand up again. Resting her head against the tree, she closed her eyes and concentrated on the chattering birds and the swish of the branches swaying in the evening breeze. She felt calmer, but still didn't know what to do next.

If I was a bird, she thought, I could fly up to the top of the mountain, right now, and they would never see me again.

The sudden sound of noisy, raucous squawking jolted her from her thoughts. A group of four or five big black crows were circling above her, screeching and calling. *Are they talking to me?* she wondered. 'Hey,' she called, 'are you talking to me?' The birds seemed to multiply in seconds. There must have been thirty of them, maybe even forty. Biddy found it impossible to count. They perched in groups, balancing on treetops, telephone lines, chimney pots and the roof of the greenhouse. Their screeches were almost deafening. Biddy wondered if the birds had come to tell her something. Perhaps they were here to help her escape from this latest nightmare. Yes, that must be it. She was certain. An enormous crow landed beside her and picked at something on the ground.

'Hello, bird,' said Biddy quietly. The crow looked at her, right into her eyes and squawked three times. Biddy held its gaze. 'Help me, will you?' she asked. 'Tell me what to do.' The bird gave another squawk, then flew up to the roof of the greenhouse where it strutted for a few seconds before flying off in the direction of the mountain, followed by the rest of the flock. They vanished almost as quickly as they had appeared, and, in an instant, Biddy knew exactly what she had to do.

She slid the tin of pins back inside her jeans pocket, tucked her sketchpad and pencil box under her arm, took a deep breath and started walking up the driveway, glancing behind her every few seconds to check that no one was following. Just as she reached the gates, she saw Mrs Abbott, Mr Patterson and Mr Boyd all standing on the steps together and quickly darted down behind the old stone wall which ran around the grounds of the house. She was too far away to hear properly, but she could faintly make out her name.

'Bideeeee! Bideeeee!'

As they called it over and over again, it suddenly occurred to Biddy just how much her name sounded like 'Birdy'. How had she never realised that before? Holding her breath, she peered above the wall and watched from behind a tendril of ivy as the three teachers went back inside the house. She breathed a sigh of relief – they hadn't seen her, then she looked around, trying to get her bearings, not entirely sure how to get onto the path they had taken earlier. She hadn't taken that much notice of the actual route this morning, lingering at the back of the group, drinking up what she could of her surroundings. Now, as she started up the narrow road which she thought might lead her onto the mountain path, she thought about the falcons, the most glorious birds she had ever laid eyes on, and hoped they would still be there, waiting for her, when she arrived.

As soon as she reached the stream and saw the stepping-stone boulders daubed with blue paint by someone called *Billy* in *April 1981*, she knew she was definitely on the right path. This was the start of Paddy's Wall. She carried on, running now, until she came to the mound of stones which marked Paddy's grave, and slumped down, breathless, beside the wooden cross, running her hand over the roughly carved inscription. As she picked at a thick bunch of wild flowers growing around the base of the stones, which smelt strong, like chives, she thought about Paddy Joyce and the story that Mr Price had told them earlier that day, and she wondered why Rory had called him a bloody weirdo. Was it just because he had liked to be on the mountain? Biddy couldn't see anything weird about that. Or was it because he built walls? But men were always building walls in Ballybrock, especially in the places where all the new houses were being made on the outskirts of the town. She couldn't work it out. People knew who *she* was. They could *see* her, so it was obvious that she was a weirdo. But Rory couldn't *see* Paddy Joyce. She shivered. It was getting chilly, and she suddenly wished she'd lifted her cardigan when she went to get her sketchpad. She looked around the mountain. It was still, and gloriously silent, apart from the occasional distant bleating of a few stray sheep. There were no birds, she realised with a jolt. She couldn't hear any birds. Where had all the birds gone?

The light had started to dim and the sky seemed to be moving closer to her. For the first time, she felt a twinge of apprehension. Maybe she was making a mistake. Maybe she should turn back. No. No, that wasn't an option. She couldn't go back there. She never wanted to see Alison Flemming again. Ever. What she needed to do was get a move on if she was going to get there before dark.

Biddy stood up and stared at the inscription on the cross. 'Goodbye, Paddy Joyce,' she said aloud. Suddenly an image of Miss Jordan popped into her head. Penny Jordan. Paddy Joyce. P.J. P.J. Paddy Joyce wasn't a bloody weirdo. He couldn't have been. He'd been a good man, gentle and kind and nice, she knew it. And somehow she was equally as certain that if he'd known her, he would have been her friend.

A familiar sound echoed across the mountain. Biddy looked up to see a raven circling high above her, its cry bouncing across the inky sky. Her apprehension vanished. She was safe on Innis. And if Paddy Joyce was here, then he would look after her. Paddy Joyce, and the birds.

25.

Biddy was out of breath and a little light-headed by the time she reached Clundaff Point. She sat down on the rock where she had eaten her sandwiches at lunchtime and pulled her arms around her knees. The falcons were nowhere to be seen. She looked at her watch. It was nearly ten to eight. Over two hours had passed since she'd heard Mrs Abbott call her name from the steps of the big house. How had the time passed so quickly? She must have spent longer sitting by Paddy Joyce's grave than she'd realised.

She turned her head and peered down the path she'd just climbed up. There was the wall, winding down the mountain in the distance. In this light, it looked more like a dragon's tail than a snail trail. It still looked wonderful, though. Biddy screwed her eyes tightly shut and imagined the dragon wall was flying up to Clundaff Point and dipping down so she could climb on board. The wall-tail became a whole dragon, and Paddy Joyce was sitting on its back. He turned to her and tipped his cap. It was the same one that her father wore. He took something from his pocket and ate it. She thought it might have been a Kimberley biscuit.

Biddy opened her eyes. She'd love to have a Kimberley biscuit right now. She was starting to feel really cold and very hungry, and she had a sudden ache for her father. If he were here with her now, he would probably have brought a packet of Kimberley biscuits with him. He always had them when she needed one. She wondered if one of the teachers had phoned her father yet to tell him that she hadn't shown up for dinner, which was disobeying the rules, and that he should come and collect her straight away.

They'd been told before the trip that any pupil who badly misbehaved or was caught drinking alcohol or smoking cigarettes would be severely dealt with. Their parents would be contacted and told to drive to Brook House to bring them home immediately. They might even face suspension. Biddy felt a stab of worry for her father. How would he even get to Brook House? Would he ask Mrs Thomas for a lift? And if she agreed, and brought him down here, what would he do when she wasn't there? Even if Mrs Abbott and Mr Patterson and Mr Boyd kept on looking for her, they would never find her up here. But they'd probably have given up by now. They'd most likely forgotten all about her. They might not even realise that she'd really gone until tomorrow – if they realised at all. Tomorrow, she thought. What would she do about tomorrow?

Biddy hadn't yet worked out a long-term plan for her escape. She had expected the birds to be here at Clundaff Point, waiting for her to arrive. She'd thought they would tell her what to do. She shivered. It was getting colder and the light was really fading now. What should she do? Should she carry on up the mountain, perhaps to the very top, to see if the birds were there? Or go back to the wall? Maybe Paddy Joyce would help her. Or should she stay here and wait? She couldn't think straight. She couldn't concentrate.

She needed to concentrate.

Biddy stood up and walked closer to the edge of the rock face, looking up to the turret where the falcons had been earlier in the day. Dropping her sketchbook and pencils on the ground, she cupped her hands around her mouth.

'Birds,' she shouted as loud as she could.

'. . . *irds*,' came the echo back.

Biddy was startled, both by the sound of her own voice, and by the echo. She so rarely spoke aloud, except to talk to her father, or to answer questions in class on the very odd occasion when she was asked something by a teacher, or to get her bus ticket, or buy something from a shop which she absolutely had to ask for. The only person she'd ever had proper conversations with was Miss Jordan. But she'd never used her voice like this before, to shout. She liked it.

'Birds,' she shouted again, even louder this time. '. . . *irds, irds,*' went the echo. She laughed. This was fun. 'Birdies. Birdies. Birdies.'

'. . . *irdies. Irdies. Irdies.*'

'Where are you?'

'. . . *R u r u r u.*'

'It's me, Biddy.'

'. . . *iddy iddy iddy.*'

'Biddy Weir.'

'. . . *Iddy eir Iddy eir.*'

'Biddy Weirdo.'

'. . . *Iddy eirdo Iddy eirdo.*'

'Bloody Biddy Weirdo.'

'. . . *Eeirdo eirdo eirdo.*'

Biddy clapped her hands together and shrieked with laughter. Even her laugh echoed back. She laughed again and spun around on the rock, her arms outstretched, her head thrown back, the darkening sky hanging just above her. Suddenly it was OK to be a bloody weirdo. The mountain liked her. It was talking to her. Maybe mountains were where bloody weirdos belonged. Maybe Rory was right after all, and Paddy Joyce was one and that's why he'd been happy here, and why he'd never left. She spun around and around, laughing and laughing and calling out 'Biddy Weirdo, Bloody Biddy Weirdo,' and the mountain called right back. She'd never felt this happy in her life. This free. As free as a bird.

Eventually the spinning made her so dizzy that she stumbled down onto the rock, breathless and giddy. She lay there panting, waiting for her breathing to settle and her heart to stop thumping. She looked up at the sky, which was spinning too. There were still some evening clouds dancing around before the black darkness of night finally swallowed them up. They were shaped like birds, really big birds with wide, fluffy wings. Suddenly a dark shadow passed over the clouds, then another, and Biddy felt a breeze blow over her face. She sat up with a start, her heart almost bursting with joy.

'You came!' she shrieked. 'You came. I knew you would.' She watched the two falcons circle above her, then glide down and perch on the turret they had occupied earlier. 'Kek-kek-kek,' they called. 'Kek-kek-kek.'

Biddy grabbed her sketchbook and pencil and began to draw the birds in a frantic, manic rush, despite the fading light. She sketched them flying, perched on the turret, together, alone. Before long, the mossy rock was covered with pages flapping around in the breeze and soon there was no more blank paper in the pad. She was exhausted, but exhilarated. A sudden gust of wind lifted most of the pages and scattered them around the mountain. Some blew down towards Paddy's Wall. Some soared up towards the peak high above her. Others danced and fluttered around Clundaff Point.

'They're flying', shrieked Biddy, 'my birds are flying.'

One of the falcons glided towards Biddy to take a closer look. 'Kek-kek-kek,' it called, as it soared over her and back to the turret. The second falcon took flight and repeated the actions of the first. Then they flew together. 'Kek-kek-kek,' they cried in unison, as they settled back on the turret.

They want me to join them, thought Biddy. They're calling to me. 'Come-come-come,' they're saying.

The turret was about 300 feet away from the mossy boulder where Biddy stood. It didn't look too far if you could just jump or fly straight over to it, but the terrain was rough and uneven, with deep drops and ragged rocks. When they'd been there for lunch earlier, Mr Price and Mrs Abbott had warned them not to stray from their picnic spot.

'This is as far as we can go,' Mr Price had said. 'You need special training to go any further. We do run residential mountaineering courses for young people during holiday periods, in case any of you are interested.'

Biddy had thought it strange that you needed to learn how to climb a mountain. She was sure that Paddy Joyce hadn't been on a mountain-climbing course. And as she stood now on the boulder, looking at the falcons, she knew she didn't need any special sort of training to get over to the turret. Suddenly everything made sense. The crows down at the big house had sent her back here to the mountain. The bird clouds in the sky had told her that the falcons were coming. Her drawings had flown away, and if they could do it, so could she. And Paddy Joyce was here to look after her. She could feel him.

A gust of wind swirled around Biddy, smearing her face with thick, coarse curls. She wobbled slightly and jumped down from the boulder, frantically pushing back her hair with the tips of her fingers. She didn't want to lose sight of her falcons for a second. The temperature was dropping rapidly and the light fading quickly, but Biddy wasn't cold at all now, or scared. Her heart was pounding, but with excitement for once, not fear; and the blood thudding through her veins was ablaze with adrenaline.

'I'm coming,' she shouted up to the turret and the waiting falcons. 'Wait for me, I'm coming.' Then, in a frenzied flurry, she began her ascent. The terrain was treacherous, but Biddy scarcely noticed. Stumbling over rocks, sliding on moss, pulling herself up a steep incline with her bare hands, she didn't think twice about what she was doing. Her concentration was focused on the turret. It was getting closer. 'Kek-kek-kek,' the falcons called in encouragement.

Biddy didn't wince when a sharp jutting rock tore through her jeans and ripped down her right leg, drenching her with blood. She didn't feel the thorns from the bracken she grabbed at to pull herself along, as they stabbed at her palms and pierced beneath her fingernails. When her footing slipped, and a black plimsoll slid from her left foot and tumbled down the slope, she carried on with one shoe.

The falcons, still perched on the top of the turret, tapped their yellow-clawed feet on the rock and watched intently as Biddy edged closer. They didn't seem at all startled. Perhaps they really were expecting her. Perhaps they'd brought her here after all. They watched and waited, and waited and watched. Then there she was, just a couple of feet away, her hair a mass of matted tats, her hands scratched and bleeding, her right leg saturated with blood, a filthy sock half-covering her dirty left foot. She looked like she'd been mauled by something on the mountain. She looked like something the falcons might well maul themselves. The swelling wind began to howl, and heavy dense clouds gathered at the top of the mountain. As the last of the light filtered away, the falcons turned from Biddy in perfect unison, spread their expansive, glorious wings and sailed away from the turret. Dipping down into the valley below, they parted company from each other, and soared back up towards the top of the mountain, one veering to the right of Biddy and the other the left.

It was the most beautiful thing that Biddy had ever seen. They were like kites, dancing in the sky, gliding and soaring with the grace of ballerinas. Her heart was so full she felt it might burst. She clapped her hands together, laughing and screeching with joy. Every nerve in her body was tingling with excitement, and energy shot through her veins like electrical charges. She felt more alive than she'd ever felt in her life. She clambered up the last few feet to the ledge where, until a few moments ago, the falcons had surveyed her journey. Pulling herself upright, she cupped her hands around her mouth and shouted at the top of her voice, 'I'm coming. Wait for me, wait for me. I'm coming with you.' Then she spread out her arms, inhaled a long, deep breath, smiled up at the heavens above her, and jumped.

Part 2: a death and a rebirth, of sorts
Ballybrock, January 2000

26.

'We therefore commit . . .'

Splat. The first handful of earth to hit the coffin was not only slightly premature, it was also so wet from the pouring rain that it made rather more noise on impact than it should have. The minister, Reverend Barker, paused and glanced up at the small troupe of mourners. He wanted this over as quickly as possible. He wasn't good with rain, and, as none of the mourners had brought umbrellas with them, he didn't think it appropriate to use his. Consequently, the rain was trickling down over his thin, fine hair, dripping onto his neck and running down the back of his dog-collar. He wished the girl had gone for a cremation. Clearing his throat lightly, he continued.

'. . . body to the ground, earth to earth,' he nodded at Biddy, acknowledging that *now* was the time to throw the soil, 'ashes to ashes, dust to dust, in the sure and certain hope of the Resurrection to Eternal Life.'

When Reverend Barker's job was done, he closed his sodden prayer book and looked over again at the mourners. All three of them. It was unusual these days to see such a small group at a funeral. He sometimes thought that people would go to the funeral of their bin man, if it meant getting a couple of hours off work. He didn't know the Weir family, as they weren't church-goers (although one of his elders at the church, Bill Dodds, had told him that his father recalled old Mr Weir's own father being a regular at the outdoor mission meetings the church used to hold many years ago). He was surprised, however, that no one else seemed to know the family either. At least they weren't having a reception that he would feel obliged to attend. There wasn't even any talk of going to the cemetery café for a cup of tea, thank goodness. Still, he needed to say a few final words of condolence. He owed them that. He'd have a quick chat and then he'd be off.

The rain was really pelting down now. A horrible, heavy, relentless wetness. Reverend Barker cleared his throat again, hoping for some kind of response from someone. He wasn't the only one who wanted to go home. The rain was agitating Mrs Thomas's arthritis. And Dr Graham, the Weirs' GP, needed to dry off before his afternoon surgery. But nobody wanted to make the first move. Nobody wanted to say, 'Right then, must be off.' The gravediggers had long since taken shelter under a huge oak tree some distance away and showed no sign of moving in to cover the grave. Dr Graham looked at his watch and glanced over at Reverend Barker who raised his eyebrows as though to say, 'I don't know what to do, do you?'

Eventually it was Dr Graham who spoke.

'I'm afraid I really do have to go. I'm so sorry.' He touched Biddy's elbow lightly and felt her flinch. 'My clinic starts shortly. I'll, ahem, I'll be in touch. Soon. I promise.'

'Yes, I really must be off too,' said Reverend Barker. 'If there's anything else I can do, well, you have my number. God bless.'

The two men, getting no response, turned to Mrs Thomas.

'Off you go, Reverend. Doctor. Don't worry. I'll stay,' she said, brushing the rain off the end of her nose. 'I'll go to the café, if need be.'

Relieved to be excused, the men dashed off to find their cars. At the brow of the hill, Dr Graham glanced back at the pathetic graveside scene, hesitating momentarily before pulling his car keys out of his pocket. Such funerals were rare these days, but then again, why was he surprised, given his knowledge of the Weirs? And what was going to happen now? Thank God he'd come. He couldn't often go to the funerals of his patients, but, despite his drenching, he was glad his morning off had coincided with this one. Taking off his sodden overcoat and throwing it in the back seat, he resolved to call at the house on his way back from work one evening this week.

Mrs Thomas lingered for a few moments longer. She was soaking and shivering, and her joints were aching. She needed to sit down.

'How about you and I go up to the café and get a cup of tea?' she asked Biddy softly. 'Well, tell you what,' she said, getting no response, 'I'll go on up myself, and you come and join me when you're ready. Then I'll take you home.' She reached out and gently placed her hand on the thin, bony shoulder of the pitiful figure standing in front of her. She felt her flinch. Poor child, she thought. Well, she's not a child, but she could be. What on earth will become of her now? She pulled up her coat collar, plunged her hands into her pockets, and trudged up the hill to the café where she had three cups of tea, a fruit scone and a caramel square.

It was almost an hour later before a drenched and dishevelled Biddy slumped into the chair opposite Mrs Thomas, dropping her wooden walking stick on the floor. Mrs Thomas looked at her neighbour's pale, translucent skin. Her eyes were dark and hollow and her long, wet, straggly hair was plastered all over her face. She looked like a ghost. Like one of the newly dead who had just risen from a recently covered grave. Mrs Thomas shivered.

'Ready to go home, love?' she asked.

'Yes,' whispered Biddy.

27.

Biddy was startled when she heard the rap of the door knocker. She looked up at the kitchen clock. It was 3 p.m. She must have been sitting at the kitchen table for a couple of hours now, maybe more. She remembered hearing the clock in the sitting room strike noon. She knew that she'd gone to the toilet shortly after that as she'd noticed there was hardly any tissue paper left on the toilet roll. She'd come downstairs and scribbled '*toilet roll*' on the notepad that lay on the kitchen table, below '*tea bags, eggs and bread*'. Had she slept? She wasn't sure. She rubbed her eyes and took a sip of tea from the mug in front of her. It was cold. She didn't remember making the tea. Was it before or after she wrote '*tea bags*' on the list? The rain was still pelting down outside, making a droning noise like background music. It had been raining like that for four full days now, ever since the day of her father's funeral.

The front door rapped again. Perhaps it was Mrs Thomas. Perhaps it had been Mrs Thomas yesterday too. And maybe it was Mrs Thomas who kept on phoning. She had said she would 'pop round, just to check', when she'd brought her back after the funeral. She had also invited Biddy to her house for tea that evening. Her son Ian was coming with his new girlfriend, Shirley. This was the first time she'd met Shirley, she confided to Biddy in the car on the way back from the cemetery, and she was sure she wasn't going to like her one little bit. Ian's ex-wife, Penny, Mrs Thomas had said, was such a lovely girl. Biddy had smiled, for the first time in days, maybe weeks. Longer, probably. She'd never been much of a smiler, especially since the accident. But the name Penny made her smile.

Mrs Thomas, of course, didn't know that was the reason. She thought Biddy's smile indicated that she was accepting her invitation to tea, and, truth be told, was somewhat shocked by this response. She wouldn't have offered if she'd thought there was any chance the girl would accept. Yes, she felt sorry for her, yes, she would do anything she could to help out at this difficult time, but the girl was odd, no doubt about it, and she didn't want her to get too close. And Ian, who was a few years younger than Biddy, wouldn't be one bit happy. She knew he had no time for Biddy, and really she couldn't blame him. She remembered over-hearing Ian and one of his school friends – she couldn't recall his name – sniggering about her years ago when they were at school, not long before the girl's bizarre accident on that field trip, calling her 'Bloody Weirdo'. Naturally she'd scolded them and told them not to use such bad language. 'But it's what everyone at school calls her, Mum,' Ian had pleaded in his defence. 'Well, that doesn't mean you boys have to,' Mrs Thomas had admonished, but secretly she'd agreed. Ian hated it when she made him go round to number 17 to cut the grass; how on earth was he going to react when she told him that Biddy was coming for dinner? Tonight would be tricky enough without Biddy to deal with, and without Ian giving her dirty looks throughout the meal. How was she going to get out of this hole?

'So, you'll come?' she asked, feigning brightness.

'Oh. No. No, thank you very much, Mrs Thomas.'

Mrs Thomas was relieved. 'Well, if you're sure,' she said.

Biddy didn't answer, so Mrs Thomas took that as a 'yes'. They had driven the rest of the journey back to Stanley Street in silence.

*

The person at the front door was really hammering now. Biddy thought they might actually break the door down. Maybe after all these years they should finally get a doorbell, so that people wouldn't have to hammer, she thought. Then again, they didn't normally get callers, apart from the postman who would knock now and again if he couldn't get something through the letter-box, although that was rare – or the man from NIE who needed to come in to read the electricity meter. Sometimes people would call at the door to try and sell them something or talk to them about God, but her father would always close the door in their faces without ever saying a word. Biddy knew he was really starting to get ill when he let a young man trying to sell him a discount voucher for some local restaurants actually come into the living room last year, and then left him sitting there and went to bed. Mrs Clarke and Mrs Farmer, the district nurses, always knocked on the door. But they wouldn't be coming anymore, so it couldn't be them. And anyway, they never banged like that. She didn't think that Mrs Thomas would bang like that either.

Anyway, there was no *they* anymore. There was only her.

Eventually the banging stopped, and Biddy breathed with relief. She took another sip of the cold tea, but a loud knock at the back door made her spit it out all over the table.

'Biddy?' a man's voice called.

Who knows me? she thought, suddenly scared. *What man knows my name?*

'Biddy?' the voice called again. 'Are you in there?'

She jumped up and stood against the wall opposite the back door. Through the glass panel at the top of the door she could make out the frame of a tall man wearing a big heavy coat. The rain and the fading light made it impossible for her to see his face. She twisted her fingers into the palm of her right hand and shoved her hand into her mouth. Screwing her eyes shut, she bit down hard, breaking the skin on her knuckles with her teeth. She'd stopped using the pins long ago – after the fall, when Alison couldn't get to her anymore and the need for them abated. Besides, following the fall, there'd been other pain to deal with. But in recent years, as the anxiety of dealing with her father's illness increased, she had taken to biting her knuckles as a form of relief. They were a mess.

'Biddy? Is that you? Please let me in. It's Doctor Graham. I just want to check that you're all right. Remember, I promised I would call?' Biddy looked around the empty kitchen. She stopped biting her hand and sucked the blood from the cuts on her right knuckles. Why was Dr Graham calling to see her? He had always come to see her father, but why did he want to see her? Why now? She didn't remember him making that promise. And she certainly hadn't asked him. If she needed to see him about her pills, she always made an appointment at the health centre. But she didn't need any pills. She had enough to do her for a while.

'Biddy, I can see you. I can see you standing against the wall. Won't you just open the door, please? Really, I just want to make sure that you're OK.'

Biddy wasn't sure what to do. She was relieved that the caller was Dr Graham and not a stranger. And he was a kind man. He was always nice to her and had never made her feel like a weirdo, not even once. And he had been so very, very good to her father. But she really didn't want to see or speak to anyone.

'Biddy, please. I'm getting absolutely soaked out here. I promise I won't stay long. Well, maybe just long enough for a cup of tea and a Kimberley biscuit. I've even brought a packet with me, just in case you haven't managed to get out to the shops this week. See?'

Biddy saw the outline of a plastic Tesco bag being held up against the glass on the back door. The thought of a Kimberley biscuit made her hesitate. She had given her father the last one in the only packet they'd had in the house last Sunday with his afternoon tea, and had intended to get some more when she went to Tesco on Tuesday to do the shopping. But then things had changed, and she never got to Tesco. And the garage at the bottom of the road where she went for basics didn't sell Kimberley biscuits. That's why she hadn't written *Kimberley biscuits* on the list. She didn't want to go to Tesco at the moment, so there was no point. But she would love a Kimberley biscuit right now, and a cup of fresh tea. Trouble was, she'd used up the last of the milk with her last cup. She went back to the table, wrote *milk* down on the list then opened the kitchen door.

'I don't have any milk. So if you take milk, you can't have a cup of tea.'

Dr Graham was prepared.

'Don't worry,' he said, squinting in the rain. 'I brought a pint of milk too, just in case you hadn't had a chance to get out in this blessed rain,' he added, pointing at the plastic bag. 'Semi-skimmed, hope that's OK?'

Biddy nodded. She opened the door wider, took the bag from him, put it on the table and limped over to the sink to fill the kettle.

As Dr Graham watched Biddy munch her third Kimberley biscuit in swift succession, he wondered if she'd actually eaten a proper square meal since her father had died. Since his collapse last Sunday, actually. He looked at her, worried by what he saw. She was painfully thin and deathly pale, with deep, dark hollows under her eyes. And, disturbingly, she looked even more shambolic than usual. Her wild, curly, copper hair was a mess of tats and frizz. It could do with a good cut, but he doubted that Biddy had ever been to a hairdresser in her life. The long-sleeved top she was wearing was at least two sizes too big and covered in stains. It looked like the type of garment some of his elderly patients in nursing homes wore, women in their eighties with senile dementia. He thought about his own daughter, Jemma, who was almost twenty-one and gorgeous – always turning up at the house with a new hairstyle, courtesy of her madcap hairdresser friend, Lulu, or some new outfit that she'd 'just picked up' at Topshop. Jemma and her friends were so vivacious, so full of life, so determined to make the most of their lives; some, like Jemma, studying for degrees, some, like Lulu, already working, others off travelling the world. Biddy was just a few years older, yet she might as well be living in a different century. She had no job and, as far as he could see, no friends or interests, apart from watching daytime TV and soap operas in the evenings. Every time he had called at the house in recent months, she was either watching some drivel on television or attending to her father. At least when her father was alive she'd had something to focus on, someone who needed her attention, a reason to keep going. But now, well, he didn't know what would become of her. He was aware, of course, that there had been a strange and terrible accident when Biddy was just fifteen. She still took painkillers, but, thankfully, there had never been a recurrence of the apparent psychosis reported at the time of the accident. Seeing her at the funeral, however, and looking at her now, he feared that she could well be heading for some kind of breakdown. He knew from her records that she had self-harmed in the past, and possibly still did, judging by the state of her raw, blood-stained knuckles, so a suicide attempt was something he had to consider. She needed help, but he'd need to be creative as he certainly didn't want to simply prescribe anti-depressants. And he very much doubted she would attend a regular counselling appointment if he made one.

A plan had loosely started to form in his head, but first he needed to win Biddy's trust, a task he knew would not be an easy one. Apart from the 'no milk' greeting, she hadn't uttered another word to him since she had reluctantly let him in, just nodding or shaking her head in response to the few polite questions he had asked. Not that this surprised him, as she'd rarely ever spoken to him when he had called to attend to her father. Watching Biddy munch another biscuit, however, the doctor was pleased with himself and saw his action this afternoon as a minor but speedy breakthrough. Every single time he had made a home visit to Mr Weir over the past three years, Biddy had presented him with a cup of tea and a Kimberley biscuit, on her father's request. The doctor wasn't really a biscuit person, never ate them at home or at coffee break in the surgery, but, as he prided himself on being an 'old-fashioned' GP, tea and biscuits came with the territory. In some houses, it was custard creams, in others chocolate diges-tives. Now and again there was a freshly baked scone or bun, which he did enjoy. Here, at number 17, Stanley Street, it was always Kimberley biscuits, and right now, they, and the painting in Mr Weir's bedroom, were his only connection with Biddy, the only tools he could think of using to reach out to her.

'Biddy?' he asked, casually.

Biddy looked at him blankly as she chewed her fourth biscuit.

'You know that lovely painting in your father's bedroom, the one with the seagull on the beach?'

He saw her swallow her mouthful of biscuit with a gulp and then bite down on her lip. He saw her cheeks burn and her neck flush a mottled red. He watched her eyes dart from him to the floor, to the kitchen table, to the door into the hall, and back to the table again. Her discomfort was obvious, but he carried on, his tone bright and casual.

'It's beautiful, isn't it?' he continued.

Biddy continued to stare at the table and didn't answer.

'The painting. It's beautiful,' he smiled. 'Did your father paint it himself?'

Biddy glanced up at the doctor, chewing her lip, a look of genuine confusion etched on her face.

'Or,' said Dr Graham, hoping that his hunch was correct after all. He had never seen her paint nor seen any evidence of an artistic hobby, but he just had a feeling the painting was hers. 'Did you?'

Biddy bit hard into her bottom lip and clasped her fingers tightly around her cup. Swallowing hard, she nodded her head quickly.

'You did?' Dr Graham leant slightly towards her across the table. Biddy instinctively leant back.

'Oh, Biddy, please don't be embarrassed. It's exquisite. Truly beautiful. It's Cove Bay, isn't it?'

Biddy nodded again, her expression now one of surprise.

'Well, I must say, you are an extremely talented young woman, Biddy. Really, I wish I had an ounce of your talent.' He paused for a second, as though lost in thought.

'You know the cottage in the background, the one with the blue shutters?'

Biddy nodded.

'Well, a friend of mine lives there now. Moved in just recently.'

Biddy looked up at Dr Graham, her expression a mixture of shock and awe. 'Really?' she gasped.

'Yep,' he smiled, taking another biscuit from the now half-empty packet, 'really.'

28.

Terri Drummond had encountered a number of complicated individuals in her years as a counsellor, and the more complex the character, the more she relished the challenge. In the beginning, her approach to her profession hadn't always sat well with many of her contemporaries. But her headstrong personality and steadfast belief in her own methods soon began to make an impact. She didn't go by the book – instead she threw it out of the window and wrote her own. Several, in fact. She was an enigma, but she got results. She knew it, her supporters knew it and, much to her delight, so did most of her adversaries.

Her friendship with Charlie Graham spanned over three decades, ever since the days they had worked together in the Royal City Infirmary back in the sixties, she as a nurse and Charlie as a young doctor. An urge to travel spurred by the onset of The Troubles took her to India, then Europe, then America, and when the wanderlust finally wore off, she decided to settle in London. She would nurse if she had to, or wait tables, or pull pints in an Irish bar, but she fancied something different. Something challenging. Something people-focused. A chance encounter with a grief-stricken, suicidal middle-aged man named Derek Davidson, on a park bench on Hampstead Heath, led her to inadvertently save a life, and started a whole new wonderful chapter of her own.

But now, in her late fifties, Terri realised that the chapter had become an incredibly long one, and she was tired. It was time to wind down, start a new chapter, or even, possibly, a brand new book. Her health wasn't what it used to be; a viral infection had left her with a weakened chest. The pace of London life was getting to her. And she was sad, still grieving the loss of her partner, Harry. Her doctor told her that she needed a change of air. Seeking a second opinion, she called Charlie. 'Come home, Terri,' he had said. So she did.

Terri's intentions had been to read, try out some recipes from her collection of cookery books that she'd rarely had the time to open, or maybe even write a novel, as she'd certainly had plenty of inspiration over the years to draw from. She would take long walks on the beach, meet old friends for lunch, see more of her brother, Patrick, and her nephews and nieces. But retirement didn't really suit Terri. She had kept herself busy for a while, transporting her old life from a rambling three-storey house in North London, to the small two-bedroom cottage at Cove Bay. But she quickly decided that she didn't have the patience to sit around and read all day, and realised there was limited satisfaction in cooking exotic meals for one every night of the week. A frustrating dose of writer's block was stalling her writing project, and there was only so much walking she could do in a day. She developed itchy feet, and twitching fingers. She missed her 'people', as she called them. Terri didn't feel complete unless she had someone else's life to sort out.

So, when Charlie Graham phoned her one especially dull day a couple of months after her return to Ballybrock, saying he wanted to have a chat about a particularly delicate patient of his whom he didn't want to refer to the practice counsellor, Terri leapt at the chance to get going again. Of course, she didn't let on to Charlie just how relieved she was. 'All right, darling,' she had told him. 'Just for you. But just this once, mind. I'm a lady of leisure now, don't forget. And there had better be a damn good lunch in it for me.'

29.

'You really will need to tread carefully with this one,' Charlie Graham said as the waiter cleared their plates. Terri had insisted they didn't talk business until after the main course, preferring to catch up on Charlie's family news and local gossip.

'She's a young woman called Biddy Weir. I've only been her GP for a few years,' he continued, scanning the dessert menu that was placed in front of him, 'but I fear she may have slipped through the net, so to speak, both when she was a young child, and then later in her teens, after an accident. To begin with I did wonder if she was on the autistic spectrum, but I'm pretty sure now that's not the case. She went to Ballybrock Grammar before the accident, so she's obviously bright. But then again, maybe she suffered some kind of undiagnosed brain injury after the accident.'

'Sticky toffee for me, please,' interrupted Terri, giving the waiter her pudding order, with a resolute 'both' to the offer of custard or ice cream. 'And pavlova for my friend here.'

Charlie raised his eyebrows. 'I'm assuming it's still your favourite?' she winked.

Charlie laughed and nodded. 'Oh, I've missed you, Ms Drummond.'

'Me too, darling,' smiled Terri. 'Now, tell me about the accident.'

'Hmm. A seriously bad fall when she was fifteen. Actually, from what I know, it's a miracle she survived. The details are hazy, but it happened up on Innis Mountain during a school field trip. Whatever the circumstances, she spent the night alone on the mountain, and was found the next morning, uncon-scious, with multiple injuries and hypothermia.'

'Bloody hell,' gasped Terri, draining her glass, then immedi-ately refilling it. Charlie could tell she was enjoying herself.

'I know,' he shook his head. 'She has never spoken to me about the incident and from her notes it's unclear if it really was an accident or a deliberate attempt to harm herself. Suicide, even. I did try to broach the subject a few times in the early days, but got nowhere. She just wouldn't talk about it. Actually, she barely speaks at all. She mostly just nods or shakes her head, and she tries to avoid eye contact. She's like a frightened bird. There's definitely something amiss. I just can't put my finger on it, but she's certainly not like any other young woman in her twenties or thirties that I know.'

Over pudding, Charlie told Terri everything he knew about Biddy's solitary existence with her father: the absence of a mother figure, the state of the house in Stanley Street. 'It's like an exhibit from the Folk Museum,' he said, shaking his head. He told her about the references to multiple pin pricks on her skin in the hospital report, and said that whilst he'd never seen any evidence of serious self-harm, he was worried about her now. And he told Terri about the beautiful painting of Cove Cottage that sat on Mr Weir's dresser and had planted a seed of an idea in his head.

'Anyway,' he bent down to take a yellow manila folder out of his briefcase and pushed it towards her, 'most of the back-ground info you need is in this file. I copied most of her notes.'

Terri raised an eyebrow. 'You naughty devil! Think what could happen to you if I were to squeal.'

'I know, I know,' he grimaced. 'I can't bloody well believe I'm doing this. I haven't done anything remotely like this before. Ever.'

'So why are you doing it, Charlie? And why now?'

'Truthfully, Terri, I really don't know,' he shrugged. 'Maybe it's something to do with Jemma.'

'Jemma?'

'Well, Biddy is just a few years older than her, yet she looks and lives like someone twice her age. Christ, three times, even. And I suspect she always has. When I see Jem and her friends, so full of life, so expectant of what the world can offer them, so free, I wonder what went wrong for Biddy. She lives a very lonely life, does Biddy Weir, and I just want, oh I don't know,' he shook his head, 'I want her to live a little, Terri, experience something of life before it really is too late. My worry is that now, without her father, she will have nothing left to live for whatsoever.' He paused and fiddled with his glass.

'I have to say, she does sound fascinating,' said Terri, licking the back of her spoon. 'It's like she's trapped. A caged bird, Charlie, not just a frightened one. And I think it's time we set her free.'

She raised her glass to Charlie who clinked it with his own.

'I knew you were just what she needed,' he smiled. 'Now then, as I'm the one who has dragged you out of retirement, I want to know what this is going to cost. I know it's highly unorthodox, but I do not want Biddy to be financing this herself. She obviously exists entirely on benefits and I doubt her father left her anything of any significance, apart from the house, so private counselling will be well above her budget. So, I shall be paying your fee, and that is to be our little secret.'

'Oh, Charlie, darling, I do love little secrets, but I shan't be looking for a penny.' Terri held her hand up to silence his objection. 'Now then, if we are to do this thing, it shall be on my terms, and my terms are one lunch a month with you in this delightful restaurant for the duration of the venture.'

'Terri, I can't expect you . . .'

'There will be no further negotiation, so take it or leave it, Charlie.'

'You drive a hard bargain,' smiled Charlie as they clinked glasses. 'Oh, and one more thing; she's addicted to Kimberley biscuits.'

30.

As soon as Terri got back to her cottage late that afternoon, she pulled her favourite red velvet armchair up to the fire, stretched out her legs, resting her feet on the matching foot stool, and opened Biddy's file. A bottle of her favourite Burgundy Pinot Noir sat on the table beside her and Bertie, her big black fluffy cat, snuggled down on her lap. The file made interesting reading, but more because of what it didn't tell her, than what it did. Unusually, there were virtually no notes prior to the accident. Biddy had had chickenpox when she was four and had been attended to at home by one of the old partners, Dr Tate, who Terri knew had been dead for quite a few years now. Then there was a bout of tonsillitis when Biddy was six. Apart from her BCG injection and the regulation health checks and boosters at school in those days, there was nothing else. No upset tummies, no more sore throats or colds or temperatures, no minor injuries or bumps or bruises, no headaches or growing pains or earaches or nose bleeds. Absolutely none of the common conditions that most children inevitably suffer from at some point in their young lives. And if the reason for Biddy's accident was, as Terri suspected, in some way psychological, her medical record certainly did not provide so much as a sniff of the catastrophe to come.

'Can't work this out, Bertie,' she said, shaking her head. 'As Biddy's mother was absent from the home, you'd think her father would have been even more reliant than normal on his GP.' She took a sip of wine and swished the pale red liquid around the glass. 'Of course, it doesn't mean that he was a bad father, Bert.

Perhaps he simply didn't know what to do. Perhaps no one ever told him.'

The most detailed notes in Biddy's file concerned the aftermath of the accident. The multiple injuries which Charlie had mentioned included a broken arm, several broken ribs, a fractured hip and a shattered knee cap. And then there was delirium and hypothermia to deal with too. It was, as Charlie had said, a miracle that she had survived the night, let alone the fall, or whatever it was that had caused the accident. It appeared the girl had spent several weeks in hospital recovering from her injuries and had been left with a permanent limp. She now suffered from associated arthritic pain in several of her damaged bones. The state of her mental health just after the accident was described as 'disturbed' and 'possibly psychotic', but a subsequent psychiatric appraisal one year after the event concluded that, while Biddy was withdrawn and possibly depressed, she was not mentally ill.

Terri finished her glass of wine and poured another. She closed the folder and put it on the table, a tingle of excitement vibrating in her spine. This was the most alive she'd felt in months.

31.

Terri Drummond didn't look like a real person to Biddy. She seemed more like a fantastical character from a children's television programme. Biddy didn't draw people, but as soon as she saw Terri Drummond, she thought she'd like to draw her. She was a very large lady, with enormous bulging breasts that looked like two extra stomachs on her chest. She wore a long, rusty brown, layered cotton skirt which came right down to her feet, just skimming a pair of purple suede boots with very pointy toes, and a wildly patterned shirt with more colours on it than Biddy could count. Huge gold loopy earrings hung from her ears, rings adorned almost every finger, and several wooden bracelets dangled on each wrist. Her eyelids sparkled with bronze eye-shadow and her orange lipstick matched the colour on her long, pointy fingernails. But the most striking thing about Terri Drummond was her hair. It was red – not copper, like Biddy's own hair, but a bright, flaming red – and pinned up at the back of her head with bits sticking out, like feathers. Biddy was mesmerised. Terri's hair was exactly the same colour as the feathers of the scarlet ibis, Biddy's favourite tropical bird, just as Dr Graham had said. Biddy had never seen anyone remotely like Terri Drummond before, and she liked her immediately. She was certain that anyone who looked like a tropical bird would be a good, nice person. Yes, she decided, Dr Graham was right, and as Terri extended her ring-clad fingers to grasp Biddy's hand and usher her into the house, Biddy was so unexpectedly glad that she'd come.

Dr Graham had been trying to get Biddy to visit his friend Terri ever since that wet, stormy evening he'd visited just after her father's funeral. Her interest had initially been sparked; how could it not have when she lived in Cove Cottage? Dr Graham couldn't have known just how much she loved that little cottage; that when she went to Cove Bay to paint she would pretend that she lived there. So when he said he thought Biddy would really like Terri, and that maybe she might like to visit her at the cottage sometime and take the painting with her, she almost shouted her reply: 'When?'

She couldn't believe what she'd said. She wasn't normally eager to meet new people and, as far as she could remember, she'd never actually been to visit anyone. But the thought of going inside Cove Cottage, actually right inside it instead of just standing on the beach staring at it, was stronger than her natural instinct to say no.

But then Dr Graham had ruined it all by saying that Terri was actually a counsellor, albeit a retired one.

'I've changed my mind. I don't want to see a counsellor,' she had said, quietly, and stood up to move the teacups from the kitchen table to the sink.

'You know, counsellors can help with all kinds of things, Biddy,' Dr Graham had replied.

'Like what? Like . . .' Biddy caught her breath. Like being a weirdo? She had wanted to ask, but of course she couldn't.

'Well, like relationship problems between married couples, or stress at work, or trauma following, say, a car accident or an attack,' Dr Graham had paused. 'Or loneliness, or grief.'

Biddy had dug her scraggy, ragged fingernails into the palms of her hands to distract the tears she felt stinging at the back of her eyes. Dr Graham obviously wanted her to see this Terri person because he thought she might be able to cure her of her weirdness. Well, it was too late for that. She took a deep breath and swallowed hard. 'Will you please go home now?' she'd whispered, staring at the floor. So he did.

But he hadn't given up. Over the next month or so, he popped in if he was 'just passing' a couple of times a week. To begin with she was irritated by his visits. Now that her father was dead, there didn't seem to be any real reason for this contact. At first, Biddy would barely speak to him at all, just nod or shake her head. But she gradually became used to his visits, looked forward to them even, and found herself feeling a twinge of disappointment if he didn't stay for a cup of tea and a Kimberley biscuit. Dr Graham was the only real human contact she had now that her papa was gone, apart from shop assistants and bus conductors. He never stayed long, but most times he did drop his counsellor friend's name into his conversation.

'Terri saw a seal in the bay the other day.'

'You know, I brought Terri a packet of Kimberley biscuits yesterday and she loved them too.'

'Guess what? Terri swears she saw a heron on the rocks by Cove Cottage on Sunday.'

But the comment that finally did it was the one about Terri's hair.

'Heavens,' Dr Graham said one morning, a few weeks after his visits began, when he glanced at Biddy's large encyclopaedia of birds which lay open on the kitchen table. Staring up at him from the open page was the resplendent scarlet ibis, which, next to the seagull, was Biddy's favourite bird. 'What a beautiful creature,' he exclaimed in awe. 'It reminds me of Terri. What is it?'

'It's a scarlet ibis,' she replied bluntly, holding his gaze, 'a tropical bird.'

'Well, it certainly is magnificent and its feathers are exactly the same colour as Terri's hair.' He shook his head in amazement. 'Exactly.'

'OK,' Biddy had said, surprising herself, not quite sure how the word had popped out of her mouth. 'OK. I'll go to see her.'

And now here she was.

'Biddy,' beamed Terri. 'Biddy, Biddy, Biddy. What a beautiful name. Is it short for Bridget?' Biddy was startled. For a start, nobody had ever told her that her name was beautiful, and secondly, she wondered why it would be short for anything.

'Erm, no, Miss Drummond,' she stuttered, feeling her cheeks flush with embarrassment. 'I don't think so. I'm just Biddy. Just Biddy Weir.'

'Well, I'm Terri,' Terri smiled. 'Might as well start off on first-name terms. Much easier, don't you think?' Biddy nodded, but Terri barely stopped for breath. 'None of this Miss or Ms or Mrs clap-trap here. Anyway, Biddy, the reason I ask about your name is that I had an aunt called Biddy. Mad as a bat she was. Bonkers. Kept chickens in her kitchen. Always knew exactly who was who. A chicken is a chicken to me, but not to Aunt Biddy. Loved that woman. Still miss her.' She paused momentarily and shook her head, then launched back in again. 'Anyway, point of the matter is, *she* was a Bridget, but everyone called her Biddy. Hadn't heard the name again, until now. Isn't it great to have a name that's a little bit different? Makes you stand out from the crowd. I'm Theresa by birth. Never liked it. Couldn't stand the name. Shortened it to Terri when I was nine, and I haven't looked back since. Causes some confusion, mind you, as most folk think I'm going to be a Mister.' She paused again, this time to chuckle. '*Anyway*, Biddy,' she continued to a transfixed Biddy, 'you didn't come here to listen to me rambling on about names. Here, let me take your coat. And what about your stick? Shall I pop it into the umbrella stand?'

Biddy winced and shook her head, tightening her grip on the stick. She did like this lady, was immediately fascinated by her, but she wasn't letting go of her stick, just in case she needed it. When she felt dizzy or sick or panicky, holding onto her stick as tightly as she could helped her to focus. She didn't actually always need it for walking support, but it had become something of a safety net for her over the years. 'You'd rather keep it?' asked Terri brightly, apparently not in the least bit perplexed by Biddy's behaviour. Biddy nodded. 'Not a problem,' Terri almost sang. 'Not a problem at all. Now Biddy, come on into my office-cum-snug-room-cum-pile-it-all-in room.'

Terri ushered her into a small, cluttered, brightly coloured room, and guided her towards one of two battered leather armchairs beside a big roaring fire.

'I've really been looking forward to meeting you, Biddy. I hear from Dr Graham that you're quite a talented artist and that my little cottage actually makes an appearance in one of your masterpieces.' Biddy felt her cheeks flush with heat. She wished for a second that she hadn't brought the painting. What if Terri didn't like it or thought it was stupid? She tightened her grip on the parcel under her arm.

'Oh, my, is that it?' Terri gasped.

Biddy blinked and swallowed. What on earth was she doing here? Why had she ever agreed to this? How had she ever thought this colourful lady would like one of her stupid pictures?

But Terri was beaming broadly and nodding at the parcel.

'I'd really love to see it, Biddy. May I?'

Biddy nodded slowly, and Terri gently removed the package from under her arm. It was wrapped in several layers of Tesco bags.

'Oh, my word,' Terri gasped as she pulled off the last plastic bag. Biddy looked at her. She couldn't quite work out from Terri's facial expression whether it was a good 'oh my word', or a bad one.

'It's fabulous, Biddy. Truly fabulous. I love it. When did you paint this? Was it recently?'

Biddy shook her head.

'A-about three years ago, I think,' she said quietly.

Actually, she knew exactly when she had painted it. It was the summer her father had become properly ill, just at the point when his mind became sick too. Her papa's body was already poorly, but when his mind stopped working, Biddy had to spend all of her time looking after him. Every second. All of a sudden there wasn't any time to go to the beach and paint anymore. Since the fall, her art and her father were all that she had in life; not that she'd had very much more before. But there was no more school, as she simply hadn't gone back. It had taken many months to recover from her injuries, and by the time her body had healed enough, it was too late to catch up in time for her O Level exams, and nothing more was said about school. If her father had ever had a conversation with Mr Duncan, or the education authorities, she never heard about it. So she drew, and then she painted, discovering that water colours were even more to her liking than pencils. The beach was her solace, and once she got used to it, the stick didn't hinder her treks along the mile or so of coast down towards Cove Bay.

But once her father's illness properly struck, she would only leave him alone briefly to nip to the shop, or to pick up a prescription from the health centre, and even then only if he was asleep. That painting was the last one she had done. She hadn't even been to the beach since. It also represented the last glimmer of sanity and lucid affection she had received from her father. The day she painted it, she had come home and left it propped up against the teapot on the kitchen table to dry. Then she went to the bathroom to wash the paint stains from her hands. When she returned, she had found her father standing in the kitchen holding the painting, just staring at it. As she walked into the room, she was sure she saw him wipe a tear from his eye.

'It's beautiful, lass, so beautiful,' he had said. 'You've a talent. A rare talent indeed. I should have . . .' he trailed off, not finishing the sentence, and put the painting back on the table. Biddy stared at him, willing him to say whatever it was he was going to say, to tell her what he should have done. Even now, all these years later she still thought about it and wondered. But he'd simply turned around and shuffled into the sitting room where he'd spent the rest of the evening staring out of the window until Biddy brought him his meal on a tray. But later, when she took the usual nightly mug of Ovaltine and concoction of bedtime tablets up to his bedroom, there was the painting propped up on top of the tallboy. And that is where it had stayed, until this morning, when she had brought it downstairs, blown the dust off it, and wrapped it in several layers of Tesco bags.

Terri was saying something else now, and Biddy had to force herself to focus. She thought she had just asked if she would paint one for her someday, but she wasn't sure. So she said nothing and stared blankly at Terri, who was holding the painting at arm's length, beaming at it, waiting for her to speak again. She had a genuine smile; like Judy Finnigan from the television. Not a fake one, like Honey Sinclair.

Terri beamed again at Biddy. 'Sit down, sit down,' she said, propping the painting up against some books on her desk. 'I'll just set it there so I can admire it while you're here,' she clapped her hands together. 'Now then, make yourself comfy, while I go and put the kettle on. Tea or coffee?'

'Tea, please,' Biddy whispered.

'Fabulous. Tea it is.'

32.

Biddy sat down on one of the leather armchairs, her mind spinning as she looked around the room. It was as colourful as Terri herself. The walls were adorned with framed certificates and child-like paintings in bold colours and patterns. On one wall hung lots of photographs, maybe twenty or thirty of them, all in different, colourful frames. There were several of young children – laughing, pulling funny faces, eating ice cream. There were lots of group shots with too many people in them for Biddy to make out, a few weddings, and three bunched together of the same dark-haired man. He was holding a tabby cat in one, bent over a desk writing something in another, and sitting on a whitewashed wall with a deep blue sea behind him in the third. Biddy wondered who all these people were: if the happy children belonged to Terri herself, if the man was her husband, or her brother. There was only one photograph in her own house: the hazy, faded, brownish one that sat on the mantelpiece, of her grandfather and grandmother on their wedding day. There were no photographs of her. And none of her mother.

She had never been in a room like this one before. There were books bulging off shelves and stacked up in uneven piles all over the floor. On a desk in the corner, which was littered with papers and files, sat a computer and an old typewriter. Candles of all shapes and sizes perched on the desk, the windowsill, the mantelpiece and the shelves. The wall, which was visible beneath the paintings and photographs, was painted in a vibrant shade of turquoise blue. Every room in Biddy's home had been decorated in the same flock wallpaper, which had once been cream but was now more like pale yellow. Her father had always been meticulous about tidiness, so there were never any books – or anything else for that matter – lying on the floor. Biddy didn't have a computer, and the only pictures on the walls in the house were two faded reproduction prints by some unknown artist which had belonged to her father's grandmother. Apart, of course, from the watercolour which her father had kept propped up on the chest of drawers in his bedroom, the painting which had brought her here. Biddy hadn't thought it possible to have a room as colourful and manically chaotic as this one. She liked it. And, as she watched her swish back into the room carrying a tray with a teapot, two bright orange mugs and a plate of biscuits, Kimberley biscuits, Biddy decided that she liked Terri Drummond too.

'Milk?' asked Terri.

'Yes, please,' replied Biddy, although she couldn't see a milk jug.

'Crumbs! I've forgotten it. Just be a jiffy.' Terri pulled herself out of the chair opposite Biddy with obvious effort and disappeared again into the kitchen. Biddy could hear her humming as she returned.

'Oh, dear,' Terri exclaimed, as she re-entered the room. 'I didn't ask if you take sugar.'

Biddy shook her head.

'Good. I take three spoonfuls myself in coffee, but loathe the stuff in tea. Biscuit? One of my favourites, these. Love them.'

'Me too' nodded Biddy, smiling, as she took a Kimberley from the plate.

'One of the best things about coming home. Kimberley biscuits. Could hardly get them in London. Oh, damn. I've forgotten the napkins. Won't be a tick.' Up she struggled again and bustled off into the kitchen, returning with a roll of kitchen roll.

'Can't find the napkins. Heaven knows where they are. Will this do?' Biddy nodded as Terri tore off a couple of sheets and handed them to her.

'Right, then,' said Terri, sitting down in the armchair again and reaching over to take a biscuit herself. 'Shall we get . . . oh bugger!' She set the biscuit back on the tray. 'I meant to switch my answer machine to automatic pick-up, so we don't get interrupted by the telephone. Now, where is the blessed thing? Bear with me Biddy, and have another Kimberley.'

Biddy was becoming more fascinated by Terri by the second. She munched on another biscuit and watched, intrigued, as Terri shuffled around the room, lifting books and boxes and cushions and magazines, looking for the answer machine. Finally she found it, flicked the appropriate switch and once more sat down in the armchair. 'My tea will be cold at this rate,' she laughed, manoeuvring her ample behind back into the chair. 'Gracious,' she exclaimed, shoving her right hand underneath her bottom and pulling out a pair of glasses, 'my specs. I wondered where these had got to.' She smiled at Biddy and shook her head as she finally picked up the Kimberley. 'I do apologise, Biddy. I'm such a scatterbrain!'

'That's OK,' said Biddy quietly. 'I'm a weirdo.'

'Really?' asked Terri, through a mouthful of biscuit. 'Well now,' she beamed, and took a sip of her tea, 'I am intrigued. So, Biddy Weir, how exactly did you come to be a weirdo?' Biddy thought about Terri's question for a few seconds. She had been a weirdo for so long now that it was hard to remember life before Alison's life-changing revelation. She didn't think of herself as a *bloody* weirdo so much these days, as she hadn't actually heard anyone call her by that name for many years. She knew of course, by the way that most people still looked at her, that she really was one, but somehow, just being a weirdo was easier to live with. And, as she had discovered, people in general paid less attention to a weirdo adult than they did to a weirdo child. Certainly if she ever encountered someone she recognised from school, on the bus, say, or at Tesco, they would generally just ignore her – which was fine. Perfect, actually. Better to be ignored than, well, than what used to happen.

'I think I've always been one,' she finally said, whispered really, eyes down, staring into the teacup she was holding onto as firmly as possible to stop herself from shaking. 'Probably since I was born, really, but I only found out in Primary 6. In Miss Justin's class. Alison Flemming told me.'

'Alison Flemming told you that you were a weirdo?' asked Terri.

Biddy nodded, still focusing on the teacup. 'She said I was a bloody weirdo, actually. Well, first of all, she called me Biddy Weirdo and everyone thought it was funny because she'd changed my name from Weir to Weir**do**. But then . . .' Biddy paused and glanced up at Terri, who was still sipping her tea. She gulped and wondered why on earth she was talking like this to a stranger. To anyone. The very act of talking was surprising her as much as what she was talking about. The only other person she had talked to in this way before was Miss Jordan, and that was almost half her lifetime ago.

'Biddy,' said Terri gently, placing her cup on the floor, 'if this is too painful for you, you really don't have to continue. This is just supposed to be a wee getting-to-know-each-other chat. I'd really like to hear more about this Alison girl and the things she said to you. But if you don't feel strong enough today, we can do it next time? There's no rush.'

She smiled that smile again – a proper warm, cosy, soft smile. The type of smile Biddy imagined a mother would have, or a sister. She thought again about Miss Jordan and her smile. Terri didn't look remotely like Miss Jordan, yet there was something about her manner that reminded her of the teacher's kindness. On her way here today, Biddy assumed that this would be a one-off visit. The idea of a 'next time' hadn't even occurred to her. But now it did, and to her astonishment she hoped it would.

'OK,' she nodded, and took another sip of tea.

33.

'Next time' happened the following Wednesday, an arrangement made at the end of her first visit. Biddy hadn't been able to get Terri or Cove Cottage out of her head, and in the days that followed, often found herself wondering if the meeting had actually happened, or if she'd dreamt it. But now, as she took the bus back again, panic rose in her chest. What if Terri wasn't so nice this time? What if she made her talk about things she didn't want to talk about? What if she'd forgotten that Biddy was even coming?

But she needn't have worried. Terri greeted her with a beaming smile, ushered her in out of the rain with the same busy manner, and had a pot of tea and a plate of Kimberley biscuits waiting for them in the study.

After a few minutes' chitchat from Terri about the relentless dreadful weather, during which Biddy simply sipped her tea and nodded politely, Terri clapped her hands together.

'So, Biddy,' she smiled, 'I've been thinking a lot about this weirdo business you mentioned last week, and this, what's her name, Angela?'

'Alison,' Biddy mumbled. 'She's Alison. And it's bloody weirdo, not just weirdo. I was,' she cleared her throat slightly, 'am, I am a bloody weirdo.'

'Ah, yes, Alison,' Terri nodded slowly, leaning back into her armchair.

'You know, I've been called a bloody weirdo once or twice myself. In fact,' she snorted, 'I'm sure some people have called me worse. But that doesn't mean I am one. Granted, I might be a bit different to them. Maybe I don't look the same, or think in

240

the same way, or dress the same,' she waved a hand over her long jade-green and turquoise-blue velvet dress and chuckled. 'Case in point. But it doesn't mean I'm weird, or a bad person. And it certainly doesn't mean I deserve to be treated badly. And you know, so what? I like it. I actually like being different, and I'll tell you what, Biddy, I use it to my advantage. Anyway, aren't we all just a little bit weird in our own unique way? What was it John Lennon said? "*It's weird not to be weird.*"'

Biddy stopped sipping her tea and glanced at Terri. She couldn't believe that anyone would ever call this woman a bloody weirdo. It wasn't possible. As far as she could see, there was nothing remotely weird about Terri Drummond at all. There'd been nothing weird about Penny Jordan either, or her father, or even Alison, for that matter. Had there? And did John Lennon really say that? She suddenly felt light-headed and, placing her cup on the table beside her, reached for her stick, gripping it tightly.

'OK, so maybe you looked different to this Alison girl,' Terri continued, lightly shrugging her shoulders. 'Maybe *you* didn't wear the same kind of clothes, or didn't play the same games she played or have the same kind of schoolbag. You didn't conform to her vision of what "normal" should be. But, well, so what?'

Biddy looked down and began picking at her nails. She was starting to perspire under her armpits now and her stomach was churning.

'Biddy,' Terri said softly, leaning forward and fixing Biddy with a kind but stern look. 'Listen to me. Just because a nasty little girl called you a bloody weirdo when you were eight or nine years old does not mean that you were a bloody weirdo then, and it certainly doesn't mean that you're one now.'

Biddy clutched her stick again, digging the nail of her fore-finger into her thumb as she did so. A mass of tangled images cluttered her head. A flash of a school bench in a gym hall, a café in the supermarket, a cherished letter. Terri's words echoed what Miss Jordan had said to her all those years ago, almost word for word. But she *was* a weirdo. A bloody weirdo. A freak. A fuck-up. A worthless waste of space. She was all of those things that Alison Flemming and the others had said she was all those years ago; that almost every person she had encountered throughout her life thought she was – even if they didn't say it. That was who she was, who she had always been. Who she would always be.

'Tell me, Biddy, how long did this go on for, this Alison busi-ness?' asked Terri gently.

'Until . . .' Biddy trailed off and started picking at her fingers again.

'Until?'

'Until I didn't see her anymore. Well, until she didn't see me anymore.'

For a few seconds, the only sound in the room was the spit-ting of wood burning in the fire. Then tears began to run down Biddy's face, slowly at first, then streaming, gushing like a river bursting through a dam. Her whole body seemed to twist and she started to shake with juddering, jolting spasms, her sobs loud and rasping. Although mortified, she couldn't stop. She couldn't work out why she was crying; and yet she knew exactly why: the memory of the Alison-years brought back to life; pain for the life that she knew she hadn't lived, that she couldn't and wouldn't ever live; and, finally, the tears for her papa that she thought she couldn't shed – her beloved papa who, despite the exhaustion of the past few years, she missed with every inch of her soul.

Terri stood up and moved over to Biddy's chair. Stooping over, she put her right arm around Biddy's back and placed her left hand on the top of her head, drawing it into her chest. She held her like that until it passed, when the light outside had faded and the fire was almost out. Then, when Biddy had settled, Terri offered to drive her home.

'It's getting late and it's pretty stormy outside,' she said, half expecting Biddy to turn her down. 'Besides, I need to get some cat food for Bertie from the garage at the roundabout.'

'OK,' Biddy whispered.

They didn't speak at all on the thirteen-minute drive from Cove Cottage to number 17, Stanley Street, except for Terri to get directions. When she drew up outside Biddy's house, Terri placed her left hand lightly on top of Biddy's right one.

'Biddy, I know how stressful that was for you, but I'd really like you to come and visit me again. Would you do that? Maybe we could set up a regular day, or time? Hmm? What do you think?'

Biddy didn't respond at all for a few seconds, then she nodded.

'You would?' smiled Terri.

Biddy nodded again.

'Well, that's great, Biddy. That's great.' Terri beamed. 'Tell you what, I'll call you tomorrow and then we can set something up. OK? A definite day and time that suits you. Will you be in at, say, eleven o'clock in the morning?'

Another nod.

'OK, then I'll phone you at eleven. Here,' she rummaged around in the glove compartment and found an old receipt and a biro, 'scribble your number down on the back of this.' She already had Biddy's number of course, from Charlie, but she knew it would be better for Biddy to hand it over herself. That way the girl was maintaining an element of control.

'Thank you,' she smiled, taking the slip of paper and setting it on the dashboard. 'It was nice to see you again, Biddy Weir.'

Biddy undid her seatbelt, opened the car door and stepped onto the pavement.

'Thank you,' she said quickly, glancing back at Terri. 'It was nice to see you again too.'

34.

Terri phoned Biddy at eleven o'clock on the dot the next morning, half expecting her not to answer. She was slightly worried that after her emotional breakdown on her second visit, she might have lost her. But, to her surprise, Biddy picked up on the second ring, and agreed without any hesitation to come back to Cove Cottage the following Wednesday. Yes, she told Terri, Wednesdays were good. The only proviso was that their appointment should be in the early afternoon, as Biddy said she couldn't leave home before 12.30, and needed to be back by 5 p.m. Terri was intrigued, wondering what required Biddy to be bound by those hours, but the arrangement suited her well, as she liked to potter and bake in the mornings. No doubt she would unravel the mystery in time. The telephone conversation was short and devoid of any small talk, but Terri understood that chitchat was not part of Biddy's language. She had to let her open up at her own pace, no matter how long it took. That familiar tingle of excitement rattled through her again: she was already in her element.

It was, just as Terri had expected, a slow process; but gradually, over the next few months, Biddy revealed some of the shocking details of her life as Bloody Weirdo. Some days, she would recount a particular incident in meticulous detail, as though it had only just happened. On other days, her memories were disjointed, fragmented and agitated. Sometimes Biddy said virtually nothing at all, and then there were days when she repeated the details of events she had already recalled. But Terri understood the benefits of patience. There was no rush. Biddy's wound was obviously so very deep and still, despite the passage of time, so painfully raw that it would take a very long time to heal. It had never been properly tended to. But heal it would. Of that, Terri was sure.

On Biddy's fourth visit to Cove Cottage, she told Terri about Red Paint Day. That afternoon, as rain pelted at the window of the study and the flames of the fire raged wildly, whipped up by the wind from the chimney, Biddy talked non-stop for almost half an hour. She hadn't ever spoken at such length before – not just to Terri, but to anyone; not even Miss Jordan. She never believed herself capable of finding so many words to say out loud. A lifetime of virtual silence was shattered in one afternoon. She hadn't even realised that she'd remembered the incident so clearly; but it was all there, to the last detail, locked inside her own private memory box with so many other hideous recollections, which were finally being given the chance to escape. Like birds flying the nest.

When she was done, Terri let silence sit in the room for a few seconds, waiting while Biddy emerged from the trance-like state she'd been in. When Biddy finally looked up, her eyes clear of tears but brimming with sorrow, she let out a long, slow, heavy sigh.

'Would you like to hear about the disco now?' she whispered.

Terri stood up and went over to Biddy's chair. Kneeling down she clasped Biddy's folded hands in her own and looked her in the eye. 'Let's save that for another day, Biddy,' she said gently. 'I think you've had enough for now. How about I make a pot of tea? I baked a chocolate cake this morning for the first time in years. I think it tastes rather yummy, but I wouldn't mind a second opinion, so let's go through to the kitchen, shall we?'

At the next few sessions, Biddy reverted to form and barely spoke at all. But Terri wasn't concerned. She simply decided that they should cut the 'official business' short and retire instead to the kitchen for refreshments. Apart from the fact that Biddy responded well to her baking, it was proving immensely pleasurable for Terri to have someone to experiment on. At last her cookery books were being put to some, if limited, use, and, thank God, she didn't have to eat those bloody Kimberley biscuits every week. And she was happy to chatter away about this and that and anything at all, while Biddy ate, and listened, and smiled. Those smiles, they melted Terri's heart. With every week that passed, Terri could see the change in Biddy. Yes, it was subtle, sometimes barely visible at all – but all the same, it was there. It was like watching a china doll slowly come to life.

35.

Two months had passed since Biddy's first encounter with Terri and, to her immense surprise, she found herself looking forward to her Wednesday visits to Cove Cottage more and more with every week that passed. She had started to feel a strange, fluttering sensation in her tummy as the bus passed through the town and the coast road came into sight: a bit like little butterflies dancing around inside her. It reminded her of the feeling she sometimes got when she used to paint the birds on the beach and they would swoop and dance and chatter, just for her. Or that surge of pleasure she'd felt all those years ago on the day Miss Jordan had taken her shopping. And on the bus journey her mouth would start to water in anticipation of what delicious treat Terri might have baked that morning.

The cottage was everything she had ever dreamed it would be, and more; and each time she stepped across the threshold, it took her breath away that she was actually going inside the quaint little house she used to sketch and had fallen in love with from a distance many years ago; into its very hall, and study, and kitchen. She'd started to use the bathroom even if she didn't need to go, just to sit on the pale pine toilet seat and wash her hands with the soap that smelt of lemons, and dry them with what must surely be the softest, fluffiest, whitest towels in the world. Apart from her own home, she had only ever been inside one other house in her entire life, and that had just been twice to Mrs Thomas's. On both occasions she'd gone to number 21 to deliver post which had been put through their letterbox by mistake, and even then she'd never been invited further than the hall. Not that she'd have gone anyway. Of course she was going to go to Miss Jordan's house once, but then, as it happened, she never got the chance.

But Biddy knew it wasn't just being in the cottage that she looked forward to – it was spending time with Terri too. She missed her father dreadfully, and wondered now if the pain she felt in her heart was partly due to loneliness? Oh, she was used to being alone, she'd been alone her whole life long, and she'd never really questioned it before; never considered loneliness as an actual emotion that applied to her. But now, as her contact with Terri rolled on from one week to another, she began to wonder if the permanent ache in her chest, which had been there since her papa died but seemed to ease in Terri's presence, was something more than grief.

Of course Biddy was well aware that, as a counsellor, Terri was simply doing her job, but with each visit to the cottage they spent less and less time in Terri's office, and more in the kitchen, drinking tea and eating cake. She had started to feel less of a 'patient' as such, and more of a . . . ? Precisely what, she wasn't quite sure. She hesitated to use the word 'friend' after her previous experience with friendship, as the last thing in the world she wanted to do was get Terri into any kind of trouble. But trouble with whom? Dr Graham? It struck her then that Terri must be getting paid by someone to help her. After all, why would she see her voluntarily? No one – apart from her father of course, and Miss Jordan, and maybe, lately at any rate, Dr Graham, and Mrs Thomas on the odd occasion, and the doctors and nurses at the hospital after her fall – had ever willingly chosen to spend time in her company. So if Terri *was* getting paid, was the money coming from Dr Graham himself?

These were the thoughts that had almost stopped her from getting off the bus at the Cove Cottage stop on this particular Wednesday afternoon. Maybe, she thought, her cheeks flushed with humiliation, Terri was only nice to her because she was getting paid to be nice, and not because she actually liked her. Who was she kidding? She almost choked on the idea; the very notion that someone like Terri Drummond would want to be her friend made her feel sick to her stomach with a wave of self-loathing. The lovely fluttering sensation vanished in a flash as she allowed the dark thoughts to take over. By the time the bus turned down Bay Road towards the shore, Biddy had decided to stay on board, get to the station in Whinport, the next village on, and wait there for the 3.30 return. She'd phone Terri when she got back and apologise. Tell her that her leg was playing up, or something. Tell her she was sorry, but she couldn't come back again. And that would be that. Tears welled in her eyes and that old familiar lump, which hadn't been around much these past few weeks, despite her father's absence, throbbed at the back of her throat.

But then, there was Cove Cottage in the distance, jutting out of the headland like a glistening pearl, its whitewashed walls and bright blue shutters glimmering in the early March sunshine. Biddy's heart lurched. She imagined Terri in the kitchen, preparing a tray of something delicious for them to eat, placing out bright floral napkins and her favourite mugs with the poppies on them. The memory of the second time she'd gone to the cottage rushed through her; when she'd somehow, strangely, easily, poured her heart out. When Terri's own words had echoed those of Miss Jordan's from all those years ago; when Terri had silently, gently, held her whilst she wept. No one would touch her if they didn't want to, never mind hug her. She knew that. No – Terri was good, and kind, and clever, and funny, and maybe even properly liked her just a little bit. And, yes, maybe some day, she might even be her friend.

'Oh,' she uttered a little gasp of panic as the bus stop came into sight, and struggled out of her regular window seat three rows from the front (far enough from the driver but close enough that she didn't have to walk too far up the aisle or pass too many other passengers) just in time.

As Biddy rang the old brass doorbell she felt so relieved, and the smile she presented to Terri when she opened the door took not an ounce of effort. And when Terri asked her if she liked scones she wondered how she could have been so stupid as to even consider not coming here today. She hadn't had a scone for months, not since Papa had become really sick, and she missed them. They used to bring home fruit scones from the Griddle bakery every Wednesday after their weekly outing to Ballybrock market. But that stopped when Papa became too poorly to make the trip. And when he told her one day that the scones from Tesco were repulsive and shouldn't be served to pigs, she never bought them again. But she'd never had a scone that had actually been baked by a person in their very own kitchen, and right now, right this moment, she was desperate for one.

'Oh, yes,' she beamed at Terri, feeling a sudden desire to hug her. 'I love them.'

'Marvellous,' Terri sang, as she took Biddy's coat and hung it on the coat stand. 'Well then, you can help me bake some. I haven't had time yet today to make anything for our afternoon tea, and there's a new recipe I'm desperate to try out. So we can do it together now. It's got raspberries in it and,' she winked, 'white chocolate.'

There was a sudden clatter. Biddy had dropped her stick.

In a split second, her smile vanished, and reality slapped her in the face. She'd made a huge mistake. She should have stayed on the bus after all. Terri wanted her to bake – and she couldn't. She still couldn't. All these years on and she'd never learnt. Oh, she'd picked up the basics of cooking from her father over the years, and could make things like stew, and vegetable broth, and shepherd's pie. When he became ill she really had no choice, and she sometimes quite enjoyed it. It was a distraction. But she wasn't adventurous; she never deviated from the limited repertoire of recipes passed on from her father – acquired over time by watching him closely as he prepared the meals, rather than any handwritten instructions. Even though she often watched the cookery items on her daytime TV shows with awe, wondering what things like pasta bakes and mushroom risotto and goat's cheese and onion tart tasted like, she didn't experiment, and she never baked. Her baking chance had passed. And that was that.

And now that humiliating truth was about to be revealed to Terri. She felt sick. What was better – to own up and make a fool of herself, or try to bake and make a fool of herself? Why was she so incapable of doing normal things? Because she was a weirdo, that's why: a dumb, stupid, bloody weirdo.

'Biddy? Are you OK? What happened? My word, you look as though you're about to pass out.'

Terri had grabbed her by the elbow and she realised with a jolt that she'd dropped her stick on the floor. She might as well get it over with.

'I can't bake,' she stuttered, her cheeks flushed with shame, as Terri retrieved the stick and handed it to her. She waited for

Terri to laugh, to tell her she couldn't be serious, that all women her age could bake. Maybe now Terri would realise what a weirdo she was after all.

'Well then,' Terri beamed, 'I shall bake the scones, and you can make the tea.'

36.

As it turned out, that afternoon turned out to be Biddy's best visit yet to Cove Cottage. The baking process fascinated Biddy and her initial tension and discomfort eased remarkably quickly. She was mesmerised by Terri's hands, transfixed as they expertly and effortlessly measured out the ingredients into a big pale blue bowl, bound them together, and moulded the mixture into perfectly formed mounds of dough – which looked good enough to eat before they had even gone into the oven. Biddy felt an overwhelming desire to grab the wooden spoon and lick it clean. There was an energy to Terri's baking that reminded her of painting and she realised with a jolt how much she missed her art. She would draw again soon, she decided. She would draw for Terri.

And she learnt so much more about Terri herself that afternoon. So far, Terri's chatter had always been interestingly frivolous: her plans for the garden and her trips to the garden centre; her constant disagreements with the snooty receptionist at the health centre who, in her opinion, Charlie needed to 'boot the hell out'; the proposed new out of town retail park; and, of course, her beloved Bertie. Biddy always loved her chatter, regardless of the subject matter. As far as she was concerned, Terri could make cleaning toilets sound interesting. And it was so wonderful to listen to an actual person talk, rather than someone on the television. But today as she made the scones and bustled about the kitchen, Terri chatted easily about her own childhood in Ballybrock, growing up in one of the large Victorian terrace houses on Shorehill Road, just behind the station. She was one of five, she said, number two, with two sisters and two brothers. She rhymed through all the names of her brothers and sisters in order of age: Patrick, herself, Caroline and Kate. 'And then,' she hesitated, 'there was Jamesy. We didn't have Jamesy for long,' she sighed. 'He died a few days before his fourth birthday.'

Biddy gasped loudly. The whole time Terri had been talking, she had been painting a colourful mental image of this big bustling family living in one of those tall regal houses on Shorehill Road that she'd always admired. She had often noticed the birds huddling in rival gangs on the majestic peaks of their roofs which were visible from the beach. The bubble was growing bigger every second. She didn't expect it to burst. 'Oh,' she said quietly. 'Poor Jamesy.' She had to swallow down a lump, fearing she might cry.

Terri wiped some flour from her hands with a tea towel. 'Well, he lived a lot longer than anyone expected him to,' she said, smiling wistfully. 'He was poorly when he was born, you see, and he suffered a lot throughout his little life. Even then we knew it was a blessing when he went. But he was such a bright wee thing, and utterly beautiful. I still think about him.'

'Oh my goodness,' said Biddy softly. 'I am so sorry, Terri. It must have been awful.'

'It was,' Terri nodded. 'Frightful. But every family has its heartache. And I'm lucky I have my sisters and Patrick. Caroline lives in Canada now, has done for thirty years or so, and Kate lives in Cornwall. I used to see quite a lot of her when I was in London; now I see more of Patrick who still lives here. We're quite close. But I do miss us all being together.' She hesitated. 'It's not that long since you buried your father, Biddy. You must miss him very much.'

Biddy nodded and lowered her head, fixing her stare on the mixing bowl. She did miss him, but she understood that, like Jamesy, it was a blessing that his suffering was over. She also realised, with a slight jolt, that if he were still alive, she wouldn't be sitting here in Terri Drummond's kitchen, watching her bake scones.

But the next question almost made her choke.

'What about your mother, Biddy – is she still alive?'

Biddy swallowed and cleared her throat. 'I don't know,' she said, her voice unsteady.

'Do you know where she is?'

Biddy shook her head and inhaled slowly. 'No. I don't know anything about her. Well, I know she was called Gracie. But,' she shrugged her shoulders slightly, 'that's all.'

'Oh, Biddy, I am sorry. I didn't realise.' Terri stopped what she was doing and rubbed her hands with a tea towel. 'I shouldn't . . .'

'It's OK,' Biddy interrupted, surprising herself. There was something about being here in this warm, cosy kitchen, watching Terri bake scones and listening to her talk about her family that made her feel unusually comfortable. She breathed in deeply.

'I didn't even know that, her name, I mean, until a year or so ago when Papa's mind was getting really muddled. He never spoke about her. Ever. And I never asked. I wanted to, all the time. I really wanted to. But I didn't. It was really stupid of me, but I don't know why I didn't ask about her. Maybe,' she hesitated and rubbed at a drop of flour on the table with her forefinger, 'maybe I was scared he'd tell me she'd left because of me. Because I was, you know,' she paused again, breathing in sharply, 'a weirdo. A bloody weirdo. When all that started, when Alison arrived, I thought that that must be it. *That* must be the reason I didn't have a mother. It made sense then. I mean, what mother would want to have a weirdo for a child? Sometimes I wondered if they had drawn straws, my mother and my papa, or flipped a coin to see which one would have to keep me, and which one could escape.'

Tears pricked at the back of Biddy's eyes now, but she couldn't stop. She didn't want to stop.

'That day, when I went into Papa's room, I can't remember why now, it must have been to give him his pills or feed him, he looked at me so strangely that I stopped and stood still at the end of his bed. "Gracie," he croaked. His voice was shaking. "What do you want?" He was really agitated. I didn't know what he was talking about or who Gracie was. "Papa," I said, "it's me, Biddy." And then he started waving his arms wildly in front of him, trying to shoo me out. "I know who you are. I know what you want," he shouted. "Well, you can't have her. I won't let you take her. You're too late." And then he started to cry, to wail. "Get out, Gracie, go away, get out, get out, get out." It was awful. I had never seen my father cry. I had never heard the name Gracie before in my life. But in that instant I knew as sure as anything that she was my mother, and I realised he thought that I was her, come to take me away. She must have looked just like me. So I turned and left the room and I sat on the top step of the stairs until my father stopped wailing. When I went back into the bedroom, he was asleep. So, you see,' Biddy looked at Terri as she sat down beside her at the table, 'I knew for sure then,' she said, shrugging her shoulders, 'that she *had* left me. That she didn't want me. But that he did. But that's all I know. Apart from her maiden name: Flynn. It was on my birth certificate, which I found in a wooden box in my father's wardrobe when I was getting out his best suit for the undertaker. It had his initials on it. The box, that is. I think perhaps he made it himself.'

The tears which had been threatening finally began to drip from Biddy's eyelids. One ran down her nose and splashed into her mug of tea. Terri handed her a box of tissues and placed a hand on her shoulder as she stood to check the oven. Biddy blew her nose loudly and dabbed a tissue at her eyes.

'You know, Biddy, there are many, many reasons why your mother might have left,' Terri said, carefully lifting the baking tray out of the oven. The kitchen was instantly filled with the aroma of freshly baked scones, and Biddy instinctively licked her lips, immediately feeling better. 'Perhaps the responsibility of having a baby to care for was too much for her. Perhaps she simply panicked, or maybe she was suffering from postnatal depression, which really wasn't recognised in those days. You know, it's even possible that your mother and father really weren't getting along and she thought you'd be better off with him. The possibilities are endless, but I am sure her decision to leave was not made easily, and was not because she didn't love you.'

'Then why did she never come back for me? Or visit? Or write me a letter? Even one letter?'

'Honestly, Biddy, I really don't know.' Terri sat down beside her again. 'But if you want, you could try to trace her yourself. There are agencies now which can help with that sort of thing. I'll support you if you do want to try.'

Biddy shook her head ferociously. She felt sick at the very thought of trying to trace her mother, only to be rejected again. 'No. No, I won't. I can't do that. She knows where I am. If she wants to see me she will come, some day. I'll wait. I'll always wait.'

'Biddy, there is the possibility that she isn't alive anymore,' said Terri softly.

'I know.' Biddy breathed in slowly. 'I do know that.'

'Well, I'll tell you something for nothing though,' Terri said as she popped a scone onto Biddy's plate, 'if your mother did look like you then she must have been quite beautiful. I mean it, Biddy,' she smiled in response to the look of shock on Biddy's face. 'You have the most exquisite eyes. And as for your hair, why, people pay a lot of money for curls like those, and I can tell you that if I had your hair colour, I'd never have gone near a bottle of dye in my life.'

Biddy smiled, despite herself. She remembered Miss Jordan saying something similar about her hair the night of the disco, telling her she had a hair clip which she wanted to give her. But she herself had never thought of her hair as anything other than an ugly mess that suited her weirdness well.

'Your beauty might not be considered standard – it's certainly not at all like those girls on the front of magazines or on TV programmes, you know, all perfect breasts and bleached blonde hair, like what's-her-name . . . Carice, no, Caprice, or that Ulrika Jonsson, or that other one . . .'

Honey, thought Biddy, her heart lurching, *she's going to say Honey*. But then the phone rang, and Terri excused herself to answer it.

As Terri chatted to her brother Patrick on the phone about an upcoming family lunch, Biddy inhaled the soft, sweet scent of the just-baked scones, and thought of her mother again. She closed her eyes and imagined Gracie floating around their tiny kitchen in Stanley Street, a blue and white gingham apron covering her yellow dress, patterned oven gloves slung over her shoulder, a dusting of white flour streaked through her copper curly hair. Since discovering that she bore a resemblance to her mother, it was so much easier now to picture her in her fantasies. If she *had* stayed, she wondered, if she *had* loved her enough, would they have baked scones together?

'Oh,' she exclaimed, suddenly glancing at the clock. 'I have to go. Now. I'll miss my bus.'

'I'll call you back this evening, Patrick. Cheerio,' said Terri into the receiver as Biddy stood to go. 'Why don't you stay a little longer today, Biddy?' Terri ventured. 'Get the next bus?'

'No,' Biddy shook her head, slightly agitated. 'I have to go home now. Thank you for the scones. I . . . they . . . I loved them.'

Terri was used to this abrupt change in Biddy's manner. It happened often: one minute she would be talking freely, openly, and the next it was as though she had pulled down a heavy metal shutter.

'OK, Biddy,' she smiled, 'that's absolutely fine. Just let me wrap up a couple of these scones for your supper. Do you think next week you could come a little earlier? Or stay a wee bit longer?' she ventured, as she covered the scones in tinfoil. 'Even half an hour? I have another recipe I'd like to try out. The trouble is, it's quite complicated and I could do with a helper, just to keep me right. No baking skill required, I promise. Just an extra pair of hands. So, if you could give me a little squinch of extra time, I would really appreciate it.'

Biddy paused, considering the request for a few seconds. People didn't generally ask her for help. She liked the idea of helping Terri out, of actually helping her to make something. And watching her bake the scones today had been wonderful. She never got to help Miss Jordan with her fairy cakes and she knew she didn't want to miss out on this opportunity too. Maybe she could come earlier, but she absolutely, definitely couldn't stay later.

'OK,' she nodded.

'Great, lovely,' Terri clapped her hands together and ushered Biddy into the hall. 'I'll give you a shout later in the week to see how you're fixed.'

37.

Biddy turned up almost a full hour earlier than normal the following week. Her excitement had been mounting for days. She wanted to mix and stir. She wanted to watch the colours of all the different ingredients blend together in a magical muddle. She wanted to eat something exotic and mouth-watering that her very own hands had helped to create.

'I'm truly excited about this one, Biddy,' said Terri as she handed her an apron adorned with little pink roses. 'It's Nigella's Boston Cream Pie.' Biddy instinctively ran her tongue over her teeth. This sounded perfect.

'I've been wanting to try it for ages; well, ever since my good friend Carla from London sent me her latest book as a belated Christmas present. *How to be a Domestic Goddess*,' Terri chuckled holding up a shiny black hardback book with a photo of a single cup cake, dripping with white icing, on the cover. 'Thing is, it seems a tad complicated,' she winced. 'Involves making a crème pâtissière. That's the trouble with Nigella –' she put the book on the table and pulled on her own brightly coloured apron, '– *she* may be a domestic goddess, but, sadly, simply owning the book doesn't put the rest of us mere mortals on the same plane. Still, we'll give it a bash, shall we? And by the end of the day perhaps you and I shall join the domestic goddess club,' she winked. 'But we're going to use the age-old traditional method: our own hands!' She held up her palms and waved them in front of Biddy, making her smile. 'I know Nigella is into using a great big all-singing-all-dancing processor,' Terri carried on, taking bowls out of cupboards and spoons out of drawers, placing them on the big wooden table, 'but personally I can't be doing with that. And she does say hands will do. So, hands it is. Okey dokey?'

A swell of apprehension tugged in Biddy's chest. It was important that she impressed Terri today; that she showed her she was capable of doing simple, normal things. Capable, at least, of baking a cake. She had barely slept last night thinking about today, but for once it was excitement keeping her awake, and not anxiety. But now, with the reality of actually having to bake this complicated cake and make a cream-whatever-it-was from this striking-looking recipe book by someone as beautiful and sophisticated as Nigella Lawson (who she'd seen on *This Morning* just a few weeks ago) staring her in the face, she suddenly felt sick. She swallowed three times to push the acid back down her throat. Domestic Goddess? Her? What was Terri thinking?

But if Terri registered the panic, she completely ignored it, and gabbled on about Nigella and her friend Carla, who actually knew someone who'd been at one of Nigella's dinner parties. So before she knew it, Biddy was creaming the butter and sugar, adding the eggs, measuring out flour and carefully adding it to the bowl; engrossed once again by Terri's chatter, and absorbed by the recipe, which, despite Terri's concerns, she found remarkably easy to follow. In fact, it didn't seem complicated at all.

As her anxiety evaporated, she felt calmer and more invigorated since, well, probably since the last time she had painted. And that, she realised with a stab of irony, was actually the painting that had brought her here in the first place. She looked up at Terri and smiled.

'Everything OK, Biddy?' Terri smiled back. 'Need any help?'

'No, thank you.' Biddy shook her head, still smiling. 'I'm fine, thank you. I'm . . .' she paused. 'This is fun.'

'Great. Terrific. Excellent!' beamed Terri. 'It is fun, isn't it? We shall be the Domestic Goddesses of Ballybrock,' she sang, and danced a little jig in the middle of the kitchen – which, for some reason, made Biddy think about the disco. Then calmly and methodically, she told Terri about the worst night of her life – and the only friend she had ever had. And she didn't even cry. Not once. And through it all, they carried on baking: the cake mixture was put in the oven, the crème pâtissière was made and left to cool, the ingredients for the chocolate ganache icing were all laid out and ready to go. By the time she had finished the story, even the washing up was done.

'Go and sit down, Biddy.' Terri nodded towards the kitchen table, as she flung a dirty tea towel into the washing machine. 'Rest your leg. You've been standing for ages and I bet you're exhausted. The cakes will take another few minutes and then they'll need to cool before we start the really fun bit – the icing!' she winked. 'In the meantime, I'll make us a brew.'

Biddy did feel exhausted, but she also felt strangely relieved. Talking to Terri about all of these events from her past, things that still felt as though they had happened just yesterday, was making her feel different. Lighter, almost. It was as though she was shedding a load she no longer wanted to carry. But as Terri opened the oven door and the smell of the cake, *her* cake, wafted out, all thoughts of Miss Jordan and Alison Flemming and that awful night evaporated.

Terri placed the cakes onto a cooling rack on the worktop.

'Look at the size of theses beauties,' she gasped. 'Biddy Weir, you're a natural.'

Biddy beamed and clasped her hands in front of her. 'I baked a cake,' she laughed. 'I baked a cake.' *Miss Jordan would be so proud of me*, she thought.

On her way home that afternoon, a strange thing happened. As the bus headed into Ballybrock along the High Whinport Road, just by the shops at the entrance to Breen Housing Estate, Biddy saw a heavily pregnant woman with bleached blonde hair scraped back off her face, a cigarette in one hand, dragging a toddler behind her by the elbow with the other. She was yelling at it over her shoulder and the child, a little girl, who couldn't have been more than three years old, was crying.

Biddy's stomach lurched. She'd seen that child before. She knew who the mother was. In fact, she would see them often around this area on her way home from Terri's. The toddler was usually crying, the mother was usually shouting, sometimes there would be another child or two in tow. And always Biddy would quickly look away for fear of being recognised. But at that precise moment the bus screeched on its brakes, the driver blasting his horn, at what Biddy couldn't tell. But the sound was enough to make the woman look up and lock her dark, tired eyes with Biddy's clear green ones. Biddy swallowed, her stomach somersaulted, she gripped the bottom of her seat. But she didn't look away. This time, for the first time ever, Georgina Harte was the one to break eye contact with Biddy Weir.

38.

As they drew up outside number 17, Stanley Street, Terri wasn't at all surprised by the state of Biddy's house. Having only ever seen the exterior in semi-darkness or evening gloom on the couple of occasions when she had dropped Biddy off, she knew it would be antiquated inside. And it was exactly as she had imagined: old-fashioned, drab and fusty, like a living museum of life in the 1950s, just as Charlie Graham had said. She knew from Biddy that her father had lived in the house his entire life, and Terri suspected that the décor had remained the same since Howard Weir had been a small boy.

It was also cold. A heavy, penetrating chill clung to the walls and shrouded the furniture. The absence of radiators in the hall and the kitchen, the only two rooms which Terri saw on that first visit, indicated that number 17, Stanley Street had never welcomed the comfort of oil-fired central heating. It reminded Terri of her grandmother's house on Park Parade, a terraced row which had been flattened years ago to make way for a modern apartment block. Yet this house wasn't exactly dilapidated. In the afternoon light, Terri could see that the exterior was in a reasonable state of repair, and she suspected that while he had been able, Mr Weir had kept it well maintained. But heavens, it was in dire need of a radical makeover! Proper heating, new windows and a bloody good lick of paint would make all the difference.

Terri watched Biddy making the tea, registering the significance of the momentary reversal of roles in their relationship. In her calf-length brown skirt, heavy brown nylons, flat black lace-up shoes and grey cardigan buttoned up to the neck, Biddy looked as drab as the house. It was almost as though the two were one and the same, as though the house had absorbed Biddy into its soul and the two of them were trapped in time together.

As they drank their tea, and ate their Kimberleys (Terri had two out of politeness), Biddy spoke about her father, her words tumbling out in a nervous, staccato scuttle, as though she was afraid to stop, to even draw breath in case her memory of him vanished. As they'd just come from the cemetery, Terri wasn't in the least surprised. She had planned on baking Gypsy Creams that afternoon, an old recipe of her grandmother's which she thought would be perfect for Biddy to venture by herself. But it was clear from the moment she had come through the door that something was afoot. The girl was subdued, distracted, and paler than normal, her eyes tired and hollow. Such a contrast from the previous week. A bit of gentle probing revealed that today would have been her father's eighty-first birthday, and on further investigation Terri discovered that Biddy hadn't been to visit his grave since the day of his funeral. *Of course she hasn't*, she chastised herself, as a distressed Biddy explained that it was too far to walk to the cemetery, and there was no direct bus route, but that she felt so very, very guilty. *You should have realised, you clut*, she scolded herself. *You should have offered before.*

Less than half an hour later, Terri watched from the car as Biddy placed a bunch of wild flowers from her garden on Howard Weir's grave. And as they drove off, when Biddy asked her if she would like to go back to her house for a cup of tea and a Kimberley biscuit in honour of her papa, she was glad she was wearing her sunglasses.

Biddy was talking about her grandfather now, Howard. He had died when her father was a boy. She didn't know exactly when. Or how. But she did know that he had liked his garden. There was a cream rose bush in the back garden and her grandfather had planted it. Her father told her that one day when she was five years old, after she had pulled every single rose in flower off its stem. It was the only time Biddy could remember her father shouting at her, really shouting. He was so cross. She hadn't realised that she had done a bad thing, and his wrath left her feeling shaken and slightly sick. But she didn't cry or run to her room to hide. And she didn't say she was sorry either. Instead, she stuck every single bud back onto the bush with Sellotape. She had watched later through the kitchen window as he stood by the bush, observing her patch-up handiwork, wiping tears from his eyes. And even at such a young age, for some reason she knew that he wasn't crying because the roses were broken, but because she had mended them. And she had realised then that that rose bush was one of her father's most treasured possessions.

Then Biddy told Terri about her grandmother, who had died when she was little. She couldn't remember her at all, but she did know that her name was Margaret because of the writing on the inside of the old sewing basket which sat in the parlour. 'This is the property of Margaret Weir', it said. Sometimes, when her father was very ill, near the end, he thought she was his mother. He would reach out for her, calling. 'I'm sorry, Mother,' he would say, or, 'Don't hit me, Mother,' or, 'Howard's been a naughty boy, Mother.' She mustn't have been a very nice woman, Biddy had concluded. She must have frightened her father. Maybe she had made him feel a bit like Alison Flemming had made her feel. It made her sad, to think that her father had suffered like that. She was glad she couldn't remember her grandmother. Maybe it was better to have no mother at all, than a mother who made you feel scared.

Biddy paused and stared into her cup, swishing the tea around.

'They obviously troubled him, my mother and my grand-mother.' She put her cup down on the table, splashing some of the unfinished tea onto the surface. 'I hope he wasn't troubled by me.'

'Of course he wasn't, Biddy,' Terri smiled and reached out to pat her hand. 'He loved you very much. And he was proud of you. The fact that he kept that painting in his bedroom proves it.'

'You think so?'

Terri nodded. 'I know so.'

Biddy exhaled again, blowing up at her nose. 'OK,' she smiled, and dipped a Kimberley into her tea.

'That rose bush you were talking about, is it in bloom yet?' Terri asked as she stood up to leave, 'or is it a touch too early yet?'

'It is,' Biddy nodded. 'It always blooms early.'

'Ooh. Can I see it? I do love roses, especially white ones.'

'They're cream,' Biddy corrected her, and Terri had to suppress a smile.

'Even better,' she said.

Biddy took her into the long, narrow back garden. There were two old shabby wooden sheds, a very small one by the side gate beside the coal bunker, and a larger one with a window at the bottom of a moss-covered, paved path which ran down the middle of the garden. Terri could see that the garden was once loved and cared for but had obviously become unruly and over-grown in recent years. In fact, the only blooming shrub was the cream rose bush. 'Your father was a gardener too?' she asked.

'Yes. He spent a lot of time out here, until he couldn't manage anymore. I feel sad when I see it like this, but I can't do it myself,' she hesitated, fiddling with her fingers. 'I can't do the weeding and the clearing. It hurts my leg. And I can't manage the lawnmower with my stick. Mrs Thomas, our neighbour, sometimes got her son, Ian, to cut the grass when he came to visit. It was really nice of her, but I know he didn't want to do it. He, well, he . . .' She hesitated, thinking about the look of disgust on Ian Thomas's face whenever she would go outside to mumble a thank-you for his kindness. She knew that he was repulsed by her. Her face flushed at the memory. 'Anyway, it was good of him. I know it needs cutting, but I don't suppose he'll come anymore, now that Papa has gone.'

'Well, he might,' reasoned Terri. 'Maybe he just hasn't been at his mother's much lately.'

Biddy nodded. 'He has a new girlfriend. Mrs Thomas told me the day of Papa's funeral.'

'Well then, that explains it,' smiled Terri. 'I imagine he's been very busy with her. Now, tell me, what are the two sheds used for?'

'Papa keeps – kept – his gardening things in that one,' Biddy nodded towards the smaller shed. 'He built them himself, I think, before I was born. He told me once that he got the wood from the hardware store where he worked.'

'My goodness, was it Morrison's?' Terri asked, remembering the old shop on the High Street.

'Yes. I think so,' nodded Biddy. The name sounded familiar.

'I used to go in there with my own father, when I was a little girl. Just think, your father might have served us.' Terri had a vague memory of bespectacled men wearing long brown aprons. Was one of them Biddy's father?

'He worked in the office, I think.'

270

'I see, well, even so, you never know, I may well have seen him at some time when I was in the shop.'

Biddy smiled. She felt a tingle of excitement at this glimpse into her father's life before she had come along. And the notion that Terri had perhaps crossed paths with her father at some time in the past was oddly comforting.

'And what's in there?' Terri asked, pointing towards the other shed.

'I don't know. Papa went in there a lot. Every day. But I've never been in it.'

'Heavens,' said Terri. 'A mystery. I love mysteries. Haven't you ever even peeked through the window?'

'No,' Biddy shook her head. Her father had told her when she was very young that the shed was his private room, and all of her life she had respected that.

'Do you know where the key is?'

Biddy nodded. 'Yes, but I still don't want to go in.'

Terri smiled. 'I understand,' she said gently, 'and I really respect the fact that you still value your father's privacy. It's an honourable sentiment. But perhaps one day, when you feel stronger, you will feel that the time is right.'

Biddy looked down toward the shed. She could never imagine feeling strong enough to do that. 'So, do you want to look at the rose bush, then?' she said in response.

'Oh yes, please,' Terri responded brightly, walking down the path. 'It's fabulous, isn't it? And it must be incredibly hardy. Mmmm,' she inhaled one of the pale cream roses. 'Exquisite. Do you ever bring them inside?'

'No,' Biddy shook her head. She hadn't cut a single stem from the rose bush since the day she had removed every bud. And as her father didn't cut them either, or any of the other shrubs that used to bloom in the garden, they never had any fresh flowers in the house.

'Well,' Terri beamed. 'They look beautiful just as they are. Now my dear, I'm afraid I really must go. Bertie will be getting quite grumpy.' She was tempted to give Biddy a hug, but knew that would be pushing it. She did, however, make a mental note to somehow, sometime, get her garden sorted for her.

39.

As spring settled and the weather improved, Terri began to introduce a walk into their weekly sessions. Not far at first, just a stroll down through her back garden to the water's edge, or a potter up the lane at the front of the cottage, where the hedgerows sparkled with pale yellow primroses. She knew that Biddy couldn't walk too far, or at much of a pace, but she hoped that being outdoors would slowly reignite her desire to paint, if only on a subconscious level. Each day they walked a little further, and with each walk Biddy seemed to blossom just a little bit more. Her posture improved, her frown faded and the breeze blew a trace of colour into her cheeks. Terri always kept a baking project in reserve, just in case the weather was poor, or Biddy wasn't feeling up to going outdoors, and she made sure there was always something freshly made that morning to have with their pot of tea when they returned from their walk.

And with every visit, Biddy appeared more relaxed. She still recalled fragments of memories from her past, but now not all of them were bad. The beach ignited positive recollections of days when she would sit at the water's edge and sketch the birds. Her eyes transformed on those occasions. There was movement to them, and life. They glistened like shards of emeralds. She still had her quiet days, but the frequency and duration of her silences were becoming shorter and shorter as time moved on.

Terri had heard things about Alison Flemming and her cronies that made her skin crawl. The 'big' significant incidents were horrendous, yes; but it was the general humiliation, the relentless, exhausting, taunting and teasing that Biddy had suffered day in, day out, for so many years at the hands of these girls, which really disturbed her. She often wondered what kind of adults they had become. Did they ever think about Biddy? Did they carry any guilt? Surely Biddy must encounter at least one of them from time to time, or other folk from school, bystanders in the cruel pantomime which Alison had directed? Ballybrock was a small town, after all, and, despite her desire to be so, Biddy was not invisible. And what about Alison herself? Where was she? What had she done with her life?

Biddy did resolve some of Terri's questions – nuggets of information gently teased from her during one of her visits. She learnt, for example, that Georgina Harte lived locally, with, from the sounds of it, a brood of children and a nicotine addiction. Julia Gamble, it transpired, worked for a building society in the town – but thankfully not the one Biddy's father had set up his account in. 'I don't know what I would do if she worked in that one,' Biddy had said, visibly shivering despite the warm spring sunshine. There were plenty of other folk from school who still lived locally, including Vanessa someone, who had started working in the library a few years ago, so Biddy had stopped going there.

'And you know that local councillor, the one who's always on TV talking about environmental stuff? Rory McBride?'

Terri nodded. 'Oh yes, the handsome one with the dark wavy hair?'

'He was in my class. He was . . .' she hesitated, '. . . he hated the mountain.'

There was a pause again as Biddy seemed to be remembering something then she shrugged her shoulders and said, 'I don't know about Jackie. I haven't seen her. And . . .' she hesitated once more and then cleared her throat.

'Anyway,' she shook her head, 'it doesn't happen often – seeing someone from, you know, school. And if it does I just turn in the opposite direction, or look into a shop window or something. But I try to look down at the pavement or the floor as much as possible anyway, to avoid making eye contact with people. It's safer that way.' She looked at Terri, with a reassuring smile. 'So it's fine.'

Terri's heart cracked a little when Biddy said that, and she had to turn her back and pretend to root around for something in her bag so that Biddy wouldn't see her eyes water.

'But,' Terri could hear Biddy inhaling a long, deep breath, 'a couple of weeks ago, I, well, I didn't look away.'

'Oh?' Terri paused her fictitious bag-fumbling and blinked ferociously a few times before turning back to Biddy, eyes wide in anticipation. 'Really?'

Biddy nodded, and smiled a half smile.

'It was on the bus home. I saw Georgina, and she happened to look up, and well, I didn't look away. She did. And afterwards I felt a bit sorry for her because she looked tired, and frazzled, and a little bit sad.'

Terri found she couldn't speak, so she simply smiled at Biddy, and patted her hand, and with the rush of pride she felt in that second, the crack that had opened was instantly healed.

On the whole, that had been a good day, Terri reflected later, but she was still none the wiser whatsoever about the whereabouts of Alison Flemming.

40.

One glorious golden Wednesday, Terri and Biddy walked to the end of the headland, the furthest they had ever ventured. The late spring sunshine and the sound of the waves gently stroking the rocks had lulled them along. Biddy was in good spirits and very excited by the large number of seagulls swooping above them, and the groups of guillemots dotted around the rocks. But as they reached the old wooden stile which led through to an uneven section of the coastal path, Terri noticed that Biddy's pace was slowing. Her limp was suddenly very visible, much more pronounced than usual.

'Are you OK, Biddy?' asked Terri, concerned.

'Oh, yes, I'm fine,' Biddy smiled, subconsciously rubbing her hip. 'Why?'

'Your leg,' Terri gestured towards Biddy's stick. 'Are you in pain?' She had only heard Biddy complain about her leg once or twice before – and then only fleetingly – but it was obviously giving her gyp today.

'Oh, it's a wee bit sore. But not too bad. Really.'

'I'm so sorry, Biddy, my fault. I didn't realise how far we had gone. I was enjoying the walk too much, and didn't think.'

'Oh, no. No, really, it's OK. It's not that bad. And I was enjoying the walk too. I probably haven't walked this far in years. We used to walk everywhere, Papa and me, when I was little. But then, after, well,' she hesitated, 'after I hurt my leg, I didn't walk anywhere for a long time. Later, when I was able, we used to walk through the park once a week until Papa couldn't manage it. So honestly, I've enjoyed it. Please don't apologise.'

'Well, let's take a break for a while anyway, sit on the rocks,' Terri smiled. She felt a bit breathless herself. 'I could do with a little rest. Not as fit as I used to be. Actually,' she chortled, 'I haven't been as fit as I used to be for about thirty years.'

Terri looked on as Biddy propped her stick against a large smooth rock and sat on it, pushing her body up with her hands until she found a comfortable position. She watched her staring at two gulls swooping and diving into the sea a few yards away. The breeze had ruffled her unruly curls so much that her hair looked a bit like something they might nest in. Terri wondered, not for the first time, what a good hairdresser would do to Biddy's locks. With a little bit of TLC, her hair could be beautiful. And a touch of make-up too; just a little. Some day she would venture the suggestion. But not now. Not yet.

'They are fabulous, aren't they?' Terri said, nodding towards the gulls. 'Have you always been fascinated by them?'

Biddy nodded. 'Always. Well, for as long as I can remember. I love all birds, actually, but seagulls are definitely my favourites.'

'Tell me, Biddy, why birds?' Terri asked, as she sat down beside her on the rock. 'I am a cat person, myself. Utterly love them. Adore them. Always have. The way they move, the way they sleep so blooming much, and most of all,' she chuckled, 'the way they have total control over us humans. So, what is it you love so much about birds?'

Biddy gazed at two seagulls who were proudly strutting along a rock close by. One looked up and appeared to hold her gaze. 'I love them because they are my friends,' she said, quietly, shrugging her shoulders. 'And they always have been. My only friends.'

'Didn't you have any friends at school at all?' asked Terri, carefully. 'There must have been someone you were a little

LESLEY ALLEN

bit chummy with?' Biddy shook her head. 'What about family friends?'

Another shake of the head. 'We didn't have any.'

'Well, neighbours then? Weren't there any girls in your street around the same age as you?'

This time, Biddy nodded. 'There were. Once, when I was really young – about five or six – I remember I was standing by the gate, watching a group of them playing in the road. They were skipping and singing rhymes. One girl, I can't remember her name – she was a bit older, I think – came over and asked me if I wanted to join in. So I went and stood beside them, but as I didn't know how to skip, or didn't know the rhymes, I just stood and watched.' She picked at the grass growing around the rock. 'I remember the girl who invited me to play smiling over at me a couple of times. Nobody else did. Then the funniest thing happened. Well,' she looked at Terri and half laughed, 'I thought it was funny, but they didn't. A seagull pooed on one of the girl's heads. A really big, runny one. She put her hand up to her scalp to see what it was, and then it was all dripping off her fingers. She started to scream, then all the others started to scream and one of them, I think it was the bird-poo girl's sister, ran into a house to get her mother.' She breathed in deeply, 'But I started to laugh. I couldn't help it. I thought it was the funniest thing I had ever seen. I actually wished that it had been me the bird had pooed on. But then the other girls stopped screaming and looked at me, and one of them asked me why I was laughing. Then the mother came out and put her arm around the poo girl and told her to come inside and she would clean her up. "She thinks it's

278

funny," the girl sobbed, pointing at me. The mother glared at me. She looked me up and down, an expression of utter disgust on her face. Then she said to the others while still glaring at me, "I told you not to play with her, girls. She's strange and she smells. I told you." So that was it. My brief friendship was over before it even started.'

'What a bitch,' spat Terri, shaking her head in disbelief. 'The mother, I mean.'

'Well,' Biddy smiled, 'one good thing did come out of that day.'

Terri looked at her, quizzically.

'That's when my fascination with bird poo started, which was a great distraction for me when I was at school. Maybe my love of seagulls goes back to that day too.'

She laughed, lightly, but Terri's heart lurched. The very notion of growing up totally alone, without a single friend to share the simple pleasures of childhood with, was devastating to her. Once again Biddy reminded her of a caged bird, the very antithesis of the creatures she so dearly loved. Looking at her now, as she watched her beloved seagulls circle above the water and dive deep into the waves, Terri shivered slightly, despite the warmth of the breeze.

'How is your leg doing, Biddy?' she asked, shaking herself.

'OK,' said Biddy.

'Feel up to the walk back now?'

'Uh-huh.'

'OK, let's make a move then. I'm in need of a nice strong cuppa, and a snack too. Fancy some of my own wheaten bread with cheese and pickle?'

'Oh,' Biddy gasped as she looked at her watch.

'What time is it?' asked Terri, sensing the flicker of panic.

'Ten past three.'

'That's fine. You've got loads of time. We'll be back in twenty minutes. You can have a quick cuppa and a bite to eat, then get the twenty past four bus, can't you?'

Biddy nodded, obviously calculating in her head.

'Come on then,' Terri smiled, helping her up.

41.

That evening, Terri was particularly agitated. The lasagne she had removed from the freezer that morning didn't interest her. Her wine tasted bitter. She couldn't even settle to watch her favourite soap. It had been a reasonably productive day, the most fruitful for weeks, in actual fact. Biddy had revealed some new information and her form, yet again, was good.

'What the hell is wrong with me, Bertie?' Terri asked her companion, as he helped himself to the untouched lasagne which sat on a tray at her feet. Bertie glanced up momentarily, but his mistress's leftovers were of more interest to him than her problems. Terri shook her head and smiled. 'You eat, my boy. One of us might as well.' She paced around the cottage, wandering from room to room, stopping every so often to drum her fingers on a window ledge or an item of furniture. Finally she returned to the living room, where Bertie lay sprawled on the rug in front of the hearth. He tilted his head and looked at her through one opened eye. 'A bath,' she announced. 'That's what I need. A big, bubbly bath, candles and some music. And another bottle of wine. This one is off.'

As Terri relaxed in her bath and hummed along to the Greek music playing in the background, the source of her pent-up agitation gradually dawned on her. She'd known for weeks that she had let herself become more personally involved with Biddy than with anyone else she had ever dealt with, apart from Derek Davidson, of course, who was still an important person in her life – so that wasn't the issue. In London there had always been several clients on her books at the same time, and a host of other exciting projects which kept her busy in between her clinics. But here, there was only Biddy. It wasn't that she was bored with her. Far from it. She was properly fond of the girl; fascinated by her, in fact. It seemed that Biddy had become her personal crusade.

She wanted to emancipate her, free her from the shackles of a stunted childhood which still imprisoned her. It wasn't too late for Biddy to live her life, and she wanted to make damn well sure that she bloody well did. Perhaps, she thought as she sipped her more agreeable wine, it was easier to connect with Biddy because she wasn't an official client. She wasn't being paid by anyone to assess the girl's state of mind, or to help sort her life out. She didn't have to submit an official report to anyone, or recommend a treatment programme, or attend meetings with several other health care professionals to discuss her case. But it wasn't just that. It was so much more. She realised, with a shock, that the discomfort which had been growing inside her wasn't purely because she was anxious for Biddy's life to begin, but because she didn't want to spend the rest of hers sorting out the lives of other people. Moving back home was supposed to put a stop to all that. It was supposed to signal the start of her own new life, to heal her own pain. Clearly, it hadn't. Oh, she loved Cove Cottage, and she didn't resent Biddy for a second. On the contrary, she was so very glad that Charlie had asked her to help. Truly. Helping Biddy, however, had made Terri realise that it really was time now to help herself. Just as Derek, dear, sweet Derek, had set her off on this journey, Biddy must be the one to end it. And as the CD played the last melodic chords of the final track, evoking a sudden, glorious memory of a certain Cretan sunset, she knew precisely what she must do.

42.

Biddy adapted to having someone else in her life remarkably quickly. Her Wednesday afternoon visits to Cove Cottage had become a source of pleasure she never imagined she would be capable of experiencing. By the middle of May, she had been to Cove Cottage fourteen times, each visit circled in red pen on the calendar she had bought in the Oxfam shop on the High Street for fifty pence at the end of February. For the first time in years, she had something to mark on a calendar other than doctor's or dental appointments. Every Wednesday afternoon when she returned from her time with Terri, the first thing she did, before she even removed her coat, was circle the following week's visit. She never circled more than one week in advance, just in case one day Terri might tell her that she couldn't see her again. It was best to take one week at a time, but each time she made a circle on the calendar, she breathed a sigh of relief.

Sometimes, as she removed her coat, Biddy caught sight of herself in the mirror which hung to the left of the coat stand in the hall. If it had been a particularly good visit, she would hold her own gaze for a second or two, and smile. She was becoming more accustomed to the stranger who smiled back, a woman who looked like her, but couldn't be. Her eyes were different. They seemed to glow; they seemed bigger. Greener, even. The smile was also more familiar now. Since meeting Terri, Biddy had caught herself smiling every now and then, for no apparent reason. Sometimes it would be in the kitchen while making a cup of tea. Sometimes when she was hanging the washing on the line. Once or twice, it had even happened while she was on the toilet.

Today, although she was tired from their long walk on the beach, and her leg was dragging more than usual, Biddy felt good as she waited at the bus stop. The bus driver smiled at her when he punched her ticket, and said, 'Hello'. She was so startled that it took her a second or two to realise that *she* had smiled at *him* first. She had actually looked into his face, and smiled. She was proud of herself, and as she peered out of the bus window and watched the goings-on of life outside: young mothers pushing prams, children playing in their gardens, people crossing roads or driving cars, someone clipping his hedge, a woman throwing a bucket of soapy water onto the pavement in front of her house, a young man jogging – Biddy realised that, for the first time in almost twenty years, she felt at ease on a bus. She was actually enjoying the journey. She didn't spot Georgina Harte, but if she had, she was sure she wouldn't have felt sick. Not today. And she'd have held her gaze again, if Georgina had looked at her. She would.

That evening, after *Honey's Pot* was over, Biddy pulled an old sketchpad out from the bottom of her wardrobe, found a pencil and a tray of paints tucked away at the back of the cupboard under the kitchen sink, and sat down at the table with her encyclopaedia of birds. She opened the book at the scarlet ibis page and began to draw for the first time in more than three years. The instantaneous rush of relief she felt was intense and consuming, electrifying even – certainly much more satisfying than the pins had ever been, and so much more comforting than sinking her teeth into her knuckles.

Biddy was writing a shopping list the next morning when the phone rang. It had been so long since she'd painted that most of the colours were dry and hard and her pencils were blunt. She could make do, she knew, but as she had lain in bed the previous night thinking about her day and planning what she would paint next, she had decided to venture into Easons on the High Street to buy some new supplies. And she would smile at the shop assistant, she vowed, as she drifted into the best sleep she'd had in months, even if it was someone she recognised from school.

The shrill ring of the phone made her jump and break the nib of the pencil she was using to write her list. She stood up from the kitchen table and walked nervously into the hall, staring at the ringing phone, not knowing whether to answer it or not. She had had a few calls recently from people trying to sell her a mortgage or a mobile phone, but they were mostly in the evenings. Sometimes the line went dead as soon as she answered. She didn't like those calls. They made her nervous. She'd heard, on one of her programmes, about companies who hound people for business. Apparently they used all kinds of tricks to get personal information. So she had simply stopped answering the phone if it rang after six o'clock. Ten o'clock in the morning, however, was a different matter. She stood by the hall table and looked at the ringing phone. Should she answer or not? Answer or not answer? She hummed the question in her head in time to the rings. Her hand hovered over the receiver, then she drew away again. She glanced up from the phone and caught her image in the mirror. 'Answer it,' her new reflection seemed to say.

'Hello?' she spoke quickly before she had time to change her mind and replace the receiver. 'Who is it?'

'Morning, Biddy. Gosh, I was just about to hang up. Hope I didn't waken you?'

It was Terri. Biddy's shoulders slumped slightly with relief then immediately tensed up again. Why was Terri phoning her? She never phoned her. Not since the day after they had first met when she said she would. What was wrong?

'N-no,' she stammered. 'No. I wake up at six o'clock.'

'Good. I'm an early riser myself. Best part of the day. Anyway, the reason I'm calling is that unfortunately I have a problem with next Wednesday. An appointment I'm afraid I can't get out of.'

Biddy's heart sank to her toes and her blood rushed to her ears. She felt herself wobble and gripped the edge of the table for balance. It was over. Terri spoke on, but she couldn't hear her words, such was the pounding in her head.

'So, what do you think?'

Biddy shook herself and breathed deeply. Think about what? 'Pardon?'

'What do you think? About Sunday?'

'Sunday?'

'Yes, you know, like I said, instead of Wednesday. Is this a bad line, Biddy? Would you like me to phone back?'

'No,' Biddy nearly jumped down the phone. 'No, it's fine. I can hear you. You want me to come on Sunday? This Sunday?'

'Well, yes, if it's OK with you. I know it's a bit of an imposition, and I generally despise changing arrangements, but I'm afraid I can't get out of this blessed thing on Wednesday. So, I wondered if you might like to come for Sunday lunch instead? That is, if you haven't got other plans, of course.'

Biddy's head was spinning. She would love to have lunch at Terri's. She would love to. Sunday lunch. A proper meal in someone else's home. Terri had asked her to stay for dinner before, of course, but always on a Wednesday. And Wednesdays didn't suit. But this was different. This was a proper invitation, by phone. This was a Sunday. And Sundays did suit.

'Yes,' she gasped. 'I mean, no. I mean, no, I haven't got plans and, yes, I'd love to come for lunch. I'd really like that. If you're sure it's OK?'

'Well now, Biddy my dear, I wouldn't have asked you if it wasn't, would I? Besides, now I won't feel guilty about cancelling our Wednesday arrangement. And I do love to make a roast dinner, especially for guests. Do you like beef and Yorkshire puds?'

'Yes, thank you,' Biddy nodded furiously. Beef and Yorkshire pudding, one of her father's favourites. She hadn't had a proper Sunday dinner for years, not since he had become incapable of cooking. It was a meal she had never managed to master herself.

'Fabulous. Shall we say 1 p.m.?'

'Yes, yes.'

'Well, I'll tell you what, you check the bus times, and if there's a problem then I shall come and get you. OK?'

Biddy was so excited it didn't even occur to her to reject the offer of a lift.

'OK.'

'Oh, and Biddy, so I can get my timings right with the meal, do you need to be home for a certain time?'

The new Biddy smiled at her through the mirror. 'No,' she shook her head. 'No time.'

'Fabulous. I'll call you back tomorrow morning at the same time, and you can tell me if you need a lift.'

'OK.'

'Great. Bye, then.'

'Terri?' Biddy gasped quickly, before Terri could hang up.

'Yes, Biddy?'

'Thank you.'

'It's a pleasure, Biddy, an absolute pleasure.'

43.

Terri was both delighted and relieved that her invitation had been accepted. Of course she could have rescheduled the appointment, but Charlie had pulled strings to get her a cancellation with Helen Potts, who by all accounts was booked up weeks in advance. Helen was the only optometrist in town worth tuppence, according to Charlie, and Terri did desperately need an eye test. Besides, it provided her with a wonderful and timely opportunity to invite Biddy to Cove Cottage for a social occasion. Now she would have a full afternoon with her. Perhaps, if things went well, she may even stay until the evening. It would be great to have the company and she would finally have the opportunity to give Biddy a proper meal. Feed her up.

Biddy arrived bang on time, clutching a bunch of pale cream roses roughly bound in kitchen roll. She thrust them at Terri as soon as she opened the door, rather like a small schoolgirl might do to an important visitor.

'Oh, Biddy, they're beautiful.' Terri inhaled. 'And the smell. Wow. Fabulous. They smell like roses really should. Are these the roses from your garden?' Biddy nodded.

Terri remembered that Biddy didn't cut the roses from that bush. She felt a lump at the back of her throat and swallowed hard.

'Oh, Biddy, thank you. Thank you so much. I know what they mean to you and I'm really touched.'

Biddy felt a tingle in her tummy. She liked the sensation. She liked this feeling of doing something nice for somebody. 'It's a pleasure,' she beamed.

'Now don't worry if you can't manage it all,' said Terri brightly as she placed Biddy's plate in front of her, piled high with tender roast beef, golden roast potatoes, perfectly caramelised carrots and parsnips and fluffy Yorkshire puddings. 'I'm never offended by leftovers on a plate, and I know a very fat cat who adores them.' But she needn't have worried. Terri watched Biddy eat as though this was the first proper meal she had had in years. Maybe it is, she thought.

As they ate, Terri chatted openly about family news. Her sister Caroline, the one who lived in Canada, was planning a trip home in the summer with her daughter, Kerry. A friend from London had bought a house in Mallorca and had invited her out for a holiday. Then there was her agent in London, who was hassling her about writing another book. Terri was done with academia and self-help books, but the problem was, she had promised him a novel. She just hadn't got around to starting it yet. And best of all, her dear old friend Derek Davidson's step-daughter, Olivia, had given birth to a little boy, Archie. Terri was very close to Olivia and her partner Benjy, as they'd lived close to her in London and she often had them over for dinner, or they her. She missed them. Their house was adorable. Olivia had such flair with interiors. And they had a beautiful garden, which had won several awards. Benjy was a horticulturist and garden designer, and was making quite a name for himself. He'd recently designed a couple of celebrity gardens and now there was talk of a television programme.

Biddy listened in awe as Terri talked. A sister in Canada, a friend in Mallorca, an agent, a new baby. People with names like Olivia and Benjy. Writing a book. Making a television programme.

Terri's world was a million miles away from her own, and it fascinated her. She didn't want Terri to ever stop talking. She wanted to hear more about her life and the people in it. She wanted to sit in this bright, sunny kitchen, in the best house in the world, eating the best food she had ever tasted in her life, and listen to Terri forever.

'Would you like a little more?' Terri asked, interrupting Biddy's thoughts. 'There's plenty, so don't be shy. But bear in mind there is a fruit crumble for afters. Mind you, we can wait a while for that, can't we?'

Biddy nodded enthusiastically. She was in no rush to leave.

'So, some more, then?'

Biddy nodded again. 'Yes please. It's delicious. I think it's the nicest meal I have ever had.'

'Well, that is the nicest compliment I have ever had. Thank you, Biddy,' Terri smiled, as she dished out more of everything onto Biddy's plate. She believed her, and that made her feel incredibly sad.

'Thank you, Terri,' said Biddy when she had finally finished, wiping her mouth with her napkin. 'That was delicious. Really, really delicious.'

'Good. Glad you liked it,' Terri smiled. 'It's such a pleasure to cook for someone again. Maybe in my next life, I will be a chef,' she winked at Biddy and began to stack the dishes in her small dishwasher.

'Well, I think you would be a great chef,' Biddy smiled. 'Roast beef and Yorkshire pudding was my father's favourite meal, so we had it all the time. But,' she laughed lightly, 'it *never* tasted like that.' A flash of guilt cut through her. 'It was still nice though, just not, well, not like that.'

'I'm sure your father was an excellent cook, Biddy,' Terri smiled warmly, 'but thank you. Actually, that was Harry's favourite meal too.'

Biddy waited for Terri to elaborate, tell her who Harry was. She'd definitely never mentioned a Harry before. But she continued to clear up, rinsing out pots and wiping down the benches. Biddy picked a tea towel from the rack, her favourite one with the blue stripes and pink roses and started to dry the pots.

'Are you still OK to have a break before pudding?' Terri asked, putting on the dishwasher. 'I thought we could maybe take a wee stroll, work up an appetite for round two.'

'Who's Harry?' Biddy blurted, ignoring the question.

Terri paused and took in a deep breath.

'That's Harry,' she said, nodding towards the framed black and white photograph which sat on the thick windowsill amidst little pots of herbs and jam jars of freshly picked wild flowers from the lane. 'That's my Harry.' She picked the photograph up and ran her fingers over the glass, as though wiping off dust, or touching a memory.

'It was taken in Donegal, on one of our trips home years ago,' she smiled, not at Biddy, but at the man in the picture. 'Harry loved Donegal. He loved Greece more, mind you,' she laughed. 'He used to say Greece was like Ireland warmed up and he'd rather have the hot version, thank you very much.'

Biddy was familiar with the photograph, which showed a much younger Terri and a large man with dark curly hair wrapped up against the elements on a windswept beach. She'd noticed it many times before, along with several others of the same man dotted around the cottage, like the ones in the study she had spotted on her very first visit. For some reason she had assumed that, as there had never been any mention of a husband, the man was Terri's brother, Patrick. But now, when she looked again at the photograph over Terri's shoulder and studied it closely, she could see something in their eyes. The way they were looking at each other. It was . . . She searched her mind for the right word, but she couldn't find it. Then she realised, with a jolt. It was love.

'Tell you what,' said Terri, taking the tea towel from Biddy and throwing it over the draining board, 'how about we go for that stroll now and I'll tell you all about my Harry?'

By the time they returned to Cove Cottage almost forty minutes later, Biddy knew all about Harry McDonald whom Terri had shared her life with for more than fifteen years, until his sudden death from a heart attack almost four years ago. That was one of the reasons she'd returned to Ballybrock, Terri admitted, she couldn't settle back into a life in London without him. They'd met at a little café Terri used to go to on her way home from work after David, her former 'asshole of a lover', had run off with 'the French floozy in the neighbouring flat'. She reckoned she'd been going to the café for three weeks before she realised that the big man in the brown suit with rugged cheeks and thick black curly hair, was sat in the same window seat every time she went in. It was another week or so before she made eye contact with him and a week after that before they finally spoke. He claimed he'd noticed her the very first evening she walked into that café. *Lola's*, it was called. They had named their first cat after it, the tabby cat from the photo in the study.

Biddy was captivated by this new, romantic story from Terri's life. It was better than anything she'd ever read in a book, or seen in a soap or watched in a film. It was beautiful and magical and full of colour and energy and life – a type of living that Biddy knew she herself would never do. Could never do. And as she listened she hoped that, somehow, Terri had got the ending wrong. For how could a love as vibrant as this one obviously was, just end? She strained with every muscle so as not to miss a word, a blink, a breath.

'We were inseparable from that very first conversation, me and my big Scottish hunk,' Terri smiled, wistfully. 'Sure, wouldn't you know he was Scottish, with a name like Harry McDonald?' she laughed. 'Ah, we were a right pair. Never married, never felt the need. Perhaps if we'd had children, we might have, but, well, that wasn't to be.'

'What did he do?' asked Biddy, still mesmerised.

'He was a writer. And a very successful one at that,' Terri told her, proudly. 'He published five bestselling thrillers. One of them, *The Casual Observer*, was named Thriller of the Year by the *Guardian* shortly after it was published. Harry was working on a film adaptation of it when he died. He was so excited,' she shook her head, smiling at the memory, 'all his dreams had come true.'

Biddy noticed Terri's eyes glaze behind her smile. 'You must miss him very much,' she said softly, almost reaching out to touch the older woman's arm.

'Oh I do, Biddy, I do. I miss him every single bloody day. I miss the life that we had and I miss the future that we planned to have. We were going to retire to Greece, you see. We'd probably be there by now. We'd set our sights on a tiny fishing village on Crete, where we used to go on holiday each year. Even had the plot picked out for our villa. But,' she sighed, 'it wasn't to be. Still. I can't complain. Like I said, I was blessed to have loved him and

I'm willing to settle for having had fifteen years of my life with that man, than never to have met him at all.'

By this time, they were nearly back at the cottage. Its white-washed walls and blue shutters sparkled in the afternoon sunshine. The window baskets which Terri had recently hung outside were starting to spill over with brightly coloured flowers. Biddy's heart leapt when she saw it. She loved the house even more, now that she actually knew it.

'Harry would have loved this place,' said Terri, almost reading her thoughts. 'But it wouldn't have won his heart the way our dream plot in Greece had.'

She winked at Biddy and pointed out a seagull who was proudly strutting along the roof, as though the cottage was actually his.

'Still,' she whispered, as Biddy walked a step or two ahead, 'it suits me. For now.'

As she left that afternoon, it occurred to Biddy that she knew more about Terri than she had ever known about anyone. More than Miss Jordan. More than her father even. And it felt wonderful. She turned quickly on the threshold of the door and flung her arms around Terri. It was clumsy and stiff, and too brief for Terri to reciprocate, but it was a hug all the same. And if Biddy had turned round to wave as she made her way down the path, she would have seen Terri wipe a tear from her eye.

44.

'Biddy, I have a favour to ask you.' It was late June, and the two women were taking their afternoon tea on the sun-drenched patio. 'Now, it's quite an imposition, so if you'd rather not, just say so and I promise you, I won't be in the least bit offended.'

Biddy wondered what was coming. People didn't ask her to do favours.

'The thing is, I have to go away for a few days soon. The week after next, in actual fact. Olivia and Benjy are having a naming ceremony for Archie. Apparently it's the done thing these days. Anyway, they expect me to be there. It's at their home in London, and, in truth, I wouldn't miss it for the world.'

Biddy wondered what this had to do with her. Then she gulped, almost choking on a crumb of the freshly baked oatmeal cookie she was munching, as the thought struck her that perhaps Terri was going to invite her along too.

'My problem, of course, is Bertie.'

Biddy sighed with relief. She was going to ask her to look after Bertie. That was fine. She could do that. She could never have travelled to London, but she could definitely look after Bertie. She'd never had much time for cats before, especially as they liked to kill birds, but she'd become used to Bertie and quite liked the way he rubbed his head against her ankles. She'd just make sure he didn't get anywhere near the birds in her back garden.

'You want me to take him home and look after him?' she said, smiling at Terri.

'Not exactly,' Terri smiled back. 'It's just that Bert is so set-tled here now; it took him quite a while after our move from

London, and I don't want to unsettle him again. I did think about putting him into a cattery, but, quite frankly, I wasn't in the least bit impressed by the two I looked at, and I did consider asking you to keep him, but I was worried that he might become disorientated and try to find his way back here and end up getting lost or . . .' she shuddered. 'Well, then I hit on the idea that you might come here? You know, take care of him here while I'm away. What do you think?'

This time Biddy did choke and spat a mouthful of biscuit into her napkin.

'Are you OK, Biddy?' asked Terri. Biddy nodded, wiping her mouth with the back of the napkin. 'Would you like a glass of water?'

Biddy shook her head and took a sip of tea. 'I'm fine,' she gasped, and took another sip. 'Really. Sorry. A crumb caught in my throat.'

'So, what do you think about my suggestion? It would be for three nights. You could sleep in the spare bedroom, it's really pretty, and I'd make sure the fridge was packed with delicious food. And of course, you could bring your sketchbook with you and paint out on the beach all day long.'

Biddy stared at Terri, aware that her mouth was actually hanging open. She could hardly believe what she was hearing. Terri wanted her to live at Cove Cottage while she was away! Actually live here, *here*, and for three whole days. Apart from the one night she'd spent at Brook House, the night on the mountain and the weeks afterwards in hospital, in her thirty years of life, she hadn't slept anywhere else but her damp, dreary bedroom at number 17, Stanley Street.

She shook her head, but in disbelief, not rejection.

'That's fine, Biddy. If you'd rather not do it, I understand. Honestly. It's a big ask. Don't worry about Bertie, I can ask . . .'

'No,' Biddy shouted. 'No. No. I mean, yes. Yes please. I'd love to. Honestly, I'd really love to.'

'Oh fabulous,' Terri clapped her hands together. 'Fabulous. This is wonderful, Biddy. You don't know how relieved I am. Do you hear that, Bert old boy?' She ran her hand along the cat's back as he stretched out on the ground at her feet. 'Biddy is going to take care of you, my darling. Isn't that wonderful? Thank you, Biddy. Thank you.'

No, thought Biddy, *thank you, Terri. Thank you. Thank you, thank you, thank you*. Her heart was thudding loudly in her chest. Her eyes were stinging with tears, and she felt that she might cry: but she didn't know why, as this was quite simply the best, most glorious, wonderful thing that had ever happened to her.

45.

The key was under the yellow flowerpot on the porch, just as Terri had said. Biddy still didn't really believe this was happening and half expected there would be no key, a note from Terri left in its place, telling her that she'd changed her mind and had asked someone else to look after Bertie. Biddy's hands were shaking as she let herself into the house and dragged her father's old brown suitcase into the hall.

She had taken a taxi rather than get the bus and have to face the short walk from the bus stop lugging the suitcase, not because it was heavy, but her stick made carrying even more than one bag of shopping from Tesco extremely difficult. She had packed very little. Just some clean underwear, a spare pair of trousers, two clean shirts and a cardigan, along with her toothbrush, toothpaste, deodorant, soap and hairbrush. Plus her sketchbook, a few pencils and the small watercolour set she'd bought in Easons to replace the old one she'd found under the sink. As she placed the items in the case, which smelt fusty and old, the memory of the last time she had packed it made her feel slightly woozy. But then she had looked at her painting of Cove Cottage, which now sat on top of the chest of drawers in her own bedroom, and a wave of calmness had engulfed her. This time, she was packing for a trip that she really wanted to go on. She decided that while she was there, she would do a painting of Cove Cottage for Terri as a thank-you for asking her to do this favour, for trusting her to look after Bertie and live in her house. Her stomach had fluttered with that feeling of dancing butterflies: a much more familiar sensation these days than the lump in her throat, or the acid in her gullet.

Biddy left the suitcase in the hall and went into the kitchen. This was her favourite room in the cottage. She loved every room, well, all the ones she had been in, but the kitchen was definitely the best. Terri had made the entire back wall into a big window with sliding glass doors out to a patio, and the view over the bay was breath taking. Biddy had often imagined herself living here, eating her meals at the kitchen table, looking out at the view. She could spend hours watching the landscape change in tone and shade and mood. The rest of the room was painted bright yellow, the colour of sunlight, and all the cupboards, the wooden chairs and the big square table were stained in a beautiful shade of blue. 'It's cobalt blue,' Terri had said when Biddy admired the colour one day, not long after her visits began. 'My favourite colour. Reminds me of Greece. Ever been to Greece, Biddy?' she had asked. Having never been anywhere, Biddy had felt her cheeks flush with embarrassment as she shook her head. 'Well, you really must go someday. You'd love it. If you're going to go anywhere, go there. The smells, the sounds, the scenery, the food, the people, the flowers,' Terri had closed her eyes and inhaled deeply, lost in a memory. 'It really is heaven on earth. Truly. And a painter's paradise, Biddy, a painter's paradise.'

Of course, Biddy hadn't known about Harry then, and the real reason why Terri loved these colours and that country, but she had thought it sounded wonderful. She'd love to go somewhere with skies the colour of Terri's kitchen cupboards one day, but she knew she wouldn't. She wouldn't have a clue how to do it.

She thought again now of Harry, and Greece, as she looked around the room.

'I know it's sad about what happened to Harry, Bertie, but I'm so glad Terri didn't go to Greece,' Biddy said to the cat, who had just come in through the cat flap on the utility room door and was rubbing his head against her ankles. 'I'm so glad she came here to Cove Cottage and I'm so glad that I met her and I'm so glad that she asked me to come here to look after you.'

She noticed an envelope on the kitchen table, propped up against a little vase of freshly picked daisies, with 'Biddy' scrawled on it in Terri's handwriting. An image of Miss Jordan's letter falling through the letterbox onto the hall floor flashed into her head – the only other handwritten, personal letter she had ever received. Hands shaking a little, she tore open the envelope and read Terri's note.

Dearest Biddy

You'll find everything you need in the fridge – I made one of my special lasagnes last night and a berry crumble – and the freezer is packed with goodies too, so just help yourself to ANYTHING. Tea, coffee, biscuits (Kimberleys, of course, as well as some of my own), breakfast cereal, etc. are all in the larder. There are plenty of tins of tuna in Bertie's cupboard – don't let him hassle you too much for food! He's a greedy old beggar!

Good news – my new television is up and running! Dean, my jack-of-all-trades friend, tuned it in for me yesterday! I do hope you enjoy watching your programmes on it. I've left all the instructions and the remotes sitting on the coffee table in the living room, but if you have any problems with it (or with anything), just call Dean. His card is pinned up on the notice board. He's a lovely young man, and will come out at the drop of a hat.

I'll give you a bell this evening but if you have any queries or worries, just call me on my mobile.

Terri.

P.S.: Hope you don't mind, but as a little thank-you for helping me out, I've asked Dean to pop round and sort out your garden while you're here. He's got terrific green fingers and I know he'll do a grand job. He's under strict instructions to treat the rose bush with extra care! If you're pleased with his work, he'd be happy to talk about a more permanent arrangement, but we'll discuss that when I get back.

P.P.S.: If you go into the utility room, you'll find a little surprise. It's my proper thank-you present for looking after my Bertie and the cottage.

Enjoy!

Terri x

Biddy re-read the letter twice. It was short, but contained a lot of important information and she wanted to be sure to take it all in. The thought of Terri's home cooking made her mouth water. She'd never been greatly excited by food until she had met Terri. Finally learning to bake with her had been a revelation. And though she'd only been for a proper meal once – that lovely Sunday lunch almost two months ago – Terri would often send her home with little plastic containers crammed with 'leftovers' like cottage pie, chicken and broccoli bake and lasagne.

She'd never tasted food like it, especially the lasagne. She loved the lasagne. She wouldn't wait until dinner time, she decided – she would have it for lunch. The new television was exciting, but worrying at the same time. It would make a change from watching her programmes on her old portable, which had been a bit fuzzy lately. But she hoped Terri's new television worked properly and that she would understand the instructions, because she definitely wouldn't be phoning Dean, no matter how nice Terri said he was. It was very kind of Terri to ask Dean to sort the garden, as it was so badly overgrown now that it made her feel sad. And she trusted Terri that he would do a good job.

That brought her to the *P.P.S.* A present. Terri had bought her a present! She flung open the door to the utility room, gasping in disbelief. Before her stood a tall easel on which sat a large, blank canvas. In front of the easel was a stool with a high back, which was set at just the right height for her to comfortably sit on, and on the floor, propped up against the easel, was a black case and another canvas. She picked up the case and opened it, balancing it against the stool, and gasped again. It was a treasure case crammed with little tubes of watercolour paints, pencils and an array of paintbrushes. She shook her head. She closed her eyes and opened them and closed them and opened them, not quite believing what she was seeing. Tears dripped from her eyes: but they were different tears than she was used to. They felt good: joyful. Biddy realised that she wasn't crying because she felt scared or worried or humiliated. She was crying because she felt happy: really, really happy.

46.

The day was as perfect as a day could be. Certainly more perfect than any day in the life of Biddy Weir had been since the Saturday all those years ago when Miss Jordan had taken her to the department store in the city to buy a bra, and then on to a café for brunch. The consequences of that day had been disastrous, but so long as Biddy made sure that Bertie was fed and that nothing untoward happened to the cottage, nothing was going to spoil the magic this time. She was so excited by her present from Terri that she immediately dragged the easel out onto the patio and began to paint the view across the bay. The morning sunlight tickled the waves, and as she painted, the gulls glided to and fro across the horizon, as though they were performing a private ballet just for her. She was so enthralled that she forgot all about *Richard and Judy*. She didn't even stop for lunch, which she always took at 12.30 p.m., as that was the time her father had always wanted to eat. It wasn't until Bertie emerged from a long, peaceful nap and demanded his own lunch that Biddy set down her brushes and looked at her watch. It was almost two o'clock. As she slid down from the stool, it occurred to her how wonderfully thoughtful Terri had been, as her leg wouldn't have endured standing for that long. She stood back and studied her work, happy with her creation. It was almost perfect, just a bit more to do. She would give it to Terri, and tomorrow she would bring the easel down onto the beach and paint a replica of the painting at home, the one which had been responsible for her bringing her here, for her friendship with Terri, and she would give that one to her too.

Bertie meowed loudly, interrupting her thoughts.

'OK, Bertie, come on. Let's get you fed.'

After they had eaten, Bertie took himself out through the cat flap and settled down for another nap on the big wicker patio chair which was bathed in the warm afternoon sun. Biddy brought her suitcase down to the guest bedroom and unpacked her things. She wished she'd brought more with her, not because she actually needed anything else, but because the little white wooden wardrobe and the matching drawers and bedside table were so pretty that she wanted to fill them up with all the belongings she had in the world. She had never imagined that furniture could be so beautiful. The room was painted white, with a pale blue gloss on the woodwork. The blue and white gingham bedspread matched the curtains and the little lamp-shade on the bedside table. On top of the drawers Terri had left another bunch of daisies from her garden, this time in a glass tumbler. On the bed sat two huge white fluffy towels, and a towelling dressing gown. Biddy sat down and buried her face in the towels, inhaling their scent. They smelt of outside in summertime. They were the softest towels she had ever felt. She stroked the dressing gown. How different it felt to the old blue nylon one she'd had for years, too many years to count. She would definitely be taking a bath tonight, she decided. As she sat on the bed holding the towels, gazing through the window at the view of the bay, a seagull swooped down and stood on the windowsill. It looked in through the glass and held her gaze for a second then flew away. 'I think this must be what paradise is,' she whispered into the towels.

She spent the afternoon pottering about the cottage, wandering from room to room, taking in the colours, the furniture, the fabrics. By four o'clock she was unusually peckish again, and took a cup of tea and three of Terri's oatmeal cookies to the patio. Collapsing into the wicker chair, she shared her cookies with the gulls, and let the afternoon sun drench her face. Yes, she decided, this was definitely paradise. She sat back in the chair and closed her eyes, semi-dozing and thinking of nothing, until a sudden breeze made her shiver. She looked at her watch. It was a quarter to five. Almost time for *Honey's Pot*, and she hadn't even figured out how to work the TV yet. Throwing the remnants of her biscuit crumbs to the gulls, she picked up her cup and went back inside the house.

Settling down in Terri's red velvet chair, Biddy switched on the television, which was enormous: more than twice the size of her own portable one, at least. Working the controls was easier than she had anticipated, and she flicked from channel to channel, enjoying the luxury of not having to get up and go over to the TV to change the programme. She found the station she was looking for, just in time to hear the female announcer say, 'And now it's time for *Honey's Pot* with Honey Sinclair,' and the familiar theme tune began to play. And then there she was: all white teeth and sparkling smile, and twinkling eyes, and glowing skin and golden hair. She looked so real on this huge screen that Biddy was momentarily startled. She sometimes thought that Honey couldn't be real, not really real, that perhaps she had invented her, that she was actually a figment of her own imagination. But as her face filled the screen, Biddy had to face it. She was real, all right. Honey Sinclair, chat show hostess, TV presenter, girl-about-town, media darling. It was definitely her. Biddy shivered. For a moment or two, she willed herself, as she always did, to turn the TV off. But the moment passed and, as she always did, she began to watch the show, hypnotised, along with half of the nation, by the myth of Honey Sinclair.

Today, the programme was all about wearing the right bra size.

'Do you know, lovely people, are you aware, that eighty per cent of the female population in the UK wear the wrong size of bra?' Honey told Biddy and the rest of her multitude of viewers in her sing-song posh English voice, head tilted ever so slightly to the right. 'And this,' she sang on, 'affects their posture, the appearance of the clothes they wear and even,' pause, blink, smile, 'their safety.'

Biddy wondered how on earth wearing the wrong size of bra could be unsafe. She'd probably always worn the wrong size, she thought. She had never had a proper fitting and was still unsure about what her real size actually was, but she was equally sure that this had never put her in any danger. She still had her first bra, the one she'd bought the day Miss Jordan took her to the city. For a long time it had been the only one she owned, and though it was now too worn to wear, and too small into the bargain, it still lived in her underwear drawer, tucked in beside the letter.

The special guests today were Cindy someone or other from a famous lingerie shop called Scarlet (Biddy imagined it must be so much more glamorous than Lorraine's Lingerie, which had closed down several years back), 'stylist to the stars' Connor Craig and a 'yoga and posture expert', Alana Lovell. They were all thin and glamorous and terribly serious, as Honey's guests always were. Alana Lovell had been on the programme before and Connor Craig was a regular. He sat with his legs crossed sideways, and he wore mascara. He was gay and often talked to Honey about his boyfriend, Demetrius. A couple of months ago, there had been a show about a campaign for a change in the law to allow gay people to get married. Connor Craig had announced on the programme that whenever it finally happened, on the very day it was made legal in actual fact, he was going to get married to Demetrius, his boyfriend, and Honey had squealed and hugged and kissed him. Then he asked her right there live on air to be one of their witnesses at the ceremony, even though it mightn't be for years yet. And she had said yes and then cried. She was crying, she said, because she was so very, very happy. And this, she said, was one of the proudest moments of her life, because she had always campaigned for gay rights and had always, always believed that gay people should be allowed to get married, ever since she had been at school, she said, where some of her very dearest friends had been gay.

Biddy had thought then about Penny Jordan and Samantha, and wondered where in the world they were, and if they would get married if the law changed and what they would make of all this. And she thought about Penny again now, as Cindy started to discuss the bras that the models were parading around the set in, explaining to the audience precisely why each of them was wearing the wrong size.

Biddy learnt about normal people's lives from *Honey's Pot* and Lorraine Kelly on *Lorraine Live* and *This Morning with Richard and Judy*. They were like encyclopaedias of life to her. She learnt about the lives of famous people too – pop stars and movie stars; but it was the normal people who really interested her. She was fascinated by the ornamental details of their lives: the kind of clothes they wore, the perfumes they liked, the food they ate, the wine they drank, the places they liked to go on holiday. She had gathered so much information from these programmes about so many things – things she wouldn't have considered to be of any interest or importance before. She had learnt about sex, and babies, and breastfeeding, and toddler taming, and dealing with difficult teenagers, and women's problems like PMT and infertility. She realised that she wasn't the only woman in the world to suffer from painful heavy periods and strange, uneasy feelings in the build up to the bleed. And thanks to nice Dr Chris on *This Morning*, she now took oil of evening primrose tablets which had made her feel much better. She watched people cooking strange, exotic dishes with ingredients and names she'd never heard of and couldn't pronounce. She discovered that there were men who liked to dress as women, and women who would happily get pregnant with other women's babies, and people who believed they could talk to the dead – and that nobody thought any of this was remotely weird at all. Well, at least none of the presenters on the programmes did. Honey Sinclair, in particular, loved everyone who was a guest on her show, and the stranger or more extreme their problem or situation happened to be, the more she seemed to love them. And, of course, the more she loved everyone, the more everyone loved her.

When watching her programmes, Biddy often wondered what her own life would have been like if she had been normal: if she'd had a father who carried a briefcase, and had a job he went to every day, and drove a car, and played football or golf on a Saturday afternoon; if she'd had a mother who loved her enough to stay and take care of her, and brush her hair, and tell her about periods so she hadn't had to find out from Alison Flemming, and show her how to put on make-up, and taught her how to cook and bake and maybe even sew, and take her shopping for nice new clothes – and her very first bra. If she had been born into a normal, regular life, she wondered, would she have done normal, regular things, like gone to the Brownies or had ballet lessons or joined a youth club when she was a child? Or studied Art at university and had a career? Or fallen in love with a man who loved her back? And married that man, and maybe even become a mother herself?

The show was nearly over. Honey blew kisses to her guests the way she always did and thanked them for their 'wonderful, valuable contributions'. She blew kisses to the studio audience, most of whom blew kisses back to her. Biddy shuddered. Then she turned to face the camera and smiled that trademark sticky-sweet, Honey smile.

'In tomorrow's programme, we'll be examining a particularly sensitive but hugely important issue: bullying.'

Biddy froze.

'As patron of BUDDI, *Bullying's Un-cool, Don't Do It*, this is an issue which is particularly close to my own heart, and it's bound to be an emotional, but, I truly hope, inspirational and illuminating show. Special guests will be the gorgeous singer Karinda, who has openly spoken of her own horrific experiences of being bullied at school, and celebrity psychologist and friend of the show, Amanda Llewellan. Until then, goodbye, my friends, and stay sweet.'

Honey blew a single, slow kiss to the camera, the audience clapped and cheered and the credits began to roll.

Biddy shivered. Despite the warm July evening, she suddenly felt very cold, like her blood had been replaced with icy cold water. The lump which hadn't been bothering her much for a while, rose now in her throat, and the old familiar knot began to tie in her stomach.

'No,' she croaked.

Her body began to shake. She closed her eyes and cupped her hands over her mouth breathing slowly and deeply for a few seconds until her racing heart slowed down. The voiceover person on the TV was giving out the number for people to call the next day if they'd had any experience of bullying and wanted to tell Honey their story or put a question to one of her guests. Biddy couldn't believe this was happening. She couldn't bear to hear the 'B' word anywhere. She flinched whenever Terri mentioned it and if she ever heard it on TV, she would close her eyes and hum loudly. Now and again the subject came up on *Lorraine* or *This Morning*, or one of the other programmes she sometimes watched, and she would keep humming until the section was over or, if it was a long slot, she would turn the television off. But she never, ever expected it to come up on *Honey's Pot* – so why did it have to happen now, here, when she felt stronger, better, happier than she had ever felt in her life? She felt as though all of the good, positive steps she had taken over the past few months were about to unravel right in front of her, in an untidy mess all over Terri's living room floor.

Still shaking, she flicked off the TV using the remote and went out to the patio through the conservatory doors. The beach was bathed in a soft amber glow by the early evening sunshine. The sea was calm and still. The only sounds were the hum of a fishing trawler chugging its way towards the harbour and the squawk of the gulls, calling to each other. She stood, leaning on the patio table, and inhaled slowly until the shaking began to subside. Bertie observed her from his spot in the sun, yawned, stretched and sauntered over to where she stood. Purring loudly, he wound his plump soft body around her ankles. The physical contact from the cat, and the melodic sound of his purr seemed to calm her and, still breathing slowly, she sat down on one of the wooden chairs. Bertie jumped up onto her lap. He looked up at her and blinked slowly.

'You know what? I won't let it happen, Bertie,' she said, stroking the cat's head. 'I just won't watch the programme tomorrow. I won't. I'll paint instead. All day. And then it'll be OK. I'll be OK. If I don't watch it, I'll be OK.'

47.

Biddy's first night at Cove Cottage wasn't as restful as she had hoped. She couldn't eat the leftover lasagne as she'd planned, as her tummy felt queasy. There was nothing on television she really wanted to watch, and though using the remote to flick through all the various channels was a distraction, the novelty soon wore off. She was agitated, uneasy, and cross with herself for feeling that way. Her leg and hip ached, probably from sitting on the stool for such a long time, and rather than take a bath as she'd wanted to do earlier, she decided just to go to bed. It must be tiredness, she thought, the excitement of the day. She'd feel better in the morning after a good, long sleep.

But even when she lay down on the soft, springy mattress and pulled the duvet, which smelt of fresh flowers, up to her chin, she couldn't get comfortable. No matter how hard she tried to push the thought of tomorrow's *Honey's Pot* out of her head, it followed her around like a menacing shadow. She tried to hum it away, she tried biting her knuckles, she tried to think about what she would paint the next morning. Nothing worked. *Sleep*, she begged the ceiling, *I want to go to sleep*. She tried counting sheep. She tried recollecting every single colour palate in her new paint set. She tried counting backwards the number of weeks she had known Terri Drummond. Still nothing worked. *Honey's Pot* was all she could think of.

Then, suddenly, she found herself high up on Mount Innis, higher even than she'd been the night she had tried to fly. She was standing on top of a sharp rigid turret, balancing on one leg, her good leg. The other leg wasn't there at first, and then it was, only it wasn't a human leg, it was a falcon's, adorned with soft brown and white feathers, bright yellow feet and black claws. A sense of elation engulfed her: she was turning into a bird, a falcon. Then two peregrines arrived and perched on either side of her. She recognised them instantly as the falcons who had been with her that night on the mountain many years before. They were strong and sleek and held themselves with pride, but when she looked down her own bad leg was back, and it started to wither, right in front of her. Then she heard shouting.

'Over here, Biddy, come to us. Over here!' She turned to her right and saw a group of people standing on top of another turret, calling at her, waving, beckoning her over. She could make out Terri, right at the front. Then Penny Jordan appeared. She cupped her hands over her mouth and shouted, 'You can do it, Biddy. I know you can do it.' Her father was there too, standing behind Miss Jordan. He didn't speak, or motion, but he smiled at her; he smiled right into the back of her eyes and all the way down her skull and her neck until he reached her heart. He looked so young and healthy. He was holding something. A sheet of paper? No, a painting. Her painting, the one of Cove Cottage.

Then she heard another voice, a shrill familiar voice which almost made her lose her balance. It was laughing and then it began to sing. Other voices joined it. She didn't want to look. She tried to stay focused on Terri and Miss Jordan and her father, who by now were joined by Dr Graham and someone else, a man she didn't recognise. He wore a uniform. He nodded his head at her and then she realised: it was the bus driver, the one who was nice to her and spoke to her now every time she took his bus. Then Terri was there again in the forefront, shouting at her.

'Face your ...' something. She couldn't hear properly, as the singing was getting louder and louder. She had to look round. She couldn't stop herself. On another turret to her right, but slightly lower, was Alison Flemming, dressed in the Ballybrock Grammar School uniform. Georgina, Jackie and Julia crowded in behind her. There were others, she couldn't remember all their names, but she knew their faces. Vanessa Parker was one of them. Jill Cleaver too. Not all of them were singing, though, just Alison, Georgina, Jackie and Julia. She recognised the tune, but she couldn't quite hear the words at first. Then the rest of them joined in the chorus:

Oh yes she's a weirdo
And she freaks us all out,
She's ugly and creepy,
There ain't no bloody doubt.

Biddy remembered now.

'Don't listen to them, Biddy,' someone shouted from the other side. She thought it might have been Miss Jordan. But the singing grew louder. It was echoing around the mountain:

There she goes again talkin' to the birds,
She's a definite nutter, she's a total nerd.

Someone else appeared. A woman. Tall and slim with long golden hair. She was laughing and hugging all the singers, telling them how funny and wonderful they were and how much she loved them. We love you too, they chorused. The woman turned around and smiled at Biddy, the glare from her pure white teeth was almost blinding. It was Honey Sinclair.

Biddy woke up with a jolt, her breathing rapid and heavy, her body drenched in sweat. It took her a few seconds to work out where she was, especially as the room was so dark and heavily quiet. The streetlight outside her bedroom window at home in Stanley Street threw a haze of grubby light into her bedroom and there was generally some kind of noise drifting around throughout the night, especially on weekends. Cars speeding around the nearby Clanmorris estate, dogs barking, cats crying, drunks stumbling home from the clubs and pubs in town, effing and blinding as they bounced off walls and collided with lampposts. Here there was nothing. Total, absolute silence. The stillness would have been pleasant, welcome even, had it not been for the fact that there was nothing to distract her from the dream. It kept replaying in her mind, over and over again. She knew she wouldn't sleep again for a while – she didn't want to anyway, in case it started again – so she pulled on the fluffy dressing gown and went into the kitchen to make a hot drink.

Biddy stood for a while, staring out through the glass doors, watching the lights of a lonesome vessel twinkling on the water in the distance. As she sipped her creamy hot chocolate, the distress of the dream, and the agitation which had been bothering her since the previous evening, finally began to dissolve. She felt strange, but not in a bad way. It was hard to describe. Lighter. Yes, that was it. She felt lighter.

She thought about the dream again, but now she wasn't frightened. She rarely dreamt so lucidly and usually couldn't remember the details of her dreams in the morning. But every detail of this one was vividly, powerfully clear. Bertie roused himself from his basket and meowed loudly. He wasn't used to being disturbed in the middle of the night. Biddy poured some milk into a saucer and placed it on his mat.

'What do you think it means, Bert?' she asked the cat, as he lapped at the milk. 'It definitely means something. I'm sure of it. What were they all trying to tell me? What was Terri shouting?'

The cat looked up at Biddy, licked his lips and sauntered back to his basket. He curled up and closed his eyes. Within seconds, he was fast asleep, but Biddy lifted the mohair throw from the small sofa in the kitchen, and went out onto the patio. Wrapping the blanket around her, she snuggled down into the wicker armchair. The trawler disappeared into the night, the dancing stars guiding its way. Biddy wondered if she had ever seen such a beautiful sight as this black night sprinkled with starlight. And then she remembered that of course she had; but on that occasion she had been cold and frightened and obviously delirious as she'd believed that the falcons could show her how to fly, and that Paddy Joyce was with her on the mountain, there to keep her safe. Now she felt soothed by the warm night air, calmed by the silence, and inspired by the star-spangled sky.

'Face your demons,' she whispered, as she gazed up at them. 'Face. Your. Demons.' *That* was what Terri had been trying to tell her in the dream. Of course it was! Terri had said that very same thing to her on the beach a couple of weeks back; the day she had told her all about the school trip, and the dull, fuzzy weeks spent in hospital afterwards: the pain, the fear, the confusion – but the relief she'd felt every night that another day had passed without Alison. Terri had listened without interrupting, as she always did. When she was done, when the whole story was out and her words had run dry, they sat in silence for a while, watching a cormorant dive from the rocks. Eventually Terri had taken her hand and squeezed it hard.

'One day soon, Biddy, you'll be strong enough to face your demons,' she had said, 'and then, puff, you'll be able to blow them all away.'

'Well, I'm ready now,' she said aloud, breathing in deeply as she headed back indoors. 'I'm ready.'

For hours she wandered around the cottage, formulating her plan. She sat down; she stood up; she drank three mugs of tea. She made toast. She made more toast. She ate three Kimberley biscuits. She talked to Terri's plants; she spoke into mirrors. She even had a chat to Harry. She watched the sun come up, and almost cried with joy at the beauty of the dawn breaking over Cove Bay.

Finally, exhaustion hit. Her head throbbed; her legs wobbled; her eyes drooped. She slid under the soft, fluffy cloud of a duvet, hugging it into her chest like a cherished treasure, and sleep took her in a second.

Part 3: an ending and a new beginning
Ballybrock, July 2000

48.

'Welcome back everyone, welcome back. Thank you all so much for joining us today.'

The sickly-sweet melodic tone of Honey Sinclair's voice greeted her adoring audience. 'Now, dear friends, if you were with us before the break, you'll know that today's show is all about the B word: bullying. My lovely guest, the talented, gorgeous, superstar-singing-sensation that is Karinda, has been sharing her dreadful story with us. Thank you, my darling, for your openness and your integrity and . . .' Honey blew a kiss in Karinda's direction, '. . . for being sooo, sooo brave. You made me cry. As an avid anti-bullying campaigner and patron of BUDDI, I truly, truly respect your courage and your candour. Don't you agree, Amanda?'

Amanda Llewellan, celebrity psychologist and regular guest on the show, dutifully nodded.

'Don't you agree, my lovely friends?'

A roar of applause and wolf-whistling rose from the studio audience.

'We need more people like you to speak out, Karinda, and, do you know, dear friends, I think we may have some more brave souls willing to share their stories with us right now!'

Another roar from the audience gave Honey the few seconds she needed to get the details of the first caller fed into her ear-piece. Female. Bridget. Thirty. Nearly died due to bullying. Spoke to Miranda. Calling from Northern Ireland. Fuck, she thought. She bloody hated talking to people from fucking Northern Ireland. Those stupid accents. And that little cow, Miranda, knew it.

'So, first off, we've got Bridget on the line. Hello, Bridget. Thank you soooo much for calling *Honey's Pot*. It's people like you, Bridget, who make our little show what it is. We couldn't do it without you.' She paused, waiting for the usual submissively complimentary response from the caller. None came. Just quick, heavy, breathing. Christ, she thought, that's all I need. A fucking Northern Irish oddball.

'Are you there, Bridget?'

'Yes,' came the wispy reply.

'Good, now don't be shy, Bridget. I'm sure this is difficult for you, and painful too, but you're going to do a lot of people a lot of good by talking to us today.' She paused to give a look of sincere concern into camera three. Honey knew how to work the studio cameras like a seasoned old pro. She was a thoroughbred; born to be on TV. Nothing fazed her. On air, at least, she could handle anything.

'Can you tell us a little bit about the awful thing that happened to you, poor, sweet Bridget?'

On the other end of the line, Biddy was shaking, violently. It was all she could do to stop herself from dropping the telephone. Her legs felt like wobbly jelly, sweat was running down her face and soaking her armpits, her throat was as dry as sandpaper. Nothing could have prepared her for this. Faced with the reality of the situation, her script was useless, and now she didn't know what to say. She didn't even think she'd be able to speak to Honey at all. How on earth had she ever believed she could do this? She squeezed her eyes shut and through a kaleidoscope of flashing lights saw Alison Flemming spitting in her face in the school toilets, telling her she was a useless scumbag, bloody weirdo fuck. She opened her eyes and saw a seagull perched on the wide windowsill outside the living room, staring in at her. She closed her eyes again and saw the people in her dream last night, calling to her: Terri, Miss Jordan, her father, Dr Graham. Then somehow, from somewhere, words began to stream from her mouth.

'Yes, I was bullied. For a long time. By a girl. There were others, but she was the leader. She did a lot of bad things to me. She humiliated me all the time. I don't know why. She made me feel sick and frightened every day. Every day,' she repeated, the memory flushing through her, creating a warm, sick feeling, which almost made her gag. 'She made me not want to go to school. She called me a name. A special name. I started to stick pins into my body to stop the pain in my head.'

Honey winced. Biddy could see her reaction on the screen, even though she still had the sound off.

'Heavens, Bridget,' she said. Biddy thought her voice sounded shaky, but maybe it was her imagination. 'That sounds dreadful, awful. Poor you.'

Biddy took a deep breath, then carried on, ignoring the host's synthetic sympathy.

'One day, I saw her doing something she shouldn't have been doing.' She had to get it all out now. Quickly. Otherwise there'd be no point. 'And before I got away she spotted me, and she knew I'd seen what she'd been doing,' she blurted, 'and I knew from the way that she looked at me that I was in trouble, that she'd do something really bad to me to stop me from saying anything. But I couldn't take any more. I'd had enough. So I ran away, and I kept going and going until,' she paused, swallowing hard, 'until I, until I had an accident and I fell and I nearly died.'

Honey was growing impatient. There was something really creepy about this one that made her feel uneasy. Mind you, most of the people who phoned into her show were weirdo creeps, but she tolerated them because they were good for her career. Bloody good, as it happened. After a whirlwind rise from weather girl on *AMTV*, to guest hostess on *Live with Clive*, to co-host of *That Was This Week*, she was now the darling of daytime TV, with her very own live chat and magazine show. She was fully aware that it was the oddball 'Great British Public' who had helped to fast-track her career so far, and whilst she detested almost every one of them, she knew their value and handled each with care. After all, if she was to conquer the States, as was her plan, and become the next Oprah, then she needed to be vigilant, on-form, and sweet as sticky honey all of the time. But this one she really didn't like. She couldn't put her finger on it, but she felt unusually uncomfortable, and she wanted rid of her. She fiddled with her right ear, the signal to Phil, the producer, that she'd had enough. But the bloody woman kept talking, going on about something else the bully had done to hurt her, something about it being the reason she never completed her education. Oh, for fuck's sake, she thought, enraged now. Why the hell did Phil not instruct her to move to the next caller? Was there a problem? Of all times for a fucking tech hitch! She'd have to take control of the situation herself. She'd move to Amanda for a psychologist's take on the whole bloody thing.

'What a vile girl, utterly vile,' she sighed, shaking her head. 'I truly hope she got her just deserts. Thank you so much for your call, Bridget. I think we'll ask Amand—'

'B.W.,' interjected Biddy. 'My "special" name.'

Honey shifted in her chair, momentarily losing her focus, her smile slipping ever so slightly. Then she laughed, a flaky, nervous laugh. She had to get this crackpot off the line. What the fuck was Phil doing?

'OK, OK, well, ah, thank you, ah, Bridg—'

'B.W.,' said Biddy, again, slowly, flatly. 'Bloody Weirdo.'

Honey Sinclair froze. She was flummoxed. Paralysed. *Is this a fucking joke?* she thought. *Is that arsehole Phil winding me up here? What the fuck? What the fucking fuck?* She looked at Amanda, and then at Karinda, then back to Amanda. Karinda giggled a little, squirming on the bright red sofa, visibly uncomfortable. Amanda's eyes widened in question, her head shaking slightly in surprise. The audience held a collective, anxious breath.

Amanda waited another two seconds for Honey to speak, then, sensing an opportunity she decided to take control.

'Oh, Bridget,' she said, quickly, her voice high-pitched and shrill. 'How awful for you. Did you . . .'

'Alison,' Biddy interrupted.

'Ah, erm, no, Bridget.' Amanda was smiling now, tilting her head to one side. 'I'm Amanda. But that's . . .'

'Alison Flemming.'

Amanda now looked to Honey for help, who by this time was as white as her own teeth.

'Her name was Alison Flemming,' Biddy continued, her voice steady now, assured almost.

Honey's face contorted. The notes she was holding slid from her hands. Phil ordered camera three to zoom in for a Honey close-up. He knew he should cut the caller off, that Honey could have him sacked for this, that she'd hate him even more than ever now, only for once, she'd have a reason. But something was up. Something was definitely up and he had an overwhelming feeling that this could be his moment. Payback time to that bitch, for making what should have been a dream job such a misery. He really didn't know what was coming next, but hey, whatever the hell was going on, this was great live TV.

Honey didn't let him down.

'Jesus Christ. Bloody Weirdo. Bloody Biddy Weirdo – my God, it's you, isn't it?' she whispered. It was barely audible, but loud enough for the mike to pick up and transmit to the nation, along with the close-up from camera three, which showed a face so unlike that of the Honey Sinclair everyone knew and loved. A face contorted with hate and revulsion. And, once she realised what she had done, terror.

49.

It was all over the papers for days to come. '*Honey's not so sweet after all*'; '*Honey's sticky situation*'; '*Queen Beetch*', ran some of the headlines. Terri came home the next afternoon, a day early, but Olivia and Benjy had agreed she should go. They'd never been able to abide Honey Sinclair themselves, and were delighted to have had an inside angle on the story. When Terri returned to Cove Cottage, she persuaded a shell-shocked Biddy to stay with her until the dust had settled, rightly predicting that certain members of the tabloid press would try to track her down. By the next morning Biddy had been identified, mostly thanks to two of her 'old school friends', Georgina McMinn, née Harte, and Julia Gamble. They regularly witnessed Alison Flemming's – a.k.a. Honey Sinclair – torture of poor Biddy Weir, they said in the exclusive interview they gave to the *Sun*. They had often tried to intervene, but were powerless against the wrath of Alison. She was ruthless, unstoppable. Whenever they had tried to help poor Biddy, Alison would turn her rage on them. It was simply awful. They only wished now that they could have done more to help. But they were here for Biddy, whenever she needed them.

Another woman came forward who claimed to know Alison Flemming from her first primary school, before she moved to Ballybrock. She sold a story about Alison cutting off her friend, Selina Burton's, long blonde hair in a fit of jealous rage. All of her hair. The papers tried to track down this Selina Burton, but it turned out she now lived in Texas and ran a successful stud farm. Her family had no comment to make.

Within days, the press had discovered Biddy's address and virtually camped out on the doorstep of number 17, Stanley Street for a couple of weeks, until it dawned on them that she wasn't coming home any time soon. Ballybrock had never seen anything like it. Most of the press had never seen anything like Ballybrock.

Biddy was bemused by the turn of events. She hadn't given any thought as to how her plan might actually play out. Her priority had been to face Alison head-on, tell her what damage she had done, not to actually expose her true identity. That had been an unavoidable coincidence. The fact that Alison's career and glamorous life as Honey Sinclair seemed to have been destroyed by her actions didn't make Biddy happy. But the fact that she had exorcised her demon did. At last, she felt free.

Eventually, when things settled down, Terri popped back to Stanley Street to check on things and lift the mound of post that had built up in the hallway. She had gone on a shopping trip to M&S on her return from London to buy some new clothes for Biddy (which Biddy loved – they were so much more stylish and comfortable than her usual charity shop garb) so there had been no real reason to go to Stanley street before that. She threw out the junk mail and the heap of scribbled notes from some of the more desperate hacks who had loitered in vain outside the house, offering various sums of money for Biddy's exclusive story, and returned to Cove Cottage with a couple of bills and a handful of letters. Some were more official requests for an interview from magazines, newspapers and television shows, including one from *This Morning*, the show that Biddy genuinely did love to watch. For a split second, Terri thought that she might accept, and worried about the fallout if she did.

But Biddy just ripped it up as she did with all of the others and dropped it into the wastepaper bin, which Terri had placed beside her.

But she did keep two letters, one with a local postmark, and one which had come from Edinburgh. The local letter, which was handwritten, came from Ruth Abbott, who told Biddy that this was the first time she had ever written to any of her former pupils. She had seen the programme by chance, she said, as it wasn't something she would normally watch. But during the summer break she had been tasked with drafting a new anti-bullying policy for the school and a colleague had called to tell her it might be useful.

Yes, Biddy, she wrote, *I'm still here. Head of the senior school now, for my sins.* For my sins. Biddy read and re-read the words several times. For my sins. What an odd thing to write, she thought. *Of course I was already aware that Ms Sinclair was actually Alison Flemming, but as soon as I heard your voice, Biddy, I knew it was you.* Where is this going? Biddy thought. Why is she writing to me? The letter rambled on a bit about school and how much it had changed in recent years and how important they now knew it was to identify bullies and provide support for pupils who *suffered at their hands.* And then came the punch line:

I am sorry, Biddy. I know now that we let you down, that I let you down, and I am truly, truly sorry. I should have read the signs better on that fateful trip to Innis. I should have been more alert. There were rumours afterwards about Alison's 'inappropriate behaviour', in more ways than one. Is she referring to Mr Patterson? Biddy thought. *But I chose to ignore them, because it was easier to do so. I have learnt a valuable lesson, and as well as offering my apologies, I would like to say thank you, Biddy.*

In truth, writing this policy was an irritant to me, a task I could frankly have done without on my summer break. But you have made me realise just how important it is to root out bullying in our schools: in this school, in particular. I promise to give this policy my full attention, and to never turn a blind eye again.

I would also like to apologise, Biddy, for not visiting you in hospital after your accident. I could give you a host of excuses, but the simple fact is that I should have, and I am truly sorry.

The letter ended with Mrs Abbott inviting Biddy to visit her at the school in September when the new term started. Biddy knew she wouldn't. She could never set foot inside that building again, ever. But the letter left her with a curious lump in her throat, a different one to the lump she'd been forcing down for years.

The second letter, with an Edinburgh address, was typed.

Dear Biddy,

You probably won't remember me, but I was in your class at school. I heard about what happened with Alison Flemming and I just felt compelled to write to you. My mum still lives in Ballybrock and she gave me your address. I hope you don't mind! Believe it or not, I have thought about you often over the years, always with a feeling of guilt that I didn't intervene when Alison was tormenting you. We all knew what she was doing, we all knew what a horror she was, but for some reason no one had the guts to stand up to her – and I for one am truly ashamed. Please forgive me, Biddy.

I now live in Edinburgh and run a small advertising agency with Tom, my husband. (We married last summer.) If you are ever in Edinburgh, Biddy, I would love to see you. I'll treat you to lunch in my favourite Italian bistro! You'll see my address, my email and my mobile number at the top of the letter, just in case. Or maybe, when I'm next home, we could grab a coffee? We're definitely coming over for Christmas this year. You don't have to reply – just send me a text so I have your number, then I'll text you when I know my dates. Of course if I never hear from you, I completely understand.

I hope you are well, Biddy, and that however tricky your life has been lately, the sun will shine again soon.

With very best wishes,
Karen Best (Robinson) X

Sitting in Terri's yellow kitchen, Biddy read and re-read each letter several times. She moved out to the patio where Terri brought her a cup of tea and a scone, and she read them again. She did remember Karen Robinson; the only person she had ever seen remotely try to challenge Alison. She looked out at the bay, the midday sunlight bouncing off the water, and smiled. Maybe she would meet her for a coffee. Some day. Maybe not at Christmas, but some day, and she would tell her that, yes, the sun was shining. Finally.

50.

Biddy was surrounded by pots of paint samples when the phone rang. She was selecting colours for the kitchen and the living room: tones of yellow and shades of cobalt blue. She had laid out a huge white sheet of paper on the kitchen table and was testing out the various samples. She planned to redecorate the whole house from top to bottom, gradually and carefully. She didn't want to make mistakes. It had to be right. When her father's estate was finally settled, she'd been shocked to discover that he'd had money tucked away in a couple of savings accounts. It wasn't a huge amount, but there was enough to do up the house, buy a new television, and frame some of her paintings. And even then, there would be some left over for safekeeping. Biddy had never known, never suspected that her papa had savings, and she wondered time and time again why he had kept it hidden from her. Had he simply forgotten it was there? What would their life together have been like if only he'd used the money to buy things for the house: furniture, or a car, perhaps, or central heating? Or even to have taken them on a holiday?

'Perhaps he felt you didn't need it while you were still together,' Terri had suggested. 'Perhaps he knew you would need it now.'

Biddy decided to look at it that way. Her father's final act of love. That, and the hoard of her old sketches and paintings which she had found in his shed when, on her return from Terri's, she had finally found the courage to venture inside. There were more than one hundred of them, carefully catalogued and stored in hand-made boxes. The first box contained a series of pencil sketches of birds, mostly seagulls, which she had drawn when she was just six years old. She knew this because of the date – 1976 – scrawled on the back in her father's handwriting. Every single piece of work was dated in some form, with either the year, or the month and year, or, on a few, the full date. All that time he had kept her work, and she had never noticed. He must have retrieved all the sketches she put in the bin, and siphoned off some of the ones she kept under the bed. All of those years, he had been proud of her, and she had never known. She had wept that morning, sitting in the shed, surrounded by her life. She wept with grief for her father, with regret that she hadn't made more of her life and shared more of his, but most of all, she wept with relief.

'Hello,' Biddy answered the phone after just one ring. It was sitting on the table beside her, as she'd been expecting Terri's call. She was going to take Biddy to B&Q to buy the first supply of paint. She'd taken her the week before to get the samples.

'I still haven't decided,' she carried on talking, before Terri could respond.

'Ahh . . . hi. Hello. Is that Biddy?'

It was a male voice, deep and velvety, with a hint of a local accent. Biddy froze. She didn't know any men, apart from Dr Graham and Dean the gardener and Ian Thomas, and this one certainly wasn't any of them. Had someone from a newspaper found out her new number? She went to hang up but the voice stopped her.

'My name is Marcus, Marcus Baxter,' it said quickly. Marcus, she thought and a memory jolted somewhere within her.

'You won't remember me, Biddy, but I met you once, very briefly, on the beach at Ballybrock, many, many years ago. You were sketching the seagulls.' A flash of a black and green stripy scarf. The Collingsford Boys' School scarf.

'I was with –' The man hesitated. 'I was with someone we both knew.'

A vision of blond floppy hair and deep brown eyes like chocolate buttons, and Alison screaming at him to get a move on flashed before her.

'Look, I really don't want to alarm you and I'm sure you're wondering how on earth I got your number and you're probably just about to put down the phone,' he spoke quickly now, a sense of desperation in his voice, 'but please, please just listen to what I have to say. It'll be worth it, I promise. Well, I hope so. My wife saw the programme. She already knew who Honey Sinclair was. I'd told her all about my fleeting romance with Alison Flemming, including the day we'd met this shy girl on the beach, a girl who was sketching the most amazing drawings of a seagull, and what an utter cow she had been to her. I have thought about that incident almost every time I saw Honey Sinclair on TV or in a magazine. When my wife saw the programme, she guessed the girl was you and she suggested I track you down. It's taken me a while, but finally I've found you.'

Finally, he stopped talking.

Biddy was utterly perplexed. She remembered the incident clearly now. The boy on the beach had been nice to her. Kind. She remembered him complimenting her drawing, and how Alison had then screamed at him. And she remembered what happened afterwards. She shuddered. She didn't want these memories back again. She didn't need them anymore. Why was this Marcus doing this? What did he want from her?

'Yes,' was all that she could muster in reply.

'Look, I'm really sorry, Biddy. Actually, this has nothing at all to do with Al – with her. It's your art. That's what I want to talk to you about. Do you still draw?'

Biddy was even more confused.

'Uh-huh.'

'And birds, do you still draw birds?'

'Uh-huh.'

'Fantastic. This is fantastic. OK, bear with me. Will you bear with me for a minute? Please?'

'OK,' she managed this time.

'So, I run a publishing company which specialises in children's books. We're based here in London. You may have heard of us. Marshmallow Moon?'

'Erm . . .'

'Don't worry. That's not important. Anyway, the thing is, one of my authors has written this fabulous adventure story about a little boy and a bird. A seagull. It's called *The Adventures of Timothy Tindall and Silas Gull*. It's fabulous. You'll love it, I'm sure. It'll be a bestseller. All her books are. She's a brilliant writer. Actually, she's a B.W. too.'

Biddy gasped. Her stomach somersaulted. This was all some kind of sick joke. Alison had found her and put him up to this. She was back. She was getting her revenge. *Oh please God, no. No.* She would hang up. Now. She would never answer the phone again. Ever. Not even to Terri.

'Bunty Walker,' Marcus said.

'Pardon?' whispered Biddy.

'The author. Her name is Bunty Walker. Biddy Weir, Bunty Walker. Two B.W. initials on the cover.'

'I beg your pardon?' she asked again. She was completely lost. Totally bemused. She didn't have a clue what this man was talking about.

'God, I'm not making sense am I? I'm sorry, it's just that I'm so excited. The thing is, Biddy, I wondered if you would be interested in doing the drawings for the book?'

Epilogue

A dedication – 17, Stanley Street, Ballybrock, October 2001

Biddy stood in the hallway and held the package in her hands. It was finally here. She breathed in and out slowly and deeply, savouring the moment. This could well be the best day of her life. There had been several occasions over the past twenty-one months since meeting Terri when she had had that very same thought, but this one, surely, surpassed them all. Outside, a man from the estate agency was sticking a 'SOLD' sign across the 'FOR SALE' board in the garden. Tomorrow, Terri would be leaving for Greece. Biddy had already booked her ticket to visit in March. Her first trip abroad. And this time next week, Cove Cottage would be hers, and Bertie would be her foster cat.

She closed the front door and went into the kitchen. The autumn sun streamed in through the window and bounced off the walls, the pale yellow paint making the room seem even brighter. The young couple who had bought the house fell in love with the yellow walls and blue cobalt cupboards the first time they viewed the house. They said it reminded them of the Greek island where they had spent their honeymoon.

Shaking slightly, she sat at the table – a mug of tea and a Kimberley biscuit on a tray in front of her – and tore open the wrapping of the package. A handwritten note fell out.

Dear Biddy,

Well, here it is, the first edition hot off the press. A job well done, I think. Congratulations. You're a star!

Be in touch soon re the launch.

Best wishes,
Marcus

Biddy turned the book over in her hands a few times, and traced the seagull on the blue and grey cover with her fingertips. That was her drawing. Hers. And there were many more inside. She opened the book slowly and turned over the first page, and then the second. There it was. That's what she'd waited to see. She took a sip of tea from her mug, cleared her throat and read aloud:

For my father, with all of my love. For Penny Jordan,
wherever she may be.
And for B.W.s everywhere.
Biddy Weir.

Acknowledgements

The journey to publication for *The Lonely Life of Biddy Weir* is a story in itself – full of drama, disappointment, reinvention, and ultimately fulfilment. Many people have been involved in the evolution of this book over the years, and consequently I have a host of folk to thank. So, please indulge me in this moment of gratitude.

First and foremost, to Mark Smith, Bonnier CEO: I now know that Biddy was waiting on you. From the bottom of my heart, I thank you for giving her a home. To Joel Richardson, my editor at Twenty7 Books, thank you for your insight, patience and diligent, thoughtful notes. Thanks also to Claire Johnson-Creek at Twenty7 and Molly Powell and Annabel Wright at Whitefox.

Enormous thanks to my agents Susan and Paul Feldstein for your years of support, patience, counsel and friendship – and for sticking with me through thick and thin. I am indebted to you both – and relieved we got there in the end!

To Damian Smyth at the Arts Council of Northern Ireland, thank you so very much for your wise words of advice on many occasions, and for encouraging me to keep going. And to the ACNI for financial support over the years, I am deeply grateful.

To Lynda Neilands, who started me off on this road, and was the first person who allowed me to think there might just be a book in me, I am truly grateful. The seeds of Biddy were planted in your writing class, Lynda, and look how she has grown.

To Catherine Murphy, Newry, Mourne and Down District Council – I am hugely grateful for the invaluable mountain of information you shared, and for helping me to get a sense of 'Innis'!

I have been extremely lucky and deeply humbled to have had words of advice, encouragement and insightful constructive criticism from several renowned authors through various stages of Biddy's journey. Heartfelt thanks go to: Bernie McGill – for your kindness and generosity over the years, and your perceptive, comprehensive notes which made such a difference; Lucy Caldwell – for an email of encouragement at a moment of despair, and for all your counsel since; Colin Bateman – for countless, ongoing titbits of advice; Jo Baker – for your perceptive and encouraging feedback all those years ago in the Seamus Heaney Centre; and to Glen Patterson – for a late night phone chat you won't even remember, way back when I was just starting out.

I'm deeply grateful to everyone who has read drafts of the novel and shared their thoughts. Special thanks must go to my dear friend Arthur Scappaticci for the formatting suggestion that transformed the book and gave it life again, and to Kathryn and Alan Thomson for hosting their own private book club, always believing, and relentlessly cheering me on. Thanks also to Natasha Geary, Caroline Nicholson, Katriona Burrow, John Richardson and Joyce Adams.

To my old Bangor Book Club – I finally got to drink that champagne, girls! To Aimee's 'Dirty Dancers' – cheers for helping me celebrate when The Call came through. To Clare and Michael Donald and to Louise Hinds – thank you all for your unwavering belief that it would happen. To Anna, Edna, Emma, Jacqui, Jane, Janet, Julie, Karen and Nadine, aka The Girls – you're the best friends in the world, and I'm glad I made you proud. To Alison Gordon, Kieran Gilmore and Sarah Kiely– thanks for helping me stay sane through the editing process. And to my fellow Twenty7 authors – I couldn't be sharing this ride with a better bunch of people.

My own schooldays were a lifetime and a half ago, but thankfully they were nothing like Biddy's, and the positive legacy of certain teachers will always be with me. So to my old English teachers, Marilyn McGimpsey and Brenda Lindsay – I am indebted to you both. I already loved stories, but you made me fall in love with words. And to my former VP, Geography teacher, and mentor, Bobby Gray (who mercifully bears no resemblance to Clive Patterson) your faith in me has finally paid off!

My family has been my bedrock these past few years, and no one has been more excited to see Biddy come to life than they. Heartfelt thanks to my sister, Karalyn, and her family, Paul, Kiera and Cameron Fields, for your unwavering support and for all of the relentless promotion you do.

To my mum and late dad, Patsy and Ronnie Allen – I owe my love of books to you. Obviously I owe *so* much more than that, but thank you for all those magical library trips, for indulging my 'secret' late-night-undercover-torch-lit reading habit, and for holding onto my dream for me. I wish you'd got to read this book, Dad, but I'm so very grateful that you will, Mum.

And to my daughter, Aimee Richardson – thank you for inspiring me every day, for being my biggest champion, and for always keeping my path so brightly lit.

Author Q&A

Biddy is such a unique and distinctive character. Where did you find the inspiration for her?

Biddy isn't based on one person in particular – she's a hybrid of several people I've encountered over the years, male and female – but there is definitely one individual who triggered the character. Before I began writing the book, I spotted a girl who had been in my year at school in a local supermarket. I hadn't seen her for many years, but she looked exactly the same as she had in our mid-teens – same closely cropped hair, same thick tan tights, same saggy cardigan and knee-length tweed skirt. Back then she was a loner who seemed to be oblivious to the teenage antics the rest of us got up to. We were now in our early forties, yet she could have passed for a woman in her sixties. I couldn't get her out of my head, and began to think of other women, and men, I'd encountered over the years who didn't necessarily conform to the idea of being 'normal', many of whom seemed to be stuck in time. Around the same time, I became aware of some bullying that was going on in my daughter's class at primary school. I personally witnessed one little girl whispering vile threats to another, then my daughter herself experienced some unpleasant behaviour from a couple of her classmates. It was so shocking and upsetting. One day, out of the blue, this character just popped into my head, demanding to tell me her story. At first I thought she was called Bunty Walker, but I knew she'd been badly bullied at school and I wrote a short story about her quest for revenge. I couldn't leave her alone, though, and kept editing the story, and adding bits on. Then I realised that she was actually called Biddy Weir, and she wasn't looking for revenge at all – she just wanted someone to talk to. So I let her talk, and I kept writing down what she had to say – until one day I realised, with some surprise, that I was actually writing a novel. As a nod to the original character, I briefly introduce a Bunty Walker towards the end of the book.

Why do you think Alison acts the way she does? Did you enjoy writing her as a character?

Alison is such a horror, isn't she – but she was tremendous fun to write. She too is based on a handful of girls and young women I've encountered over the years, a couple of whom certainly left a lasting impression on me – though I have to add I was never, ever bullied in the way Biddy was. Not even close to it. But it's so easy for a carefully chosen insult, or even a throwaway comment, to leave a lasting scar, and I found writing Alison deliciously cathartic at times. She's a controversial character, I know, and no doubt she'll cast up that age-old question about nature or nurture. Personally I think she's just a nasty piece of work – some children are. And some, like Alison, never grow out of it. She's also highly sexualised from an early age, which again is both controversial and entirely plausible. And, of course, she's ridiculously spoiled and pampered by her parents, who are equally flawed, and have never impressed on her the meaning of humility. She has so much going for her, but virtually everything that should be a positive turns her into a deeply unpleasant individual.

The bullying in the novel is so well described. Was it hard to write those scenes?

Extremely! I found myself in tears sometimes and wondered on occasion if I was pushing the boundaries too far. But I also knew I couldn't hold back; I had to make the bullying as realistic and hard-hitting as possible, otherwise Biddy's internal dialogue wouldn't ring true. It does make for uncomfortable reading at times – but it's supposed to.

Why do you think children like Biddy are picked on?
Because they are easy targets. Because they don't have the strength or the voice to fight back. Because someone, an Alison figure, is always going to be around to lead a group in the picking-on process, and it's easier to go along with it, than challenge his/her behaviour. I think as adults we need to actively impress upon our children the value of individuality, idiosyncrasies, oddness. If they are taught that 'weirdness' can be intriguing and endearing, rather than threatening and repellent, then so many children would escape the torture of being bullied simply because they don't conform to the 'norm'. Weirdo doesn't have to be a dirty word!

Did you always know the way Biddy's story would end? Did anything surprise you as you wrote the story?
I didn't entirely know what would happen, but from the outset I did want Biddy to find some form of peace. The ending had to be hopeful, but realistic – to have her running off into the sunset with Marcus, for example, just wouldn't have rung true. And everything surprised me. Everything. That is the joy of writing!

Are you a big reader? What books inspired your journey to becoming an author?
For as long as I can remember, reading has been essential to my wellbeing. I get anxious if I don't have at least three books on my bedside table at any given time, and my first thought when I'm embarking on a trip is 'how many books can I bring'? ('How many pairs of shoes' comes a close second.) I think I probably first had the feeling of wanting to write a novel way back when I read Louisa May Alcott's *Little Women*, and there were many more books over the years that poked the writer in me on the shoulder: Plath's *The Bell Jar*, Austen's *Emma*, Lee's *To Kill a Mockingbird*.

But in my late teens I buried my adolescent ambition deep within me – folded it up and tucked it right inside my ribcage. Two decades on I read *The Lovely Bones* by Alice Seabold, and the old ache started to unravel. Something about that book triggered a physical reaction: it dragged the need to write out from its hiding place and slapped me around the face with it. It still took me a wee while to get going, but that book made me realise I couldn't ignore my dream forever.

This is your first book – was it easy to write?
I wouldn't say it was ever easy, but sometimes it was less difficult than at others. For me, writing is a bit like that little girl with a curl in the middle of her forehead – when it's good, it's really, really good, and when it's bad, it's horrid! There were many times during the writing of this book when I paused – sometimes just for a day or two, at one point for almost a year. But no matter how despondent or consumed by self-doubt I became, I never gave up on Biddy. She wormed her way into my subconscious and has been a part of my life now for several years – and I guess she always will be.

What would be your top piece of advice to aspiring writers?
Read. Read often, and read well. Choose books in the genre you want to be published in. Study your genre, keep abreast of debut publications in your field, read different styles and examine POVs. I know a lot of authors don't agree with me on this, as they feel reading other writers' work can influence them, even on a subconscious level. But for me it is essential. It's my springboard – when I read something magnificent, I want to dive into my own work and swim around in it. And never give up. It sounds like such a cliché, but if I'd given up, well, you wouldn't be reading this now!